PETER LEWENSTEIN

PALA PALA KILLER

GET REAL
BOOKS

First published by Get Real Books, London 2023

Cover design by Books Covered Ltd
Photograph by the author
Typeset on Reedsy

First edition
ISBN: 978-1-91-962563-8

www.peterlewenstein.com

'For a colonized people the most essential value, because it's the most concrete, is first and foremost the land: the land which will bring them bread and, above all, dignity.'

Frantz Fanon, The Wretched of the Earth

PART I

Ngoso é mabotea nde na isese

The man who sings learned first to whistle
(Douala Proverb)

Chapter 1

He stopped dead in his tracks.

'Na wetin that?'

Whatever it was, it was nearby. But the sounds of the forest played tricks on a man's ears.

His eyes swept from side to side, squinting through the bushes and between the trees and into the darkness; then up, from the carpet of fallen leaves to the sparkling canopy high above.

Nothing stirred.

He listened, trying to filter out the creaks and groans of the giant ironwood trunks, the chirps of the birds and the soft buzzing of the flies.

But he didn't hear it again, that single, sharp snap.

He noted his position on the GPS and moved on more cautiously, alert to the danger but also to the opportunity. Twenty years patrolling Bakunda National Park had taught him the signs to watch out for. If it was an elephant – and it could be – its next move was hard to predict. It could bolt, or stay put, watching him, waiting for him to leave.

He looked around again. It was six months since he'd last seen one. The animals had learned to be wary of men and their guns and rarely ventured near the edge of the forest, except sometimes at dawn when they came to drink at the river.

But it might not be an elephant. His heart beat faster. He shouldn't have come on his own.

He tutted. He knew the forest. He knew how to look after himself. He cut open a hanging tree root and let its water trickle into his mouth to refresh himself, then continued on his way. It was a dead branch breaking off, he told himself as he checked his rifle was still hanging over his shoulder.

The trail was overgrown. Like so much else here, it wasn't maintained. He hacked a way through with his machete, all the time looking out for signs of poachers, like a clearing used for a bush camp, or cartridge shells, or wild snares.

Bakunda National Park was virgin rainforest. It needed to be protected. It needed him. His colleagues – most of them – they didn't care; they were lazy and unreliable. His bosses didn't care; for them, it was another job, a stepping stone in their civil service careers. And the government didn't care; the forest for them was a bargaining chip in climate change negotiations. These people didn't know the forest, they didn't love it; and they didn't understand its importance, for Cameroon and the whole world. One day, hopefully, they'd wake up. Hopefully before it was too late.

He was thinking about these things when he came to another abrupt halt. Not because of something he heard but because of something he saw, right in front of him.

He scratched his head. Checked his GPS. Switched it off and on again; checked it once more. Shook his head in disbelief.

'*Mamami yee.* This can't be.'

Chapter 2

The door is shut behind him but not locked. They know he will not try to escape. They have given him two rooms, well appointed. How typical of these people that now they should spare him no comfort.

Through the open window he can see lights from the trading ships anchored in the bay. He leans out and listens for sounds of the river, like a night fisherman paddling his *pirogue*. But all is quiet. The river has been the lifeblood of his people and has made them rich, and it strikes him only now that he will not see it again.

He carries the newly-lit candle to the desk, sits himself down, adjusts his bow tie, pinches at the front corners of his starched shirt collar, and starts to write.

DOUALA, CAMEROON
AUGUST 7TH 1914

I am Rudolf Douala Manga Bell, son of Manga Ndumbe and Tomedi Mwasso. I am King of the Douala people – until tomorrow. I leave this brief memoir so that the truth may be known; otherwise, I fear it will follow me into my grave and stay buried for ever.

Today, my faithful assistant Ngosso Din and I were brought before a court, accused of treason against the German Kaiser and the German people. The hearing lasted three hours. No evidence was presented. No witnesses were called. We had no lawyer.

The prosecutor was also the judge, a man by the name of Neidermayer, who has lived in our country ten years and rejoices in telling us how much he loathes it; who enjoys his large mansion with his hoard of cats, and the services of a cook, a washer-woman, a sweeper, and a nanny for his children – an army of domestic servants whom he does not hesitate to flog with hard rope should he judge them not to be sweating enough ...

Let me not be diverted.

I was arrested three months ago. I have not seen my family since. My wife Emma Engome and four of our children are, I am told, at home in the royal palace in Bonanjo, a few hundred metres from where I sit. They were not at the hearing; no one from the public was present. Our eldest son Alexandre Ndoumbe is in Germany, being schooled in the court of Kaiser Wilhelm II. I doubt he knows his protector has sanctioned his father's execution.

It was alleged I was plotting a rebellion against German rule in Cameroon; that in this enterprise I had been seeking to enlist the support of my fellow chiefs. According to Neidermayer, I wanted the British to take over. That was a lie. What I wanted was for my people to be free.

Did I turn their heads? the despicable prosecutor asked. I replied I had opened their eyes to the wrongdoings of the Germans, the Germans who will not accept us as human beings, let alone as equals. And I had warned our neighbouring chiefs: should they allow the Germans to take the Douala land now, it would be their land next.

Neidermayer said I was a snake. 'Never compare whites and

blacks,' he protested. 'Without us whites, you would not know how to live.' He said this though we Africans have lived well for many centuries, indeed since long before the Europeans came to our shores. To think I once admired these people.

The trial was as we expected. The only surprise was that it took as long as it did. Now that the Germans are at war with the British, they are in a hurry.

Tomorrow they will take us to the gallows.

Ngosso Din and I are not afraid to die. We are prepared. We all have to die someday. And though we will miss our families, and will not ever enjoy the company of our grandchildren and our great grandchildren, we know it is better to die young with honour than to die old in shame.

Chapter 3

'Now, my friend, the game is up.'

Patrice Le Congo stood behind the door, arm raised, ready to strike. He kept perfectly still. He knew it was there, camouflaged against the dark wood panels. He tapped gently to coax it out, saw the movement and smacked the door hard. But when he pulled back his hand there was nothing. He looked around and saw it drifting up the wall, silently; strange how they only ever made a noise when you couldn't see them, dancing around your ears as you lay helpless in the night. It came to a stop. Out of reach. But not for long.

'You've got wings, I've got brains.'

He went to the low table in the middle of the room and picked up a newspaper, rolled it up, walked quietly back to the wall, stretched up … and … thwack.

'Justice!'

A bloody stain and a few squashed threads were all that remained. Patrice left the battle scene and went downstairs.

'Good morning, *oga*,' the waiter said. 'You sleep fine?'

'No. A mosquito kept me awake. But this morning I got my revenge.' He held up the newspaper to show the other half of the bloody mark left on the wall.

'You don't have mosquitoes in Congo?'

'In the forest, of course, but not in Bukavu. They don't like the altitude.'

'You are leaving today, *oga*?'

Patrice nodded.

'You don't like Cameroon?'

'I don't like mosquitoes.' He did like Cameroon and he'd been happy to get away from the troubles in Congo. He'd *needed* to get away. But now he was looking forward to going home; looking forward to fresh tilapia, caught in Lake Kivu and grilled in a chilli pepper marinade …

The waiter brought his omelette and plantain and instant coffee. Patrice ate while he read the newspaper, then went to his room to pack. Before he could finish, there was a knock on the door.

A young man he'd been working with was there, crying. 'Please, Mr Congo, come. My mother is in the hospital.'

Patrice checked the time. 'Let's go.' They hurried downstairs and climbed on to a waiting *okada*.

A hazy sun was up. Bakingi town was warm and wide awake as the motorcycle taxi sped down the main street, weaving through the throng of traffic, to the hospital. The young man's mother was sitting in a waiting area. Her face was bruised and swollen.

'*Mami*, you know this Mr Congo …'

The woman stared into space. She looked shell-shocked.

Patrice took her hand. 'It's okay, *Mami*, you can talk to me. Tell me what happened.'

'The indigenes came,' she said, quietly. 'This morning. They said they want to take back their land. I said, "No, I won't go; it's my land now, my farm is here." They hit me with sticks and stripped me naked. That is how my sisters found me.'

'I'm sorry, *Mami*, for your suffering. Did the police come?'

'You know the police never take our side in this business.'

Patrice sighed. 'I will emphasize in my report that this dispute in Ekindila village is getting worse. I wish I could do more to help. But I'm leaving today.'

He patted the woman gently on the arm and wished her and her son well, and took an *okada* back to his hotel. He would update his report and submit it to the African Union's Human Rights Commission, but would it help these people get the protection and justice they deserved and desperately needed? The Commission meant well but it had no powers to enforce any recommendations. Its offices in Banjul in The Gambia were a long way from the forests of Cameroon.

As if to make the point, as Patrice was about to walk down to reception to pay his bill he got a call on a crackly line from the head of the Commission's investigations unit, his boss. He held the phone away from his ear. Josie Mwinga always shouted when she spoke on the phone.

'Hello, Patrice, can you hear me?'

'Hello, ma'am, yes, I can hear you.'

Mwinga congratulated him on his work and said she was looking forward to reading his report. She promised to flag up the urgency of the situation. She said she had a friend who worked in Cameroon's Ministry of Justice, who would ensure the matter came to the attention of the relevant authorities. Then her voice softened and climbed to a friendlier pitch.

'So, Patrice, when's your flight?'

'Tomorrow; I'm leaving for Douala this morning.'

'Okay, good. Before you go, would you mind checking out something for us?'

Patrice recognised this was a command not a request.

'It won't take long. It's a favour for a colleague who works on the AU's Environmental Protection Committee. I bumped into him at a meeting in Addis the other day and he was asking if we had anyone in Cameroon …'

The long build-up was ominous.

'… so, what it is, Patrice, there's a man who's been in contact with members of that committee, warning of serious problems in Bakunda National Park … he's a park ranger and he says security in the park is being neglected, despite promises by the government to do something about it, and now the wildlife is being threatened by poachers to the point of extinction; and as you know, Patrice, the AU is committed to safeguarding the continent's rich biodiversity …'

'I'm sure this is important,' Patrice said. 'But with respect, ma'am, it doesn't sound like a human rights issue.'

'No, no, you're absolutely right there. It's just, well, they've lost contact with this man and it's a bit tricky because no one in that place knows he's been talking to people at the African Union. So rather than calling from Addis or Banjul and arousing suspicions, we were thinking you could get in touch with this man, to check he's alright …'

She gave Patrice the man's name and said, 'Thanks so much.'

Patrice looked at his suitcase with a sinking feeling. Bakunda was hours away and not in the direction of Douala. He noticed the blood-stained newspaper on the table and wondered how many millions of mosquitoes lived in the national park. Then he remembered something …

He flipped through the newspaper. He found what he was looking for on page eight, below a report about an armed robbery on a group of cattle traders; a headline he'd half noticed while eating breakfast: *Elephant Tramples Ranger*.

Chapter 4

The smell of fish cooking over charcoal drifted across the dark, open courtyard of Mama's, a backstreet restaurant in the Bonabéri neighbourhood of Douala, Cameroon's largest city. Mama was fanning the coals in the kitchen, in a corner; her daughter sat on an old sofa watching a Nigerian soap on TV. The night was hot and still.

The only customers were two men who sat on white plastic chairs at a white plastic table. In contrast to the informal setting, they wore well-tailored Western clothes: Pierre Mponda in a dark blazer over a white tee shirt; the deputy minister in a grey business suit.

Mponda enjoyed the moment as his boss took in the surroundings. The deputy minister had come from the airport and Mponda was his host for the evening. *'J'espère que votre visite à Londres a été un succès, monsieur?'*

'*Nous verrons*, Pierre. We shall see. Those people say one thing to your face but something completely different when your back is turned. There were handshakes but nothing is certain until there are signatures on pieces of paper.'

'I am certain you will have done the utmost to promote the opportunities in our country to them, sir. I hope also you were able to relax and go sightseeing?'

'Alas, no. I was in meetings all day long. At this level, that's how it is. Somehow, the minister made time to visit his sons, who are schooling there, and to take his wife shopping …' The deputy minister raised a mischievous eyebrow.

'Aha.' Mponda showed he understood the gesture. He was excited his boss had such confidence in him. 'But you have a night in Douala. I hope this evening will make you feel that whatever happens, your trip has not been wasted.'

The deputy minister looked around. 'I admit, I am curious as to why you have brought me here, Pierre, for the one evening I have in this city. There are restaurants across the bridge where we may have been more comfortable. But then I know you like to play games.'

Mponda grinned. 'When you taste the fish, sir, then you will appreciate why we came here. Out of all the places to eat in Douala, this is my favourite. But there's another reason. For here, it is quiet, as you can see. We will not be seen, nor heard.'

He turned in his chair and called across. 'Mama, *des boissons*. Bring us drinks, Mutzig and 7up.'

Mama sent her daughter over with the bottles. The girl placed them on the table without a word and went back to her television.

'You won't take some beer with me, Pierre?'

'I don't like the taste of alcohol, especially when I am working. It disturbs my concentration.'

'And you are working now?'

'I am always working, sir.'

His companion chuckled. 'I was teasing you. So tell me what it is you wish to discuss, that is so secret.'

Mponda took his time, careful not to come across as

over-enthusiastic. 'I know our country well, sir, and not just Douala. My work takes me to all parts. I understand our people; their wishes, their fears; their strengths, their weaknesses. I am also a man who gets things done.'

'I'll drink to that, Pierre,' the deputy minister said, taking a sip of his beer. 'But you don't need to sell yourself to me. We have worked together long enough to know we make a good team, that we have the same vision.'

'Thank you, sir.' Mponda raised his 7up and they clinked bottles. 'You observed that I like games. Did you know that I play chess?'

'I did not. But I am not surprised.'

Mponda was getting close. He needed to show he had thought everything through. His boss was greedy but he was also cautious.

'I like chess because you have to look for opportunities and to work out the different possibilities, to predict how your opponent may react. And I believe I have spotted an opportunity now; let me say, a situation that could be exploited to our mutual benefit.'

With the single bar of light fixed to a wall behind the deputy minister it was hard to see the look on his face. But the way he sat up made it clear he was interested.

'It's not so far from here. You could say it's an opportunity rooted in economic development; recent and not so recent; personal and political.'

'I'm intrigued, Pierre. Tell me more.'

Mama brought their fish: a single large carp, charred, the juices sparkling in the gashes scored on its side, topped with rings of onion. The plate stretched across the table.

'Let's eat,' Mponda said. 'I think you have an appetite now.'

Chapter 5

A gust of wind blows in, the candle flame sways and stretches. There's a crack of thunder. The night-time storm begins. King Rudolf Douala Manga Bell walks to the window. Cool, wet air slaps his face. The palms outside are bent over double, fronds twisting and flapping. He holds out a hand. The raindrops sting like needles.

Paradoxically, the tempestuous night helps him to see things clearly - perhaps because it is his last. As he looks back over his life, he understands that everything that's happened has been leading inevitably to this point. From the day he was born, it was destined to be this way; such is the relentless force of history.

He dries his hand and returns to the writing desk.

My grandfather and my father were kings before me, and it was they who educated me about my kingdom-to-be. They made me understand how the Douala people had prospered, first through fishing, then from river trade. They initiated me into our culture and traditions. They related the epic stories of the Douala folk heroes; my favourite was Jeki la Njambe.

I can recall, as a boy, sitting with my grandfather in front of a fire late one night when I was supposed to be sleeping. Spellbound by the old man's rasping voice, I listened as he told me how Jeki la Njambe once threw a spear over Mongo-ma-Lobo, the Mountain of Thunder.

What, I ask myself now, would Jeki la Njambe do in my current situation? He was strong and brave. He overcame the snake, the crocodile, the lion and the eagle and assumed their powers; but in Jeki la Njambe's time it was easier to distinguish between good and evil.

My grandfather and my father told me we must also learn the white man's sciences, otherwise we will be their slaves. So it was the Germans who educated me about the wider world. As a young prince I attended the German school in Douala, and at the age of twelve I was sent to Germany to continue my education at the secondary school in Ulm. I shared a boat to Hamburg with a cargo of ivory and palm oil.

It was in Ulm that I met Hermann von Roehm. At first, we were friends. While other boys made no secret of their disdain for me, calling me names I don't wish to repeat, Roehm was happy to share my company. He took me to his house. I met his family. I dined with them. The two of us shared a taste for fine clothes and for learning and for culture.

All was fine between us until a strange incident occurred. It was the summer of 1890. I was seventeen. We had gone with Roehm's mother and his older sister Rosa to attend the grand opening of Ulm Minster, the tallest church in the world. When the ceremony was over, Roehm and I climbed the staircase inside the steeple to the viewing platform at the top level. From that high point, one could see far across southern Germany, as far even as the snow-capped peaks of the Alps.

I confess, looking down at the miniature people on the ground below brought on me a feeling of dizziness; the stiff breeze swirling around the corners of the stone balcony caused me to reach for the back wall to steady myself. My companion, however, was not so unsettled. He jumped on to a narrow ledge and, with the sheer drop behind him, declared, 'Lang lebe Deutchland! Douala Manga, this is proof that of all the people in the world, God wishes us Germans to be closest to Him.'

I thought nothing of that remark at the time, partly because I took it for youthful bluster, and partly because Roehm slipped. He cried out. His arms wavered. He teetered on the edge. Other visitors screamed as he began to fall backwards. I jumped forward, grabbed him round the knee and pulled him hard so that he landed flat on his backside, but on the safe side of the ledge. Two men ran up and helped Roehm to his feet. 'You need to be careful here', I recall one of them saying. He was talking to Roehm but looking at me. 'And about whom you choose as your friends.'

Roehm dusted himself down. When the men had returned to their friends, he turned on me. 'What on earth came over you, Douala Manga? You could have killed me. As it is, you have humiliated me in front of some of our most prominent citizens.'

How ironic that I saved Roehm's life.

From that day, things turned cool between us. The invitations for dinner at the von Roehm family home ceased and he, like the others, now shunned me. Until, that is, one evening the following year, when I was soon to leave Ulm to go to study law at the University of Bonn and Roehm had been offered a position in Berlin in the office of the Secretary of State for the Colonies. A carriage was sent to collect me from my lodgings and take me to the von Roehm residence, a large town house with a garden that sloped down to the old city wall, beyond which was the River Danube. I can still remember what I wore that evening: a blue double-breasted suit, high white collar and check bow tie.

The family were in the garden when I arrived. The younger children were singing and making daisy chains. Roehm's mother and his sister Rosa were sitting in a wicker swinging chair. I greeted them with a bow. Frau von Roehm said it was delightful to see me again and Rosa smiled warmly. I cannot deny I would happily have spent the entire evening in their company, as they had both always made me feel welcome. But a sense of obligation led me to join Roehm and his father and his older brother Franz, who were standing by the house discussing a recent exchange of territory between Germany and Great Britain in which Germany had ceded the Indian Ocean island of Zanzibar to Britain in return for the island of Heligoland in the North Sea. The conversation went like this:

'Ah, the young lawyer-to-be,' Herr von Roehm announced. 'Lange her, seit wir uns das letze Mal gesehen haben. It's been a long time.'

'Sir,' I replied.

'We were asking ourselves what interest the British could have in Zanzibar. Was ist Ihre Ansicht? Do you have a view?'

'I would say cloves, and a position of nuisance near to Dar-es-Salaam. But I would be guessing. I think I may better understand what advantage Germany seeks to gain from the transaction.'

The old man snorted. His sons frowned.

'Offensichtlich,' I said. 'It's obvious. You wish to build a naval base in Heligoland.'

'Young man, the exchange from Germany's point of view is simply to get the British off an island that is geographically part of Germany. I advise you to stick to subjects about which you are qualified to speak.'

'Such as matters concerning Africa?'

'There is no call for facetiousness. As you know, Hermann is

going to work for the Secretary of State for the Colonies. I trust we can be assured you will offer him all the help you can? Who knows, you may one day be working together.'

The reason for my being invited back to the von Roehm family home became clear. 'If he feels able to accept my help, I will be honoured. Provided our interests concur.'

'Young Douala Manga, you have developed an arrogant streak. What is in the interests of Germany is in the interests of your people too. I believe your grandfather has done well both for himself and the Douala people as a result of our partnership.'

'That is true, sir. And long may it continue like that.'

Throughout the conversation, the young Roehm was focussed on his shoes, not uttering a word. I had long since assumed our friendship was over, as he must have too, and he was now embarrassed by the prospect that he might one day be calling on me for favours. At least, that is what I thought then.

I remember that evening so well, not just for that tense exchange that now, looking back, I see held so much foreboding but also for another altogether different reason.

Douala Manga glances up at the slanting rain. It is a long time since he has reflected on his years in Germany and his last visit to the von Roehm residence in Ulm. Regardless of the way it ended, and indeed his present circumstances, a faint smile pulls on his lips.

The conversation over dinner was more relaxed. Frau von Roehm asked how I was looking forward to studying in Bonn, and the young children asked for stories about encounters with wild animals in Africa. Afterwards, Herr von Roehm announced he would be enjoying a cigar and schnapps, and asked us young men to join him. But as I made for his library at the front of the house, his son Hermann grabbed my arm and insisted we take a turn in the garden instead.

We had not walked far before he began speaking. 'Douala Manga, I hope you realise this was my father's idea.'

'To what do you refer?'

'I feared you would find this situation difficult. My father seems to think I shall end up in Cameroon, but there is much more likelihood of me going to Tanganyika; that is where the real German imperial expansion is taking place. That is where the future is, would you not agree?'

I found Roehm's failure to acknowledge that we had once been friends immature and disrespectful.

'The future can be unpredictable,' I said. 'But if you do come to Cameroon, I hope that we can talk to each other as men and that we can be honourable in our dealings.'

Roehm walked to the house without inviting me to follow.

It was a warm midsummer's night. I strolled down to the bottom of the garden and through a door in the wall that opened on to the riverside, unaware that it was in fact I who was being followed.

A full moon was shining brightly on the calm water. I had not been home for six years and I longed then to be there, standing by the banks of the Wouri River. It had not been easy being an African in Germany, but I had remained resolute. I never forgot why I was there. And if I felt alone at that moment, it was a feeling that did not last long, because out of the night a voice called to me.

'Douala Manga, komm her!"

I looked around and could see no one. Then it called again.

'The willow tree.'

I walked to the tree by the riverbank and parted the curtain of hanging leaves. Standing inside was Rosa. Before I could say a word, she pulled me towards her. She pressed her body against mine and we kissed. One thing led hastily to another. Before long we were lying on the ground, in the darkness under the willow tree, breathless and amazed.

But then the curtain parted again, and her brother, my former friend, appeared above us.

'Hermann!' Rosa cried in horror. She jumped up, smoothing her dress.

Roehm's face was filling with rage, like a balloon about to burst. I struggled to my feet as Rosa made off. Roehm pushed me back to the ground. Then he undid his belt and started lashing out.

I will not write the words he said as he whipped the buckle down on me, for I accept he was in a fury. But as I cowered below and glanced up from under the arm I had raised for protection, I saw on his lips a hateful smile.

Remembering how he accused me of raping his sister, though he had seen us lying peacefully together, it is strange that I did not conclude then as I do now: that there is nothing our colonial masters enjoy more than an excuse to flog an African.

I left that night without saying goodbye to my hosts, being forced to flee along the riverside path. I have no idea what, if anything, Roehm said to Rosa. But I am sure he said nothing to his father, otherwise I would have heard from the police.

Soon afterwards I went to Bonn. I never saw Rosa again. Sadly, I cannot say the same for her brother.

Chapter 6

Patrice picked up his phone to call Josie Mwinga and tell her what he'd read about her colleague's contact in the national park. One short paragraph:

A park ranger has been trampled to death by an elephant in Bakunda National Park. The ranger, named as Alex Ebot, aged 42, was crushed by the beast while on patrol in a remote area.

He'd tell her the sad news then he'd be on his way. He'd be in Douala that evening, putting the finishing touches to his report and enjoying his last dinner in Cameroon. That port city was famous for its fresh fish.

But then he imagined her voice exploding out of his phone. *'Oh yeah? Killed by an elephant?'* She'd be right to be sceptical. The man had been complaining about a lack of security in the park and now he was dead. And Patrice, as an investigator, relied on such people - people prepared to speak out even if it meant putting themselves in danger.

He leafed through the pages of the newspaper and found a list of its reporters. *Bakingi Bureau: Sally Bintu.* He called her and told her he had information about the land dispute in Ekindila. She told him to take an *okada* to the Green Oil filling station near the chief's palace and she'd meet him in the bar next door.

Ten minutes later he was sitting at a blue plastic table on the terrace in front of the bar when a young woman with a pale complexion, fine features and a red streak in her loose-curled hair walked up and joined him.

'Patrice Le Congo?' she asked, pulling a notebook out of her bag. She wore a sleeveless yellow shirt, tight jeans and white trainers.

'Sally Bintu? How did you guess?'

'We don't get many visitors in Bakingi, not from other countries.' She looked at him more closely as she spoke, tilting her head to one side. 'Your Afro?'

Patrice returned her look.

The reporter touched her own hair with her finger tips. 'I'm not from here either.' She smiled tightly.

They ordered soft drinks; Coke for her, lemon Fanta for him. Patrice told her about his investigation and about the attack on the woman who was now in the hospital.

The reporter listened and made notes. 'That's terrible,' she said, when he'd finished. 'Naked aggression.'

'You could put it like that. I hope you won't. To make a play on words ...'

'I'm sorry. I was thinking out loud. I try to offer headlines for stories I'm writing. I believe it's good practice, and helps me to get the right angle.'

'I see. This is not a game, you know, for these people.'

The young woman glared at him. 'Are you a reporter?'

'No.'

'Then don't tell me how to do my job.'

'All I'm saying is, treat this business sensitively. The family are distressed.'

She turned up her nose and looked away.

They sat for a while with their drinks, watching the traffic, not talking. Then she said, 'It's strange. You've been here how long?'

'Three weeks.'

'And we haven't met before?'

'We keep a low profile. The idea is to raise human rights issues with national governments but quietly. "Soft pressure." So, please keep me and my mission out of your story.'

'*No wahala*. No problem. But thank you for the tip. I'll go to the hospital right away.' She made to stand.

'Wait. There was something I wanted to ask you.'

'I thought so,' she said, settling again in her chair. 'Nothing's ever for free.'

'I was interested in the report on the park ranger who was killed by the elephant.'

'I don't know why you should be. It's not very interesting. If human rights is your area, there are other things you could investigate down there, like the farmers who are losing their land – not the death of a careless park ranger.'

'Well, it's ironic, if nothing else. His job is to protect the elephants, and then one of them kills him.'

The reporter frowned, as if this hadn't occurred to her. 'Elephants cause damage and destruction,' she said. 'Villagers complain about them.'

'But a park ranger would know how to look after himself.'

'Accidents can happen. To be honest with you, I wrote the story because there was nothing else that day. I was surprised the paper found room to print it.'

She sounded defensive. Either that or she lacked curiosity. Patrice guessed she hadn't been in the job for long. 'How did you find out about it?'

'*You no dey ever tire for ask something?* A contact tipped me off. He works in the park's tourist centre in Bakunda town. I confirmed the details with the park authorities.'

'Can I speak to your contact?'

'It's fine,' she said. She pulled out her phone and read out a number. 'His name's Adam Tarkang.'

'Do you know of problems at the park, like a lack of security, poaching ...?'

'Of course, there's poaching in all the national parks. Like all public amenities in Cameroon, they suffer from a lack of investment. Even if funds are allocated, it doesn't mean they reach their destination.'

'I understand. Thank you, Sally Bintu, for your time.'

'It's no problem,' she said, putting her notebook in her bag. 'You can call me Sally. As a matter of fact, apart from the story you've told me about I didn't have much on today.'

'There's no other news here?'

The reporter narrowed her eyes. '*Chai this man*! Are you sure you're not a reporter like me?'

'Quite sure,' he said. 'But our work is similar: pestering people for information, writing reports.'

She nodded, seriously. 'Well, if you want to know, right now all my paper's interested in is the preparations for the fiftieth anniversary of reunification, and there's little to say about that here in Bakingi.'

'Reunification of what?'

'Of Cameroon – when the former British part of Cameroon joined the rest of the country after independence. Well, half of it joined, and half of it joined Nigeria. There was a plebiscite; it's complicated.'

'Oh, maybe I did read about that. When is the anniversary?'

'Another question! But that's a good one. Because nobody knows. The actual date was two years ago, but they keep postponing the celebration. Now there are rumours it will happen soon, and the president will come to South West Region, and that's what the paper writes about, these rumours.' She shrugged her shoulders.

'Knowing your country's history is important.'

'I know that,' she said, her face lighting up, like a child's. 'I like history. I did a history module when I was studying journalism and mass communication. I'm actually doing some historical research at the moment in my spare time for a story proposal.'

'That shows initiative,' he said. It was good to know she was interested in something and hard not to smile at her enthusiasm.

'My editor will probably tell me it's not news, but I believe you cannot understand the present if you don't know what happened in the past.'

'Well, good luck. I'll look out for your reports. And your headlines. As a journalist, you're already writing history; you're writing the history of tomorrow!'

She laughed. 'Thank you. And good luck to you too.' She rose from her seat. 'And safe journey.'

She handed Patrice her business card and he gave her his. 'You can call me Patrice.'

'Okay, Patrice. I like that. But your family name is strange.' She screwed up her nose. 'I don't know anyone called Cameroon, or any other country's name.'

'There is a story behind my names,' he said. 'A historical one. I'll tell you next time we meet, if we ever do.'

'Intriguing!' she said, 'I'll keep you to that. I'll tell you about my family history too. It's said we are descended from kings.' She raised her chin in a mock show of nobility and then broke into a smile.

Patrice wasn't sure what she meant, but he smiled back.

'About the ranger,' she said, turning as she walked away, 'let me know if you find out anything.'

Patrice waved and watched her climb on to an *okada* and speed off through a puff of black exhaust.

Then he called the number she'd given him.

'Hello, Adam Tarkang?'

A young man's voice answered. 'Yes, who's this?'

Patrice introduced himself, and said he was calling on behalf of a friend who knew Alex Ebot, the park ranger. 'The reporter, Sally Bintu, gave me your number.'

'Oh, okay. But I don't think there's anything I can tell you than I didn't tell her.'

'My friend just wants to understand what happened. Was the ranger with anyone at the time of the ... incident? A witness? Who I could talk to?'

'No. Alex, the ranger, was alone.'

'So, just so I can explain it to my friend, how do they know it was an elephant that killed him?'

'Well, I don't know, I don't know anything, but when they found him, that's what they said. His ribcage was damaged, so I suppose ... and they probably saw tracks ...'

'Where in the park did it happen? Is it a place where elephants are known to be?'

'Yes, it was in the south of the park. There are elephants there but not as many as in the past. It's the same with all the animals, they're still being hunted.'

'Is the park not protected?'

'The rangers patrol the park as best they can, and a few soldiers guard the main entrance. But it's a large area. I mean, you'd need an army to keep the poachers out.'

'It's the same in Congo. Thank you, Tarkang. You've been helpful. I'll tell my friend.'

'Thank you, Mr Le Congo, you are welcome. You know, there is one thing ... it may not be important, but there was something strange about the route Alex took that day.'

'Strange?'

'Yes. The place where he fell, he was walking back the way he'd come.'

'Is that unusual?'

'Well, yes, the park is big, so they don't waste time covering the same ground twice.'

'How do you know he did this, if he was on his own?'

'We have the signals sent from his GPS tracker. You can see where he went. It's hard to explain, but if you come I can show you what I mean.'

Chapter 7

Sally looked back over her shoulder. Through the exhaust smoke she saw the Congolese investigator on his phone. He probably thought she was crazy for saying she was descended from kings. She quite liked him. He'd been a bit patronising, but he had kind eyes. And she liked the way he went about his business dressed casually, in a tee shirt, jeans and sandals, as if he didn't care what people thought about him. It was odd, though, how interested he was in the death of the park ranger.

She bit her lip. She hadn't been thorough in the way she'd followed up the story. She'd written down what the park official had told her, but she hadn't stopped to think there might be more to it.

The week before, her editor had told her that her story count was too low. Sally had said it wasn't her fault that Bakingi was a quiet town. He'd said there were stories everywhere; it was her job to find them.

Hopefully the story she'd been told about today would make him see she had potential. But as she paid the *okada* and climbed the steps to the hospital, she was left with a nagging feeling that she wasn't cut out for this work.

A receptionist told her to wait while she sent for a doctor.

When the doctor came, he told her she couldn't see the woman who'd been attacked because she wasn't in a fit state to talk and had been admitted. He suggested she speak to the woman's family, but he didn't know when they would be coming.

Her phone rang. It was a colleague at the *Courier*.

'Lucy. How are you?'

'Hey, sister, I'm fine. You?'

'So so, you know.'

'Are you busy?'

Lucy Kometa worked at the Douala bureau, the paper's second biggest after Buea. She was the one reporter at the *Courier* who took an interest in Sally.

'You know this place. Not much happens here.'

'Sally, we need your help. A job's come up, an interview, something I've been trying to arrange for a long time. But it means coming here, to Douala. The day after tomorrow.'

'I don't mind, Lucy. What's it about?'

'Sugar daddies. It's a series I'm working on, about HIV. I've been trying to find a girl who'll talk, a girl who's got a sugar daddy, about the risks they take. It's hard to find them, and then to persuade them to share their story. But a friend's daughter, who's at university, she knows a girl who's got this man who gives her things, her tuition fees and more, in return for, well, you know. But she won't talk to me.'

'Why not? Why will she talk to me if she won't talk to you?'

'She wants to talk to a young woman, she says, someone who'll be able to understand her. I thought, you're young, you were recently in university, so she'll feel comfortable with you. Anyway, it has to be you, because you're the only young woman reporter we have!'

'Well, okay, thanks, sister.' It sounded promising to Sally. She wasn't especially interested in the subject – girls who did that kind of thing, well, they must know they were taking risks – but it could raise her profile. She pictured herself at a meeting with the senior editorial staff. 'Shall I come to the office so you can brief me?'

There was a pause the other end before Lucy came back, speaking more quietly, as if her hand was cupped around her mouth.

'The thing is, our editor doesn't know about the story yet. I want to wait till I've got all the angles in the bag before I put it to him – you know, he's conservative about sex and moral stuff. But don't worry, I'll cover your expenses – I'll pay your fare, and you can stay in my apartment, if that's okay with you?'

'But then … the interview will be under your byline?'

'Let's say, I'll owe you one. And this will be good experience for you.'

Sally kissed her teeth. 'What if something happens here and I'm not around to cover it?'

'Like you said, not much happens there! But if it does, you can return, and no one will ever know you were gone …'

Sally said she'd see her colleague in two days, ended the call and sat down in the hospital reception area to wait.

It was late evening by the time Sally had talked to the old woman's family and been to the cybercafé to write her report and email it to the *Courier*, and eaten rice and stew, and finally climbed the steps to the small room she rented above a hairdresser's salon. Feeling, at last, at the end of a long day, that her time was her own, she sat on her bed, propped up with pillows, and opened an old book she'd bought at a stall in the market, a torn and battered biography of King Rudolph Douala Manga Bell.

It was funny, she reflected, remembering her conversation with Patrice Le Congo, how her interest in history had been sparked by the story her mother used to tell, about the family having a secret royal heritage, and how she'd spent hours as a girl reading a book about the kings and queens of England and looking at the colourful pictures.

And now here she was conducting research into the life of a Cameroonian king. The book Sally had found was part of a series called *Heroes of the Resistance*. As the title suggested, it was a favourable account. "What must his state of mind have been," the writer asked, "to leave his wife and family, and to go knowingly to his death?"

Very little had been written about Douala Manga, so Sally devoured every word. Making notes in the margins, she soon became engrossed, and forgot all about story counts and sugar daddies and the poor woman in the hospital and the unfortunate ranger in the national park.

Chapter 8

The storm has passed but the air outside is still dark and muggy. Douala Manga could climb through the window and slip away, unheard, unseen. His captors would like it if he did - they would say it proved his guilt. And it would give them an excuse to go through the town, door to door, exacting retribution on his people.

It occurs to him that his decision not to flee could lead it to be said of him one day that he was a brave man. But, in that case, those who said it should know that, really, he had no choice in the matter.

The only time in my life I can say I was truly afraid was the day I came face to face with an elephant. It was ten years ago.

I had travelled upriver by canoe with a dozen men after news came that a marauding herd of elephants had gone on the rampage in the village of Ngembum. A guard in the service of the chief had been killed when he tried to stop the animals entering the village. One of the elephants had picked up the man with his trunk and smashed him on to the ground.

We arrived with guns. The aim was not to kill the elephants, but to get them to return to the forest. We spotted them close to the river, below the falls that lie upstream from the village. We spread ourselves out in a semi-circle. I counted to three, and we fired in the air as one. It was a deafening blast which sent the animals running off across the water and into the trees on the other side. But then, from behind us, a single bull came charging. Before we had time to reload our rifles, the elephant was bearing down on us. We scattered, looking for cover.

Even now, so long after the event, my heart races as I recall what happened next.

I turned to run like the others but slipped in the mud as I tried to scale a steep path by the side of the falls. The giant beast was almost upon me. Without time to think, I threw myself to the side. I felt the elephant's front foot brush against my waist. The ground shook, as the animal thundered by.

But the danger was not over. My balance was lost and I tumbled over the side of the riverbank and into the swirling waters below the falls. I was thrown around, head over heels underwater. Reaching out in all directions, one of my hands by chance slapped against a boulder. I held on to it and pulled myself to the surface, spluttering and gasping for air.

When my father found out about my encounter with the elephant, he lectured me with a wagging finger. By putting my life in danger, he told me, I had put the future of my people in danger too. 'Do not forget,' he told me, 'one day you are to be king.'

The Douala man has more respect for the elephant than for any German. He reveres the forest in which the elephant resides, and its mighty rivers and waterfalls, more than he does the so-called German empire. The Douala man may know, like I do, of the secrets that lie within that forest. When the white man comes to our land, he sees darkness. He does not think black people can teach him anything, yet the white man has a lot to learn!

I returned from my studies in Germany by the same ship I

had taken to Hamburg all those years before. On the way back I accompanied a cargo of munitions, alcohol and tobacco, as well as chests full of watches, pipes and umbrellas.

With a degree in law, I was sent by my grandfather to work for the colonial administration as a judge. It is with deep shame now that I admit to being blinded by loyalty to my royal lineage and hoodwinked by my German education. I allowed myself to believe that I belonged in social status with our German masters and was superior to other Cameroonians. And that is how I was able to sit in a velvet-lined black robe and white shirt and white tie, dispatching my own countrymen to jails far worse than the one where I now sit, sometimes for the most menial offences.

Recalling now how I once sentenced a man to three months' forced labour on a plantation (a plantation owned by my family) for stealing a single fish from the market, I can but hang my head and beg for forgiveness. For the record, let me state that in the three years I dispensed German justice, I never once ordered anyone to be flogged. But I suspect this nuance was lost on my people, for whom the arrogant young dandy presiding over the court must have appeared as German as the Kaiser himself. Perhaps it is the case that a man will not see he has wronged others until others have wronged him.

It was during this period that my grandfather died and my father succeeded to the Douala throne. My grandfather, Ndoumbe Lobe Bell, was a formidable character who left ninety-nine widows. He had managed to assert the authority of the Bells over the other big Douala families, persuading most of them to sign, along with him, a treaty with the Germans in 1884.

The treaty accepted that the Germans would be in charge of the administration of Cameroon, but the land would still be owned by Cameroonians. This suited my grandfather well, as he owned a lot of land, and now the Germans would help him protect his property with their laws. When another clan leader challenged him shortly after the treaty was signed, my grandfather sent a hundred men to set fire to his opponent's villages.

My father, Manga Bell, was - in contrast to his father - a man of peace and compromise and believed in the importance of economic development for the people of Cameroon. I helped him expand our territory, convinced it was for the benefit of the entire country. Our palm and cocoa plantations were vast, and we travelled up the creeks in a motor boat to inspect them together. When we arrived in a village, there would be a grand reception, with canoe races and wrestling tournaments, singing and story-telling.

And then it was my turn.

Douala Manga watches a drop of wax slide down the half-burned candle. His thoughts turn to a night such as this four years earlier. Then, as now, he was waiting for the dawn. But then he was looking forward to a day that marked the beginning, not the end.

On the eve of my coronation, as on this night, I didn't sleep; then, it was out of excitement, in anticipation of what I would able to achieve for my people as king.

My father had died two years before, but my succession had been challenged by jealous rivals of the Bell dynasty. Eventually they fell into line, and the Douala nation celebrated my enthronement - if not as one, at least in peace. The elders stepped forward on the morning of the coronation to wash their mouths with the leaves of the dibokuboku tree, ensuring in the customary way that their words would not contain hatred or rancour, and took it in turns to denounce past greedy actions of their chiefs. Then Mukekele

Kum'a Mbape, the most senior of the elders, brought out the sceptre and the fly whisk.

'Douala Manga,' he said, 'take first the fly whisk, the symbol of peace and harmony; and now the sceptre, the symbol of strength and war, to be used only as a last resort.'

Finally, in keeping with tradition, I carried across the courtyard a bag containing symbolic Douala possessions, like salt, soap, palm oil, plantain – a heavy load I was duty-bound to carry with courage and patience, to show I understood the weight of the responsibilities I now shouldered.

That day there was joy on the people's faces as they watched the wrestling tournament and heard the great Douala songs and poems. It was a time of high hopes; after two years of feuding, the Douala were united again. We thought better times lay ahead, but we were mistaken.

Chapter 9

The bush taxi bumped along the unpaved road, a Toyota Corolla saloon with seven passengers. Patrice had climbed in over the fold-down seat and was in the back with three others. Three more were in the front. The woman next to the driver had been complaining since they'd left Bakingi that she had to sit with the gear-stick between her legs.

'This is undignified,' she said.

The driver was leaning out of his window, trying to see through the thick clouds of red dust thrown up by the vehicle in front, his right arm stretched inside to guide the steering wheel.

A five-hour drive to Bakunda lay ahead.

A man sitting to Patrice's left said, 'I don't like these one-doors. They're stressful. It is like we are trapped.'

The four of them in the back took it in turns, in pairs, to lean forward or sit back, till the aches or numbness forced them to change positions.

The woman on Patrice's right said, 'This is how we suffer.' The side of her buttock was wrapped around his hip.

'Hey, *mami*,' the man who'd been complaining about one-doors said, 'you think this man from Congo doesn't know what is suffering? Compared to that place, we live in paradise.'

'I suppose everywhere has its problems,' Patrice said.

'Sure, but here in Cameroon we have plenty to eat, and there is no war.'

The man sitting on the other side of the woman said, 'They were supposed to pave this road years ago.' He was a tall man who, like Patrice, was perched forward, but because of his height had to curl his neck down under the roof. 'We were told the money was there, then it disappeared.'

'What happened to the money?' Patrice asked.

'*Wetin really happen with the money*? We will never know. But rest assured the road that leads to the governor's village is in perfect condition.'

'International standard,' someone said.

There was a pause in the conversation before the man who didn't like one-doors asked, 'You know why this road here was cut through the forest in the first place, years ago?'

Nobody answered.

'For slaves,' he said. 'They marched them along this road in chains. The slave raiders came from the neighbouring districts. They caught the slaves and sold them to the Douala, who took them by canoe to the Europeans in Fernando Po, or set them to work on their own plantations.'

Still no one else said a word.

'Many Cameroonians will not know that some of us were free men and some of us were slaves. We learn how the Portuguese came here and named our country after the shrimps in the river; we learn how the Europeans brought us religion and education and took away our slaves and palm oil; we learn that we gained independence. But we are ignorant of the history that is truly ours.'

Patrice was inclined to agree. So much of Africa's past was

missing, lost. 'The Europeans were good at writing things down,' he said. 'So history is theirs.'

'Uh-huh, that is what I am saying. In Africa our history is that which touched the Europeans.'

The road ahead was clear now, the driver back inside his window. But another red cloud swirled in the distance; a truck carrying three huge tree trunks was approaching. As it passed, the taxi was plunged into a dust storm. The driver slowed but there was no visibility, and they thumped into a pothole. A clunk echoed from below, followed by a scraping rattle. The taxi pulled over. The passengers got out to stretch their legs and relieve themselves in the bushes. The driver slid under the car and started tinkering.

Patrice stood by the side of the road, hands on hips, looking over the forest that stretched to the horizon. Douala, with its fresh fish and international airport, was far, far away.

The one-door Toyota Corolla made it to Bakunda around midnight and dropped Patrice at a hotel on the main road into town. In the morning, he took an *okada* to the Bakunda National Park Tourist Centre, which was housed in the park headquarters, a low, red-brick building with a tin roof, set back from the road among palms and other tropical trees.

Adam Tarkang, the young assistant, a short, skinny man, was waiting at the gate. After a brief greeting, he hurried Patrice through to a back office. Tarkang sat in front of a computer terminal and invited Patrice to stand beside him.

'You see these dots here?' Tarkang was pointing at the screen. 'They show the ranger's position. Join them together, and you see the journey he made.' He traced an imaginary line. His face was serious and intense, his brow furrowed.

'The GPS tracker sends out the signal automatically every hour, but these may not get through depending on the density of the tree cover. But the operator can also send out a signal manually; for example, to mark where he spots an animal or when he finds signs of poaching.'

The young assistant was speaking rapidly, and kept glancing over his shoulder at the door. He zoomed into an area of the map about ten kilometres square. Thin black lines divided it into a grid.

'What the rangers do on patrol is methodically explore an area, using this grid to go through it square by square. You can see the ranger was heading for the southern part of this block to begin his reconnaissance.' He pointed again. 'When you look at these records, and join the dots, you normally see a criss-cross pattern as they make their way backwards and forwards. But here it's different.'

He glanced up to confirm Patrice was following.

'The ranger reaches this point, but then he turns back the way he came. He gets five hundred metres and then … this is where he was found.'

'I see. Could it be that he dropped something and then retraced his steps, looking for it?

Tarkang rubbed his cheek, his eyes still fixed on the screen. 'All I'm saying is I haven't seen this before. As I said, usually they are methodical.'

'Did you show this to other people here?'

'I told my boss. He said it wasn't important.'

Patrice jotted down the co-ordinates from the last two locations. 'Is it normal for the rangers to go on patrol alone?'

'It happens sometimes. They are supposed to go in pairs, but the other ranger was sick that day. That's what …'

He broke off mid-sentence, as the door swung open and a big-bellied man in a striped polo shirt stepped in.

'Sir,' the assistant said, unfolding a map of the park trails, as if he'd been about to show it to the visitor. 'This is Mr Le Congo, from Congo.'

The man looked Patrice up and down, disapprovingly. 'I am Ngwa, the tourist centre manager. Can we help you?'

'Thank you. I work for the African Union. I believe you have a beautiful national park here in Bakunda.'

'Indeed. One of the oldest in Africa. We are proud of it.'

'I was sorry to hear about the death of the ranger …'

'I see. It is sad. Alex Ebot had worked here for many years; twenty, I believe. We are in a state of shock.'

'Do you know the Kahuzi-Biega park? It's near where I live. We have a lot of problems there with poaching …'

'Yes, it's a problem all over. But this was not to do with poaching. The ranger was killed by an elephant.'

'Yes, I read that. Has that happened before?'

The tourist centre manager hesitated. 'Not that I know of, no. Not a park ranger. But two villagers were killed by an elephant, some years ago …'

'Did you know the ranger had contacted officials at the African Union to say there was a lack of security in the park? He said he was worried for the safety of the animals.'

'I did not. How …'

'Did he complain to you about this?'

Ngwa looked like he was about to answer, but then he checked himself and changed tack. 'Mr Le Congo, thank you for your concern, but what precisely is your interest in this matter? Just because you live near a national park in Congo, I am not sure what this has to do with you.'

'I'm actually an investigator with the AU …' He let the words hang; the man didn't react. '… with the Human Rights Commission. I was on assignment here in Cameroon, and then I heard about this, and … it's … I know from experience that things might not be what they seem. In my country …'

'This is not Congo,' the tourist centre manager cut in sharply. 'This is Cameroon.'

'Of course. The situations in our countries are different. Still, it must be a challenge to protect an area as large as Bakunda National Park.'

'It's no secret we lack resources. We are a developing nation, like Congo, and there are competing needs, so we must be patient.'

'You didn't find the circumstances of the ranger's death suspicious?'

The dark eyes beneath the bald head looked straight at Patrice's. If Ngwa knew something, he wasn't showing it.

'The police have investigated this tragedy and for them the matter is closed. If you are here to carry out a further investigation on behalf of the African Union, then you must go through the correct channels, and you will receive all the necessary assistance. But if not …'

'Thank you, I understand. And thank you for your help. I'm not here on business. In fact, I have a few days off now I've finished my work, and I would still be interested to visit the park as a tourist. Can I arrange that here?'

Ngwa glanced at his assistant. 'I'm afraid not. The park is closed to visitors, since the ranger's death.'

'But if the investigation is complete?'

'As I said, the park's closed, for now. I'm sure it will reopen soon, and then you will be welcome.' The tourist centre manager took a step back and held his arm through the door, inviting Patrice to leave.

Patrice walked out through the main reception area, where fading posters were pinned to the walls showing the park's exotic inhabitants: primates including the chimpanzee and red colobus, and birds he'd never heard of - the vermiculated fishing owl and chocolate-backed kingfisher. There was a large visitors' book on a table. He flipped through it – tourists from Germany and France and the United States; a group of birdwatchers from Britain. It was a large book, with a lot of empty pages. Fewer than a hundred people had visited the park in the previous year.

Outside, he hailed an *okada* and asked the rider to take him on a tour of the town. It didn't take long. Bakunda was a rural outpost; a few wide red dirt roads coming together in the midst of lush, green forest, farmland and plantations – about ten kilometres from the park itself. The whitewashed town hall and courthouse were the only buildings of more than one storey. The *okada* took Patrice down to the river then to the market, which was next to the motor park. He pointed across a dusty football pitch to a bar which he said was the most popular place in town.

Patrice spent the afternoon working on his report on the land dispute. He ate dinner at his hotel; meat with eru leaf soup and yellow garri – cassava fried in palm oil, giving it a rich texture and dark colour. He took a bottle of Mutzig beer outside and sat at a table in the garden in the warm night air. He called his boss and told her he'd be staying in Bakunda a while longer.

Chapter 10

The sound of drums started somewhere in the distance as Patrice was ordering a second beer.

'Pala pala match dey oh,' the barman said. 'Wrestling contest.'

Patrice thought about going to take a look, but he was tired. He let the barman bring his second beer instead.

*

A crowd was gathered in a circle between two streetlights in an empty corner of the motor park, forming a floodlit ring. Two drummers sitting cross-legged at the front pounded a fast and relentless rhythm. Pierre Mponda, in his white tee shirt and black Western-style blazer, stood at the back, out of the light, observing the scene with curiosity and expectancy.

Two young wrestlers entered the arena in shorts, their torsos glistening with sweat. They stood either side of the referee, who introduced them to the crowd.

The first, Namange, received a ripple of applause. He had a shaved head and chest muscles that looked like armour plates. A couple of men on one side of the ring shouted his name. The wrestler waved to them and grinned, revealing a missing front tooth.

There was no applause for the second, Jeki, who was a few centimetres shorter than his opponent. His hair was cut short. His brow was knitted, his lips pouted as he took a shy bow.

A voice called out, 'Jeki, *come show us that power wey you claim you get.* Show us how strong you are!'

Some of the spectators tittered. The wrestler frowned. Mponda had followed Jeki's progress from a distance. He'd heard he'd won a couple of fights. But the crowd weren't taking him seriously. Someone said he was a loner who worked as a porter at the motor park.

The referee stepped out of the way, and the men assumed their positions, legs apart, knees bent, leaning forward. The crowd cheered them on, the drummers keeping up the beat. The wrestlers moved sideways, circling, eyes fixed on their opponent, waiting. Namange stepped forward and got hold of Jeki by his head and neck. Jeki responded by grabbing Namange's waist. Locked together, they continued circling till the referee signalled to them to let go, and they parted, and began their opening ritual again.

This time Jeki straightened his legs and, still bent over at the waist, placed his outstretched hand on Namange's shoulder. Namenge's legs were also straight. They circled, then Jeki pushed Namange's shoulder down and tried to grab him from behind; but Namange spun round and the two men crashed together, chest to chest, and bounced apart.

The crowd cheered and the drummers upped the tempo, raising expectations that the next encounter would be decisive. Jeki hurled himself forward. Namange held out his arm but Jeki dodged underneath; he locked Namange's neck in his arm, twisted Namange's head round and turned him on to the ground, lodging a knee into his back. Namange yelped and the referee jumped forward to end the bout. The drumming reached a crescendo then stopped abruptly.

The winner, Jeki, got to his feet. The referee lifted his arm. Jeki didn't look at the crowd and didn't celebrate. There were a few coughs and no applause. A couple of Namange's supporters said bad luck to their man.

Pierre Mponda, still standing back out of the light, kept his eyes fixed on Jeki, the wrestler who looked so disconsolate in victory. 'My secret weapon,' he thought. '*Mon agent provocateur*. Who'd have believed it?' He slipped away into the night before the wrestlers had left the ring.

*

The drums had fallen silent. Three empty beer bottles stood on Patrice's table. He walked across the hotel garden to his chalet, ready for bed, but as soon as he was inside there was a tap on the door. Adam Tarkang, the national park tourist centre assistant, was standing there, looking nervously over his shoulder. Patrice let him in.

'I couldn't talk to you outside,' Tarkang said, the dim light shining off his young face. 'I mustn't be seen with you.'

Patrice fetched him a glass of water. 'Sit down ...'

Tarkang shook his head. 'I won't stay.'

'What's happened?'

'After you left today the manager was angry with me. He said visitors are not permitted to enter the office. So please, sir, be careful what you say. If he finds out I have told you things, I am worried I will lose my job. And it is hard to find a job here.' The young man held his hands together, pleading.

Patrice said, 'I won't say a word.'

'Thank you, sir, thank you. The manager is not a bad man, but he doesn't want any scandal.'

Quietly, Patrice asked, 'So he doesn't believe the elephant story?'

'I don't know. He wants to believe it.'

'What can you tell me about the police investigation? Was it thorough?'

Tarkang tutted. 'You know, the police here ... They came with the divisional officer - that's the government administrator for Bakunda district - and they talked to the park director and my manager. I don't know what they said. But the police didn't go to the park.'

'Who found the ranger's body?'

'When Alex didn't return from his patrol, the other rangers looked at the signal record and saw the last one had been sent the previous day. They said the GPS tracker batteries had run out, or the instrument had been damaged. The park director said they couldn't be sure and told them to organise a search party. Two rangers and two soldiers went to the spot where the last signal came from, and they returned with his body. I didn't see it but my manager said it looked like he had been trampled by an elephant.'

'What did the rangers say?'

The young man hesitated. 'I haven't heard anyone disagree with that theory, but ...'

'But?'

Tarkang looked from side to side, as if to make sure they couldn't be overheard. 'The other men didn't care for Alex. They said he was a bossy man, finding fault with their work, telling them they should take their responsibilities more seriously. I heard them complaining.'

'But he was an experienced colleague. They didn't ask any questions?'

'I heard one say we cannot understand the work of God.'

'Where did they take the body?'

'To the hospital mortuary. Two days later, I heard Alex's family came to take him to their village.'

'Is that nearby?'

'No. It's some hours from here, somewhere near Mamfe.' The young man looked at his phone. 'I should go now. If you want to know more about Alex, you can speak to the man who owns the San Siro, the bar across from the motor park. I believe he knew him. But please don't say anything about me.'

'Thank you, I appreciate your help.' Patrice patted the assistant on the shoulder as they got to their feet. 'But tell me, how did you know where I was staying?'

'The *okada* men know everything in this town,' he said, smiling for the first time.

Patrice opened the door and checked no one was around to see his visitor leave. 'There's one more thing,' he said. 'Can I borrow one of the park's GPS tracking units?'

'What for?'

'I want to see for myself where the ranger was found.'

'Sir, you heard what my manager said, the park is closed now.'

'Yes, so if I can't go in as a visitor with a guide, I'll need to find my own way. I won't be gone long.'

Tarkang averted his eyes. 'I'd like to help you, but I can't. I'm sorry. Goodnight.'

The young man turned and walked away.

Chapter 11

'They came with guns, they came with lies; they hate the sun, they hate the flies ...'

From the window, Douala Manga hears the cheery, mocking voice of his assistant, Ngosso Din, who's being held in another room – a locked one.

A guard shouts, *'Halt die Klappe!* Shut up!'

Douala Manga is pleased his assistant has retained his sense of humour. At their trial, Ngosso Din was asked if he acknowledged the charges against him. He replied, 'The cat plays with the mouse before the kill.'

How right he was to throw their hypocrisy back in their faces. The trial was a show. And it turns out these people have been playing a game all along.

The candle flickers as he picks up his pen again.

The Germans wanted me to succeed my father as king; having conducted affairs to their satisfaction with him, and with his father before him, they assumed it would be the same with me. At first I was happy to co-operate with them. I encouraged my people to educate themselves and take jobs in the colonial administration as I had done myself. And the Germans rewarded me with a handsome annual pension of 3,000 marks.

Let me be clear, at this stage, I doubted their true intentions. I knew they did not respect us as people; in their minds we were inferior to them. But I trusted their education and their institutions. With their laws laid down in writing, I thought, we had protection and resort to the courts.

Things were changing, I could see that. The German traders who had previously been happy to stay on their boats, do their business there, and return to Hamburg, were now coming ashore. They wanted our land. They bought houses by the river and paid a good price; three marks a square metre or more, and some of my people were happy to sell. But then the colonial authorities intervened and said the price must be set at a mere 40 pfennigs a square metre. I could see where this was leading: soon my people would find themselves dispossessed of all the good riverside land in Douala. So we stopped selling.

It was shortly after this development, as I was attending to some papers in my office one morning, that a messenger arrived with a letter from the governor informing me of the appointment of a new Kaiserliche Bezirksamtmann, the imperial district officer for Douala. When I read the name, I knew at once that my faith in German laws and institutions was about to be put to the test. It was Hermann von Roehm.

Through gritted teeth I dispatched orders for a reception in his honour. Invitations were sent to the colonial district office and to my fellow chiefs. There was to be dancing and a feast (I considered a wrestling tournament inappropriate). However, when the day came and the drummers played to welcome the guests, the new imperial district officer was not among them. We were informed that Herr von Roehm was unwell with fever.

Evidently, he made a brisk recovery. Two days later it was my turn to receive an invitation, though from the wording it could equally have been read as a summons. The new imperial district officer was expecting me that afternoon. A car was sent to collect me and take me to his office.

Fifteen years had passed since I had seen him last. He had filled out somewhat, and he had grown a moustache resembling the Kaiser's, styled with a tweak at each end.

He came out from behind his desk and shook my hand with unconvincing eagerness.

'My dear Douala Manga,' he said. 'Wie schön Sie wiederzusehen, nach all den Jahren! How good it is to see you after all these years! It is strange that our life journeys should once again converge, do you not think?'

It was clear his ability to forget, or at least to pretend to, had remained intact.

'A man cannot always control his destiny, sir,' I replied. 'I hope you have recovered from your fever.'

'Yes, thank you. I was sorry to miss the feast and not to meet all the Douala chiefs.'

'I am King Douala Manga now,' I said.

'Yes, of course. Though I think you know in Germany we translate the Douala word for king as chief.'

'I see you have adopted the arrogance that your father used to find unappealing.' Roehm's face turned crimson. 'Were you so keen as to meet all the Douala chiefs, you could have invited them here today.'

'Douala Manga,' he said, 'I am looking forward to us working together for the good of the empire that I know you admire. For this reason, I think it we should get to know each other again, so that I know that I can trust you to be on our side.'

'Your side?'

'I hope we are on the same side.'

'As I said the last time we met, so long as our interests align, we are on the same side.'

'Good,' he replied.

Roehm's manner was condescending. I should have cracked his head against a wall there and then. Instead, I stepped back to stop myself from doing exactly that.

'And what are your impressions of my country?' I asked.

'As you warned me, the climate here is hot.'

So, I concluded, he didn't forget everything. He wiped his brow and neck. I could see he did not care for my country at all. One day, hopefully, these people will pack up and leave and return to their frost and snow.

The following week, Roehm summoned me again. He outlined his solution to what he described as the land problem. He called it the Appropriation Plan. This was to involve forcibly removing all Douala people from the riverside areas into new suburbs away from the water, from where we were to be separated from the Germans by a 'no-man's land'. This, he said, would protect the Germans from African diseases, and prevent the development of a tendency – as was happening, he said, in British West African colonies – towards social and political equality between Europeans and natives, as he liked to call us. He asked for my full support.

The Appropriation Plan amounted to robbery, and it was illegal. The treaty my grandfather signed with the Germans in 1884 explicitly stated that land ownership would remain in the hands of the local people. The land was ours. Without it, we had nothing. I vowed there and then to do everything in my power to fight Roehm's plan. I would challenge it in the courts; I would appeal to the Reichstag; but if all else failed, I had not forgotten the sceptre that had been placed in my hand.

Chapter 12

Bakunda's district hospital comprised a cluster of single-storey buildings with tin roofs set among well-kept lawns off the main road. Patrice ignored the *okadas* and went there on foot. He asked a porter where he could find the mortuary and was directed to a room at the end of a veranda. He knocked on the dark wood-panelled door, heard a cough from inside and let himself in.

A short man with white hair forming a crown on his head was at work. He was wearing a blood-stained apron and latex gloves and was bent over a corpse lying on one of two trestle tables. The corpse's stomach was sliced open and the man was prodding at the innards with a scalpel. The room smelled like vinegar.

'Yes?' the man asked, not looking up.

'Good morning,' Patrice said.

The man didn't respond.

'I'm trying to find out if a post mortem was carried out on the park ranger, Alex Ebot.'

The man peered at Patrice over the steel rims of his glasses. 'And who are you?' He didn't sound unwelcoming.

'My name is Patrice Le Congo. You might say I'm a friend of a friend of the ranger.'

'Are you a reporter?'

'I'm an investigator with the African Union's Human Rights Commission, but I'm not here officially …'

The man looked back at his work and picked around again with his scalpel. 'Good,' he said, chuckling. 'Neither am I.'

'Excuse me?'

'This is a small district hospital, Mr Le Congo. It has no resident pathologist, officially.'

'I see …'

'I am the mortician. Sylvestre Atemkeng, at your service. *Doctor* Sylvestre Atemkeng, formerly Senior Pathologist at Yaounde General Hospital. What you see me doing now is merely a hobby.'

'You do that for your amusement?'

'More like professional curiosity. And yes, to relieve the boredom.' Atemkeng made another move with his scalpel then stuck his hand inside the corpse and pulled something free to expose it. 'There, look at that.'

Patrice peered at a dark, pock-marked organ.

'It's as I thought when he came in. Swollen ankles, jaundiced eyes. The signs were there, but you can never be sure until you open them up. Cirrhosis of the liver. You see? This scarring? These bumps?'

Having confirmed his suspicions, the mortician stuffed everything back and began stitching up the incision. 'This man liked his palm wine,' he said. 'A kindred spirit, you might say.' He winked at Patrice.

He peeled off his gloves and went to a desk in the corner of the room. From one of the drawers he pulled out a dark bottle with no label. 'Drink?'

'No, thank you.'

The mortician put the bottle to his lips and took two gulps. 'This is what got me into trouble,' he said. 'Not that I couldn't handle it. It never interfered with my work, but it's what they used against me.'

'Who? Why?'

'The bureaucrats. I discovered the mistress of a government minister had been poisoned. They told me if I wrote that in my report, they would let it be known I was a drunk to discredit me. So we did a deal. I had to leave my position, and the capital city, but if I kept quiet, I would retain my pension. And here I am. In another two years I will claim my pension.'

'That's a sad waste of your skills,' Patrice said, watching the man take another gulp. 'Did you, out of professional curiosity, take a look at the body of the ranger?'

'I might have,' Atemkeng said, staring at Patrice, expressionless. 'It depends.'

'On what?'

'That whatever you hear, you didn't hear from me. Do you understand?'

'I understand.'

'Good. It's the pension, you see. Now, what is it you want to know, unofficially?'

'I want to know how he died.'

Atemkeng took one more gulp and put the bottle back in the drawer. 'You are the first person to ask me that question. Not even the divisional officer or the park director, who together accompanied the body here, sought my opinion. They know I still like to tinker. I asked them if they wanted it sent to Buea for a post mortem, but the divisional officer said there was no need. The ranger had been trampled to death by an elephant; keep the body here till the relatives come to collect it. That's what he said. And when the relatives came, they didn't ask any questions either.'

'So, *was* he killed by an elephant?'

'Be patient, please. I am a pathologist. *Was* a pathologist. As such, I thought to myself, I'll take a look. And so I did.'

'And?'

'After the divisional officer and the park director left, I went to work. The injuries sustained by the ranger were: eight broken ribs; two of these had punctured his lungs, and this is what killed him. Now, do you know how much a forest elephant weighs?'

'No.'

'On average, four or five tons. Being trampled on by such a beast would be similar to being run over by a pick-up truck. There would be massive internal haemorrhaging. We wouldn't be talking about a few ribs. His ribcage would likely have been crushed. And he'd have suffered external wounds too; serious abrasions at the very least. Yet once the dirt was washed off him, apart from bruising around the ribcage, there was not a scratch.'

'I see. So how do you think he did sustain his injuries?

The mortician opened the drawer, took another drink and wiped his lips. 'I have come to no definitive conclusion,' he said. 'I have an alternative theory, but I'm afraid it is as unlikely as the elephant. Eight ribs were broken. The four lowest, right and left. So, was he attacked by someone who grabbed him from behind and literally squeezed him to death? It's hard to believe ...'

'Is it possible to be killed that way?'

'Only if the victim's bones were weak, which in this case I have no reason to believe they were, or the perpetrator was a man of unimaginable strength. Or a gorilla. But there are no gorillas in this park.'

'What about an elephant, grabbing him like that with its trunk?'

'People can be attacked by elephants that way, but they are not squeezed to death. In such cases, the animal swings its victim violently against trees or the ground, and there would certainly be other wounds.'

The more Patrice learned about the death of the ranger, the harder it became to believe the official explanation. 'Surely, after discovering this, you had to tell the divisional officer and the park director of your suspicions?'

'They would have laughed at me, and searched for my bottle.' The mortician took off his glasses and wiped them with a piece of cloth. 'It was not for me to interfere. They had made it clear there was no need for further investigations. In a small town like this the divisional officer is a powerful person, and the park director is an old man, like me … and as I said, I can't be sure and ….'

'… and there's your pension. What about the ranger's family?'

'The divisional officer said they had sorted everything out with them to their satisfaction. Those were his words.'

'They paid them off? All this to avoid some bad publicity for the park?'

Atemkeng pursed his lips. 'All I would say is if you continue with your unofficial investigation, you should be careful.'

Chapter 13

The young footballers in their yellow kit made a noisy entrance into town. They were squeezed into a saloon car - the whole team; two on the bonnet in front, three sitting in the open boot at the back and the rest inside. They were singing and slapping the sides of the car while the driver beeped the horn. Patrice watched from a seat in the San Siro as they came over the brow of the hill and down towards Bakunda town centre. They made a circuit of the dusty pitch in front, which Patrice guessed was where they played their home matches, before heading off into the dusk to continue their victory parade.

The San Siro was a bar made out of a shipping container. The drinks were stored inside and drunk outside, under a tin roof supported by wooden posts. There were a dozen tables. A group of teachers were sitting round three of them, talking loudly so they could be heard above the makossa music blaring out of two large speakers. There were two light bulbs, one for the bar area, one for the man roasting meat at the side.

Patrice ordered a Mutzig and a plate of beef, which came with chilli powder.

'Excusez-moi ...'

He looked up.

'*Puis-je rester ici?* May I sit here?' A man wearing a white tee shirt under a black blazer was pulling back a chair.

'*Bien sûr, pas de problème.*' Patrice looked around – there were other tables free, but he was happy to have company.

The man sat and began a conversation immediately. 'I think that you are not from here?' He spoke English with a French accent. He looked to be in his forties. He was well groomed and he spoke with self-assurance.

'No. How did you know?'

'Because this is a small town,' the man replied. 'But also, your haircut is unusual, it is … er … quite wild for a young man. People have not worn this style here for a long time.'

Patrice was thirty-three, so he was surprised the man should describe him as young. 'It was wilder when I was a student,' he said, holding his hands out from his head. 'But people in Bukavu, where I'm from, also think my hair is from another time, and that I might be from somewhere else.'

'A stranger in his home town; can such a man be trusted?' The man grinned. 'But you are a visitor from Congo, so you are welcome.'

'Thank you. My name is Patrice Le Congo.'

'I am glad to make your acquaintance. Pierre Mponda.' The man made to shake hands, revealing a heavy gold bracelet round his wrist.

'Are you the owner of this bar?'

'No, no. You won't see the owner here tonight.'

'Why not?'

'He is with the football players. He's the team coach and the driver. I'm sure he will be here tomorrow.'

'It looks like they won,' Patrice said.

'Yes, I suppose, though I don't care for football.'

'A Cameroonian who doesn't like football; can such a man be trusted?' Patrice joked. The man smiled awkwardly. Patrice asked him if he'd like a beer, but he declined.

'Tell me,' Mponda asked, 'how do you find it in Cameroon?'

'I like it a lot. The people are hospitable and the scenery is spectacular. The only thing I don't like are the mosquitoes, and the only thing I miss is tilapia from Lake Kivu.'

'Ah, you like fish? Then you should go to Douala. It is where I'm from. There you can eat any fish you want. Here it is mostly the dried fish, as you know.'

'Yes, but mostly I like the food here. Ndole is delicious.'

'Ndole too is a Douala dish. So you *must* go to Douala! I can recommend the Hôtel Alexandre. They know me there. Say my name and they will make sure you are comfortable.' Mponda paused and leaned forward to get closer. 'You know, there are people here who do not think this is my country? They think the English-speaking part of Cameroon should be separate. They say us French-speakers take their jobs.'

'And what is your job?'

'I am with the Ministry of Foreign Business and Investment, in liaison.'

'Liaison?'

'I work with our partners, foreign investors, to help them with whatever they need help with ... logistics, infrastructure, local knowledge. It can be difficult for newcomers to find their way around, isn't that right?'

Patrice didn't answer.

'I was a teacher once,' Mponda said. 'Then a policeman. But I found I was looking for more in life, more opportunities, to rise up.'

'I was also a teacher once.'

'So we have something in common.'

'Except I was not interested in rising up, as you put it.'

'Yes. I understand now you work in the field of human rights?'

'This really is a small town.'

Without acknowledging Patrice's comment, the man continued. 'It is an interesting concept, is it not, human rights? A Western one, not African.'

'It's a universal one now.'

The man chuckled. 'What rights do we have? We are born into this world, but why does that mean we should have rights? Obligations, perhaps.'

Given they'd only just met, it felt like the conversation was covering a lot of ground. Patrice wondered where it was heading. 'Rights and duties are both enshrined in the African Charter on Human and People's Rights,' he said, feeling he should defend his work. 'As an example, I can quote you Article 4: "Human beings are inviolable. Every human being shall be entitled to respect for his life and the integrity of his person. No one may be arbitrarily deprived of this right." You can read it all on the internet ...'

'That's commendable. But these are mere words, my friend. How many of the governments that signed this charter abide by its ideals?'

'That's a different issue. It doesn't mean we as individuals shouldn't respect and cherish those ideals.'

'I see you are a man of high principles.'

It was hard to gauge if the man was being serious. Patrice drank some beer.

A discussion between the barmaid and a group of men at

another table was becoming heated. The customers wanted the music turned down so they could hear the commentary of an English football match between Manchester City and Chelsea showing on an old television. The barmaid said they could make do with just the picture, as the other customers were enjoying the music.

'In that case, we will leave,' one of the men said.

'Not without paying.'

'We haven't finished our drinks yet.'

'It's up to you,' the barmaid said. 'You can't be demanding this and that without regard for everyone else.'

The men looked at each other, then carried on drinking, looking at the small, flickering screen.

Patrice's table companion leaned forward again.

'I hear you were asking questions about the park ranger, the one who was killed by the elephant?'

Patrice tried to read the man's eyes, but they gave nothing away. 'You have friends at the tourist centre?'

'I have friends everywhere. That is my job, to have friends and to know what is going on. What is your interest in this sad affair, may I ask?'

'I'm always asking questions. What do you make of it?'

'It was a tragedy. But these things can happen.'

'It didn't strike you as odd, that an experienced park ranger could let himself be killed by an elephant?'

Now it was Mponda looking at Patrice, as if trying to read *his* eyes. 'Careless, possibly. But anyone can make a mistake.'

'A mistake?'

'Well, to be in the wrong place at the wrong time ...'

'Is that a mistake, or bad luck?'

'You must excuse me, my English is not so perfect.'

His English was no worse than Patrice's. It was the man's offhand tone that grated more than his words.

'What I am trying to say is there is no need for a human rights investigator to waste his time on this. There must be more pressing matters that require your attention. But good luck with your work.'

'GOAL!' The men watching the TV with no commentary were slapping each other and doing high fives. Patrice craned his neck to see a replay of Samir Nasri scoring a second for Manchester City.

When he looked back, Mponda was gone. Strange, Patrice thought; another person suggesting the death of the park ranger was of little interest or importance; someone else, it seemed, who didn't give a damn. The thing was, with Patrice, the more he was told not to do something, the more determined it made him to do it.

He finished his beer and left the San Siro, making for two *okadas* parked under a dim streetlight. As he approached, he could hear the riders were comparing their motorcycles.

'Sanili is more stable.'

'I like Nanfung. It can go smooth through streams ...'

'*Okada*!' they shouted in unison when they noticed Patrice.

He chose the Sanili. Back at his hotel, he found a small package outside the door to his chalet. There was no one around. He opened the package. Inside was a GPS tracking unit. He jogged to the gate. The *okada* was still there.

'How much to the park, first thing in the morning?'

'Five thousand.'

'How much for you not to tell anyone you're taking me there?'

'*No wahala*. You don't have to pay me for that.'

Chapter 14

The rooftop terrace at the Hôtel Alexandre in Akwa, Douala's business district, was not as glitzy as Sally had imagined. Paint was fading on the tables and chairs and cracks zig-zagged up the low perimeter wall. The bar prices meant it was not the kind of place you'd expect to meet a student, but the drinks that afternoon were on Lucy, Sally's colleague at the *Courier* – it was her story, after all.

Though it was six floors up, there was no breeze. The air was hot and clammy, muffling the noise of the traffic below. Sally took in the hazy view: the tin roofs and courtyards nearby and the factories and cranes by the port a few blocks away. She was checking the time when a young woman approached.

'I hope I'm not late,' the woman said, with a smile that exposed two rows of perfect teeth.

'Estelle? Actually, you are on time, which is unusual. I'm Sally, Sally Bintu.'

'Nice to meet you.'

She was medium height, taller than Sally, skinny but flat-chested, Sally thought. She was wearing jeans, flat sandals and a tee shirt; little make-up; hair in cornrows. In fact, she looked quite plain. Her nails, though, were long and manicured and made Sally aware of her own, which were short and chewed.

They sat and ordered drinks, soft ones.

'Thank you for agreeing to meet me,' Sally said. 'I hope we can talk frankly.'

'Sure, why not? As long as you don't use my real name, I'm happy. I want to set the record straight.'

'How do you mean?'

'You know. Women in my … situation, we get a bad press. Like we're only in it for the money. But who's to judge me and the relationship I'm in?'

For someone who must be younger than Sally, she was strikingly confident and self-composed. Or was it naivety? 'How old are you?'

'Twenty-two.'

'And your …'

'Don't call him my sugar daddy. I hate that expression.'

'Why?'

'Because of what I said. It implies the relationship is only about his money and my youth. But it's not like that. That's what I want you to understand.'

'What *do* you call him?'

'My boyfriend, I guess.'

'And how old is your boyfriend.'

'Forty … something.'

'How long have you known him? How did you meet?'

'It was a couple of months ago. I was a waitress in a bar, and we got talking, and got on … and one thing led to another. There's nothing unusual about it. It's the age difference that people seize on, as if to say it's wrong because of that.'

'But now you don't have to work as a waitress, right?'

Estelle tutted. 'That's the attitude I was talking about.'

'Listen,' Sally said, 'I want to hear your story. You say you get on; what would you say you have in common with this man who's double your age?'

'Lots of things. An interest in fashion, in clothes. And art. And architecture. He's cultured ... like I want to be.'

'What are you studying?'

'Accountancy. I'm the first person in my family ever to go to university. And I want to make something of it. I think you're the same?'

'Actually, my parents went to university. They met there.'

'Well, I see determination in your character, and you must be determined to have this good job.'

'Sometimes,' Sally said. 'Sometimes it's a good job.' She didn't say that her father was now a successful businessman and an old friend of the owner of the *Courier*.

They sat and sipped at their drinks. A middle-aged couple walked past; the man in a Western suit, with shiny black shoes; the woman in a black blouse and short, green skirt and high heels. They stood together across the terrace, holding hands, looking out over the city.

'Is he married, your boyfriend?'

'He's a successful man. Of course he's married!'

'Does he have other mistresses?'

'I expect so.'

'Aren't you worried, about getting HIV, for instance?'

'We take precautions.'

This woman knew what she was doing. If Lucy had been expecting a story about a dumb gold-digger who was risking her life, and the lives of others, she wasn't going to get it. 'But he does give you things? Gifts? Your fees?'

'Sure. And I take them. The fees are helpful - they enable me to study. When I worked full time, it was hard to find time for studying. But the gifts? I take them, but it's more to please him. He thinks that's what I expect. And in return, I flirt with him, because I think that's what he expects. So it's not what people call love, but that doesn't mean that we don't get along or that our relationship is not genuine.'

There was a warm glow in the late afternoon sky as the sun sank towards the horizon.

'Does your boyfriend know you're talking to a newspaper about your relationship?'

'No. I don't think he'd like it. I mean, as I said, he's married, so he might worry that people could recognise him?'

'How do you know he won't come here, to this bar, and see you? I'm guessing he introduced you to this place?'

'He did. But he's travelled, for work.'

'What does he do?'

'He's in government. I can't say more than that.'

'Do you *know* more than that?

'There you go again, still doubting what we have, the sincerity of our connection.'

Estelle still sounded confident, but, for the first time during their conversation, she avoided Sally's eyes when she spoke, as if she too was having doubts.

Sally had a sip of her drink. 'It's my job to ask questions,' she said. 'And I suppose the big question people would want me to put to you is, would you be seeing this man, would he be your boyfriend, if he didn't have money? If he wasn't able to pay your fees?'

Though Estelle was still looking away, Sally could see a tear was forming in the corner of her eye.

Estelle sniffled and dabbed at the tear with the back of a finger. 'It's not fair to put it like that,' she said. 'Look at that couple there. You could say that woman is too old to wear that skirt. So, she is flirting with her man. And I bet he is paying for their drinks. But nobody is going to challenge their motives.'

'I'm sorry. I didn't mean to upset you.' Sally looked through her notes. She had enough now. Even if the HIV angle hadn't come out the way Lucy had been expecting, the woman had talked openly about a taboo subject. She thought of a headline: *Me and My Sugar Daddy: a Sweet and Sour Story*.

Estelle was still sniffling. Then, out of the blue, she announced, 'I don't feel comfortable now, about talking to you.'

'What? But you agreed …'

'No. I don't want to do this. I'm sorry but I hadn't thought it all through. And now I've changed my mind. You've made me think about things I hadn't thought about before, and I need some time.'

'Well, it's too late.'

'Please, Sally, listen to me. I … I feel like I'm revealing too much about myself.'

'Nobody is going to know it's you who's talking except me, so relax.' She couldn't let this story slip through her fingers, even if it wasn't her story. Lucy would be furious if she messed this up.

'But I want to explain …'

'No, Estelle, you can't be wasting my time like this.'

'Hear me out, please.' The young woman who had looked so confident before now looked pitiful and lost.

Sally sighed, impatiently. 'What is it you want to explain?'

'About ... how things ... how I came to be in this situation, so you understand. I come from a long line of maids. My mother was a maid. Her mother was a maid ...'

Sally was listening, but all she could think about was how she was going to get away without agreeing to drop the story.

'They worked for rich people, even for a queen. But now, I want to be the one who has a maid.' She pulled a tissue out of her bag and wiped her tears and blew her nose. 'Not a queen, but a rich person ... you see? Is that so bad? Is it shameful to want to improve your situation?'

Sally was getting to her feet but sat down again. 'Wait,' she said. 'What do you mean, your grandmother worked for a queen?'

'Not my grandmother, but a long time ago; my grandmother's grandmother, I think – she worked for Queen Emma. My mother told me; she was proud of it - proud of someone being a maid.'

'Well, hang on, Estelle. There's maids and maids. I can see why someone would be proud to have a connection to a royal household. You know, I'd like to talk to your mother.'

Estelle was checking herself in a mirror. 'You want to write a story about maids now?'

'No. I'm doing some historical research of my own. Your mother may be able to help me.'

'Huh!' Estelle was smiling again, showing her perfect teeth. 'So, we can do a deal. I can ask my mother if she wants to talk to you. In return, you drop the story about me.'

A short while later, Sally called her colleague, Lucy, and told her the young woman never showed.

Chapter 15

The dawn is overcast and wet. Despite what the day will bring, King Rudolph Douala Manga Bell enjoys the moment. This is the climate the Germans do not like. This is why they moved their capital to Buea on the cool slopes of Mount Cameroon. From there they look down on Douala. But not for much longer, he thinks. He dips his pen in the ink.

An image springs to mind that illustrates how things have deteriorated these past few years. A boatman is strapped face down over the upturned keel of his pirogue on the banks of the Wouri River; two German soldiers stand over him, taking it in turns to deliver full-blooded lashes on his bare back. The cuts are deep. Six other soldiers have their guns aimed at the watching crowd, warning them to stay back. The boatman's 'crime' was to refuse to take a German businessman to a ship anchored in the estuary. The crowd's faces betray no expression, and tell the soldiers: 'You can beat us till we die, but we are not afraid of you.'

Through incidents such as this – and there are hundreds more the same – the Germans united the people of Cameroon behind me in a way I could never have achieved on my own. Those rivals of mine, who had grudgingly sworn their allegiance at my coronation, now pledged their unconditional support. After Roehm's plans were announced, I embarked on a tour of the country, from the coastal areas to deep inside the hinterland. And it was not hard to make the people everywhere see that what was being threatened now in Douala would soon be threatening them.

At the same time, I sought support for our cause from old friends in Berlin, for there are still Germans who truly respect their laws and institutions, and the rights of others. One such is Hellmut von Gerlach, the journalist and Reichstag Deputy, who wrote articles in the liberal press and made speeches to his fellow parliamentarians to raise awareness of our plight in Douala.

Faced with this combined challenge, from his own people and from Cameroonians, Roehm reacted with violence. Before he even had the Reichstag's approval, he set about destroying our houses.

That was last December. I was up-country. When I learned what was happening, I sent my assistant and dear friend Ngosso Din to Southern Nigeria to make arrangements, contingencies; not to invite the British to Cameroon, as the prosecutor Neidermayer alleged, but so as not to leave ourselves defenceless.

On my return I was greeted by a street of flattened houses, their former inhabitants destitute. The promised dwellings built for them in an area the Germans call New Bell turned out to be shacks, often without windows. I am proud to say the Douala people did their best to resist these plans, withdrawing their labour from German businesses and the administration. They suffered floggings in return.

Ngosso Din travelled on in secret to Germany to rally diplomatic support for our cause, and for a time it appeared this peaceful approach might succeed. The Reichstag's Budget Commission ordered a halt to the appropriation programme until it was properly investigated. The other chiefs and I shared palm wine the day we heard that news.

But we were to be out-manoeuvred. Roehm messaged Berlin to say the civil disobedience in Douala could spread to other regions, which would threaten German rule. Then, when Wilhelm Solf, the Secretary of State for the Colonies, was summoned before the Reichstag, he produced a telegram with the claim that I had sought support for a military uprising from the Sultan of Njoya in Foumban, a man I have met but once, a man I had no reason to trust. The sultan is said to have betrayed me to a missionary. The Budget Commission members could not know this was a lie and agreed the colonial authorities should do what they must. Too late, I realised it was a waste of time to appeal to German law.

The next day, I was arrested. Ngosso Din was detained and sent home in chains. I have been informed that other chiefs who were sympathetic to our cause have been jailed or exiled or worse. They include my noble friend, the Chief of Ngembum, in whose custody we entrusted our last hope. No such fate awaits the Sultan of Njoya, but then he never was a friend of ours.

The resistance is broken, for now at least. The sceptre lies hidden, waiting to be found, and wielded.

Douala Manga folds the sheets of paper, and looks out of the window at the grey sky. He spits on his fingers and extinguishes the candle.

Chapter 16

The *okada* sped down a dirt road that cut through the middle of an oil palm plantation. Patrice looked from side to side, down the corridors of trees which fanned out in all directions. They passed a few children walking to school and farmers carrying machetes, but mostly the road was quiet in the dull, damp early morning. Through a break in the palms, a river came into view, and on the far bank, thick virgin forest tumbling down to the water's edge. The river marked the eastern border of Bakunda National Park.

The *okada* rider pointed ahead at a footbridge that drooped across the river. 'Park entrance,' he said. He pulled up and nodded in the direction of a small brick building. 'Three soldiers live in that house. You must walk from here by the river to the bridge.'

Patrice got off and paid the fare. He waited till the *okada* was out of sight before heading off through the palms to the riverbank. As he approached the bridge, he could see the front of the house and one of the soldiers, a blanket draped round his shoulders, squatted in front of a fire of sticks. He was stirring a pan with his back to the river.

Patrice climbed the steps to the bridge. Shielded from the house by trees, he trod cautiously over the rickety cross-planks, down to the bottom of the sag in the middle then up towards the forest which loomed ahead, absorbing the light of the early morning and the sound of the gushing water below. When he reached the far side and stood at the top of the steps there, he could see over the roof of the main canopy, lush and green, stretching to the horizon, out of which the tallest trees protruded like giant slender mushrooms.

Below, faded signposts pointed to different trails. He switched on the GPS tracker and marked his co-ordinates on the map he'd picked up at the park office. He headed for a trail that led south and walked through an archway of tangled vines and leaves - the entrance to the forest.

It was not as dark as he'd expected. Breaks in the canopy allowed shafts of light from the brightening sky to shine through. It smelled of tree bark and earth. The forest floor was a spongy carpet of dead leaves littered with rotting branches, small bushes, and coiled tree roots. Birds were chirping amid the hum of insects.

He kept a good pace. It was fifteen kilometres to the spot where the ranger was found. The trail led him over ridges and through mud-filled gullies. Soon his shirt was saturated with sweat. His stops for a drink of water became more frequent as the hours passed. He came to a large stream, where powerful rapids roared between rounded boulders. The trail ended here, and he had to clamber and jump from boulder to boulder to make his way across.

He checked his position on the tracker and carried on through the forest on the other side. At times he thought he was following a path, cut possibly by the ranger or the men who came looking for him, but then he would lose it. The going was slow. The vegetation was thick. Hanging vines curled around his neck. Stinging leaves tore at his skin. It felt like the forest was telling him to turn back.

It was well into the afternoon by the time Patrice reached the position from where the ranger's last signal had been sent. He sat on a log and drank more water and ate some nuts, and looked around. The grid reference on his GPS tracker pinpointed his position to within ten metres square.

In front of him was an area where the leaves on the ground were flattened in a way that could be consistent with a group of men arriving and laying a stretcher on which to carry the body. He walked back and forth, bent over, looking for clues as to what had happened, but he found none. And there was nothing resembling an elephant's footprint.

He headed off in a southerly direction. After a few minutes he saw light through the trees ahead. He checked his position. He carried on until he was at the exact spot from where the ranger's penultimate signal had come. He scratched his head, and checked the map.

He was standing two kilometres from the south-east edge of the park, in what should have been dense rainforest. Yet stretching out ahead of him was cleared farmland. He recognised cassava plants, maize and young oil palms. All that remained of the forest were a few of the tall trees, which looked even taller now with all the others gone. An area the size of several football pitches had been cut down.

A cold feeling came over Patrice. He edged backwards, into the cover of the trees. Remembering the mortician's theory, that the ranger could have been grabbed from behind, he swivelled round. He stared into the forest, ears pricked up, looking and listening for signs of movement. All was still. Keeping inside the tree line, he skirted round the edge of the clearing. He narrowed his eyes and scanned the fields. Then a shout rang out. Two men jumped out from behind a bush by a small tree in the clearing and started towards him; one was wearing a red baseball cap and waving a machete.

Patrice turned and ran into the forest. He could hear the men behind him, twigs snapping beneath their feet. He thrashed his way through the trees and soon came to the big river. The plantation was on the other side. Far off, between two rows of trees, a truck was driving away, laden with bunches of palm fruit.

He slid down the bank. More shouts followed him as he began to cross the river, using rocks as stepping stones. He reached the main channel, where the water was deeper, and turned to see the man with the red cap and machete emerging from the trees. He waded in. The water was up to his waist, then his chest. Then the current swept him off his feet and he was carried downstream.

He steered himself to the far bank, where he pulled himself out, holding on to tree roots. Turning again, he saw his pursuer had stopped where the rocks sloped into the water; he was standing, hands on hips, machete dangling at his side, yelling in a language Patrice didn't understand.

Patrice dragged himself up the bank, wrung the water from his clothes, and headed into the plantation. The truck he'd spotted from the other bank had stopped; three men were standing below nearby trees using sickles on the ends of long poles to cut down the fruit. They turned and looked.

Patrice waved. 'Hello. Can I get a ride with you? I was in the park, but I got lost.'

The men exchanged a few words, then laughed. The driver leaned out of his cab, chewing on a piece of sugarcane.

'Get in,' he said.

Patrice climbed in the other side. 'Thank you.'

The man chuckled. 'They say if they had another sickle you could help with the harvest.'

Patrice smiled, still wet and out of breath, but relieved. He watched the men outside. 'That looks like tricky work,' he said to the driver.

'It is. These trees are old, so they are tall now, and the harvest is difficult. It takes two hours to fill this truck.'

'Where will you take the fruit?'

'To the mill, that way,' he said, pointing in the direction they were facing. 'You can find *okada* there.'

There was a creaking sound, then a crunch, as a bunch broke from the tree and fell to the ground. It was the size of half a sack of flour, and it looked as heavy. But the harvester picked it up and tossed it to a colleague standing on the back of the truck as if it was as light as an empty cardboard box.

'Whose plantation is this,' Patrice asked.

'Pamol. You know Pamol? It's the state-run oil palm company. This is one of the biggest plantations in Cameroon, eight thousand hectares.'

'What about that area?' Patrice asked, pointing at an area of younger trees to the south.

'That's a new plantation,' the man said, picking his teeth with his finger. 'Private.'

'And on the other side of the river? What about the farm over there?'

'That's the National Park, there can be no farming there.'

'But ...' Patrice looked. The cleared land couldn't be seen from this side of the river. 'Of course,' he said, and let the subject drop.

One of the harvesters knocked on the side of the truck. The driver rolled it forward past a few more trees and stopped again. Patrice sat with him in the cab as the men outside worked. Patrice could feel the man's eyes on him.

'Tourist?'

'Yes.'

'Normally it's white people who go to the park.'

Patrice shifted in his seat. 'Have you ever been?'

'No. There's nothing there for me.'

Patrice nodded. He'd only once visited the national park near where he lived, and that had been in pursuit of a corrupt army colonel. 'I suppose not,' he said.

'Did you see animals?' the driver asked.

'Two elephants. They didn't like me being there.'

With a full load, the truck set off for the mill, lurching from side to side on the uneven ground between the palms. They turned on to a dirt road and after ten minutes came to the mill. It was an old factory with corrugated iron walls and smoke belching out of tall chimneys and open windows, surrounded by a rambling collection of outbuildings and sheds. The driver steered his truck round to a weighing station and pointed the way to the entrance.

Patrice walked through the facility, accompanied by the deafening noise of engines and hissing steam and an overpowering smell of palm oil. By the main structure, he saw vats of cleaned fruit bunches lined up below conveyor belts and elevators. Inside, he caught glimpses of control panels with cracked glass dials and porcelain buttons. Men in headscarves and flip-flops were shovelling fibrous husk into open white-hot furnaces, and every surface was covered with a greasy red sheen.

As he passed a storage tank, a man called out to him. 'You want to buy palm oil?' The man was grinning. He had a bony face and wore spectacles. 'The oil in that tank will cost you a million dollars.'

'Really?'

'Palm oil is big business, my friend.' The man held out his hand. 'Norbert Ekellem, Chief Engineer.'

'Patrice Le Congo, from Congo. I'm just visiting. In fact, I'm looking for the exit.'

'Over there.' The engineer pointed behind Patrice. 'I thought you were American. You're not in the business yourself?'

'No.'

'That is a pity. I saw you looking around the mill. As you can see, this place is dilapidated. We need investment, especially for purification. Our machines are outdated. They cannot achieve the same quality as the newer presses. I can tell you it is impossible now to compete with the big plantations in Malaysia and Indonesia, where they have all the latest equipment, or even with the new private companies here with their foreign backing.'

'And your trees are old ...'

'You are right. They still produce, but when they are ten or twelve metres high, then harvesting is slow. A tree that is twenty-five years old is not economically viable and we have many that are reaching that age.'

'Can't you grow new trees?'

'We have planted some areas, but not enough.'

'Is there a shortage of land here? I mean, couldn't you expand into the National Park?'

'Absolutely not!' The man stared at Patrice through his

glasses. 'That is protected. But there is other forest land, not part of the park, on the other side of the plantation; but to develop that, we need more investment. This is what I'm saying. So you are interested! If you want, I can show you round?'

'No, thank you.'

Patrice left in search of an *okada,* and within a minute he was riding away from the mill, up a road lined on both sides by rows of single-storey concrete buildings, like army barracks but with no doors in the doorways, nor glass in the windows. Groups of men were standing or sitting outside in groups.

'Who are these people?' he asked.

'Plantation workers,' the *okada* man answered. 'This is their accommodation.'

Patrice thought about what it would be like to spend a day shovelling oil palm fibre into a white-hot furnace and return to this. He looked at the men more carefully. They were young and strong, like the harvesters in the plantation. He thought about the man who'd chased him into the river. He'd looked strong too, with powerful round shoulders – like any farmer who spent his day bent over, harvesting his crops with a machete. It was hard to judge if he was strong enough to squeeze a man to death. But the fact was the park ranger had seen something, and it looked like someone had made sure he wasn't going to tell.

Chapter 17

The Guinness delivery truck pulled up outside the San Siro around midday. Samson Eta emerged from the doorway of the shipping container in a vest, black tracksuit trousers and open sandals. He stretched his arms, then walked through the covered seating area and out into the sun to lend a hand.

'Oga Coach, how things dey go?' the driver's mate asked as he started unloading the crates.

'Everything dey fine, no wahala.'

'Your boys won again yesterday, I heard.'

'Yes. They're playing well.'

'People everywhere in town are talking about them. Can they win the championship?'

'We're praying they can, but we're not taking anything for granted. Let me take these …'

Samson stacked up two crates and carried them through to the storeroom, then came for more. In five minutes they were done, and the truck went on its way.

'Good luck oh, oga Coach!' the driver's mate shouted from the back, standing among the crates of empties.

Samson punched his fist in the air.

There were five or six customers in the bar. One of them, a security guard from the money transfer office two plots up the road, was complaining about the size of his portion. 'I said, "Give me rice for two hundred and meat," but look at this. I tell you, the food is little but the money is great.'

Samson looked over to the grill. His wife, Monique, who was cooking this lunchtime, replied to the security guard, '*I give you food for the money wey you pay*. What do you expect for two hundred?'

Samson walked across and helped himself to a piece of roasted goat, dipping it in chilli pepper powder.

'Ah,' the security guard said, 'I see I am paying for the owner's food as well!'

Monique laughed but stopped when Samson put a few pieces on a plate and went to serve it to the dissatisfied customer.

'What are you doing?' she asked across the terrace. '*You want give away all the food for free? How we go fit make any profit*? How will we even feed ourselves?'

Samson had heard this complaint before. He walked around the terrace, straightening chairs and wiping tables.

'When will we have a proper house to live in instead of a shack?' Monique asked, pointing in the direction of the slatted wooden structure Samson had built behind the San Siro. 'You're not a businessman, I'm telling you.'

The security guard sniggered in his corner. '*You dey for big trouble, Coach!*'

Samson leant against one of the wooden posts that supported the tin roof and looked out at the football pitch on the other side of the road. A group of women were walking towards the motor park carrying onions and tomatoes in baskets on their heads. They saw him and waved, then squatted and laid out their produce on the ground in neat pyramids. Samson waved back, but his mind was elsewhere. Despite the success of his football team, he felt disturbed by recent events.

First his old friend Alex Ebot had died in a freak accident in the forest. They hadn't been close for a long time, it was true, but Alex had come to watch the Bakunda Lions, and his death had reminded Samson of the times they'd spent together. A link with the past had been severed, and it left him with an empty feeling. He had his health and his strength for now, but what happened to Alex showed you never knew when your time was up.

And then there was the rumour that a Chinese businessman was planning to build a hotel on the piece of land between the San Siro and the motor park, the piece of land Samson was looking at right now – the Lions' football pitch. He jerked his head involuntarily to the side and blinked twice.

'Well done, Coach!' Adam Tarkang from the national park tourist centre was approaching the bar, with his boss, Ngwa, a regular customer. The young assistant came to watch most of the Lions' home games. 'The Lions are roaring!' Tarkang held out his hand.

'Five wins in a row,' Samson said, slapping Tarkang's palm and trying to push his troubles off the pitch to the back of his mind. 'We're third now. If we keep winning, we have a chance for the title, and that would be a first for the Bakunda Lions.'

'It would be a first for the town,' Tarkang said. 'No team from here has ever won anything!'

'Is the team's success a result of your tactics?' Ngwa asked, though sounding uninterested.

Samson pursed his lips. 'Tactics play a part; they are part

of the preparation. But, you know, a lot is confidence. When you're winning every week, the possibility of losing doesn't cross your mind, even when you're playing better teams. The important thing now is to stay focussed but calm.'

The two men sat down. Tarkang ordered a Coke, Ngwa a large bottle of *Trente-trois* Export. It occurred to Samson that the tourist centre manager might have heard about the new hotel, so when he returned with the drinks, he pulled a chair over and asked him.

The man grinned. 'Yes, I have,' he said. 'It's very good news. The better the infrastructure, the more the tourists will want to come to the park.'

'But aren't there enough hotels? And they're not full. And who is this man who's building it? I mean, how did he get permission from the municipality? These things usually take years ...'

'I don't know all the ins and outs, but this hotel will attract a different class of visitor. Four stars. This will put Bakunda National Park on the international map.'

Samson shrugged.

'What will you do, Coach?' Tarkang asked. 'Where will you play?'

'I don't know. We can train at the district school if we have to, but the condition of the pitch is bad. And it's too small for matches ...'

'Well, hold on a minute, Coach,' Ngwa said. 'I may not know everything there is to know about football, and I don't want to sound rude, but Bakunda Lions are a youth team in South West Region, Cameroon; it's not English Premier League.'

'I tell you, other teams will refuse to play there.' Samson jerked his head and blinked twice and looked over at the pitch outside. It was not Wembley Stadium, for sure. There was no grass. But it was flat, relatively smooth and the correct dimensions. 'If this hotel comes, we'll have to look elsewhere, another town: Mbimbia or Mabengi, or even in Bakingi.'

'It would be bad for the town if it lost its football team,' Tarkang said.

Ngwa glared at him.

'It will not be easy,' Samson said. 'There are my fuel costs if we have to play far from here. And the extra time travelling,' he added, glancing at his wife, who was carrying a plate of meat to two customers. 'This could spell the end for the Bakunda Lions.'

There was a short silence. Ngwa cleared his throat. 'Talking of visitors, have you come across our human rights investigator friend from Congo? A strange little man with bushy hair ...' He held his hands away from his head.

'No.'

'He's been nosing around, inquiring about Alex Ebot; it seems he's intent on causing trouble for the park.'

'What does he want to know? I didn't see much of Alex, so there's not much I could tell him.'

'That's just as well. If I were you, I wouldn't engage with this man. Didn't you and Alex have a big falling out?'

Samson looked across at the football pitch again. 'That was a long time ago and long forgotten,' he said.

It was mid-evening when an *okada* pulled up outside the San Siro. The passenger's clothes were crumpled and covered in dust. He got off the motorcycle, shook himself down, patted his thick hair, and stepped across the drainage ditch and on to the terrace. Samson knew at once this was the Congolese man Ngwa had talked about. He wasn't so little. He had a puzzled look on his face, but he didn't look like a trouble-maker.

The Congolese ordered a bottle of Mutzig.

Samson brought it over. 'The roads are dusty at this time year,' he said.

The man looked up as if he was far away in thought but replied like he was grateful for the distraction. 'It's the same where I'm from, everywhere in Africa; it's either dust or mud.'

'You're from Congo, right?'

'News travels fast in this town. And let me guess how you knew – my hair?'

Samson laughed. 'No offence, I hope,' he said.

'None taken. I'm Patrice Le Congo, nice to meet you. If you're the owner of this bar, then I also know something about you. You coach a football team, and …' the Congolese lowered his voice '… you knew Alex Ebot, the park ranger who died in the forest?'

Samson pulled out a chair and sat. 'This is a small town. I'm Samson Eta. People here call me Coach. What you say is true. I'm glad to meet you. I heard you were asking about Alex.' He could see Le Congo sizing him up.

Chapter 18

Jeki picked up a handful of dust from the ground and rubbed it between his palms and fingers, trying to clear his mind and focus on the task before him. It was a new weight. A mechanic had welded it together for him using steel piping and four wheel-shaped bits of iron that came from an old bus. Jeki had no idea what it weighed in kilos, but it had been a struggle for the two of them to get it into the "gym", a corner of the shack that was his home.

He glanced at himself in the mirror. It was his dream to become a champion wrestler. He'd worked hard since his last fight in the motor park. He flexed his biceps and they bulged like ripe melons. The feeling sent a rush through his whole body. Then he went down on his haunches and placed his hands on the bar, shifting them around till his grip stuck. Slowly, he stood up, bent over, gripping the bar. He took a breath, pushed out his chest, held in his stomach, and jerked the bar up to his neck. It was heavy, heavier than anything he'd ever lifted. He steadied himself, brought his breathing under control, and prepared for the final push, telling himself over and over to keep calm.

But at the moment he needed to concentrate most, he saw himself in the forest. Suddenly, the weight felt twice as heavy. He was losing his balance, his palms felt sweaty. The bar slipped out of his hands and he jumped backwards as it crashed to the floor with a thud. He kicked the ground and slumped into his chair.

It was an accident. Jeki had told himself that again and again. If he didn't mean it, it couldn't be his fault. Gnawing at what was left of his fingernails, he looked for comfort and inspiration to the drawings pinned to his wall of the first Jeki, Jeki la Njambe, the mythical hero of the old Douala folk tale, after whom his mother had named him.

What, he asked himself, would Jeki la Njambe have done in his place? He wouldn't have let himself be used. Jeki la Njambe was his own man. He wasn't plagued by doubts. He was born with a spear in his hand, and in all he did, in all the tasks he was set, the goal was the same: to avenge the mistreatment of his mother by his father. If only things were so clear-cut for this Jeki, who never knew his father and whose mother had passed away ten years ago. Since then he'd lived alone. He depended on no one, and no one depended on him. Yet for some reason he felt he had to please other people, people he didn't even know well.

It was later that afternoon, when Jeki was breaking firewood outside his shack, that a vehicle pulled up in front. Few vehicles ventured to this corner of town. His shack was on its own, off a narrow track that led down to the river. He looked up to see a man in a black blazer and white tee shirt step out of a four-by-four with blackened windows. Under normal circumstances, Jeki would have assumed he was lost, or had come to the wrong house. But not now, not after what had happened. He froze.

The man stopped and waved. Jeki didn't usually trust men who were dressed well and rode in smart cars.

'*Ebíamu á bwâm,*' the man said. He was speaking Douala. 'Good evening. I am looking for Jeki, and I see I have found him!'

He spoke in a friendly tone, not like someone who was about to arrest him. Jeki relaxed a little.

'I hope I am not disturbing you?'

'*Bepayédí bá bwâm.* You are welcome.' Jeki avoided eye contact.

'I saw your bout the other night.'

Jeki hung his head.

'I was impressed,' the man said.

Jeki gave the man a sideways glance. 'I can do better.'

'That's what I think. With coaching, you could be one of the greats.'

It took time for his words to sink in. The man was smiling. Jeki's face lit up. 'Are you a promoter?'

The man looked to the left and right, then answered in a quieter voice. 'I think I can help you, Jeki. And you can help me. Is there somewhere we can sit and talk?' He started towards the shack.

Jeki moved across and blocked his path, not wanting the man to see the pitiful state of his home. 'We can sit here,' he said, pointing at two bits of sawn tree trunk.

The man looked over Jeki's shoulder. 'You train in here as well?'

'Yes. I train here, I eat here, and I sleep here. I don't have anywhere else.'

The man pulled out a piece of cloth and wiped the seat, then lifted his trousers at the knees to sit. Jeki asked him if he'd like something to eat or some water. The man said no and patted the other seat, gesturing for Jeki to sit next to him.

'You know you could go far, Jeki. With the right people behind you.'

'Thank you, sir. I know I can.'

'I know lots of people, Jeki. Powerful people who can make things happen. If you're ready to work with me?'

Jeki was taken aback. 'I am definitely ready, sir.'

'That's good,' the man said, sounding serious and businesslike. 'Because you will have to work hard, and show tremendous discipline.'

'I can do that, sir.' If the man thought he was ready, then he must be. His dream was about to come true.

'Before we get carried away, Jeki, there is something we need to sort out. I think you know what I'm talking about?'

'Sir?'

'The misfortune that befell the ranger in the forest. People are beginning to talk.'

Chapter 19

After the day Patrice had had – his trek through the forest, his escape across the river – the beer tasted good.

'How well did you know him?' he asked the bar owner.

'We were best friends when we were young, but we went our own ways, so ...'

Coach Samson looked like he might have been a football player once: a big man, well built, in good shape. He seemed happy to talk but he had a nervous tic, which made it look, perhaps unfairly, like he might have something to hide.

'So?'

'Well, so, we didn't stay friends.'

'Did something happen?'

'More like, something *didn't* happen. I can tell you about it. But why are you asking about Alex? Have you come to my bar to accuse me of something?'

'I'm not accusing you of anything. The ranger had been in touch with the African Union, warning about a lack security in the national park. And then he died. I think he discovered something he wasn't supposed to know about.'

Coach Samson did that thing again and blinked. 'Like what?' he asked.

'Wait. First let me hear more about you and Alex Ebot.'

The man sighed, then began his story. 'It's a silly thing, looking back. We were from the same town, Mamfe, and we were friends ... and we loved football. We were a gang of two. We called ourselves the Indomitable Lions, after the Cameroon national team – that's their nickname. So ...'

He glanced up and must have caught Patrice smiling. 'Yes, this is all about football ...'

'So, carry on – I like football.'

'So, when Cameroon qualified for the 1990 World Cup in Italy – we were eighteen at the time – we made a pledge that we would go there to watch them play. We worked every evening and weekends in bars, saving money. But, of course, it wasn't enough for an air ticket and visa and everything, so we decided we'd go by truck, over the desert, and somehow get across the Mediterranean. But when the time came, Alex pulled out. He said he was going to university to study forestry, and he was going to use his money for that. I was upset. We argued. He claimed he'd thought I was joking about crossing the desert. Well, I wasn't going to go on my own. But that was the end of our friendship.'

Patrice said, 'Maybe it was for the best. A lot of people don't make it across the desert, or the sea.'

'For me, football was my life. Playing, watching, it was all I wanted to do. I didn't think about anything else. I thought Alex was the same. But he had more sense than me.'

Their bottles were empty. Patrice asked for another and invited Coach Samson to have one too.

'Try this one,' the bar-owner said on his return, carrying two bottles of Isenbeck. 'It's lighter than the others.'

Patrice tasted it. It was cool and sharp. 'It's good,' he said, licking his lips. 'Is it Cameroonian?'

'No. It's brewed here but owned by a foreign company, like Mutzig, *Trente-trois,* Guinness ... this one's German, I think. You know, I would like to drink Cameroonian beer, but it is rough against the throat. I sell it, but nobody drinks it, unless they have not been paid. If you want a Cameroonian drink, you drink palm wine.'

'The Europeans have got us hooked on their beer!'

'It's true!' Coach Samson said. 'And their football!'

They laughed and clinked bottles.

Their conversation was interrupted by a shout from a table where three men were sitting. 'Hello! Is anyone working in this bar tonight? We need more beer ...'

Coach Samson excused himself while he tended to other customers.

Patrice drank some more. A mouth-watering smell of roasting meat wafted across the bar. He ordered a plate from the cook.

Two boys on a bicycle pulled up outside the bar; one was riding, the other sitting sideways on the crossbar. Both had football boots draped round their shoulders.

'Papa,' the passenger shouted. 'Tell Mama I'm sleeping at Tico's house tonight.'

Coach Samson came over. *'You dong do all your school work?'*

'We go do the homework for Tico their house, Papa.'

'Okay, Sonny. *Wuna waka fine oh.* Go safely, boys.'

'We go see tomorrow, Papa,' Sonny said as they rode off into the darkness. 'See you tomorrow.'

The coach sat down again and swigged his beer.

'Are they in your team?' Patrice asked.

'Yes. Sonny plays Number Ten, like his papa used to. He's thirteen now. If he keeps fit and keeps growing, I think he could make it. You should come and watch – they'll be playing Saturday, on this pitch right here ...'

Patrice said he would if he could but wasn't sure of his plans. 'Did you ever play professionally?' he asked.

'I played for teams here in Cameroon, but you couldn't call it professional, as we were never paid. Then I had a trial for a team in Cannes, in France. They flew me there, but it didn't work out. It didn't happen for me ...'

He was a grown man, and this had all happened a long time ago, but he looked like he was close to tears.

'I remember the 1990 World Cup,' Patrice said, 'and the opening game, when Cameroon beat Argentina.'

'I should have been there! But it was a wonderful moment; it made me so proud to be Cameroonian.'

'All of Africa was proud. Cameroon were playing for the whole continent.'

'We took the world by surprise. After that, everyone was interested in Cameroonian players, and that's how I got the trial in Cannes. As I say, it didn't work out. But then I stayed on and did different jobs: driving, working in bars. I stayed in France four years and saved some money, and then I went home, to Mamfe.'

'And how did you end up here?'

'My wife is from here. We came to visit her family one time, and I saw this place, this bar, and I suggested we give it a go, try and make something of it. This is our home now. I built our living quarters behind.'

'San Siro – I get the name now. That's the name of the stadium in Milan where Cameroon won that match!'

'Yes, that's right.' The coach chuckled. 'And then, by coincidence, Alex came to work here, in the park.'

'You two didn't renew your friendship?'

The man twitched and blinked. 'No. He spent most of his time in the forest with his conservation work and what have you. He didn't ever come here to have a drink and relax.'

'Because it's your bar?'

'I don't know. He wasn't one to socialise. The other rangers come here, and they told me Alex was the same at work, keeping himself to himself, and strict about things, filing his reports, getting angry if people were late, complaining the park management didn't take their duties seriously ...'

Patrice chose his next words carefully. 'From what you say, it sounds like he'd be angry if he found out someone had cut down part of the national park and started farming there?'

The bar owner didn't look at him, but gazed across the football pitch to the motor park. 'Yes. He would. He'd be angry.' He paused and his head jerked to the side, as it had done before. 'But is that possible?'

'It's happening. I saw it myself today, with my own eyes.'

Coach Samson blinked twice. 'And you think that's why Alex was killed?'

'It looks like it.'

'We heard it was an elephant,' Coach Samson said, getting to his feet. 'Anyway, I have work to do. It's been nice to meet you.' He went to serve more customers.

Patrice finished his beer. He felt like he'd been going round in circles and was somehow back at square one. He picked up his phone and texted Josie Mwinga in Banjul or Addis, or wherever she was, to say he'd be staying on longer in Cameroon. Then he called the reporter, Sally Bintu.

'Hello, Sally,' he said. 'I need to speak to you. Can we meet?'

'Sure,' she said. 'But I'm in Douala.'

Chapter 20

The ride from the military camp to police headquarters, King Rudolf Douala Manga Bell's last journey, takes fifteen minutes in heavy rain. He assumes they've waited for the deluge to ensure as few people as possible are on the streets. No one can doubt their organisational skills.

The wheels skid in the mud. The rain gushes down the windscreen like a waterfall. Ngosso Din is in a car behind. The convoy is protected by soldiers on foot with rifles pointed outwards. The people of Douala watch the vehicles pass from their verandas in silence.

Douala Manga is accompanied by Colonel Zimmerman, the German military commander in Cameroon, a man he has got on with well. They even went hunting together.

'Was it you who arranged for me to be so well fed today?' he asks, reflecting on a breakfast of pineapple and pawpaw and a lunch of fish, ndole and garri.

Zimmerman's mood is sombre, matching the rain. 'It was the least I could do,' he says. He turns to face his captive. 'Douala Manga, *es nicht zu spät ist Ihre Meinung zu ändern.* It's not too late to change your mind.'

'And announce that, in order to save my skin, I agree to the subjugation of my people?'

Zimmerman winces. The raindrops falling on the car roof sound like stones. 'Who knows what's going to happen now. I can tell you, as a friend, I am not confident that Germany can hold on to Cameroon in the face of an attack by the British and French. And that attack is certain to come.'

Douala Manga pats the colonel on his forearm. 'In which case, were I to accept your conditions, the British and French would find a defeated people, a ready-made colony of slaves. You should know, it matters not to us whether the white man with the whip is counting his twenty-five lashes in English, French or German.'

Zimmerman turns to the window.

As Douala Manga looks outside at the faces partially obscured by the rain, he can see in their eyes that these people know where he is being taken. But they will see a man who is not afraid, a king who is true to his people, who will suffer for them. Out of a habit he acquired as a boy in Germany, he pulls his collar forward and checks his tie is straight.

They pass the post office and the customs house, and in between Douala Manga catches a glimpse of the German battleship that arrived the year before with eight hundred and fifty troops on board, and which has remained in Douala's port ever since in an ugly show of strength.

When they reach police headquarters, Douala Manga is escorted into a bare waiting room.

A few minutes pass. Then the door opens and his wife Emma Engome rushes towards him, her arms flung wide. Two guards armed with rifles follow her into the room, and stand either side of the door.

'Douala Manga, they are going to murder you!' She sobs and shakes against his chest.

He tries to comfort her in his embrace, his cheek pressed against the top of her head. Emma Engome's father was an English trader; her mother was the daughter of another chief. Douala Manga's father, who was educated in England, arranged the marriage. Douala Manga and Emma Engome were grateful; for them it has been a union of love. Until his detention three months ago, he shared with her his struggles as he sought to challenge the German land appropriation plan. He knows, though, that her priority is the wellbeing of their family.

She looks up at him. Her face is wet with smudged tears. 'What will become of us without you, Douala Manga? We depend on you, as do your people …'

'A struggle that relies on one man is a struggle doomed to fail,' he says, determined to maintain his dignity. 'Our struggle is for the honour and freedom of all Cameroonians. Others will rise to lead it, do not fear.'

He wipes away Emma Engome's tears with his thumbs, and bends to kiss her gently on the lips. He cannot pretend to himself that he is not worried for his soon-to-be widow and their children, and the thought that they might suffer is unbearable. He takes a breath to compose himself. Then he makes as if to kiss her hair, and whispers in her ear. His words make her wail and drop to her knees in front of him, and bow at his feet.

She cries out, 'Douala Manga, you are strong and brave, and we will be strong and brave like you.' Three times she repeats this phrase while praying at her husband's feet.

The king pulls his queen up gently and holds her again, her hands clasped against her chest. She slips the sheets of paper she has removed from under his shirt into her dress.

One of the guards steps forward. '*Bewegung!*' he commands. 'Time to go!'

Douala Manga gives Emma Engome one last embrace. She bows again and turns and is led out of the door.

And Hermann von Roehm enters. He is sneering. 'So, Douala Manga, you prefer to die than to admit the truth.'

'I prefer to die than to lick your boots, Roehm.'

Roehm's sneer vanishes. 'Well,' he says, 'they are ready for you.' The *Kaiserliche Bezirksamtmann* swivels on his boot heels and walks away.

PART II

Njibàa mulema e sí malángabe

It is hard to read another's heart
(Douala proverb)

Chapter 21

'That's where they did it.' Sally Bintu, the young reporter, was pointing to the back of a dusty courtyard next to the former colonial police station in the Bonanjo district of Douala. 'It's been neglected, so you'd never know something so dramatic happened here.'

Patrice looked through the railings. The building was now used by the Ministry of Transport. Behind a rusty flagpole with no flag attached he could make out two vehicle tyres lying flat with plants growing in them and the torn shreds of a plastic wreath on top.

'There was a tree there. King Rudolf Douala Manga Bell and his assistant Ngosso Din were hanged from one of the branches. They say Douala Manga put the rope around his neck himself.'

Patrice listened obligingly. He'd spent twelve hours travelling the previous day. His body ached from the journey. But it was a relief to be away from the claustrophobic atmosphere in Bakunda.

'Was it a public execution?'

'No. There would have been a riot. Everyone knew the charges against them were fabricated.'

'So who said he put the rope around his neck himself?'

'Ugh.' She made a noise like she'd cut her finger. *'You dey still ask too many questions!* It's according to legend that he did that, okay? Afterwards, he and Ngosso Din were taken to what the Germans called the native cemetery and buried. And it was another twenty years before Douala Manga's remains were moved to the Pagoda.'

'The Pagoda?'

'That's what people call the old palace, because it looks like a pagoda. Come, it's not far.'

They turned and headed for Place du Gouvernement. It was late morning, baking hot and humid. The short walk was long enough to make Patrice sweat.

The square was quiet but for the distant car horns and heavy hum of the traffic that clogged Douala's main streets.

'There,' Sally said. 'In the far corner.'

The pagoda stood amidst a cloud of black dust thrown up by roadworks going on in front of it. In contrast to the neighbouring colonial buildings and modern, concrete blocks, the former seat of the Douala kings looked like a Buddhist shrine; four tapering stories of whitewashed walls with verandas and green tiled roofs, topped by a small tower.

'It's offices now, and in a poor state,' Sally said as they approached. She pointed out the broken shutters and peeling paint. 'It should be a beautiful museum dedicated to Douala culture and the history of the resistance to colonial rule.'

She led Patrice to the rear of the building, to the royal burial vault. 'Douala Manga's wife, Emma Engome, was still alive when they brought his remains here, to their rightful resting place. It's nice she got to see that. She died the following year. The people loved her. She was a connection with their past because after the French took over, after they and the British defeated the Germans, the Douala were sidelined. They never had any power after that.'

Patrice looked at the plain stone monument marking the spot. The young reporter was gazing at the Pagoda behind them. 'I'm guessing this is all related to the historical research you told me you're doing.'

'You remembered! Yes. It's a hundred years since Douala Manga died. I want to raise awareness about him. He should be a national hero, yet many Cameroonians don't know his story.' She swished her long hair with its red streak to one side.

'Have you won round your editor?'

'I haven't told him yet. Actually, you're the first person I've told. To convince my editor, I'm going to have to come up with something new about Douala Manga, so I've been looking for original sources of information. And I've made a good contact here in Douala. Anyway, my editor is still obsessed with stories about the reunification anniversary ...'

'Oh, yes. Any news on that?'

'Still no date. Meanwhile everything else is on hold. So,' she said with a smile, 'are you hungry? Would you like to buy me lunch? I know a place where we can eat fresh fish.'

'Let's go,' he said.

She hailed a yellow taxi and told the driver to take them to *Base Naval*. The driver made a U-turn, causing three cars and a motorcycle to brake sharply, then drove around the edge of the port down to a group of restaurants on the bank of the Wouri River estuary. They were greeted by the hypnotic smell of grilled fish. Sally pointed at a restaurant she said she knew, and after haggling with the manager over the price of a carp that weighed a kilo, they found a table on the edge of the deck, below which a small sandy beach sloped into the water.

'Fish from here fine but e too dear,' Sally complained.

Patrice said, 'Don't worry about it. I'm paying.'

She tutted. 'If we had more time I could take you to a place in Bonabéri, where it's as good as this but cheaper.'

The carp the waiter brought them thirty minutes later was scored on the sides, cooked over a charcoal fire and served with onion, pepper and a side plate of plantain. They tore off the firm white flesh with their fingers. It was delicious, Patrice thought, and worth every centime.

'So,' Sally said as they ate, 'it's my turn to ask the questions. I don't know anything about you.'

'Me? There's not much to know.'

'Well, there's your name, to start with. You told me there's a story behind it.'

'So, yes. As a baby, I was left outside an orphanage with no note. It was Independence Day, the anniversary of Congo's independence, so Mama, the lady who ran the orphanage, she named me after our country. And because she was an admirer of Patrice Lumumba, our first leader after independence, she chose that for my first name.'

Sally was looking at him, wide-eyed. 'I like that. No one knew anything about you, but she gave you a history. And then what?'

He shrugged. 'I went to primary school in the nearest town, secondary school in Bukavu. I won a scholarship to the Catholic university and studied economics. I became a teacher ... really, you know, as I said, there's not much ...'

'And now you're a human rights investigator. So how did that happen?'

'There was a war in my country – actually, it's not over. When you see people suffer, all around, well, you have to do something. I was teaching children French, which is useful for them, but it felt like there were more urgent things ... so I left teaching and set up a small organisation to assist people in trouble. But it was hard to keep it going. We lost our funding, then a lady from the African Union offered me a job, so that's why I'm here now.'

'And is there a Madame Le Congo, in Congo?' Perhaps she was simply being nosy, but her smile was open to interpretation.

'No,' he said, not smiling. 'There was once, but not now.' Patrice's wife, Annette, had died three years earlier. He didn't feel like talking about it.

Sally took the hint. 'Okay, sorry to pry.'

'No problem. What about you? And your royal ancestry?'

She laughed. 'I don't know why I told you that. It was just something silly my mother used to say. She said it was a family secret, passed down through the generations. I used to ask her why we didn't live in a palace, and she'd change the subject. I suppose she thought all little girls want to be a princess.'

'It would be unusual for a princess to become a reporter.'

'Yes,' she said, laughing again. 'I still ask my mother about it when I go home, just to tease her.'

'And where is home?'

'Bamenda. It's a city in North West Region. It's quite far from here. But now back to you, and my last question: what is it that you wanted to speak to me about?'

The waiter came to clear their table. Patrice waited till he was gone before answering. 'It's that story of yours, the one about the ranger in Bakunda National Park. He wasn't killed by an elephant.'

'That's it? Really? You came all the way to Douala to tell me that? What did kill him? A gorilla? But I don't think they have gorillas in that park … A crocodile?'

'I think he was murdered.'

Sally stared at him. 'What? Why?'

'Because he discovered a corner of the park has been cut down and is being cultivated by farmers.'

Her mouth dropped open.

'You mentioned some farmers there were being displaced. So I'm thinking …'

'How do you know this?'

He told her about his visit to the park with the GPS tracker and being chased by the farmer with the machete.

'*Mama-ye!* My God, Patrice! *Take care oh.*'

'That's what everyone keeps telling me. But the strange thing is, in the town, it's as if people know something's not right, but no one wants to investigate what's going on. And this is a national park. It's supposed to be protected. But even the people who run the park aren't interested, apart from your contact Adam Tarkang, and he's petrified he's going to lose his job.'

Sally looked out across the estuary. 'I thought you wanted to go home?' she said.

'I did, and I do.' He pulled a small fish-bone from between his teeth. 'But you know how it is; one thing's led to another. Anyway, the thing is – and I'm not trying to tell you how to do your job – I thought you might want to come to Bakunda to write a follow-up. It could help to get things out in the open.'

Sally bit her lip. 'Not now, not with the president going to Buea. I told you, that's all my paper's interested in. I'll tell my editor about it, but I know what he'll say. For him, what the president eats for breakfast is more important than the life of a park ranger; what the president's wife is wearing is more important than a threat to our rainforest.'

'You could go for a couple of days, while you're waiting. You might as well be there as in Douala ...'

'Patrice, *I know how for sort myself out!* From here I can be in Buea in an hour. If I'm in Bakunda, forget it, I'll be stranded. And ...'

She looked away.

'And?'

'Well, there's this research I'm doing, about Douala Manga. I have ... an appointment.'

Patrice rolled his eyes. 'No problem. I'll go back on my own.'

'I'm sorry, Patrice. I'll come when I get the chance. Let me give you a contact ...' She scrolled through her phone. 'My predecessor in Bakingi gave me his number ... I don't know him, but he's an activist who's been working with the farmers ... here it is. He owns a bar. His name's Samson Eta.'

Chapter 22

Jeki reeled. 'The ranger?' The smartly dressed man was looking at him like a teacher looks at a naughty boy. He felt short of breath. 'But … I didn't mean …'

'I know that,' the man said. 'And you know that. But not everyone may believe that. That's what I meant when I said we can help each other. I can protect you, Jeki. I have friends in high places. If you ever run into trouble, these are people who can get you out.'

'Who told you? It must be …'

'Now, now, Jeki. Keep calm. Everything will be fine. You will be a great champion. Help me so I can help you.' The man got to his feet.

Jeki did the same. He bowed, holding his hands together. 'Please, sir, I am a hard worker, what is it you want me to do?'

'Stand up straight, Jeki, and maintain your dignity at all times. I'm sure you know the story of the other Jeki, from long ago?'

'*O bí munía mwá Jeki lá Njambe?* You know the story of Jeki la Njambe?'

'Of course. He is a Douala legend and that's what you can be. In fact, I believe that is what you have been chosen to be.'

'Chosen?'

'*A Loba*. By God. God has empowered you with the strength of Jeki la Njambe. It is a sign He wants the Douala people to be respected again, as we once were. But Jeki, you must share the great legend's belief. Ask yourself: did he ever cower before anyone?'

Jeki lowered his head in shame.

'You must show you are worthy of the name. And I know you are. Because the spirit of Jeki la Njambe is within you.'

At last, Jeki looked into the man's eyes. The man exuded great power, and now Jeki could feel this power in himself.

'Why do you think you are built like this? It is not natural for a man to have such incredible strength. Why do you think your mother named you Jeki? Like the mother of the legend, she knew she had given birth to a special child.'

Jeki was speechless. Apart from his mother, no one had ever had a good word to say for him.

'You are the reincarnation of Jeki la Njambe.'

Jeki drew a sharp breath.

The man lifted Jeki's chin with his fingers. 'And Jeki, as Jeki la Njambe was set some tasks, so you will be set some tasks, to show you are worthy of his name, and of my support and protection. Like the challenges faced by Jeki la Njambe, these will not be easy. They may be dangerous. But believe in yourself!'

To be like Jeki la Njambe! It was what he had always aspired to, but had not thought possible.

'Each time you complete a task, you shall reap a reward. But if you fail, the consequences will be serious. It was the same for Jeki la Njambe.'

The man leaned forward and looked Jeki straight in the eye. He was so close Jeki couldn't look away.

After a long pause, the man asked, *'Oe mbáki na o e bebe ó bola níka?* Do you think you are ready for this?'

Jeki lifted his shoulders and pushed forward his chest. *'Ee! Na e bebe!* Yes! I am ready!'

'Good. Very good.' The man stepped back and adjusted the sleeves of his jacket. 'Before I set the first task, there is one more thing, Jeki. You will never know my name, and you must never speak of me to anyone. If you do, you will be on your own, and then there will be problems, with the police. Do you understand?'

'I understand,' Jeki replied, still standing to attention. 'But if I am not to know your name, what do I call you?'

'Bébé mbá na Sáŋgó. You can call me Master.'

'A Sáŋgó âm! My Master!' Jeki took another bow. 'I am ready for the first task, *Sáŋgó*.'

The man gestured for him to sit again. Even though there was no one around, he leant his head close to Jeki's ear to issue his instructions in a whisper. Then he placed a small packet of folded newspaper into the palm of Jeki's hand. 'With this, you will be able to disguise yourself, the way Jeki la Njambe used to do.'

As he watched the four-by-four turn and head towards town, Jeki felt strong again. He got the fire going for his dinner then went into his shack and stood above the metal bar. The weights that looked so daunting before now looked no heavier than coconut shells. He dusted his hands, gripped the bar and without hesitation, jerked it on to his chest. Barely pausing, he roared, and straightened his arms above his head. He stood still, counting to ten, then threw the bar down in triumph. The ground around his feet trembled.

What *Sáŋgó* had said was right. He needed not just to admire Jeki la Njambe, he needed to behave like him too. Hold his head high, be proud. As he thought these things, the cloud that had been hanging over him before began to lift.

He ate a double portion of garri with his dried fish that evening. After his meal, out of curiosity, he opened the small package. The powder inside had a strong smell. He wouldn't brew it up in a potion yet, but to see what it was like he licked his finger and dabbed the powder on his tongue. It was bitter, as *Sáŋgó* had warned him it would be.

Jeki sat outside in the dusk and watched the trees on the other side of the track fade into the darkening night. He felt a rush through his body and a warm glow that brought a rare smile to his face. He lay in the grass. Soon he was recalling one of his favourite stories about Jeki la Njambe …

Jeki has gone to his father's village for a wrestling tournament. As his father, Njambe, had banished his mother before Jeki was born - believing her to be unable to bear him children - neither he nor anyone else in the village recognises Jeki. The night before the wrestling, there's to be a game of ngoti, where spears of bamboo are thrown at a gourd hanging from a tree branch.

Jeki arrives as the game is starting. His opponents are three other sons of his father, three brothers whom Jeki has been ordered to swallow in order to avenge his mother's honour. As is the case in a game of such importance, the last one out will be killed.

His brothers are big and strong and boast that none of them will be last out. They take it in turns to throw their spears; first, Etrungwe, who strikes the gourd, and is out; then Krubete and Ekunto also hit the gourd, but their spears hit exactly the same spot, and the game must start again. The night has turned cool and even Njambe, Jeki's father, shivers. Jeki stands side-on to the gourd. He feels a morning breeze and knows soon the cock will crow; when that happens, all competitors left must be killed. But he doesn't panic. He raises his spear and touches the sharpened point. Then he calls out his mother's name: 'Bekele, you are the one that trusts in me; as I stand in the court of your husband, my father, let my spear fly true.' He hurls his bamboo with such force that it pierces the gourd, breaks it open, and sends it crashing to the ground.

There is silence, broken by a distant cockerel. Realising what this means, Njambe orders that it must be Jeki who is killed, for he has interrupted the first round. The crowd surge forward to attack Jeki with sticks and machetes, but Jeki has anticipated this. He has been to the village before and, having transformed himself into a bat hanging from a branch, has watched his father preside over games such as this; he knows his father cannot accept defeat. He grabs his three brothers and holds them out as a shield against the advancing mob. They cry out as they take the blows. The crowd step back. Then Jeki swallows his three brothers, one after the other. He rises before the crowd, his chest and shoulders now bulging but his stomach still small, and he shouts, 'Njá nú matée mbá besna? Who will strike me now?' No one comes forward ...

Jeki looked at the stars. He was remembering the story as his mother used to tell it to him, and as he did, he heard her scratchy voice, wise and reassuring. 'These are the stories from where we come,' she used to say.

But, on this night, something was different, for the story Jeki heard his mother telling him was, it seemed, about him.

Chapter 23

'May God bless this bus and all who travel in it, because the journey of fate is a journey of ups and downs, and the road you take today will be a road of ups and downs …'

The preacher chased the minibus out of the motor park waving his bible. A passenger clutching a crucifix pushed a banknote out of the window for him. The preacher cried out, 'God loves Jesus.'

Patrice sat drumming his fingers on the bag on his lap, resigned to another long, uncomfortable journey. The sky was grey, the landscape green. They crossed the Mungo River, then entered South West Region. As they passed a sign for Buea, the man next to him tapped him on the shoulder and said, 'It is pronounced *Boya*; like *soya* but with a B.' Perhaps he mistook Patrice for a newly-arrived tourist.

Patrice nodded. He wasn't in the mood for chitchat. He was kicking himself for not having seen there might be more to Coach Samson than a football-crazy bar owner. He looked out of the window for a glimpse of Mount Cameroon, but it was hidden by the clouds, shrouded in mystery – like the death of the ranger Alex Ebot.

On reaching Bakunda town, he checked back into his hotel, showered under a trickle of cold water and, around dusk, walked to the San Siro. Boys were playing football in the fading light on the pitch across the road from the bar. He noticed Sonny and Tico among them, and guessed the Bakunda Lions were preparing for their next match, though he couldn't see their coach.

As he entered the bar, three men with machetes slung over their shoulders emerged from the shipping container at the back. They looked like farmers, and they were followed by Coach Samson, who patted them on their backs. The men looked downcast. They trudged across the terrace, past Patrice, and left without saying a word.

'Le Congo.' The big man approached. 'I thought you'd gone home.' He blinked and his head twitched.

'Hello, Coach.'

They shook hands.

'I was thinking of leaving but I realised I'm not finished here yet.'

'You are welcome.' Coach Samson showed him to a table while glancing down the street the way the farmers had gone. 'Isenbeck?'

Patrice nodded. 'Thank you. I was looking for you out there on the pitch ...'

'I was there before. We had a training session ... but I had to attend to other things. It's late now, they'll be finishing soon.'

'Will you join me for a beer?' The bar was quiet. There was no point in delaying the conversation.

'Thank you, I will.'

Before the man could move to get the drinks, Patrice continued. 'I tried calling you from Douala but I couldn't get through. A young reporter with the *Courier* gave me your number. She says you're an activist, working with displaced farmers. So, I've learned something else about you.'

'She? I don't know any woman reporter.'

'Sally Bintu. Her predecessor in Bakingi gave her your number ...'

Coach Samson blinked again. 'You can say I'm a bar owner, or a football coach, but I'm not an activist, whatever that is.'

'Fine. But I'm guessing those three men I saw walking away from here are not players in your football team ...'

*

Le Congo's tone was accusatory, but he was jumping to conclusions. Samson sat down and set about trying to explain. 'I'm a friend of the farmers, and believe me, they need friends. They came to me with their problems because they think I know things, because I've been to other countries and might be able to help them. And because they don't trust the people who *should* be able to help them, people in authority, and they've got nobody else they can turn to. I think you have met people in that situation.'

The Congolese raised an eyebrow but said nothing.

'Let me get those beers.' Samson went into the container and picked up two bottles of Isenbeck from a crate on the floor. He noticed the large envelope on the counter and picked that up too.

'Actually, I'm glad you're here,' he said as he rejoined Le Congo and they clinked bottles. 'I believe you're a man who stands up for the rights of downtrodden people.'

'Hang on, Coach, what about the rights of a park ranger trying to do his job?'

'I'm coming to that.' Samson pulled some papers from the envelope. 'As I said, people here are not sure who to trust.'

Le Congo said, 'I know the feeling.'

'Let me tell you how things are. Those three men you saw are from a village west of here, near the park. As a matter of fact, I got to know them because two of their boys play for the Bakunda Lions. They're good kids and they come from good homes. These men have been farmers all their lives; they've worked hard, but now they've lost their farms, and they are asking me, what are they going to do?'

'Have they started farming in the park?'

'They're in a difficult position, through no fault of their own.'

'The other day I was in a difficult position, when I was chased by someone – a farmer I believe – with a machete. And I'm wondering if that's what happened to Alex Ebot, except he didn't get away.'

Samson steadied himself to think. He leaned forward across the table and lowered his voice. 'I asked to see those three men today to ask them about Alex, if they knew anything. They told me they didn't, and I have to believe them. But if you show me the place you went to, we can meet the men farming there. They'll trust me.'

'Trust you? To do what? To keep quiet?'

'No. Listen, it's not like that. I – we, you and me – will explain to them that if ... if they know something about what happened to Alex, then they must come forward. Not just for Alex's sake, but because they can't hide that kind of thing for ever, and when it comes to light, it will be bad not just for them but for their whole village. As you see, they are not the only ones who've gone into the park.'

'Jesus! Who else knows about what these farmers are doing?'

'Shush, please.' Samson looked into the man's eyes, hoping to find compassion. 'I know some of the rangers know. Those from round here, they understand it's not easy for the farmers.'

'Did Alex Ebot know?'

'I don't know. If he did, I don't think he would have turned a blind eye to it.'

'He was once your friend, and you're trying to excuse ...'

'I'm not trying to excuse anything. I'm trying to enlighten you.'

The Congolese looked out at the dark football pitch, drinking his beer. Then he asked, 'How has this all happened? Why did these farmers lose their farms in the first place?'

Samson breathed a sigh of relief; for the man to ask such a question, it must mean he cared. 'The village and their farms are on land that's been leased to a foreign company that wants to create one of the biggest oil palm plantations in Cameroon – twenty thousand hectares. The company's called New Deal Plantations; it's half British, half German.'

He flipped through his pile of documents and pulled out a map. 'Those farmers you saw, they don't read and write well, so they ask me to look after their papers for them. Here's the proposal for the plantation, made six years ago. This area shaded green is the land the company wants. This part, where it's darker, that's the concession they've already been granted. You can see, it starts outside Bakunda town, and stretches halfway to the Nigerian border.'

'Did the farmers have to give up their land, if they didn't want to leave?' Le Congo asked.

'The problem is they don't own the land, even though their families have been farming it for generations. No one owns it. But the Government of Cameroon claims all untitled land for the state and leased it out to New Deal Plantations. Work started even before the concession was granted.'

'How?'

'It was a simple thing for them. They sent in the chainsaws and bulldozers.'

Le Congo frowned and studied the map more closely. After a while he asked, 'So the land leased for this plantation goes right up to the river that forms the eastern border of the national park?'

'It's a huge area,' Samson said, circling his finger round the map. 'So many farmers are affected by this.'

'We have similar cases back home,' Le Congo said. 'A few years ago, an international mining company was awarded a concession and wanted to evict hundreds of local miners who panned a river for gold. The company was going to mine underground but still they wanted the miners out. We fought a campaign and although the miners had to move their homes, they were allowed to carry on panning the river.'

Samson pointed at the envelope. 'I'd like to do something like that for the farmers here. But I don't know about these things. All I know about is football. But you, Le Congo, you have the experience, you can help them fight a campaign like you did for your miners ….'

'I can try. I can't deny this kind of thing makes me angry. It happens all over the world, and it has been happening like this for centuries. Poor people trampled on by the rich. But to encroach into the national park – a precious natural resource, an irreplaceable one – that can't be a long-term solution.'

'You're right.' Samson turned his bottle of beer round on the table. 'But, for now, what else can they do? In the view of these farmers, the government has taken their land and sold it to a foreign company. Bakunda National Park is big and doesn't have a fence around it.'

Le Congo looked at the map again. 'I swam across that river when the farmer chased me. The young trees I saw next to the Pamol plantation must belong to New Deal. The clearing I saw is close to that point.'

'These farmers I was talking to, their village is here …' Samson pointed to a spot on the map. 'It's called Bafuke. You saw them, they are real people, their families have been farming here for generations, like I said, and they have treated the forest with respect. But they have children to feed. And there are thousands in their position, in villages across this region.' He paused for a swig of his beer. 'And they're getting desperate.'

'Desperate enough to kill someone if they got caught?'

Samson blinked and jerked his head. 'That's what we're going to find out.'

Chapter 24

It was gone ten when Sally and Lucy emerged from the elevator into the car park below Lucy's apartment building and got into her car.

'Thank you for doing this for me,' Sally said.

'Lock your door. Will you tell me where we're going?'

'Bonanjo.'

Lucy drove out through the electronically controlled gates and set off across the city. The streets of Douala were dark and deserted apart from groups of street boys loitering on shadowy corners. Sally directed her to the *Palais de Justice,* then said to park under a tree in Place du Gouvernement.

'You're my friend,' Lucy said, looking around the empty square. 'So I'm happy to help you. But this is mysterious.'

Sally grimaced. 'It's better it stays that way.'

'I hope you know what you're doing.'

'It's okay. I won't be long, so don't move. If you have to, sound your horn twice, so I know, and I'll wait for you to return. Okay?'

'Okay.'

'Thanks, sister. After this, it'll be me who owes you.'

Sally got out of the car and waited for Lucy to lean across again and lock the door, then she set off along the sidewalk, keeping close to the edge, where the shadows were deepest. White trainers didn't seem like such a good idea now, glowing like they'd been dipped in luminous paint. Faint bass rhythms floated over from a nearby nightspot, muffled in the humid night air. As she came round the corner, she saw the yellow asphalt-laying machine she'd noticed before, when she'd been here with Patrice Le Congo. It was parked against the wall of the Pagoda.

She stepped into the road and looked up at the building, specifically at a first-floor window she'd also noticed before. It was still open. She went over to the vehicle, took one more look around, saw no one, and climbed on to the roof of the driver's cab. From there she was able to step on to the roof of the Pagoda's ground-floor veranda, holding on to a baluster supporting the next level up. She paused to take some deep breaths, trying to calm herself. Then she edged carefully along the sloping copper roof, across to the open window, and climbed inside.

It was pitch black. She waited for her eyes to adjust to the darkness. It felt like she'd crossed a line, and there was no going back.

Gradually, shapes began to form. She was about to step forward when a buzzing sound stopped her. She cursed under her breath as she fumbled for her phone inside the small bag on her back. Her editor was calling.

'Yes?' she whispered.

'Sally, where are you?'

'I'm sleeping.'

'The president is arriving in the morning. You must be at Tiko Airport by six. You're going with Raymond.'

'Okay, sir. Thank you.'

She hung up and called Raymond, one of the *Courier's* photographers, and told him she'd make her own way to the airport. She'd have to go to the motor park at four and wait for a vehicle. It was going to be a long night.

Distracted, she tried to get her bearings. She could see now the room she was in was empty. She walked across to the black shape of a door and turned the handle. It creaked open. Queen Emma Engome's bedroom. It too was empty.

She was away from the front of the building, so Sally risked the torch on her phone. The cupboard was in a corner. She walked across to it over a carpet of dust. The room was quiet and stuffy, like a padded cell. She pulled on the cupboard door. With a sharp tug, it jolted open, revealing a forest of cobwebs arched across the corners, shining silver in the torchlight. She got on her knees and tapped the floorboards. As she'd been told by Estelle's mother, one of the boards was loose. Her heart felt like it was in her throat. She edged up one end of the board with her finger tips and lifted it free. Another cobweb was between the joists, and a spider, which scuttled off. She brushed away the web and there it was, the package, wrapped in cloth, tied with a cotton ribbon.

It had lain there undisturbed for a hundred years, a secret known only to the queen and her maid, then the maid's daughter and her daughter's daughter – and now Sally. She'd been told the queen had refused to read Douala Manga's memoirs, having been too upset, and not wanting ever to be reminded of the circumstances of her last meeting with him. Sally's hands trembled as she picked up the package and felt the folded paper inside.

A car horn made her jump. She swung round. Headlights raced round the wall. She replaced the board and ran into the first room and over to the side of the window. Lucy's car was outside. But a police car had joined it. Sally stood against the wall, breathing deeply.

She couldn't stay where she was. She put the package in her bag, tiptoed back into the former bedroom, and went out through another door, which opened on to a landing and a stairwell. She made her way down the wooden stairs in total darkness. She felt a wisp of fresh air and followed it along a corridor, feeling the wall with her hands, too scared to use her torch. She came to a half-open window, which she crawled through and lowered herself into a courtyard. Then she heaved herself up and over a wall, and she was out of the compound. The streets were still deserted. She dusted herself off and headed round to Lucy's car.

'Lucy,' she called, seeing her colleague with two policemen. 'Is everything alright? I'm sorry I took so long.'

'Sally, I am glad to see you. These officers didn't believe I was waiting for my friend. Next time you go to Club 69, don't ring for me until you are ready to leave.'

The policemen looked Sally up and down.

'ID,' one said. Sally handed it to him. The policeman shone his torch at it and frowned before handing it back. '*Wuna be both journalists?*' he asked. 'You're both reporters?'

The women nodded.

'*We be small kaki boys.* We're policemen. *Wuna get small thing for us?*'

Sally gave them some small banknotes and wished them a good night. She got into the car with Lucy and let out a long breath. 'Oh my God,' she said. 'I'm so sorry, Lucy.'

'You owe me double now,' Lucy said as she pulled away. 'What's that?'

Sally didn't answer. She'd pulled the package from her bag and opened it. She was staring at the top sheet of paper. Then she read aloud. *'I am Rudolf Douala Manga Bell ... I am King of the Douala people – until tomorrow.'* She flipped the edges of the sheets of paper with her thumb and guessed there were some thirty hand-written pages. '*Chai, papa God*!' she said.

Lucy shook her head. '*Mamami-ye*! Holy Jesus! *Where you come get all these?'*

Sally looked at her with eyes wide open but mouth shut.

'The Pagoda? You broke in? I don't believe it! What are you thinking? You'll have to give that to the living descendants of the Bell family.'

Sally bit her lip. 'I don't see why I should. I mean, I found it. They don't even know about it.'

'But it's theirs, no? I know the different branches of the family have been in dispute about what should happen to the Pagoda, but something that's found there ... it must belong to them, or at least to some of them.'

'They won't miss what they didn't know they had,' she said. She was gazing again at the top page, running her fingers over the writing. '*Douala, Cameroon, August 7th 1914* ... it's history, in my hands!'

Lucy pulled over and brought the car to a halt. 'You know, sister, you're guilty of breaking and entering. Removing anything from that place is theft, plain and simple.'

Only then did it occur to Sally that there could be a problem. She'd been so excited to find the memoirs actually existed, she hadn't thought through the implications of her taking them. As Lucy had said, she'd broken the law. She could go to prison and lose her job. The package in her hands now felt like a sack of burning coals.

Chapter 25

Coach Samson was a man who'd been prepared to risk his life to watch Cameroon play football in the World Cup, so it didn't exactly come as a surprise to Patrice when he said they'd have to wait a day till they could travel to speak to the farmers who'd cut down a corner of the national park because his boys, the Bakunda Lions, had a match.

'You said you might come to see them,' the coach reminded him. 'And the farmers won't be going anywhere.'

Patrice used the time to track down someone else he'd been wanting to talk to. He found him where Adam Tarkang, the tourist centre assistant, had said he'd be on a Saturday morning - by the river, under the shade of a tree, gutting fish.

'Good morning,' Patrice said.

The man was lean with a thin face and thin moustache, aged about forty. 'Good morning,' he replied.

'Catch much?'

'What you see here,' the man said, working with his knife.

'Pike?'

'Today, pike. Are you a fisherman?'

'No, but I eat a lot of fish. That's a nice-looking rod you have, may I look?'

The man passed it over. Patrice examined the skilfully

crafted length of bamboo with a spindle of cork and wire attached above the handle.

'Do you fish for sport?'

'I suppose. I used to be a hunter, so this is similar.'

'I tried fly-fishing once. You need patience …'

'Like any form of hunting. But if you go to the right places, you can be lucky. Pike's what we get most up here. Further down there's more, like bone back and other bigger fish.'

'Bone back? Is that tilapia?'

'I don't know. We call it bone back.' The man looked up again. 'If you're looking to buy, you must go to the market. I don't have extra to sell today.'

'No, I wanted to talk.'

'About fishing?'

'About Alex Ebot.'

The man gutted his last fish and placed it in his icebox, but didn't say anything.

'You're Fidelis Nganje, the park ranger?'

'Are you a reporter?'

'I'm a human rights investigator. My name is Patrice Le Congo, from Congo.'

'Investigator? Why are you investigating Alex Ebot?'

'I don't believe a ranger who'd been working in that park for twenty years would get trampled by an elephant. Do you?'

There was a split-second hesitation. 'That's what they said. You know different?'

'What I know is nothing adds up.'

The ranger rinsed his hands in a bucket of water. 'Who told you where to find me?'

'I asked at the park office. Is there a problem?'

'What do you want to know?'

Patrice handed back the fishing rod. 'Did you know Ebot well?'

'Not well. Just to work with.'

'How long have you been a ranger?'

'Two years. I used to be hunter, as I told you, but there's less and less forest now where you can hunt, so I decided to use my skills another way, helping to protect the animals instead of killing them.'

'Like a poacher turned gamekeeper?'

'I was a hunter, not a poacher, there's a difference. When I was a boy there were many places you could hunt freely, but not now.'

'But that's a difficult switch to make, trying to catch hunters when you used to be one yourself.'

'As I said, they're poachers. What they're doing is illegal.'

'What about Ebot, did he have any ... sympathy, any appreciation of the life of a hunter?'

The fisherman leant his rod against the tree. 'If Alex had his way, hunters - poachers - would be shot on sight,' he said, pointing his finger at Patrice like a gun.

'What about farmers? What would he do if he found they were encroaching into the park?'

The man swallowed.

'I was told you were supposed to go on patrol with Ebot the day he was killed, but you were sick. What was wrong with you?'

'Malaria.'

'Did you know where he was planning to go?'

The man paused. 'Yes,' he said quietly.

'So you knew what he'd find?'

Silence.

'Did you tell anyone where he was going?'

The man's eyes were turning moist and a tear dropped to the ground. 'I don't know what happened, I swear. I know a farmer there, we're old friends. We used to drink palm wine together. There are a few farmers, they've lost their land; they're not a big problem. But I knew Alex would go crazy if he found out.'

He sat down on his icebox, his hand rubbing across the back of his head. Patrice squatted on his haunches in front of him.

'I called my friend, to warn him Alex was coming that way, and to be on the lookout, to be sure Alex didn't find him. I didn't want to be there, so I said I was sick.'

There was a pause again. Patrice didn't interrupt.

'The next thing I heard, Alex was dead, and they were bringing his body. I was distraught. I knew I'd have to tell them I'd told my friend. And that's what I meant to do. But then they said it was an elephant and …'

He glanced at Patrice, pleading for understanding. 'I told myself it was possible. But deep down inside me … I don't know …'

'Didn't you speak to your friend, the farmer, afterwards?'

'I didn't want to call him, in case he told me … something else.'

Patrice weighed up the ranger's story. It was plausible. 'What's the farmer's name?'

The ranger replied in a whisper. 'Daniel Ajebe.'

'Does he wear a red baseball cap?'

'Yes … no … I don't know. He's not a bad man, he's a farmer. I can't believe this was anything to do with him.'

It was midday. A group of children were playing in the

river, running down a jetty and jumping into the water. Washerwomen were laying out clothes on rocks to dry. Patrice left the ranger with his gutted fish and his guilt and headed into town.

In the afternoon he watched the Bakunda Lions, along with a couple of hundred other spectators. The boys played the Cameroonian style of game, with strength and skill, but their winning streak came to an end with a 3-1 defeat. Patrice waited by the touchline as Coach Samson walked over, holding his hands up apologetically.

'I told the boys we lost a battle, but we can still win the war,' the coach said. His head jerked to the side and he blinked. 'But it's going to be tough.'

His son, Sonny, and his friend, Tico, came running up. 'We can still do it, Papa,' Sonny said, jumping on to his father's back, clinging to his shoulders. 'We can be the champions!'

Coach Samson laughed and swung his son round, giving him a hug and a friendly pat on the head. 'My boy's a winner!'

The boys scampered off. The coach turned to Patrice. 'They're good boys. And they have the ability.' He blinked again. 'It's a lack of concentration and discipline that can lead to mistakes. They're going to have to work hard from now on in, or they'll be disappointed.'

Patrice got the impression that winning the league might be more important to the coach than his players.

They walked to the San Siro. Patrice told Coach Samson about his conversation with Alex Ebot's colleague.

'That's bad,' the coach said. 'Poor Alex. He was doing his job. If it's true the farmer attacked him, it'll be a big problem. We'll need to be careful when we meet this man.'

Chapter 26

Jeki was there early - he had walked through the night so as not to be seen. He hid beneath the roots of a tree on the edge of the clearing and ate some cold garri and dried fish. He was ready for the first task.

He unscrewed the cap of his flask. He smelled the steam and remembered *Sáŋgó's* instructions: drink the *niya* hot and all at once; only in that way would the potion's full powers be unleashed. He braced himself and tipped the brew into his mouth. He clenched his fists, suppressing the urge to scream. It was liquid fire, scalding his tongue, burning his throat, flowing like molten steel into his stomach.

The pain subsided as the heat surged through his body, through his arms and legs to the tips of his fingers and toes. Now Jeki felt exhilarated and ready, like a rocket at the point of lift-off. The worrisome thoughts that had been confusing him before he'd met *Sáŋgó*, that had caused him to doubt his strength and ability, had vanished.

The sun had risen, a bright white ball in the dull grey cloud, when Jeki felt a new sensation: a tingling, buzzing glow behind his ears that quickly engulfed his whole head. His surroundings looked different. The forest merged with the sky. It was as if he was floating inside a giant dome ...

He was in a world of colours and shapes - inside an egg his mother had laid. It was here that he would receive his training and his equipment, and it was from here that he would emerge in his new form, ready to deal with whatever challenge confronted him. He was invincible. He flew as a bird above the forest, he swam like a fish in the river; he could be whatever he wanted to be ...

The shell wasn't thick. He pushed his head through and he could feel the air on his face and see the light. It was tinged with grey. The trees that bordered the clearing were grey too, but darker.

Something stirred. The two rats he'd been waiting for emerged, and scuttled across the fields. One of them was carrying a gourd. Jeki's tongue twitched. He watched them settle beneath a small tree. There was a taste of palm wine in the air. He would wait some more and let them drink.

When the time came, he made his move. He slipped out of the egg and along on his stomach under the cover of the cassava plants towards the tree, approaching from behind, stealthily, silently. It was like he was swimming, his body winding from side to side, sliding over the grass. As he got nearer, he felt vibrations in his jaw. The rats were squeaking, like they were laughing. He hissed.

He raised his head above the grass to check his bearings. He opened his mouth and flicked his tongue. The smell of palm wine was strong. The rats were within spitting distance, sitting with their backs to him, their outlines burning brightly. He stayed calm and poised. He slunk down again and slithered quickly. Then he struck.

He coiled himself round both of them at the same time. They squealed and kicked out as he tightened his grip. He squeezed them hard. They were gasping. He could feel them wriggling, throwing their heads back and forth. He felt something crunch. But then one of the rats squirmed free, coughing and spluttering. It twisted and reared. There was a flash of light as it lunged forward, baring its front teeth. Jeki was alert. He turned and used the rat in his arm as a shield. There was a tearing sound and a groan and the rat in his arm slumped over. The teeth came again. Jeki stepped towards them and threw a mighty punch that smashed the teeth into the monster's mouth. The rat made a strange croaking sound. Jeki swiped it hard in the face, again and again. Then both the rats were still and quiet.

Slowly, things returned to normal. He looked at the scene in front of him and held up his arms in disbelief. *Sáŋgó* would be pleased, Jeki was sure of that; and he'd earned his reward. But he still had things to do. He heard what sounded like a motorcycle engine, distant but coming his way.

Chapter 27

Sally looked at the backgammon board, but she couldn't concentrate. All she could think about was Douala Manga. She'd read the memoirs twice now and wanted to read them again, properly, in a quiet place where she could make detailed notes and a considered assessment of their significance.

'It's your turn,' Raymond, the *Courier* photographer, reminded her.

She threw a three and a five and moved two counters.

She'd have to discuss the memoirs with people who knew about Douala Manga, like a historian or one of the cultural experts in Douala. But she couldn't do that yet. They'd ask where she got them, especially someone in Douala.

'It's your turn again.'

She threw two fours and was forced to focus on the game. It was mid-morning. They were sitting in Raymond's Peugeot 504, parked on a grass verge outside the entrance to Tiko Airport, waiting for the president. The doors were open but it was stiflingly hot. She considered her options and made her moves.

Not being able to share her discovery with the world was tying Sally's stomach in knots. She couldn't tell her editor yet; he'd go straight to the police. She couldn't tell Raymond; she didn't know him well. And, anyway, journalists were the worst people in the world at keeping secrets. She'd had to make her colleague Lucy swear on her mother's life she wouldn't tell a soul. In return, Sally had promised she'd go to the descendants of Douala Manga and hand over the manuscript and be honest with them about how she'd got it - and it would be for the family to decide if they wanted to report her to the police. But Sally hadn't specified when she'd do that.

'First I'll read it,' she'd said as they'd driven out of Douala over the Wouri Bridge. 'I mean, I have to do that ... then I can make a copy and give that to the family? Or even the original, I could give them the original, and I keep a copy. Then I've helped them ... How's that?'

'Keep me out of it,' were Lucy's last words on the subject.

They'd arrived at the airport at 4am, before the other reporters. Sally had given Lucy a hug and said, 'Thank you, sister. I owe you triple now!'

By late morning there were two army vehicles and a four-by-four inside the airport but no planes. Outside, Sally and Raymond, along with a dozen other reporters, photographers, and TV and radio people, were still waiting.

'What made me believe for even one minute the president would arrive at six o'clock?' she said. *'That one dong ever happen before?* I didn't have to rush. I could have had a good night's sleep. And poor Lucy, bringing me here in the middle of the night. It's not safe driving at that time, but I said I had to be here. *And for wetinsef?* For what?'

Two more games of backgammon and it was time for lunch.

Raymond, a lanky man who always wore the same worn-out sleeveless jacket, with lots of pockets, strode into town and returned with plantains and rice. They ate and played more backgammon. Around four in the afternoon a security man ambled across from the airport gates.

'My friends,' he said, 'I don't know what you've heard, but the president is not coming today. You can go home.'

'When is he coming?' one of the TV reporters asked.

'I don't know. I'm sure your editors will be informed.'

'Like they were informed yesterday?' another reporter sniped.

The security man turned and walked back through the gate. Sally rang her office and told her editor.

'Who told you that?' he asked.

'Security.'

'Name?'

'I don't know his name. Since when do those people tell you their names?'

He told her to wait. He rang an hour later. 'The president's not coming today,' he said.

She ended the call, exasperated. *'See how man waste one day for nothing!'*

Raymond said, 'Let's be thankful we have employment and a salary.'

He offered Sally a lift to Buea, which she accepted. The thought of reading the stolen memoirs there, away from Douala, made her feel less guilty about taking them. She'd hide herself away and go through them again while she waited for the president to actually arrive. And there were lots of academics in Buea with whom she could cross-check facts without them having to know where she was getting her information. The more she thought about it, the more she became convinced that what she had was worthy of much more than a feature in the *Courier*; only a book could do it justice.

Her editor rang again. 'Sally, I've got a job for you tomorrow. Instead of sitting around twiddling your thumbs you can cover the *pala pala*.'

'What? Wrestling? I don't do sport. I don't understand sport.'

'You're a journalist.'

'Meaning?'

'Write about the spectacle. People say traditional wrestling is dying out. So why is it still popular in Buea? That's the angle. It will make an entertaining feature while Buea waits for the president, and we have lots of pages to fill.'

She wouldn't have minded putting her research to one side for something important, but for a feature about wrestling? 'You know, there's that story I told you about in Bakunda National Park? I could go and investigate ...'

'Don't argue, Sally.'

Chapter 28

The truth was that Samson didn't know why things had gone wrong for the Lions the day before. He'd blamed the boys but they hadn't played badly; they'd stuck to their positions and passed well and created a few openings, and worked hard when they'd lost the ball to get it back.

'I know this road,' Le Congo was saying - they were riding on Samson's motorcycle. 'I came this way the other day on my way from the mill.'

Samson nodded, half listening. In the end, he supposed, it all came down to those split seconds in front of goal, when you either took your chances or you didn't. They'd lost 3-1 but it could easily have been the other way round ...

'Is this all Pamol's plantation?' the Congolese asked.

'Yes,' Samson replied, nodding his head again absentmindedly. 'All this, on both sides.'

It wasn't over yet, he thought. There were still two matches to play. But the boys needed to be sharp, mentally as well as physically, so when those chances came, in those split seconds, they'd keep calm. That's what they'd work on this week.

They were riding west towards the big river and the spot where Le Congo had seen the farm inside the national park. The forest had given way to endless rows of palms.

'I hope we're not too late,' the investigator said, checking the time on his phone. 'If he did kill the ranger, and he heard we're coming, he may make a run for it.'

'Where will he run to? These farmers don't know any other place.'

There was little traffic. To appease his passenger Samson pulled on the throttle, but round a bend he was forced to skid to a stop. A fully laden logging truck lay jack-knifed across the road, the cab tilting into a ditch by the side.

'Mon Dieu!' Le Congo said.

Samson spotted the driver squatting underneath the trailer. He called to him. *'You dey ok?'*

'I no wound myself, thank God. A tractor is coming to pull it right.'

'What happened?'

'It was in the night. *Okada* came in front of me. I had to steer the truck like this. He had no lights.'

Samson tutted. 'It's dangerous for a big truck to be on these roads, especially at night. *You get good luck say no person no die*. What speed were you doing?'

The driver didn't answer.

Samson turned to Le Congo. 'Come.'

They pushed the motorcycle up a steep bank and round the back of the trailer, where the sawn ends of three tree trunks jutted out.

As they were riding off again, Samson asked, 'Did you notice the mark on the timber?'

'No.'

'New Deal. They must be clearing more land.'

They continued on their way. It wasn't long before they reached the river and the narrow, fast-flowing stretch that Le

Congo had swum across before. Samson turned downstream, then, where the water was wide and shallow, turned again and took them across on the motorcycle, then back upstream on the other side. He parked the bike on its stand and they set off into the forest on foot.

Le Congo was leading the way. Samson wondered what kind of reception they were going to get. The man was in a hurry, but he needed to be calm. 'Slow down,' he said as they approached the area that had been cleared for farming. 'We don't want to scare him.'

They stopped and scanned the fields from the cover of the trees. There was no one to be seen. They walked out between crops of cassava and maize to a small tree, one of the few that had not been felled. The distinctive, sour smell of palm wine greeted them.

The Congolese said, 'It doesn't look like he's been farming here today.'

Samson had reached the same conclusion. The grass around the tree was flattened. There was a log where one or two people could have been sitting. But there was nobody there now. All that remained of the palm wine was a cracked gourd, pinned to the ground by a bamboo stick.

Le Congo pulled on the bamboo stick. It was buried so deep it was stuck fast.

'Let's go to his village,' Samson said. 'But we will need to tread carefully. If it comes to a confrontation, with other farmers around, it could be awkward.'

They walked back through the trees, then rode back across the river and headed downstream along a track above the bank. After a short while, Samson pulled over. 'I want to show you something,' he said.

'Now? Can't we go and find this man?'

'Relax, he's not going anywhere. It's Sunday. If he drank that palm wine this morning, he'll be sleeping now, for sure!'

They walked over a ditch and up the side of a bank. Before them, lines and lines of young trees stretched away towards the low grey hills in the distance.

'This is New Deal, Cameroon,' Samson said. 'From here to those hills is five kilometres. Then in this direction, where the river's flowing, the plantation goes on for ten kilometres. And this is only a quarter of their plantation.'

The Congolese opened his eyes wide.

Samson nodded. 'It's big, huh? Like I told you. These trees are among the first they planted. But come, I'll show you something else.'

They rode on what was now little more than a footpath until they reached a point where a wide stream joined the river. Samson parked again and led Le Congo through some bushes, behind which was a barbed wire fence. On the other side of the fence was an area the size of two or three football pitches, where thousands of seedlings were growing in black plastic pots, again arranged in straight lines.

'This is one of the palm nurseries. When the newly cleared forest is ready, they'll plant these.'

Le Congo surveyed the scene. 'It's an industrial operation,' he said. 'You can see a lot of money's going into this, the kind of money that won't allow the rights of a few villagers to get in its way.'

'Exactly.'

'Is it legal to clear the forest here?'

'No! They haven't been officially granted the concession. The land is not legally theirs to cultivate. But they did an unofficial deal; the government let them start work in return for the proceeds from all the timber that's felled. Even the government is breaking the law.'

'So it's not just farmland they're taking over?'

'Most of it is forest. Not protected forest, like the national park, but still forest. The area we saw heading to the hills, that was forest a few years ago. So you can imagine the profits made from the timber alone - the trunks we saw on that truck are worth thousands of euros each, and there are thousands like that coming out of the forest here. That's why they're allowed to get away with this, because some Cameroonians are getting rich from it.'

The Congolese rubbed his chin. 'Lots of things happen here unofficially,' he said.

Samson pulled him by the arm. 'Let's go and find that farmer. His village is near.'

Back on the motorcycle, they crossed the stream and continued along the path above the riverbank before turning up a track into Bafuke village. They rode past groups of houses with slatted wood walls and tin roofs. Children were playing a game of chase. A boy was herding a few kid goats. Samson beeped and pulled up by one of the houses, outside which a man and a woman were sitting under a tree.

'Andre, Alice, *wuna morning,*' he said, waving.

'Morning, Coach,' the man replied, getting to his feet in a lemon-coloured tee shirt and loose-fitting black trousers. '*How far?* How are you? What happened to the Lions yesterday? 3-1, I heard?'

Samson felt himself blink twice. 'It's not over yet,' he said. 'We'll do some light training tonight and go through a few things. *How things dey your side?*'

'Thanks to God, we are surviving.'

Alice smiled. *'Hungrey dey do you, Coach?* You want lunch?'

'Thank you, Alice, but I don't know if we can stay. We're looking for a farmer called Daniel Ajebe.'

The man and the woman looked blank.

'His farm is near to Pamol, on the other side of the river.'

The couple glanced at Le Congo, their welcoming smiles replaced by suspicious frowns. This was the kind of reception Samson had been afraid of.

*

Patrice sensed the change of mood as keenly as if the temperature had dropped ten degrees. It was clear the couple were asking themselves who the outsider was and why he was there in their village, aware apparently of their secret.

The coach held up an open hand. 'Don't be alarmed, this man is not police.'

'If he's not police, what is he?' Andre asked.

Patrice noted his rounded shoulders and the hard skin on his hands. 'I'm a human rights investigator. Patrice Le Congo, from Congo.'

'He helps people in trouble,' Coach Samson added. 'I've been showing him the New Deal plantation and explaining to him how you farmers have been pushed off your land.'

'Is Daniel Ajebe in trouble?'

The man was sharp as a whetted machete blade. 'He could be,' Patrice said.

Andre looked him up and down. Then he nodded in the direction of a track that led off the main street. *'E house dey up there.* But I haven't seen him today.'

'He went to his farm yesterday with Louis, who works the land next to his,' the woman called Alice said. 'They may be there still.'

'We've come from the farm,' Coach Samson said. 'They're not there.'

Alice shouted over to the house next door, and two other men and another woman emerged. *'You dong see Daniel Ajebe or Louis Sone?'* she asked.

There was a shake of heads.

'Can you call him?' the coach asked Andre.

Andre pulled out his phone, but his call didn't go through.

'He could be sleeping,' the coach said.

This suggestion caused a few chuckles.

'I'll go to his house,' Alice said, dusting off her pink floral dress. She walked up the street and round the corner.

'What's this all about?' Andre asked, looking at Patrice.

Patrice glanced at the coach, then answered. 'You know the park ranger who died? It was after he found Ajebe's farm.'

'So? We are all upset about the ranger. No one would want that to happen to anyone.'

'But what if it wasn't an elephant that killed him?'

Andre didn't respond. His neighbours came closer to listen. No one was chuckling now.

'Ajebe was warned the ranger was going to be in the area. If something happened ...'

There was a hostile silence. Patrice felt the stares coming his way. He could tell from the way Coach Samson narrowed his eyes that he was pushing his luck.

'They should leave us alone,' a man in a white vest said, stepping forward. His loud, gruff voice suited his burly appearance. 'It's true there is some small cultivating there.

But it's not much. We have to survive. We've lost our farms. If the rangers are concerned about the rainforest, they should talk to Pamol and New Deal. They're the ones who are depleting our forests, not us.'

'Francis Akwanga here is right,' Andre said, resting his hand on the other man's shoulder. There were a few murmurs of agreement.

'This is also why we came here today,' the coach said. 'That's the main ...'

He was interrupted by Alice, calling out as she came round the corner. 'Ajebe is not at his house. His family don't know where he is.'

'Leave this to us for now,' Andre said, wrinkles tightening on his forehead. 'We will talk to him when he comes. We'll find out if he knows anything more about this business.'

Patrice tutted to himself; they should have come the day before, instead of waiting for a game of football.

'Okay, good,' Coach Samson said. 'You've all made your frustration clear. You've said it well. And if something did occur between Daniel Ajebe and the ranger, then I know you people of Bafuke will make him do the right thing now.'

One or two heads nodded hesitantly and the coach paused, as if to let the words sink in. Then he patted Patrice on the arm, and continued. 'Like I was saying, we understand the problem between the farmers and the park is because of the plantations. And this is why I have brought Le Congo here today, because I think he can help you.'

It was Coach Samson who was pushing his luck now. Patrice turned to the villagers. Judging by the look of incredulity on their faces, the coach might have told them this man from Congo was going to take them to the moon.

Chapter 29

Sally was sitting in the marquee, fuming. Wrestling! It was no surprise to her that the sport was no longer popular in most of Cameroon; it belonged to a bygone era, when men depended on their physical strength. 'There's no point to it now,' she said to herself. 'We use our brains, we have machines, we aspire to modernity …'

A big crowd had come to the Buea town wrestling ground to watch the tournament. They were sitting and standing up to a dozen deep all the way round the field, cheering, dancing and singing.

The *Courier* photographer, Raymond, came and sat next to her and showed her the pictures he'd taken of competitors and spectators, which included lots of cheerful faces. 'You might not like it, Sally, but these people do.'

'I know. I've talked to them. But I still don't understand it. All I see is half-naked men rolling over in the mud.'

'And women – did you see the women?'

Sally gave a reluctant nod.

'It's exciting,' Raymond added. 'It's tradition.'

She kissed her teeth.

'It's important, don't you think? Tradition, culture, history. Like King Douala Manga?'

She stared at him hard. *'You dong dey spy on me, Raymond?'*

He giggled. 'I'm a photographer. It's my job to keep my eyes open.' He showed her one more photograph, taken over her shoulder - the first few words from the opening page of the memoirs were clearly visible.

'You have been spying! *You dey try me!* How dare you ...'

'Take it easy, Sally. I'm only curious. I saw you reading, and this zoom lens is powerful.'

'Please delete that, now.'

'Okay, okay.' He turned the camera so she could see him do it. 'There, it's gone. But it looks like you're on to something interesting!'

'Why? What's it to you?'

'He's a resistance hero.'

'You think he is?'

'He was a leader who was willing to die for his people. Not like the leaders we have now, just out for themselves.'

Sally had spent most of the past two days with Raymond, but she didn't feel she knew him well. 'Raymond, please don't tell anyone about this, please. I ... I'm not supposed to have it. I want to write a book about Douala Manga, but I could get into a lot of trouble ...'

'Don't worry. I can keep a secret.' He patted her on the shoulder and went to the front of the seating area to take more pictures as the village chiefs and notables handed out trophies for categories such as Best Village, Strongest Wrestlers and Best Chest Vibrator.

Sally nibbled at a fingernail and scolded herself for being so careless. That was two people who knew her secret now. Her obsession with Douala Manga had become dangerous. It was distracting her from her work as well and interfering with her professional judgement. Like Raymond had pointed out about the wrestling. For the people here, this tournament was important, and it was her job to reflect that and put aside her prejudices. She forced herself to focus on the story in front of her by trying to think of a headline: *Holding on to History? Attention Grabbers?*

It wasn't long, though, before her mind drifted, and she was casting her eyes down, looking at her bag, and thinking again about the manuscript inside. Like an alcoholic who tells herself she's going to stop drinking even as she lifts a bottle to her lips, she peaked again at the hand-written pages. The more she read it, the more she became convinced it was going to cause a sensation.

She heard the crowd cheer, and she looked up vaguely to see more bodies twisting around and entwining and falling to the ground. But she wasn't paying any attention to the wrestling tournament.

The thing that intrigued her most was a reference Douala Manga made to the sceptre. He had tried to make the Douala case to the Germans peacefully, appealing to their parliament, the Reichstag; that was using the fly whisk, the symbol of conciliation. And that had failed. *But I had not forgotten the sceptre that had been placed in my hand.* And then he'd sent Ngosso Din to *make arrangements ... so as not to leave ourselves defenceless.*

The accepted wisdom was that Douala Manga had been leading a campaign of civil disobedience and had been falsely charged by the Germans with treason so they could get him out of the way. He wrote in his memoirs that it was a lie to suggest he wanted the British to come; and it was a lie to say he had sought the support of the Sultan of Njoya. But could he still, nonetheless, have been planning an armed rebellion? And *the sceptre lies hidden*. It was tantalising!

There was also the curious passage where Douala Manga had lain with Rosa von Roehm. If Rosa had had a child as a result, there'd have been a scandal. The baby could even have been taken from her and sent to Cameroon to be adopted. Sally knew she was being ridiculous but she couldn't help wondering, if only for a moment, if her mother really was joking when she'd said they were descended from kings.

She was so consumed by all the questions thrown up by her discovery of the memoirs that she took no notice when an open contest for wrestlers from all across South West Region was announced, and one of the competitors was introduced as Jeki.

Chapter 30

Patrice had all but accused one of the villagers of murder. Now he had to gain the others' trust. Coach Samson had put him on the spot, but it was what they'd agreed. Whatever the missing farmer had done, wherever he was now, the fact was the villagers of Bafuke were victims of a severe injustice, and Patrice wasn't going to turn his back on them. If he could help them get their farms back, he'd have a go. Someone had to stand up to the corporate bullies.

'I'll do what I can,' he said, addressing the group gathered outside Andre and Alice's house. *'If you want make I help you ... I do gladly ... do so.'*

More silence greeted his hesitant attempt at pidgin.

'Le Congo here is a good man,' the coach said, wrapping his arm round Patrice's shoulders. 'In his country, he challenged an international mining company and won a famous victory for the local people who were being threatened with eviction.'

'But this is not his country,' the farmer in the white vest said, the farmer called Francis Akwanga. 'Things are different here, and he is a stranger.'

'I will need you to explain to me how things are here,' Patrice said. 'But some aspects of these cases may be similar. If you don't want my help, that's fine.'

'The man is offering to assist us,' Alice said. 'I say we hear what he has to say. But first, he must eat with us.'

A chair was brought out for Patrice and one for Coach Samson, and Alice served them lunch of maize fufu and chicken and eru. After the meal, they sat in the shade of the tree and the villagers shared their stories with Patrice.

Andre went first. Though his hair was greying round the temples, his eyes were bright, and there were few lines on his face. He twiddled a stick in his hands as he spoke.

'Mine was a small farm,' he said. 'Three hectares. I inherited it from my father, who had twelve hectares and divided the farm between his four sons. He had inherited his share from his father before him. I had my farm ten years. I grew cassava, potatoes, maize, and for cash, some oil palms. I sold the fruit unprocessed to Pamol, or I used a small mill in another village to make oil myself, and my wife Alice would sell that at the market in town.'

He paused as he stabbed the stick into the earth. 'We had enough, but no more than enough. I knew if I was going to leave any land for my children, I would have to go into the forest and clear some myself, like my grandfather had done. I agreed an area with our chief. But it didn't happen because now New Deal have taken that land, and they have taken my farm as well.'

He sat, staring at his stick.

'What happened on the day they took your farm?' Patrice asked.

'They came with their chainsaws. They cut down the oil palms first, then they stood aside, and the bulldozer moved in and cleared everything into piles. I sat and watched my past and my future disappear in front of my eyes.'

Patrice shook his head in disgust. 'Did you receive a warning?'

'I knew it was my turn that day because they had done the same to my neighbour the day before. But what could I do?'

'But, I mean, you hadn't been told before that this was going to happen?'

'The government told us New Deal were coming here, but I didn't know it meant there would be nothing left for us.'

'The divisional officer said it was for our benefit,' the woman from the next-door house said. 'Can you imagine? He said we were hungry and we were suffering, but we were not suffering. We can grow many things here; cassava, cocoa, oil palm, maize, bush mango, kola nut: so many things we can sell. We didn't need these people to come and disturb us.'

'Our farms were productive,' Andre said. 'But the government said the plantations would make more for the country and they leased the land cheaply.'

'So was there a consultation process?' Patrice asked.

A chorus of voices answered, 'No!'

Andre looked at Francis Akwanga, who took up the story. 'They held some meetings,' he said. 'The company will say this was a consultation. But it was not. The meetings were in another place, forty kilometres from here, at short notice. That place is remote, and it was last August, in the middle of the rains. To go there in the rainy season you need a four-by-four. We were told afterwards there were six or eight people present, when what they were talking about was something that would affect thousands.'

'No one from this village went?'

There was a pause. 'One man went,' Francis said. 'But he did not speak up for the people you see before you now.'

Patrice wrote some notes. It was, sadly, a familiar tale: a big company, in cahoots with government officials, riding roughshod over the rights of powerless villagers. But in this instance, there was an added complication.

He cleared his throat. 'What's important, from my experience, is that you organise yourselves and agree on what action to take; individual farmers going off and … doing things on their own … that can damage the cause.' He could see out of the corner of his eye glances being thrown at Coach Samson. 'United, you will be strong. But your protest must be legal and non-violent …'

'We've heard that before,' Francis said. 'But New Deal has acted illegally, and violently. Look how they destroyed our farms.'

'It can be done!' Patrice looked the villagers in the eye, one by one, searching for signs of belief. 'You are in the right. And that is how you must fight this. You need to let the world know what is going on here and bring shame on the company, till it gets to the point where they'll have to give in to you because if they don't, no one will buy their palm oil.'

Now there were one or two nods of approval.

'But as soon as you use violence, you will no longer be perceived as innocent. You will lose the moral high ground. You will lose support. And you'll be on your own, once again at the mercy of these brutes.'

As he finished speaking, Patrice noticed that all eyes were not now on him, but on something behind him. He turned to see a dishevelled-looking man wearing a necklace of animal teeth, leaning on a staff with a handle carved in the shape of an eagle's head.

'What is this?' the man asked. 'Who is this?'

At first, no one answered. Then Coach Samson spoke up. 'He is a visitor from Congo, Chief. I brought him here to meet the farmers, he has experience in …'

'If he is a visitor to our village, then he should come first to the chief. And he should bring something for the chief. That is how it is done. Bring him to my compound. Let him address me if he wants to talk about matters that concern the whole village.'

'Yes, Chief.'

'Come this evening. I will be waiting.'

Though the chief was standing several metres away, the smell of palm wine on his breath was unmistakable. Patrice watched him turn and walk unsteadily up the main street, supporting himself with his stick.

'You asked if anyone from this village went to the consultation with New Deal,' Andre said. 'Well, that's the man who went. Chief Adama Takubi. He got a lift with the divisional officer. It will be interesting to hear what he has to say to you about the meeting because what he said to us was that everything would be fine.'

Chapter 31

What a crowd! What a reception! Jeki raised his arms. He turned his head and scanned the faces, looking for *Sáŋgó*. He spotted him in the VIP seats, next to a white man with silver hair. As instructed, he didn't acknowledge him, though he wanted to, to thank him for this opportunity.

He'd called *Sáŋgó* the night before. *Sáŋgó* had said he was pleased with Jeki's work. And *Sáŋgó* had kept his promise – telling Jeki to report to a trainer called Mbella here in Buea this morning.

Mbella had shown no interest in Jeki. He'd just told him to get ready, while he stood counting money.

Jeki had said he was ready. He was tired but he felt strong.

'Well, let's see what you can do,' the trainer had said.

Jeki was so distracted by the enormity of the occasion that he didn't catch his opponent's name. He didn't care about that. But his opponent was bigger than him. Jeki would have to be careful, not be overconfident.

The wrestlers circled, bent over, arms out, facing each other. The crowd was whooping and whistling, the drums beating, women dancing. This was what Jeki had been waiting for, a big stage to show off his skills.

His opponent put a hand on Jeki's shoulder. Jeki rippled

the muscles there, and he could feel his opponent shift his weight on to the back foot. The man was afraid, Jeki could see it in his eyes. Jeki lunged, clamped his arms round his opponent's waist, and twisted him on to the ground. The crowd cheered. The referee signalled for Jeki to step back.

The circling ritual began again. Jeki told himself to be patient. He could sense it wouldn't be long before his opponent attacked. He was right. His opponent tried to grab him by the upper arm and twist him. But Jeki stood firm and, instead, it was his opponent who spun round, and Jeki grabbed him with both arms from behind.

The position was familiar. Jeki found himself increasing the pressure. He felt the tingle, and the rush of strength through his body, like he had the day before, yet he hadn't drunk any potion today. He looked up and saw *Sáŋgó*. He could see the crowd waving. But he wasn't hearing them.

Everything was quiet. The only sound was coming from inside his head. It was a voice, his mother's. She was calling his name. '*Ya o wân,*' she told him. 'Come on Jeki. *O léye má njá o éná!* Show him what you can do!' He increased the pressure.

Then there was another voice, from a distance but getting closer, and someone was pulling hard on his shoulder. He shook his head, as if shaking himself awake. The referee was ordering him to let go. He relaxed his grip. His opponent gasped and slumped to his knees. The crowd was silent.

The trainer came running across and pulled Jeki away. He told him he'd been disqualified. Jeki followed the trainer out of the arena, his head hanging low.

'Hey, strong man,' the trainer said. 'Do you know the rules of *pala pala*?'

Jeki glanced over his shoulder and saw his opponent clutching his ribs. He looked for *Sáŋgó,* but he was gone. He'd disgraced himself, and *Sáŋgó* would be cross. He'd never get a chance like this again. Something had come over him. 'I … I don't know what happened. I lost my concentration.'

'It didn't look that way. It looked like you were concentrating hard. Did he say something to you, to make you angry?'

'No, no. He made a move I wasn't expecting and …' Jeki's lip wobbled. 'Is that it? Is there another fight?'

'Not today. And not with me.'

Jeki sat on a wooden box behind the crowd, where a few other wrestlers were warming up. He hadn't slept for thirty-six hours. This was why he'd lost his concentration. He thought of his mother again. He wanted to cry.

There was a tap on his shoulder. *Sáŋgó* was standing behind him, beckoning him.

Jeki trembled as he followed the man to his four-by-four, which was parked alongside other cars behind the VIP tent. He climbed into the back as instructed. He'd never been inside a vehicle with blackened windows before. The seats were leather.

'Jeki, my boy.' *Sáŋgó* was sitting in the front.

'*A Sáŋgó âm!*' Jeki was breathing heavily.

'*Esímo!* Congratulations! You have served a warning. There is a new wrestler in town!'

'*A Sáŋgó âm, o sí liŋgi?* Master, you are not angry?'

'Angry?' The Master, wearing the same black blazer with a white tee shirt underneath, turned in his seat to face back. 'Quite the opposite. You were very good.'

'I was disqualified.'

'Jeki, Jeki, this is the beginning. What you have done today is to reveal your strength, the strength of Jeki la Njambe, after whom you are named, in whose likeness you have been created.'

Jeki felt his despair lifting as if he was throwing off a heavy blanket on a hot day. 'His likeness,' he repeated, amazed.

'As Jeki la Njambe astonished his father's wives when they witnessed him coming out from his mother's womb with a spear and a trident and a swordfish machete, so this crowd here today, and the other wrestlers, saw a new Jeki born, with a strength they have never seen before. It was dramatic, Jeki.' He patted Jeki's arm.

'But I …'

'It's a matter of discipline, Jeki. That is something you will learn. But now you must rest. You must be strong for your next task.'

Chapter 32

The night air was warm and humid, and saturated with the shrill, incessant gabble of insects and frogs. Patrice followed Coach Samson and Andre along a track off the main street, close to the river. The coach was agitated and kept shaking his head. It was clear he wasn't relishing the prospect of an audience with Chief Adama Takubi. Judging from the state the chief had been in earlier, it was likely his guests were going to be on the receiving end of a drunken lecture, which they would have to endure politely. And for Coach Samson, every minute spent there in Bafuke village was a minute less on the training ground with his football team.

They entered the chief's high-walled compound, in which stood several single-storey dwellings. By the door to one a woman was pounding yam under a weak solar light. A young man appeared behind her and told the visitors to wait. A few minutes later a voice sounded from the side of the house and the young man came to escort them to a circular, open-sided shelter with a conical grass roof. Chief Takubi was seated inside on a high-backed upright chair; the guests were offered stools.

Andre greeted his chief by bowing and holding his right wrist in his left hand. '*Mbeh, mbeh, mbeh*,' he said.

Coach Samson bowed and introduced Patrice.

The chief ignored the coach. 'What have you brought for me?' he asked Patrice. His breath reeked of palm wine. His eyes were bloodshot.

Patrice bowed, and with both hands offered a banknote.

The chief nodded and took the money. 'Now let me offer you something.' He looked into the darkness outside the shelter, and a boy entered with four glasses and a jug on a tray. 'I hope you will drink with me. It is not so strong. I tapped it myself this morning.'

The boy poured the milky liquid into the glasses and the men drank. It was sour, but fresh.

Chief Takubi let out a loud burp. 'You see,' he said to Coach Samson, 'this is how we do things here.' He took another drink and turned to Patrice. 'Now tell me, Mr Congo, what has brought you all the way from your country to our small village here?' Without waiting for an answer, he continued. 'I am told you have been asking questions about New Deal Plantations?'

Patrice was about to reply, but the chief cut him off. 'You know Pamol? Pamol used to be owned by white people ... Unilever owned it before ... but now there is a big fuss because white people are growing a new plantation.'

This time Patrice cut in. 'The fuss is not because they're white but because the forest is being cleared and farmers are losing their land. Some of them are farmers from your village.'

'Did I ask you to speak?' The chief snapped, before swallowing a burp. 'You talk like a white man. You interrupt. You interrupt a chief when he is speaking. You don't respect our traditions and our culture.'

He finished his glass and held it out for more. The boy leaned forward to top it up. The chief drank another mouthful.

Patrice drank some more of his. It slipped down easily. But he knew he had to be careful. If it loosened his tongue too much, he might make him himself unwelcome in the village.

Coach Samson must have sensed the need to smooth things over. 'I think, Chief,' he said, 'what our friend here is trying to say, is that he has been talking to the villagers and is concerned for their welfare.'

Chief Takubi frowned. 'I am their chief. If they have problems, they come to me. I look out for their welfare.' He finished the glass. 'Let me tell you this, Mr Congo. It is true we in Cameroon used not to know the value of our land. We thought we had so much, it was not worth anything. Now we know, and we are getting a good price for it. And we are not even selling. We are leasing. And we are being offered compensation. And because it takes a lot of work to maintain a big plantation, so there will be many, many jobs.'

The chief stared at Andre, who looked at the ground.

'Now you want to ask me something?' he said, turning to Patrice. 'You can ask now, now I have finished speaking. That is the way we do things here.'

The chief grunted and the boy brought another refill. Patrice knew the importance of showing respect for traditions and local customs, but it was hard to show respect for the custodian of those traditions when that custodian was drunk and rude.

'What does a plantation worker earn?' he asked. 'Does that compensate for losing a farm?'

Chief Takubi drank more of his palm wine and wiped

his dripping lips with his wrist. 'Despite what some people say, New Deal do understand our ways here, and do respect our traditions. And part of that is showing respect for the chieftaincy. That is why they have given scholarships to my children and the children of the other chiefs in the district, as a sign of respect. And on behalf our communities, we have accepted this small gift.'

'Scholarships for what?'

'Science scholarships at the university. And when they graduate, they will be offered jobs with New Deal. So, like the rest of the community, they will be working on the plantation.'

Patrice noticed Andre was still staring at the ground. 'And the farmers who've encroached into the national park, will they be offered work too?'

The chief took a long time to answer. A flicker in his bloodshot eyes betrayed his discomfort. 'There's work for everyone.'

'Did you know two of them have gone missing?'

The chief's eyes narrowed.

Patrice kept prodding. 'Daniel Ajebe is one of them. Do you know him?'

'I know all my people.'

'Did you know he knew the ranger who died was coming near his farm in the national park that day?'

There was another long silence. 'How would I know that?'

'You said your people come to you when they have problems.'

Chief Takubi scowled and took another drink. 'I thought it was New Deal you were interested in, Mr Congo. What has this got to do with New Deal?'

'The reason the farmers have cleared a corner of the park is because New Deal have taken their land.'

The chief looked at Andre and Coach Samson before responding. 'I am chief of this village,' he said. 'I will deal with these matters.' He looked away, making it clear the audience was over.

Patrice stood to leave. It seemed unlikely to him that Chief Takubi would *deal with these matters*; he was more part of the problem than any solution. 'Thank you for your hospitality, Chief, and for explaining how things are.'

The chief waved his guests away. The three men walked to Andre's house in silence. Patrice and the coach thanked Alice for the meal and set off on the motorcycle. After the stuffy encounter in the chief's compound Patrice welcomed the breeze on his face. But the meeting had left a sour taste in his mouth, and not only because of the palm wine.

The road to town took them past the main entrance to the New Deal plantation. Coach Samson pulled over briefly and turned his headlight to illuminate a wrought iron double gate, two metres high, hung between brick pillars. Given that the fence around the plantation was two strings of barbed wire, which anyone could climb under, it looked unnecessary and ostentatious.

'The company has bought off the chief,' Patrice said, still thinking about the meeting. 'But the villagers respect his title – you saw how Andre kept so quiet. This could undermine their determination to fight for what's right.'

'It's like that here,' the coach concurred. 'But you've given the farmers something to think about. The chief talks about jobs, but Andre and the others know that the workers on this plantation earn less than half what a farmer can make.'

It was late by the time they reached Bakunda. Coach Samson dropped Patrice at his hotel. He patted him on the shoulder and shook his hand. 'Thank you, Le Congo. It's good of you to take this on.' Then he rode off.

Clearly it was a relief for the coach. He was free now to concentrate on the Bakunda Lions and their last two matches of the season.

As Patrice sat with a bottle of beer in the hotel garden, he got a call from Josie Mwinga.

'Patrice,' she said, shouting down the line. 'I've heard from my friend at the Ministry of Justice that three young men have been arrested in Ekindila for the attack on that poor old woman, the one who was left without her clothes.'

'Oh, that's good news for her and her family, and unexpected. Let's hope it serves as a warning to any others planning on harassing the settlers.'

'And it's thanks to your report, Patrice. You see, your work is making a difference.'

'My work, and your friend.'

'It's important to have contacts. Now, Patrice, how is it going? I've been meaning to ask. I didn't intend for you to stay there so long …'

He brought her up to date.

'Good,' she said when he'd finished. 'It sounds like you've done all you can. It's sad but there's nothing to suggest the park ranger was killed because of any contact he had with the African Union.'

'Well, with respect, we don't know the full story yet. It's definitely tied in with the farmers losing their land to make way for the plantation, and it sounds to me like the village chief knows more about what happened to the ranger than he's letting on ...'

'Patrice. I think I know where this is going. You've done the job I asked you to do. Now I'm telling you to go home and take a well-earned rest.'

'Ma'am, the eviction of these farmers is a serious human rights issue.'

'That's enough, Patrice. It's time to leave.' She wished him well and said goodnight.

Patrice looked at his phone. The plight of the villagers of Bafuke was essentially the same as that of the settlers being harassed in Ekindila village; one way or another, they were being forced off their land. The difference was that the African Union had officially sanctioned an investigation into the latter. Josie Mwinga was a bureaucrat and followed the rules. He wasn't, and he didn't.

He finished his beer and soon forgot about Josie Mwinga as his thoughts turned to the events of the day. He went to bed with a disconcerting vision in his mind of Chief Adama Takubi lying by his palm tree, guzzling fresh palm wine from a gourd and burping.

PART III

Songa diwo di boise bona masonga

One bad tooth can rot the whole mouth
(Douala proverb)

Chapter 33

'Here come the chiefs in their traditional robes, dignified, respectful, resplendent as they approach the president …'

Sally Bintu glanced round at Radio Cameroon's commentator as he described the scene in Buea's main square, where thousands of people had gathered for the long-delayed celebrations marking the fiftieth anniversary of reunification.

'… they step forward now, taking it in turns, to bow before the head of state … symbolising the power-relationship in modern-day Cameroon ….'

Sally considered what Douala Manga would make of this, but only briefly, because for once she wasn't thinking much about the old Douala king and his memoirs. She wasn't thinking much about the chiefs or the president either. She was mostly watching the far side of the square, waiting for a signal from Raymond, the *Courier* photographer, and checking the time. Patrice Le Congo had messaged her that morning to say the farmers were planning a demonstration.

The public-address system relayed the chief's greetings:

'Thank you, Mr President, for the marvellous job you are doing for our country.'

'Mr President, you are the Number One manager of the nation. You are the Chief of Chiefs.'

The chiefs presented the president with a life-size statue of himself.

Sally rolled her eyes at her colleague Lucy Kometa, who'd joined the *Courier* Reunification Anniversary Reporting Team for the big day.

Lucy pulled a pained expression. 'Three hours,' she said. 'Three long hours. We've seen the police, the military police, the army, the navy, the air force, the military band, the fire brigade, the chiefs … I'll run out of pages in my notebook before this is over.'

Sally nodded. 'Our newspaper devoted so much coverage to this event in the run-up. Yet now it's happening, it's tedious.'

'Can you believe it? And all the editor wants from me are the names of the VIPs in the grandstand and the groups taking part in the march-past. It's not challenging for me.'

'All he wants from me is *colour*.' Sally made inverted commas with her fingers. 'That's what he said. That's all he ever wants from me. "Describe the atmosphere, Sally. Find out what ordinary people think about it." What does he mean by *ordinary* people? I tell you, he doesn't trust me with anything serious.'

'It's because we're women, sister.'

'Well, he'll soon find out I can be a news reporter too, and as good as any man.'

Sally looked out across the square again. She and Lucy had got there early and found a vantage point up a scaffold being used by one of the state broadcasting teams – from there they'd watched the president arrive in his black limousine flanked by ten besuited bodyguards, five running each side. A cordon of police now surrounded the area in front of the grandstand and heavily armed soldiers were everywhere. That could be a problem. The security forces would not take kindly to anyone trying to spoil the party. Sally wanted to warn Patrice, but there was no phone signal in the square. She feared the farmers might be biting off more than they could chew.

The Radio Cameroon commentator picked up again. 'The chiefs are now continuing on their way, and next we have the schoolchildren … representing the future of our proud nation. Here they come, marching confidently before the most important people in Cameroon …'

Sally scanned the faces in the grandstand. They looked pretty *ordinary* to her. She recognised some of the senior ministers and military leaders, but most of them there were unknown to her and, she was sure, to the public.

'Who be that man?' she asked Lucy, pointing at someone she was sure she'd seen somewhere recently, but couldn't place. 'The one in the black jacket with no tie …'

Lucy strained her eyes. 'I don't know him. But the one sitting next to him, in the shadows, I think he's Number Two in the Ministry of Foreign Business and Investment. I must check his name. Thanks, sister, I hadn't noticed him.'

Sally kissed her teeth. *'Na big people*. I mean, what do they do? What have they done to be where they are?'

It was as the chiefs moved on after delivering their gift to the president that Sally saw Raymond, in a corner of the square where the schoolchildren were assembling, waving his arms. She waved back, descended the steps, and headed over. The square was packed. She had to push her way through, passing in front of banners bearing proclamations such as *A UNITED CAMEROON IS A PROSPEROUS CAMEROON* and ducking under placards with the words *YES* on one side and *OUI* on the other, before squeezing out the other side of the crowd.

'They're coming up there,' Raymond said, nodding at a side street. Like all the roads in and out of the square, it was blocked; a line of two dozen black-uniformed police stood across it, backs to the square, forming a black wall.

Sally peered through the gaps between their legs. The farmers were marching, about thirty of them, in silence. They carried banners with slogans very different to the ones in the square: *END FOREIGN LAND GRAB! GIVE US BACK OUR FARMS!*

Raymond held his camera above his head and took photographs. 'These are the spiritual descendants of Douala Manga!' he said to Sally, and he winked at her.

*

As they approached the wall of police, Patrice feared the worst. He was at the front of the march with the farmers Andre and Francis. 'You're sure you want to go on?' he asked. 'People may get hurt.'

Francis glared at him. 'You said we should organise ourselves. We haven't come all this way just to turn back.'

'So long as you're ready. Because there's no way through to the square.' The demonstration had been a good idea. The farmers were fearless – and tough – but the point was for them to be seen.

Andre turned as he walked and addressed the farmers. '*We dey march peacefully with causing no wahala*. We have a right to be heard.'

Francis shouted, 'United we stand!'

There were calls of support from among the other farmers. One of them chanted, *'We dey with you! We dey with you!'* Another cried out, *'Make we all go!'*

They carried on, banners held high. Patrice steeled himself and moved forward with the others.

The police stood firm as the marchers approached and got close. Then they raised their batons. Andre stopped and held his arms up as a signal to the farmers to stop too.

Sweat trickled down the policemen's cheeks. Their eyes were hostile. They were ready to react, and it wasn't going to take much to set them off. And they were within striking distance.

Andre called to a sergeant standing at the end of the line. 'We are farmers who've lost our land. Please let us pass so we can stage our peaceful protest.'

The response was a blow from a baton on his shoulder.

The police charged into the farmers, lashing out with their sticks. Patrice turned, dipping his head, trying to protect it with his arm. He felt a whack on his back, followed by another to the side of his waist. He tried to run, but he got caught on the shin and stumbled to his knees. He saw Francis taking some heavy blows. The farmers were defenceless. Those carrying placards tried to use them as shields. Some slipped away, but few escaped the vicious assault as the police trampled through them, striking indiscriminately.

Police pick-ups arrived. Farmers were bundled in, among them a bruised-looking Andre. Two policemen took Patrice by his arms and hauled him towards a vehicle. He resisted and got a punch in the stomach. He buckled over. Then there was a deafening sound of sirens.

The two policemen dropped Patrice and ran to the top of the road to join a newly re-formed wall. Behind it, in the square, Patrice could see a procession of motorcycles and blue lights and black limousines. He picked himself up and fled down the road with the farmers, who were clutching their beaten bodies as they ran, abandoning their banners which lay broken and torn.

They made their way to the truck that had brought them to Buea and was now waiting at the motor park. They sat on the back, nursing their wounds.

Patrice turned to Francis, who was wrapping a piece of cloth over a gash on his forearm. 'Are you alright?' he asked.

Francis scowled. 'It's a scratch.'

An incoming text on Patrice's phone indicated the return of the mobile network, meaning the president had left the town and normal activities could resume. It was from the reporter, Sally Bintu: *R u ok? I saw what happened.*

Good for her, he thought. The protest hadn't gone unnoticed. He replied: *Battered and bruised but alive.*

'Look, they're coming.' One of the farmers was pointing at the road. Andre and four others were hobbling towards them.

'They let us go,' Andre said as he reached the truck. 'They just didn't want the president to see anything.'

Patrice helped him up.

Francis rallied the farmers. 'Now we see what we're up against,' he said. 'We took a beating. But we're not giving up!'

'No!' the farmers responded.

Francis raised his fist in the air defiantly.

Chapter 34

Jeki took an *okada* as far as the Pamol mill. He told the *okada* man he was looking for work.

The man gave him a strange look. 'You won't find any here today.'

'Why not?'

'It's a holiday.'

Jeki saw the main gate was closed. He felt hot behind his ears. 'It doesn't matter. I'll wait till tomorrow.'

'Okay!' The man laughed. 'Good luck!'

Jeki paid the fare. He didn't like the way the man laughed, like he'd caught him out.

He waited till the *okada* was out of sight, then turned and started walking down the road that led to the river. What was important from now on was that no one should see him. *Sáŋgó* had said there would be few people about, and he was right. *Sáŋgó* thought of everything.

When he reached the river, he walked along the bank till he came to the stream that *Sáŋgó* had told him about. He pulled off his bag to check the contents again and stroked his thumb across the blade of his machete. It was razor sharp. He crossed the stream and crawled into the bushes. From here, hidden from view, he could see into the nursery. A dozen men were working among the potted seedlings, carrying tools, pushing wheelbarrows, sweeping, watering. There was no holiday for them.

Jeki sat and waited. He closed his eyes and imagined he was back in his mother's arms as she told him the tale of Jeki la Njambe and the giant crocodile …

One night, as a trick, Jeki's father Njambe ordered Jeki to fetch him the giant crocodile that lived in the river, saying he wanted to eat it with his couscous. 'Bring it to me in the morning,' he said, 'as I have already brushed my teeth.'

In fact, Njambe was hoping the beast would kill Jeki. Fearless, Jeki paddled out into the river in the darkness, until he came across a great green cliff-face. He asked the ngalo, his amulet, what it was. 'It's the crocodile,' the ngalo replied. 'Be polite and he will not harm you.'

Jeki told the crocodile the village elders were holding a meeting and wished to consult him, knowing he had great wisdom. The crocodile followed Jeki to the riverbank. Before they reached it, Jeki spun his paddle with such strength that he created an enormous wave that carried his canoe, and the crocodile right into the centre of the village.

The crocodile snapped, and a house vanished. He flipped his tail, and two houses flew away into the air. Jeki called out to his father, asking what he wanted to do with the crocodile.

His father, Njambe, was shocked. He waited till morning before coming out of his house, whereupon he sat in his grand armchair and asked for his garri. When his wife, not Jeki's mother, brought it to him in a ball on a plate, Njambe picked it up and placed it on the crocodile's nose and then picked up the giant animal, with the garri, and swallowed them both in one gulp.

Njambe had shown his strength to Jeki; but after this incident, he was left in no doubt as to the great power of the son he so despised.

Jeki smiled to himself. It was one of his favourite stories. Jeki la Njambe's father had tried to trick him, but in the end it was Jeki la Njambe who had tricked his father and outsmarted him.

By late afternoon the nursery workers had finished for the day. At dusk Jeki saw them outside their bunkhouse, eating dinner and drinking bottles of beer. Jeki took the flask out of his bag and unscrewed the lid. Steam hissed out, reminding him of the pain he'd have to endure when he drank the *niya*. But he felt a rush of adrenaline with the anticipation of what was to follow, the power he would command. Tightening his stomach muscles, he downed the scalding potion in one.

He let out a long breath and waited a little longer, till the men went inside and the lights were out.

Then he crawled under the barbed-wire fence, snapping his teeth and swiping his tail, and went about his business.

Later, Jeki was by the water's edge, where the stream flowed into the river. He felt like he'd just woken from a dream. He crouched over to wipe clean his machete, the reflection of the rising moon sparkling on the blade.

Chapter 35

'Two paragraphs!' Outraged, Sally passed the Special Anniversary Edition of the *Courier* to Raymond. 'All that trouble for two paragraphs!'

Raymond rubbed the bandage on the side of his head. 'Without the pictures, that's all it's worth.'

'But they took your flash card!'

The photographer shrugged. 'Like I said, without the pictures, it's not big news.'

'You're very philosophical, considering a soldier did that to you with his rifle butt.'

'I'm thankful he didn't shoot me; an AKM assault rifle fired at close range would have blown my head off.'

'You know the name of the gun?'

'I'm interested in all things that shoot; guns and cameras.' He giggled.

Sally rolled her eyes. '*Na only man pickin fit think like that,*' she said. 'Only a man could think like that.'

It was the morning after the big anniversary event. They were sitting in front of a bar in Buea, drinking Cokes.

She took back the paper and read the two paragraphs again. It was the second story in a section headlined, *What you didn't see at the Reunification Celebrations* (the first was a piece about how the president had actually been sitting in the chair intended for his wife, upsetting the carefully planned seating arrangements in the grandstand). 'I don't like this sub-heading: *Farmers' Protest Quelled*. It suggests they were causing a disturbance. I've told our editor I'm not happy with the coverage.'

'What did he say?' Raymond asked as he fiddled with his camera.

'He told me not to be upset. He said the farmers were out to get publicity, and we've reported on their grievance with New Deal before.'

'Okay. But he liked the colour piece you did; he's given it half a page.'

'I know, but why?'

'It's entertaining – more entertaining than those long-winded opinion pieces he's always running by ageing professors about the unresolved Anglophone issue.'

'What I mean is, what's happening to the farmers in Bafuke, for an example, is more important than a celebration to mark reunification. The way these editorial decisions are made makes me ask if I'm in the right job. I've been at the *Courier* two years but it's like I still don't get it.'

The *Courier* photographer held his camera to his eye and took a series of pictures of the traffic passing by. 'What's there to get? You write a story. If the editor likes it, he puts it in the paper. If he doesn't, he spikes it. The important thing is you get paid at the end of the month.'

'I can't believe you think like that. For me, journalism is about raising the consciousness of the people, holding the government to account.'

Raymond looked at the pictures he'd taken. 'For me it's a

job. If you want to change the world, then pick up an AKM assault rifle!'

She looked at him quizzically. 'I never know when you're joking and when you're being serious. But talking of ageing professors, I've got a meeting. Then I'm taking a few days off. See you soon, Raymond.'

He waved goodbye and she left him to his camera. She'd actually enjoyed working with Raymond the past few days. He was an experienced journalist and despite his blasé attitude, he'd shown an interest in her research into Douala Manga, which showed, she thought, he had a broader world view than other colleagues at the *Courier*, including her editor.

She hailed an *okada* and rode into the hills beneath the former German governor's residence, up a track that took them out of the town centre. Most of the houses in this part of Buea were large - some from colonial days, others newly built. The one that belonged to Professor Arthur Mbinglo, a renowned expert on Cameroon's colonial history who had recently retired, was a pink-coloured bungalow surrounded by a lush garden.

The *okada* left Sally at the gate. Flowers and shrubs spilled over low walls. The only sounds up here in the hills were of birds and insects. Sally knocked on the door. A maid answered and showed her through to a dark reception area, with armchairs lined against the walls and a set of low tables in the middle. Sally walked across to the window, pulled aside the curtain, and looked out at the view over the grey rooftops to the grey town below.

'Don't believe it if you ever hear anyone say the Germans used to look down on Douala from up here.'

Sally looked round to see the professor shuffling in, a smile on his face.

'Buea is a town of mist and rain. The Germans came here for the cooler climate, certainly not the view.'

Sally hadn't met the professor before. He looked no older than fifty, not a wrinkle in his oily skin, though she knew he was over seventy.

'How do you do?' he said, in a very English accent. He introduced himself.

'Hello, Prof, it's nice to meet you,' Sally said, shaking a hand that was older than the face. 'Thank you for agreeing to speak to me.'

'It's a pleasure. For an old man like me, an honour. If you were coming as a reporter, it would have been a different matter because I don't trust the newspapers, but if it's for serious historical research, I am happy to help you, if I can.'

He gestured for them to sit. 'Can I get you a drink? Tea? Or beer?'

Sally declined.

The professor told the maid to bring him a bottle of Guinness. 'Now, young lady … Miss Bintu … what is it you'd like to know about Douala Manga?'

She opened her notebook. 'As I told you when I called, I'm researching for a book I want to write about him, it being a hundred years since his death. One thing that's puzzling me is how far he was prepared to go to resist the German land appropriation plan. After all his diplomatic efforts had failed, is it possible he was considering an armed rebellion?'

The professor lowered his head and looked at Sally over his wire-rimmed glasses. 'Of course, this is what he was accused of. But it is highly unlikely. To begin with, there is no credible evidence to suggest this was something he was contemplating, let alone planning.'

The maid brought the Guinness. The professor drank a mouthful and licked his lips.

'You see,' he continued, 'even if Douala Manga had wanted to stage an armed rebellion, how could he manage it? Where would he get the arms?'

'From Southern Nigeria? From people who sympathised with his cause … they might have wanted to help Douala Manga?'

'But how?' Professor Mbinglo pursed his lips as he carefully emptied the bottle into a glass. 'I don't see how the Nigerians could have helped him. What I mean is, look at the Bussa rebellion, for example, in Northern Nigeria, which took place the year after Douala Manga's execution; that was undertaken with bows and arrows and was easily suppressed by the British. These people didn't have the resources to pose a serious threat.'

'Could the British have armed Douala Manga so he could rebel against the Germans?'

'There's no evidence that they did. Besides, by this time, the British could see the war coming and felt confident in their own strength to defeat the Germans in West Africa. So why complicate things by giving arms to the natives, who might not want to give them up afterwards? You see?'

'But the thing is, Douala Manga had a duty to defend his people …'

'His people?' He gave her that look over his glasses. 'We should ask, who were his people? The Douala, and certainly in this struggle they were united. But who among other groups saw Douala Manga as their leader? The other coastal people were glad to see him trying to resist the German land-grab – let's call it what it was, a land-grab – because they could see, as he told them, that they could be next. But don't go getting it into your head that Douala Manga was any kind of Cameroonian nationalist. The inland groups were still suspicious of the Douala. For two centuries the Douala had made their fortune partly by trading slaves with the Europeans, slaves caught in the hinterland. They listened to him politely, but they did not trust the Douala any more than they trusted the Germans.'

He downed the glass into which he'd emptied the bottle and licked his lips again.

'What is it, my dear, that makes you think he was planning a rebellion? I hope you're not trying to build him up into something … something more than he was, in order to make your book more interesting?'

Sally felt herself blush. Perhaps she had begun to romanticise the role of Douala Manga in Cameroon's history. 'No, no, Prof. Definitely not. Something I read …'

'I'm afraid to say there are some among the Douala community who – having lost the privileged position they held among Cameroonian groups because of their dealings with the Europeans – have sought to rekindle the memory of Douala Manga in an attempt to win back some of the former glory they used to enjoy. They have sought to mythologise him by calling him a hero-martyr who sacrificed his life for the dignity of the community.'

'But he did sacrifice his life!' Sally blurted out, louder than she intended. 'He could have saved himself by agreeing to the German appropriation plan, but he didn't, and that was for the sake of the pride of his people.'

'Well, we don't know what he was thinking,' the professor said, quietly.

'I do.'

'How's that?'

'I … I mean … I suppose I have a strong feeling about what was going on his mind at that time.'

The professor called to his maid to bring another bottle. 'Forgive me, Miss Bintu, if I have upset you - I did not intend to offend. I know, because I have been told before, that I can speak too bluntly on occasion …'

Sally took a breath to calm herself. 'No offence taken. Please, carry on. I just think there might be more to Douala Manga than he's given credit for.'

'Well, that may be. I suppose the point I was trying to make by including the historical context is that a serious piece of research must be guided by facts, not conjecture or … to be blunt again, forgive me … wishful thinking. And, based on what we know, we can conclude that Douala Manga had no plan for an armed revolt, above all because he knew the Douala could not defeat the Germans militarily.'

'Thank you, Prof.' Sally sat up straight in her chair. 'I do appreciate your time, and your speaking frankly with me. But I do want you to know that this latest line of my research has been guided by some original documentation that I don't believe has been seen before.'

'How intriguing!' the professor said, smiling. 'Would you like to tell me more about that?'

'I'm sorry, I can't, not yet.' She couldn't resist teasing him. 'But I'll be happy to share it with you when the time comes.'

'That would be an honour,' he replied. 'And please, if you have any other questions, I am here and happy to help.'

Sally smiled a thank you. 'There is one more thing. Do you know if Douala Manga fathered any children when he was studying in Germany? And if so, if they could have been sent for adoption in Cameroon?'

The old man chuckled. 'What kind of book is it that you're going to write, I wonder? It is unlikely he had relationships with any German girls … most unlikely. Such a liaison would have been frowned upon by German society in those days, and Douala Manga would have been sensitive to what was acceptable to his hosts. But I take it you're referring to the story of the German prince?'

'What story is that?'

'It's a made-up one, my dear. Like so many, that get passed down through the generations and embellished with every telling.'

'Oh. But what was the story?'

He looked at her over his glasses again. 'It went like this: a woman arrived one night in the village of Ngembum, not so far from here. She had a baby boy. No one there had seen her before. She said she'd been to work in Germany as a maid but had had to leave when it was clear she was with child, because the father was a German prince. And, would you believe it, the baby had fair skin. The woman said her family had disowned her so she could not return home. The people in the village took pity on her and built her a house. It was said that when Douala Manga heard about the German prince, he went to visit, which led to rumours that the child was in fact his, and that the woman was not the real mother. But of course, no one knows what became of the woman or the boy. Just a silly story, with no evidence to substantiate any aspect of it.'

'But still ... Where was she from?'

'She said her family lived near Bamenda, I believe. I can see you are interested, but as I said before, historical research should always be evidence-based.'

'Of course,' Sally said, squeezing the corners of her lips. She wasn't going to get carried away, or jump to conclusions. But ... she was from Bamenda, her skin tone was relatively light, and her mother had said the family were descended from kings. It might be ridiculous, but she couldn't ignore the possibility, however remote, of a personal connection.

'Thank you again, Prof. You've been so helpful.'

Professor Arthur Mbinglo had made his points well; he had his facts. But Sally had new evidence of her own. And the prof's arrogant self-assurance made her even more determined to get to the bottom of Douala Manga's story – or stories.

She walked back into town and went to a hair salon. She felt like a change and opted for a natural style with twist-outs on top.

Chapter 36

Still sore from the battering he'd taken at the demonstration the day before, Patrice rode Coach Samson's motorcycle to New Deal's oil palm nursery. He parked by the river.

Andre greeted him. 'It's good of you to come,' he said. The farmer held out a hand, but he looked troubled. 'Where's the coach?'

'He sends his apologies. He has to wash the Bakunda Lions football kit …'

'Never mind. Come. It's bad.'

They walked up the bank, to the fence at the top, and Patrice saw the scene of the massacre – a massacre of plants.

Hardly a single seedling palm was left standing. Hundreds, thousands of pots were strewn all over. It looked like a herd of elephants had run amok, except that in the pots that were still upright, the plants had been scythed with a clean cut. And elephants didn't carry machetes.

'Someone's gone berserk,' Patrice said.

The farmer pointed to a group of policemen by the fence further along. One of them was holding a red baseball cap. 'That's Ajebe's. They found it there.'

Patrice shook his head, disappointedly. 'So much for the moral high ground.'

Andre said, 'We must go to the village. There'll be trouble now for sure.'

Patrice rode them down the track by the river, glancing up at the police as they passed. 'It's definitely *his* hat?'

'Yes. They found a phone too. They think Ajebe fell as he made his escape. They called the last number dialled on the phone, from a week ago, and got through to the chief. He confirmed the phone was Ajebe's.'

A week was a long time to go without making a phone call, Patrice thought. He was trying to think what else it might mean when they reached the road into Bafuke, and he brought the motorcycle to an abrupt halt. Ahead of them, all the way up the main street, armed men were walking in and out of the houses; some were police, others wore military-style beige-coloured fatigues with matching baseball caps and were carrying automatic weapons.

'Who are they?' Patrice asked.

'Land Security,' Andre said. 'A South African security company hired by New Deal.'

They rode to Andre's house. As they arrived, Alice came stumbling out of the doorway as if she'd been pushed. Two of the beige-uniformed men followed.

'They're searching everywhere for Daniel Ajebe,' she said, holding her arms out wide. 'We told them he's not here, but they've come into our houses, looking under our beds.'

The security men went to the next house, thumped on the open door and barged in.

'No one's seen Ajebe, or Louis Sone,' Alice continued. 'Louisa is worried.'

'Ajebe's wife?' Patrice guessed. 'Can I speak to her?'

'You take him, Alice.' Andre said. 'I'll stay by the house.'

Alice led Patrice further up the main street. Villagers were outside their houses, watching on as the security guards moved from one to the next, trampling over laundry laid out to dry on the grass by the side of the road. They turned off along a track. Alice pointed to a yellow generator the size of a small car.

'A gift from New Deal, for the whole village. It has never worked. That's why we continue to live in darkness here.'

There was no need for Alice to point out Daniel Ajebe's house, a small wooden structure with a tin roof. Six security guards were standing in front of it, next to a police pick-up. A woman was sitting on a step below the porch, her face buried in her hands. She was sobbing. Alice went to sit beside her and wrapped an arm around her shoulders.

'I nova see him since Saturday,' the woman said. *'I nova see him since Saturday.'*

A teenage girl appeared at the doorway, a baby strapped to her back, a toddler on her hip, a young boy at her side holding on to her leg.

'Their children,' Alice said.

Patrice went to look inside the house. A table and chairs had been upturned, drawers pulled open, contents emptied on the floor. The mattress on which he guessed most or all of the family slept had been pulled off the bed and upended. He stooped to pick up a photograph, its frame broken, of a young couple on their wedding day. The groom was a short man with broad, round shoulders that stretched the jacket of his dress suit, and Patrice recognised his face. The bride – the woman now sitting outside – was in a white dress, her hair in locks. They were smiling, looking happy and excited about their future together. Patrice propped it on a shelf.

Outside, a security guard was talking to a police inspector. The guard's cap was embroidered with the words *Land Security* and a silhouette of a dog's head. Patrice looked at Ajebe's wife and her children and approached the men.

'Let me see your search warrant,' he said.

They looked at him blankly, then at one another. 'Who are you?' the police inspector asked.

'You need a warrant to search a house. Where is it?'

'You are hindering a police investigation into a serious crime. Get out of my way or I will have you arrested.'

Patrice didn't move. 'I'm an investigator with the African Union's Human Rights Commission.' If it got back to his boss that he was making out he was acting officially, he'd lose his job. He was sure it wouldn't.

'If you work for an international organisation such as that, you should dress more smartly than this.' He waved a finger at Patrice's jeans and sandals. 'And get a haircut.'

'I'll be making a full report on what's going on here.'

The police inspector spat on the ground by Patrice's feet. 'Go and make your report.' Turning to Daniel Ajebe's wife, he said, *'Tell your man say e get to surrender for police.'*

The security guard added, 'If he doesn't, we'll hunt him down.' Then he addressed the other villagers who'd assembled outside Daniel Ajebe's house. 'One way or another, you'll pay for the damage that's been caused.'

Chapter 37

Jeki loaded the taxi boot with luggage: two jerrycans, a large carrier bag full of yams, and other bags and cases and boxes. As he covered them with plastic sheeting to protect them from the dust and fastened everything with rubber straps, he noticed two policemen in the motor park. They were stopping to talk to people.

The driver came to inspect the packing and found a loose knot. He barked at Jeki, saying he should take more care, before handing him a couple of low-value banknotes. Jeki checked the money. He'd worked all morning and barely earned enough for one meal.

Soon, he hoped, he wouldn't need to come to the motor park to work. That's what *Sáŋgó* had told him. But as he watched the policemen now standing at the ticket counter, he felt uneasy. He wasn't booked for any new wrestling contests. And he still had more tasks to do for *Sáŋgó*.

'Hey, Jeki!' One of the other porters came up. 'Don't you like it here?'

It was like the man could hear Jeki think. 'It's not that, but everyone should look to improve himself.'

His colleague laughed. 'Is it better working at Pamol?'

Jeki felt his ears burn. 'What do you mean?'

'I heard you went there looking for a job?'

'I … I was thinking of it, but I changed my mind. I want to be a professional wrestler. I've been told I can make it. A promoter is interested in me.'

'A promoter? Well, if that's the case, next time you fight, let me know. I'll put my money on you!'

'What money? Porters don't have any money to make bets with. I know that.'

His colleague laughed again and slapped Jeki on the shoulder. *'Mama-ye!* What do you feed yourself, Jeki? Your shoulder's hard as rock.'

'I eat the same as everybody else, but I train. That's the difference …'

He trailed off as he saw the two policemen were talking to one of the drivers and showing him something. The driver was shaking his head. The policemen walked over to Jeki and the other porter.

'Have you seen these farmers?' one of them asked, holding two photographs in front of Jeki's face.

'No!' He almost shouted the word. His heart was thumping. He swallowed, and, trying to sound more natural, he added, 'Wait. Let me see.' He made as if to study the photographs. 'No,' he said again, 'not today.'

'You've seen them before, another time?'

'No, no. I mean I haven't seen them ever.'

The policeman pushed the photos into his hand. 'Think carefully. They may not have had bags. Did you see them waiting around?'

Jeki swallowed again. His mouth was dry. He tried to lick his lips but his tongue stuck to them, so that he had to raise his other hand and ease it free with his fingers while pretending he was giving the matter extra thought. 'I ... I don't know,' he said at last. 'I haven't seen them.'

The other porter leaned over. 'Aren't they the farmers who come to watch the wrestling, here in the motor park?'

Jeki felt like he wanted to empty his bowels. He was speechless.

'What about today?' The policeman snatched the photos from Jeki and showed them to the other porter. 'Were they here today? Or yesterday?'

'No. I don't think so.'

The policeman stared from one porter to the other. 'Let us know if you see them.'

'What have they done?' the other porter asked.

'Something they'll regret.'

'Are they dangerous?'

'They are to plants.'

The policemen went off to talk to a group of waiting passengers.

The other porter turned to Jeki and screwed up his face. 'How can a farmer be dangerous to plants?'

'I don't know.' Jeki was chewing at his fingernails and taking deep breaths. *Sáŋgó* had said their plan – as he called it – was working. But there were things *Sáŋgó* was telling him to do that he didn't fully understand.

'You don't remember them, Jeki? I'm sure I saw them talking to you one time. Not last week, but before ...'

'Not me. Another wrestler maybe.' Jeki was relieved to see a minibus taxi approaching. 'Look, work,' he said. 'But you take it, I'm going for my lunch.'

The other man patted him on the shoulder and ran off to greet the new arrival. Another porter rushed out to join him and the two men shouted through the windows to the passengers, offering their services.

Jeki slipped away into the dark midday shadows cast by the trees at the edge of the motor park. He walked down towards the river then up the short track that led to his shack. Inside he saw the weights on the floor but decided not to attempt them until he'd composed himself. He ate cold garri again for lunch and rested, and he felt better about things when he woke. He must have been tired earlier.

Standing over the bar, he bent down and grabbed it. Without hesitating, barely breaking sweat, he lifted it to his chest, then up above his head, before letting it drop to the ground.

He was ready. He sharpened his machete on the whetstone and went on his way.

Chapter 38

Observing his furrowed brow and frightened eyes, it was hard for Patrice not to sympathise with the taxi porter. A police interrogation could make anyone appear guilty. He was half expecting the officers to pull out their sticks and beat a witness statement out of the sorry-looking man. Then the minibus arrived, and Patrice went to meet Sally Bintu.

'Hello,' he said. 'You've made it, finally.' He'd called her the previous day to tell her about the attack on the plantation nursery and the search for the missing farmer.

'Just about,' she said as she alighted and slapped the dust off her clothes. 'Ugh, that road is bad.'

He took her bag from a porter on the roof.

Sally shouted up, complaining the luggage had not been properly covered.

He noticed her hair was different. The red streak had gone.

She patted the sides of her head. 'Like it?'

'Yes, it's nice. It looks modern.'

They rode an *okada* to the hotel, where he'd booked a room for her. Over tea in the garden, he filled her in. 'It's good your paper's taking an interest in this business. Tensions are running high. We can go to the village tomorrow. You can meet the farmers and get the full story.'

Sally fiddled with her fingers. 'You know, Patrice, I haven't sold the story to my editor. He says a few plants being cut down is not a big deal.'

'It was more than a few. But then why has he sent you?'

She paused. 'He didn't. I'm here on my own time - I took some days off.' She screwed up her face apologetically.

'Oh, I see,' he said, not wanting his frustration to show; if he'd doubted her commitment when they'd first met, at least now it seemed she was taking her job seriously, and being resourceful – even if her editor's attitude was disappointing. 'Once you've been there and told him how things are, he may change his mind.'

'I'll do my best.' She didn't look hopeful.

'Cheer up. He'll be impressed with your dedication. As it happens, I'm here on my own time, too.' He told her how Josie Mwinga had ordered him to stop his investigation.

Sally tutted. Then she said, 'There's actually another reason I came ... I wanted to show you something.'

'Yes?'

'Not here. Can I come to your room?'

'To my room? Why the secrecy?'

'I'll explain once we're there.'

He wondered if she was planning to seduce him. If so, it was a bad plan. She was attractive but young, and he was busy and not looking for diversions.

They finished their tea and walked round to Patrice's chalet. He offered her a seat on the large sofa while he sat opposite on a chair.

'So, what is it?'

She lowered her voice. 'You remember I told you about the research I was doing in Douala? I've decided now I'm going to write a book. And this is why …' She handed him an envelope. 'Will you read it? Please? It won't take long.'

He pulled out a manuscript. He could feel her eyes fixed on him. From the dateline alone it looked intriguing. And the more he read, the more he was drawn into it. To see the words of the Douala king, written in his own hand on the eve of his execution by the colonialists, sent a chill down his spine.

'That's amazing,' he said, when he'd finished. 'Where did you get it?'

'You should know you can't ask a journalist for that kind of information.'

'Did you steal it? Who does it belong to?'

'It's not clear,' she said, coughing. 'But aside from how I come to have it, what do you think about the content?'

'It's sad. A man writing his memoirs as he awaits his death. I found it moving.' He sensed she was waiting for more. 'And it's interesting for me, not knowing about that period in Cameroon's history. Of course, it's an indictment of European imperialism. It's an exciting discovery. But why are you showing it to me?'

'Because I can't trust anyone else. History is a sensitive issue. You can never be sure where people's loyalties lie. For now, I have to be careful. You are the only person who knows I've got this apart from two colleagues at the *Courier*. I think I can trust them, but they're Cameroonian and already have their opinion of Douala Manga. You're an outsider, and you're an investigator. And I was hoping you could help me.'

'Help you what?'

'Solve a mystery. Reading this, as you've done, what would you say were Douala Manga's intentions before he was arrested? Do you think he was planning an armed insurrection?'

Patrice shrugged. 'He talks about defending his people. It sounds like he was up to something. But, even if he was, it didn't happen, so I suppose it's hypothetical.'

'*E be important!* Don't you see? It's evidence that Douala Manga really was a hero of the resistance.'

'Okay, well, I'm sorry, but it's not clear …'

'What about the sceptre! And the Nigerians!' Sally was shouting. She put her hand to her mouth.

Patrice gave her back the manuscript. 'Sally, this all happened a hundred years ago. It's interesting, but important things are happening here and now that need your attention, things affecting the lives of people living today.'

She looked away like a scolded child. 'I know,' she said, quietly now. 'That's the main reason I'm here. And we'll meet the farmers tomorrow.' Then she looked at him with a smile. 'Don't think I came all this way just to see you!'

*

Sally's paper had carried a few reports about the New Deal plantation, but she'd never been there. Now, as they rode to Bafuke village and Patrice pointed out the endless rows of small palms, she made the connection.

'I know you don't want to hear any more about Douala Manga,' she said, 'but this is what he predicted.'

'What?'

'That we would lose our land to the Europeans. Things have come full circle since his time. We gained our independence, but now we're losing it again.'

'We Africans never gained our independence; it was a myth. They left and let us choose the colours of our flags, but they still control everything. It's called neo-colonialism. Kwame Nkrumah wrote about it.'

Sally smiled to herself. Now she understood the Afro; Patrice was from another time. 'I don't know about those old theories. But this, it's real. It's our land we're giving away. That's what I mean - it's what Douala Manga was trying to resist. And it adds a new dimension to my book.'

They were travelling on Samson Eta's motorcycle. They'd gone to his bar the previous evening; the coach had said he was sorry he couldn't come with them, but he had an early training session with his football team ahead of a big game at the weekend. They reached a river, with thick forest on the far side. That's how it would have looked a hundred years ago, Sally thought - how Douala Manga would have seen it.

They rode on. She couldn't help asking another question. 'Patrice, do you think it's a truthful memoir?' She didn't give him time to answer. 'Do you think he was telling the truth when he described what happened between him and Rosa von Roehm?'

There was a pause. She guessed he was rolling his eyes. 'I suppose so,' he said, eventually. 'He had no reason to lie. You think it's significant?'

Sally said, 'No, no, not at all.' Then she added, 'But I'm thinking I might take a DNA test.'

'What? Why? You mean, you think ... because of the story your mother told you?'

'It's not just that. I found out something else, but it doesn't matter.'

He shook his head. 'Sally, has it occurred to you that

you might be getting too personally involved in this Douala Manga project?'

'I was speculating, that's all. It's no big deal.' Sally nibbled a fingernail, wishing she hadn't mentioned the idea to him.

It was market day in Bafuke, though it wasn't much of a market - half-a-dozen women seated on one side of the road, selling produce Sally guessed they'd grown in their gardens, like onions and tomatoes, and cobs of maize. They sat forlornly under their umbrellas.

Along with some dark clouds above, it felt like the village was shrouded in gloom.

Patrice parked by a tree outside a house and knocked on the door. A man and a woman came out, and Patrice introduced them as Andre and Alice.

'This is the reporter I told you about,' he said.

'You are welcome,' they said together.

Andre said he'd fetch a few other villagers so the reporter could talk to them. Sally and Patrice waited with Alice outside by the tree.

'Five years ago, this whole road was used for the market,' Alice said, as if apologising for its sorry state now. 'On both sides. There were pineapples in piles like this' – she held her hand at waist height – 'and cocoyams. People brought these things from their farms, but now there are so few farms. And traders came from Bakunda town and other places with shoes and CDs and many things. But now they don't come because people have no money here.'

An elderly woman with a basket of laundry was passing by. Alice called to her. *'Mama, you fit still remember how market day used to be for Bafuke?'*

'Everybody used to glad plenty for market day,' she said.

'Mama's right,' Alice nodded.

The elderly woman sucked on her lips. 'You could walk around and hear all the news and gossip. There was a woman who came from far down the river with dried fish, and she'd knock at my door to offer me first choice. But she doesn't come now.'

'Look how things bad for here now,' Alice said. *'Our village dey die small small.* Our village is dying.'

Sally took notes and asked about the history of the village, but it felt like she was going through the motions. She couldn't imagine her editor would print any of it. Andre returned with two other farmers who greeted Patrice with a nod of recognition.

'Take her to see the generator,' Alice said.

'Yes, come,' Andre said. 'We tried to fix it this morning, but we don't have the parts.'

Sally didn't want to go and look at a broken generator, but she followed obediently. It was as they were showing her why it wasn't working that Andre got a call. From the way he stood staring at his phone after the call was finished, it was clear he'd had a shock.

'They've found the two missing farmers,' he said. 'They've been murdered.'

Sally turned to Patrice and whispered, 'I think my editor will be interested now.'

Chapter 39

Her shoulder blades were sharp, her buttocks round. Pierre Mponda watched as she walked naked from the black silk sheets of the bed to the white marble tiles of the bathroom. He propped himself against the pillow and let his gaze drift round the apartment, his *deuxième bureau,* secretly acquired in the upmarket Douala suburb of Bonapriso for the purpose of entertaining his mistresses. His gaze came to rest on the chandelier that had arrived the previous week from Italy. It was large – Estelle had said it was too large for the room – but what style!

He threw off the sheets, went to the wardrobe and picked out black trousers, a grey blazer and white tee shirt. He laid the clothes on the bed then went to take a shower. Estelle feigned surprised embarrassment as he entered the bathroom, covering her breasts with her hands. Then she smiled coquettishly as she pulled her fingers aside, revealing her nipples between her long, pink nails.

'Do you think my boobs are too small?' she asked, looking sideways at herself in the large mirror.

'No, Estelle,' he assured her. '*Ils sont parfaits.*'

She pushed against him, wriggling her body suggestively.

'Not now,' he said, pulling away. 'I have work.'

'Take me with you.' She ran a fingernail down his spine as he turned for the shower.

He felt a quiver in his groin and thought for a moment about turning back. But he ran the water instead. 'What would my wife say if she heard a young woman was coming to my office with me?'

'I never get to see you,' she said, pouting but smiling at the same time, still teasing him with her fingers. 'Are you ashamed of me?'

'You're seeing me tonight. Remember? We're going out.'

'But that's with your business friend, and because you want me to bring Dorothy to entertain him.'

Mponda lifted her hand off him. 'You must visit me in Yaounde then. I will be going there soon.'

He'd been seeing Estelle for two months. She was lucky. He paid her university fees and she knew better than to make demands on his time. If that happened, he'd let her go. For now, though, he thought as he showered, she knew how to please him and played the game.

He got dressed and put on his watch and the heavy gold bracelet that he'd acquired after seeing a senior government minister wearing something similar. He checked his phones, which had been on silent. There was a missed call from his wife on the gold one, which he ignored. And there was a missed call on the cheap phone he'd bought recently. He walked through to the salon to return it.

'Jeki.'

'*A Sáŋgó âm.* My Master. I want you to know I have completed the latest task.'

'Did you think I would doubt you? You must learn to be more confident in yourself.'

'*Ee, Sáŋgó.* Yes, Master. But I also want to ask if you have arranged any further wrestling contests?'

'No, not yet. It will take time after what happened.'

'But how long must I wait, *a Sáŋgó âm?*'

Mponda looked through to the bedroom and saw Estelle at the dressing table doing something with her hair, but looking at him in the mirror. He lowered his voice. 'You will wait as long as I say. In the meantime, you must keep up your training, and be prepared for your next task.'

'But *Sáŋgó*, you promised me …'

'Are you forgetting why it is that you must do as I say?'

There was a pause. '*Kém, Sáŋgó*. No, Master. I will wait to hear from you.'

Mponda ended the call. He went into the bedroom and bent to kiss Estelle on her neck and told her he'd see her later. 'Now I must work,' he said.

The walk from the apartment block entrance to his four-by-four was twenty metres, twenty metres enveloped in Douala's early afternoon heat. He drove, air-conditioned, to the port, where he had what he called an unofficial office in a warehouse. There he was able to check on the progress of various shipments through customs.

The first was a container from Genoa full of lighting and electrical appliances destined for a new conference centre being built in Yaounde. He scrolled through the list of contents and checked that the adjustments had been made correctly to show one less chandelier had been ordered.

Next was a large delivery of agricultural machinery from Marseilles, which had been cleared through customs exempt of import duty. In return for this concession, the manufacturer would be offering developmental assistance to Cameroon in the form of sponsoring a student through business school in France. Bearing in mind his current focus, and not knowing when he might need further favours, Mponda had arranged for the beneficiary of this scheme to be the son of the divisional officer in Bakunda. He thanked his contact in the port and pushed a roll of banknotes into his hand.

He stopped off in Akwa to buy a case of St Emillion grand cru for his wife. Returning to his car, he received a call on his third phone, the black one with the large screen.

'*Bonne après-midi, monsieur*,' he said.

'*Comment ça se passe?*'

Mponda made sure not to rush his words - to sound calm and confident, in control. 'Everything is going well, sir.'

'When will we start to see results?'

'I think things will move rapidly now. I have a meeting this evening ...'

'Everyone's onside?'

'I'm making sure of that.'

'And the Congolese?'

If anything, it was the deputy minister who was sounding nervous. It would not be surprising; he had a lot to lose. 'He has no idea. He's like a blind man lost in a thick forest. For the time being, without knowing it, he's actually helping us.' Mponda chuckled. 'But you can be sure, if he gets in the way we will deal with him.'

Chapter 40

Patrice and Sally stood with the villagers and their chief, looking at two dead farmers. The bodies of Daniel Ajebe and Louis Sone were lying on the bank below the fence around the New Deal Plantations seedling nursery. Their heads had been cut off and left in two plant pots next to the bodies, their eyes staring.

'This is how I found them,' the farmer who'd raised the alarm told the chief. 'I saw them from across the river.'

Patrice looked over. He and Sally had ridden past this spot. A bush obscured the view from the track.

The villagers turned to the chief, but he didn't speak. He gazed at the brutalised corpses, which looked disturbingly anaemic. For a while, no one said a word.

The silence was broken by the farmer Francis Akwanga, who climbed the bank, took hold of the barbed wire fence and shook it.

'Nyamfukas!' His cursing was aimed at the bunkhouse at the far end of the nursery, though there was no one around. Plants and pots were still strewn about after the act of vandalism three days before. 'You think these men's lives are worth the same as a few trees? *Na so you think wedey?* Is that what you think of us?'

Andre climbed up and put his arm round Francis' shoulder, trying to calm him. Francis shrugged him off and continued his tirade. 'You take our land, now you take our lives!' He pulled on the fence so hard he wrenched a post from the ground. Only then did he let go and come down. The barbs had torn into his palms, which were covered in blood.

It was Francis' reaction, rather than the grisly death-scene itself, that seemed to rouse the chief from his stupor. 'We must call the police,' he said. 'This is a matter for them. We cannot take the law into our own hands.'

'*Make we call police make dem do wetin?*' Francis had regained his composure, but his tone was hostile. 'What's the point? The police won't take any action against New Deal.'

The other villagers looked from Francis to the chief.

'You are challenging my authority?' the chief asked. 'The authority handed to me by my father, who was handed it by his father?'

Francis squared up to the chief. 'What have you done to help us?'

The chief looked startled. There were murmurs among the villagers.

Andre said, 'This is no time for disagreement. We must be strong and united. The chief is right, we should call the police.'

Francis raised his chin dismissively but backed off.

The chief made the call and spoke to the inspector in Bakunda town. 'They will be here soon,' he announced.

Patrice went to examine the flowerpots. Sally followed. The dead farmers' faces looked drained and ghost-like. One of their heads was tilted, revealing the severed neck, which was coated in mud. The other head was horribly swollen and bruised around the mouth. He turned his attention to the bodies, which were clothed and also muddy. Sally took photos with her phone from different angles, then went to talk with people who had known the two men.

There was something incongruous about the scene, but before Patrice could think what it was, he was distracted by an approaching vehicle, a small four-by-four, inside the nursery. It came to a halt the other side of the fence. Four men in beige uniforms got out, armed with rifles, and walked over to the uprooted fence post.

'What's going on?' one of the men said. He had two stars on his shirt lapel. Patrice noticed Francis hide his hands behind his back.

'That's what we want to know,' the chief said, prompting voices of support from the villagers. He pointed at the two corpses, which had until then been out of the sight of the security guards. All four leaned over the fence and saw the carnage. Two of them reacted by aiming their rifles at the crowd.

'This is the farmer accused of damaging the nursery,' the chief said, pointing at Ajebe's head. 'Who did this?'

The guards didn't answer.

'Where's your leader?' the chief asked. 'The one who came to our village.'

'The one who said you were going to hunt this farmer down,' Andre added.

'We … I know nothing about this,' the security guard with two stars said. He pulled out a radio and spoke into it. 'We're by the riverside nursery. We have a situation here.'

The villagers stared at the two men with their rifles still pointed at them. Strangely, Patrice thought, given that things were this way round, it was the security guards who looked more threatened, as if they were calculating what would happen if the crowd charged, or how many shots they could fire before they'd be set upon and torn apart. Patrice looked at Francis. He could tell from the farmer's hardened eyes he was wound up tight. He had to control himself; one false move and a twitchy finger could pull on a trigger.

Two more four-by-fours arrived, then the police inspector from Bakunda town accompanied by six men and two stretchers; they'd had to leave their vehicle upstream and come on foot along the path by the riverbank. It was the same inspector who'd been in the village during the search for Ajebe, and among the new security men to arrive was the one who'd warned they'd hunt the farmer down. Patrice now saw he had three stars on his shirt lapel. The police inspector noticed Patrice and glowered at him.

The chief briefed the inspector while the guard with two stars briefed the one with three, and finally the men with rifles lowered them. The inspector took a cursory look at the two bodies and addressed the villagers.

'This is a crime scene now,' he said. 'You must all leave while we carry out an examination of the area.' He tried to shoo them away, but no one moved. All eyes were on two of the beige-uniformed men who'd stepped over the torn section of fence and were about to pick up the plant pots containing the heads.

The police inspector yelled, 'Stop! Don't touch!'

The guard with two stars said, 'These pots are nursery property.' The one with three ordered the men to retreat.

'These people!' Andre said what all the villagers must have been thinking.

'We'll leave the pots,' the three-star guard said. 'But be our witness to the damage that's been caused to this fence.'

Even the police inspector seemed taken aback by the lack of concern for the two dead men. 'We're talking about a murder investigation here,' he said, 'Not two plant pots and a fence post.'

The inspector persuaded the villagers to back off. Then he set about examining the scene, making notes and instructing one of his men to take photographs. He came and talked to the chief and took a statement from the farmer who found the bodies.

'What about them?' Francis asked, pointing at the security guards. 'Aren't you going to interrogate them?'

'I will talk to everyone,' the inspector said. 'But those men are doing their job.'

'They made threats. They must be suspects.'

'Go back to your village. There's nothing more for you to do here. My men will search this area and then take the bodies to the mortuary in town.'

Patrice remembered what the mortician Sylvestre Atemkeng had told him, and guessed it was unlikely that post mortems would be carried out officially.

That evening, Patrice and Sally ate dinner as guests of Andre and Alice, who made fish stew with corn fufu.

'I was going to cook ndole with fish for you,' she said. 'I wanted to make something special. But it didn't feel right after today. Who could do such a thing? And why? Because they cut down some plants?'

Little else was said, conversation suffocated by the sombre mood.

Patrice and Sally were preparing to leave when a convoy of vehicles drove through the village; three four-by-fours, heading for the chief's compound.

'Make we go see wetin happen now,' Andre said.

They arrived to see the beige-uniformed security guards escorting a white man into the chief's compound.

'MacGregor,' Andre said. 'New Deal's general manager.'

The chief appeared and, seeing Andre and the others, invited them to join him. His manner suggested he wanted support. Greetings were exchanged, and the chief clapped his hands and ordered his boy to fetch the palm wine. The chief led the visitors to his open-sided shelter and settled on his chair. After the formalities of inquiring after the chief's health and that of his family, the New Deal man came to the matter that had brought him there that evening.

'Chief, it's good to see you again, but I am sorry it is in these terrible circumstances.'

The chief nodded.

'New Deal is aware of tensions between the plantation and some of the villagers here in Bafuke, and we will do all in our power to make things work between us, to improve relations, because we consider ourselves to be a company with the interests of the community at heart. And Chief, I know you have said so yourself and praised our efforts.'

The chief coughed awkwardly and looked away. Patrice took a sip of his palm wine. He was getting a taste for it. He looked at MacGregor, a man in his forties, his short straight hair parted to one side and turning grey. He spoke articulately, with a Scottish accent.

'Chief, the reason I have come tonight is to offer the company's heartfelt condolences for the loss your village has suffered. We understand that these men may well have been responsible for the attack on our nursery. But I have come also to assure you, absolutely and with my hand on my heart, that despite what may have been suggested in the heat of the moment, their deaths had nothing to do with us.'

The chief raised his head and swallowed a mouthful of palm wine. 'It is good you have come here tonight personally. It shows respect. And I know you to be a man of your word. As you know, this matter is now in the hands of the police, and as such we must wait for the results of their investigation. But I hope, in the meantime, you can also assure me that there will be no further harassment of my people over the matter of what occurred at the nursery.' As he spoke these last words, the chief waved a finger in the direction of the Land Security men, hovering around the compound gate.

It was the New Deal General Manager's turn to cough. 'Chief, I hope there has not been any harassment, as you call it. As I am sure you appreciate, these men have a job to do, and as I understand it, they go about that job in a professional manner. And what I can assure you of now is that any further action with regard to compensation for damages at the nursery can be undertaken through the courts, in accordance with due legal procedure.'

There was a stunned silence. 'Did I hear you correctly?' the chief asked. 'You want compensation? From whom? The man you say is responsible is dead.'

MacGregor slapped a mosquito on his neck. Sweat was spreading around the armpits of his white shirt. 'No, no,' he said. 'That's what I mean. It will be a matter for the courts to determine. It's not about what New Deal wants.'

'You think his widow, who has four children, will pay your

compensation? Do you think she has property other than her house, a wooden shack with two rooms and leaks in the tin roof? We know your insurance will pay for this damage, so please don't threaten us.'

'Of course, of course, Chief,' MacGregor said. 'I'm sure any appeal through the courts will be purely a formality, but it has to be done in order to satisfy the insurers, as I am sure you're aware.' The general manager leaned forward towards the chief. 'But Chief, let's not forget, the future of New Deal Plantations and the future of the communities here, not least that of your own family, are closely tied together.'

'Get out of my compound,' the chief snapped. 'You have overstayed your welcome.'

MacGregor got up from his seat and said goodbye, nodded at Patrice and the others present, and left.

The chief took a drink of palm wine, his hand shaking.

Patrice and Sally rode back to Bakunda town on Coach Samson's motorcycle. In the warm night, the headlight beam was thick with insects.

'What a nerve!' Sally said. 'That general manager is lucky the villagers didn't string him up.'

Patrice nodded in agreement, but he was thinking of the chief. Earlier by the river and now this evening, the drunkard had stood up to the bullies and their threats. And he'd done so in front of his people, which might help restore their trust in him. But after the confrontation with the general manager, he had, for the second time that day, looked scared. Patrice wondered if, at last, but possibly too late, it had dawned on Chief Adama Takubi that his past disregard for his ancestral duties could be the ruin of his village.

Chapter 41

Estelle's skirt was so short he thought she'd forgotten to put it on, until he caught a glimpse of it below her loose blouse. Her friend Dorothy was dressed - undressed - in a similar way. Their legs glistened blue and green and red under the spinning lights as they approached his booth in the downstairs section of the Phoenix nightclub in Akwa, one of Douala's best-known venues for live music.

Pierre Mponda saw the girls were having the desired effect on his guest for the evening, Thomas Schmidt, Vice-President of New Deal Plantations, who was on one of his 'catch-up' visits to Cameroon. Already sweating from the heat in the club and a large brandy, the sight of the women made the German drool. He stood to greet them and held out a clammy hand. They smiled politely.

Mponda clicked his fingers to summon a waitress and ordered more drinks. Estelle sat beside him and crossed her legs. He couldn't help looking again to check the skirt was really there. Dorothy sat the other side of Schmidt; the company vice-president took her hand and placed it on his thigh.

Shouting to make himself heard above the warm-up DJ's hip-hop music, Schmidt told Mponda about a phone call he'd had that evening from his general manager. The two women stared into the middle distance.

'There's trouble with the villagers,' he said. 'They think our security people killed the farmers. It's absurd. And you know these people caused us a lot of damage.'

The German drained his glass of brandy.

Mponda sipped his bottled water. 'I'm sure things will blow over,' he said. 'As they do. Your company has been in our country five years. Most people accept it is for the benefit of our development.'

'That's what you would hope. But even the chief is acting strangely. After all we've done for him.'

'The chief?'

'MacGregor says he started protesting when the subject of compensation came up. Can you believe it? We are taking his kids through college. He's supposed to be on our side.'

A six-piece band had made its way on to the stage. On a nod from the bass player, the American music ended abruptly and the Cameroonian music began. Couples stood in their booths and danced to the makossa rhythms. The singer, a dreadlocked man in his forties, stepped off the stage with his radio mic and serenaded the dancers, who showed their appreciation by placing folded banknotes behind his ear.

Schmidt seemed to forget about the problems at the plantation and got up to dance, pulling Dorothy with him. He jumped about with a gormless look on his face, his silvery bouffant hair flapping over his forehead, dark sweat patches breaking out on his light blue shirt. She barely moved and showed no expression.

Estelle leaned across. 'That man has no shame,' she said. 'He drinks so much, it's disgusting.'

Mponda was deep in thought and not listening. He was interrupted by someone calling his name.

'Hello, Pierre.'

He looked up. 'Oh, Jean-Philippe, hello.' Jean-Philippe, a tall man in a dark, well-cut suit with a white shirt and tie, was his banker. 'How are you?'

'Very well. But I won't detain you, I can see you have company.' The man nodded and grinned at Estelle. 'Pretty company!'

'Yes, indeed. But it's good to see you. In fact, it's good timing. I hope to have some business for you soon.'

'Ah, good. It's always a pleasure to work with you, Pierre. Have a pleasant evening.'

The man returned to his booth. Estelle asked who he was.

'He's a friend of mine, a financial adviser. He's well connected here in Douala.'

'You know I am studying accountancy. Perhaps I can come when you meet him, to learn and make contacts?'

Mponda patted Estelle's leg. 'I don't think so.' She was bright, but it was not a good idea to mix business with pleasure.

There were more whoops and cheers as the band started playing the old-time classic, Sweet Mother. Schmidt clapped his hands above his head. Dorothy signalled to Estelle and they went off to the bathroom together.

Eventually Schmidt sat down, breathless, and wiped his brow. 'Fuck them,' he said. 'The villagers. New Deal only now is beginning to make money, and it's about time. You know what we've invested, in the palms, in the mill. And it's only now we're producing oil. And we must give the revenue from the timber to the government. We were not anticipating that beforehand. That's another loss I've had to explain to the board.'

'Of course, Thomas.' Mponda made an effort to sound sympathetic. 'But much of the land is cleared, no? And you are producing. From now on your annual yields will increase. You knew it would take time, I think?'

'But it's taking longer than we planned. Our investors are asking when they will start to see a return. And now the natives are getting restless.' He smiled in a conspiratorial way, as if Mponda should be flattered that this term was not being applied to him. 'They're going to have to pay for the damage to the nursery. Those seedlings were due for planting - they must pay for us to replace them.'

The German businessman wiped his brow and tried to get the attention of a waitress by clicking his fingers, but they were wet and slippery.

Mponda did it for him. 'Why did you have so many seedlings in the nursery?' he asked as Schmidt snatched his brandy from the waitress, downed it in one, and ordered another.

'The land was not ready. The logs are piled high in that area, waiting to be taken to Douala. It's the government. These 'people don't know what they're doing.'

'You forget perhaps that I work for the government,' Mponda said with a straight face.

Schmidt paused. Then he laughed and patted Mponda on the back. 'But you're different, Pierre!'

The women returned and Mponda took the opportunity to slip out for a minute, giving Estelle a pat on her buttock and leaving Schmidt with a young woman in a short skirt sitting either side of him.

It was warm outside, but a gentle breeze made it pleasant. The bass guitar thudded through the walls of the nightclub. Cars were waiting with their drivers, and two bouncers were on the door. Otherwise, the street was deserted.

Mponda brought up a number on the black phone. 'Good evening, Chief. How are things?'

'Mr Mponda. How are you?'

'I am well. But I've heard not all is good in Bafuke?'

'It is true, sir. You know the farmers I told you about? The ones who had the … the problem with the park ranger and asked the wrestler to help?'

'Yes, you told me about them. But that was all blamed on an elephant.'

'Yes, an elephant, that's right. But now … it's bad. The farmers cut down all the seedlings in the New Deal nursery, and now someone's killed them. And New Deal, you will not believe it, they want compensation. For all I know, their men did this.'

Mponda used the time it took the chief to go through what had happened to check his fingernails were clean.

'Mr Mponda, you helped me before … and my children. But now … my people are not happy, and we are afraid for the future.'

'Don't worry, Chief. I will sort something out. Leave it with me.' Mponda ended the call, then made another on the cheap phone. 'Jeki.'

Chapter 42

'One touch, pass. One touch, pass.' Samson instructed from the touchline. The session was simple: no goals; keep the ball from the other team; concentrate on passing. He wanted to drum it into them. Get their heads in the right place. The rest would follow. 'One touch to control the ball, then pass. If you can do that, you can beat anyone.'

It was eight in the morning. After the terrible news Le Congo and the young reporter had told him about the night before, it was hard to concentrate on football, but he couldn't disappoint the boys. They were depending on him to get them back to winning ways.

The day was warming up. Another thirty minutes would be enough for now. A pass went astray, and the ball landed at his feet. He juggled it a few times then held it under his arm and summoned the players for another lecture.

'Think ahead,' Samson said. 'This is about awareness, of what's going on around you ... *for make we understand everything weydey happen for your corner. Where your mates demdey, where your opponents dey, who dey run go where, where space for control dey ...*'

The boys stood before him, sweating, hands on hips or leaning over, panting.

'Anticipate! You must know who you're going to pass to, even before the ball is passed to you. When the ball is passed to a teammate, you must think, who is he going to pass to next? Look around. Think *three* passes ahead ...'

Out of the corner of his eye he saw Ngwa, the national park tourist centre manager, and his assistant, Adam Tarkang, walking over.

'... read the game. *Football no only be about playing, you need for use sense too for play well.*' He threw the ball to the boys and they carried on with their passing.

'Good morning, Coach.' Ngwa wiped his brow. He looked worried. 'I thought we might find you here. Working on new tactics?'

Samson felt his head jerk. 'No,' he said, turning the movement into a shake from side to side. 'We are working on basics. How are you, sir?'

'Good, thank you. But you've heard about the farmers in Bafuke? It's a bad business. Really, very bad. You know the police are saying it might have been these farmers who killed Alex Ebot, and then vandalised the plantation nursery. Now the villagers think New Deal security men killed the farmers in retaliation.'

'Well, the Congolese investigator never believed Alex was killed by an elephant.'

'Yes, um ... well, we don't know,' Ngwa said. 'That's what I wanted to talk to you about. I wanted to ask you something. We heard there was a newspaper reporter down there, a woman? And that you know her?'

'I don't know her. She had my number and she gave it to the Congolese, and they've been over for a drink the last two evenings. Her name's Sally Bintu, from the *Courier*.' Samson noticed Adam Tarkang look away. 'She wrote the first report about Alex's death and the elephant.'

Ngwa screwed up his face. 'Well, do you know what she's going to write this time? Because I was hoping it might not be necessary for her to go into the business about Alex. I mean, in fact, nothing's been proved, so it might be confusing, and it would be wrong to spread unfounded rumours.'

Anything to protect the reputation of his park, Samson thought. 'It's not my place to interfere, and like I said, I don't know her. But you can call her.' He searched his pockets and showed her card to Ngwa.

'Oh, good, right. Thank you.' Ngwa took down the number. He looked far from satisfied. 'By the way, Coach,' he added, his tone brightening, 'the hotel people are coming to see us today with their plans. They're offering us space for a desk in the reception area, which is very generous.'

'Is that right?' Samson blinked twice.

'Yes. The developers say the hotel want to sponsor new infrastructure for the park. They'll repair the bridge. They're even offering to rebuild one of the camps destroyed by poachers and to make it available for hotel guests to stay in. These are exciting times for Bakunda National Park.'

Samson sighed and turned his attention to the training session. The players were working hard, calling to each other for the ball. 'One touch, pass,' he repeated. 'One touch pass.' There were cries and scuffs of dust as the team without the ball tried to intercept it.

'You never know,' Ngwa added, as he and Tarkang turned to leave, 'these people may like to sponsor a football team.'

'They're taking our pitch, so I don't think so.' Samson kicked the hard ground and blew his whistle to end the session. 'Well done boys,' he told them as they trooped off. 'Keep at it and you'll see the results when we next play. Ball control, passing, awareness ... they'll all be improved.'

Samson picked up the ball and headed for the San Siro. Ngwa might be excited, but with all that had been going on, it felt to Samson like Bakunda was under a cloud.

'*Papa no worry. We fit still do am.* We can still do it.' Sonny was shouting from the roadside, grinning and punching the air. 'The Lions will win the league!'

'*Na so, Sonny*. That's the spirit.'

The boy waved. Samson smiled. Without knowing it, he thought, kids had a way of picking you up when you were down. His own big dreams, of going to Europe to watch Cameroon play in the World Cup, then to play in Europe, had come to nothing. But little dreams still meant something. And it struck him now that success for the Lions – if it came – would be a boost for the whole town.

Chapter 43

Patrice knew when he woke that something was wrong. His head hurt. He felt sick. It wasn't a hangover. He wanted to stay in bed, but he had things to do. He staggered to the bathroom and turned the shower tap, but no water came out, so he tipped a few cupfuls from the bucket over his head. It made no difference to the grogginess inside.

He didn't want breakfast. He walked out to the road. The morning heat was thicker and heavier than usual, the white sunlight brighter. It was an effort to lift his arm to hail an *okada*. Getting on the motorcycle left him breathless and giddy.

As they approached the San Siro, he saw Coach Samson striding off the dusty football pitch, bouncing a ball up and down.

The coach beckoned the *okada* to pull over. 'Good morning, Le Congo.'

'Coach ... how's it going?' It was exhausting to speak.

'Everybody's shocked by what happened. And you? Is there more news from the village?'

'No, I don't think so. I don't know.'

'Where's the reporter? The tourist centre manager was asking after her.'

'She left early. She went to Buea, I think. Her paper comes out tomorrow.'

'Okay. That's good. See you later.' The coach turned to walk off but turned back. 'Are you alright, Le Congo? You look tired.'

'No, yes, I'm fine.' Patrice wasn't sure what he felt, except it wasn't fine. 'I had a bad night's sleep.'

The coach waved, and crossed the road to his bar. Patrice rubbed his fingers through his hair, trying to focus on what he had to do. He tapped the *okada* man on the shoulder and they sped off to the district hospital. He got off outside the iron gates as a funeral procession was passing out. He wiped his sweaty brow and made his way to the room at the end of the veranda, and tapped on the dark wood-panelled door. Whenever it was that he'd visited this room before, it felt like a long, long time ago.

A familiar cough came from the other side and Patrice let himself in.

'Well, well.' Dr Sylvestre Atemkeng was looking up at him over his glasses. 'You've come back for more. One visit's enough for most people.'

The stench alone testified to the mortician's comment. Patrice tried to cover his nose and mouth, but there was no escaping the sickly smelling cocktail of rotting flesh and human waste. Both tables were occupied. Both the bodies were decapitated. Atemkeng was bent over one of them. He had a young woman with him this time, wearing a white coat smeared with blood, like a butcher's apron. She held a clipboard and was making notes.

Patrice wiped his brow again. 'Good morning, Doctor. I hope you don't mind. These are the farmers ...'

The mortician nodded. 'I have no objection,' he said. 'This is Veronique, my unofficial student.' The young woman glanced at Patrice, apparently unmoved by the smell. 'We've finished our unofficial examination.' Atemkeng pulled off his gloves, walked to his desk and gulped some palm wine. He held out the bottle. 'You look like you could do with a drink,' he said.

'No, thank you.' A drink was the furthest thing from his mind. 'What did you find out?'

'You know, young man, I believe, extraordinary as this is going to sound, that these two men died the same way as the park ranger.'

'What?' Patrice looked at the severed necks of the two bodies before him.

'Yes. They were decapitated, but after they died. Some days after. What is not so obvious is that both men suffered broken ribs and punctured lungs.'

The former pathologist was talking rapidly and Patrice was having trouble keeping up. 'You mean they were killed by the same person who killed the ranger?'

'Mr Le Congo, I can talk about what, not who. But, having said that, I can confirm the method to be almost identical.'

'Almost?'

'You will recall the ranger suffered broken ribs on both sides of his body. These men's ribs were broken on one side each.' Atemkeng pointed with his finger at the naked bodies. 'This one here, on the right side; that one on the left.'

Patrice's head was spinning.

'Incredibly, it appears he held them both, one in each arm, and squeezed them to death at the same time. It was not so easy for him; there are signs of a struggle. One of the victims suffered lacerations to the side of his body, but not fatal ones.

The other has been punched hard in the mouth and all around his head.'

Patrice looked for a chair, and sat. He looked at the student, who acknowledged the hypothesis with pursed lips.

'I say *he*,' the mortician continued, 'though it's hard, as I said before, to imagine a human being with such strength.'

Patrice rubbed his head again, trying to work it out. 'So this means … when do you think they were killed?'

'I can't say precisely. But given the state of decay of the food in their stomachs, I would say up to a week ago, maximum.'

Patrice put his hand on his chest, fearing he was about to be sick. 'And minimum?'

'Four days? Are you alright, young man? You look pale.'

'I'm fine.'

Atemkeng took another drink from his bottle. 'I believe they were killed and then left in the forest, partially buried - hence all the mud they brought in with them. I can tell from the way the blood has settled and clotted in their backs and buttocks that they were buried front side up. As you know, they were found lying on their sides, so we can be sure they were moved there after they died. And it was after that that their heads were cut off. This would explain why there was little blood around the neck wounds. It would have been like chopping a piece of dried meat.'

Patrice recalled the scene; the two farmers lying outside the nursery fence and the looks of horror and astonishment on the faces of the villagers. 'So … let's get this straight … this means it wasn't them who killed the ranger …'

Atemkeng put his bottle in the drawer. 'If you want my opinion, unofficially, like last time, I would point out that they succumbed to the same injuries as the ranger. I would also suggest that neither of these men had the necessary strength. Look at their arms ...' He picked up one and let it drop. 'Good for working in the fields but they don't look to me like they are capable of causing such damage.'

It was hot and stuffy in the room, but Patrice felt cold. He swayed in his chair, trying to lift himself up. He was salivating. He had to get outside. He wanted to thank Atemkeng, but he was scared to open his mouth. He got to his feet and made it to the door, but his hands were so sweaty he couldn't turn the handle. The student opened it for him, and he fell outside into the sunshine, vomiting.

He was on his hands and knees. He couldn't get up. He heard the mortician tell the student to fetch a doctor. His mind was swirling but another thought came to him and stuck firmly: if the farmers had been dead four days, it couldn't have been them who vandalised the nursery.

He struggled to his feet. He had to tell Andre and Francis about this. But he crashed back to the ground. He was gasping for breath. His energy was draining. The student was dabbing his forehead with a rag. The mortician was saying something, but Patrice couldn't make out what.

The next thing he knew, he was lying on a bed in a strange room. The sheet beneath him was wet. He was sweating and shivering. He had to get to Bafuke. But he couldn't move.

Chapter 44

It was a moonlit night. Jeki poured the powder into the pot on the fire and stirred it for five minutes, as the old lady in the market had instructed. He filled a cup with the *niya* and let it cool a little. The old lady had said the *niya* would taste different; it would be stronger. *Sáŋgó* had told him she was a wise woman.

He could smell the potion was bitter. He clenched his fist, lifted the cup, and drank it all in one. Like a red-hot rasp, it burned and scoured his throat. Immediately he felt a rush, intense and compelling.

Inside his shack he tore off his shirt and stood over the weights, and lifted the bar with ease. He saw himself in the mirror, in the golden candlelight, and roared so loudly that the walls shook. He was invincible.

He let down the weights gently, as if laying a baby to sleep, and picked up his machete, turning it in his hand so the freshly sharpened blade sparkled and flickered. He tucked it in his belt and set off for the river.

By the time he reached the water he was on all fours. He untied his canoe and hopped in, then slipped downstream with the gentle current, holding the paddle in his claws.

On seeing him, the crocodiles moved out of the way to let him pass. And when he moored the boat and got out on to the bank, he heard snakes slip to the side. These creatures respected his authority, but with the dogs it would be different. They would not pay him his due respect. He would have to use his trickery.

As he approached their den, he heard barking. At least some of them were awake. They might even be expecting him. He circled round the area Sáŋgó had told him about; it was as he had described. There was a high wall. He climbed a tree and leapt over, landing without making a sound. A guard dog lay by the door. Jeki threw a stone on to the path in front. The dog jumped forward, pouncing on the spot where the stone landed. As it did so, Jeki sneaked through the unguarded door.

It was dark inside, but he could hear the alpha male breathing; its breath smelled of palm wine. He readied himself. There was a growl and a bark, and the dog's silhouette bounded out of the shadows. It was huge. And now the guard dog was coming. They were brave but no match for Jeki.

With a roar and a mighty swing of his claws he sliced the alpha dog's throat, releasing a torrent of blood that flowed like a tidal wave and carried the guard dog out through the door it had entered. A howl turned into a gurgle as the alpha dog collapsed on to the floor. Blood was filling the house like a lake. Jeki had to get out before he drowned. He jumped through an open window, over the high wall, and made for the river.

Barks followed him. The pack had been roused and were after him. Jeki raced to his canoe and paddled hard upstream. They'd lose the scent now.

It was morning when he tied the boat in its place and walked to his shack. All was still. He felt like he'd been away for days; far, far away. He was sure that *Sáŋgó* would be more pleased than ever with his latest accomplishment, for this had been the most daring. He felt a warm glow of pride. He had become as strong and cunning as Jeki la Njambe.

But something changed once he was indoors. The warm glow was gone. He felt cold and tired and edgy. He caught a glimpse of himself in the mirror. He looked across to the picture on the wall then back to the mirror. He didn't look at all like Jeki la Njambe. He looked like Jeki the motor park porter, who wrestled for next to nothing in front of sniggering crowds.

Chapter 45

There was something Patrice had to do. But he no longer knew what it was. The answer lay behind the door. But every time he went to open it the mosquito was there, blocking his way. It was bigger now than when he'd killed it. Its legs were bulging with muscles, its eyes were as big as dinner plates, and its proboscis was the size and shape of a machete.

He was struck down with malaria.

For two days he lay prostrate on the bed, hallucinating and feverish. At times when the visions receded, he was able to get up, to be sick and to go to the toilet, crawling across the floor to get to the bathroom.

His brain was in a fog. At some point, Coach Samson came to visit. Patrice was aware of him standing at the foot of the bed, having a conversation with the nurse. He could hear them but he couldn't understand what they said. He could see them, and he saw the coach turn to him and talk. He heard his name. He could hear other words, but they were flying past and he couldn't catch them. He wanted to tell the coach there was something important behind the door. He opened his mouth, but he couldn't speak.

On the third day, he woke, and for the first time it felt like the fever was breaking. His body felt weak and drained and he was soaked in sweat, but he could think. He was in a ward with seven other beds. His was in a corner.

The nurse was there. 'Welcome back,' she said. 'You're a lucky man.'

'To get malaria?'

'To fall ill here, in the hospital.'

She had a young face and a radiant beam which Patrice thought, on its own, would be enough to make most patients feel better. 'I haven't been ill like that for a long time,' he said. 'I thought I was immune.'

A doctor was walking into the ward. 'That's a mistake a lot of us make,' he said. 'Especially if we come from a different place and encounter a different strain.'

'I know the mosquito that gave me this. We had a long battle one night. I thought I'd won, but it's got its own back from beyond the grave.'

'And you're not out of the woods yet. The fever may return. You've had two doses of quinine and you'll need at least one more. In the meantime, rest.'

'You can read,' the nurse said. 'Your friend left this for you.' She handed Patrice a two-day-old copy of the *Courier*.

With a dizzying effort, Patrice propped himself on the pillows and began to look through the paper. On page 3 he saw a headline that made him sit bolt upright: *VILLAGE CHIEF SLAIN*. Below, in smaller print, was a sub-heading: *Latest victim in dispute with Anglo-German plantation*.

The report was thin on details. The chief of Bafuke had been hacked to death in his compound. It said his death followed those of two farmers from his village who were "believed to have been responsible" for an attack on a nursery that caused damage worth thousands of euros and an “angry confrontation” with the general manager of New Deal Plantations over demands for compensation.

Patrice let the paper drop to the floor and stared at the ceiling. Then he leaned over to the chair next to the bed and rummaged in his trousers for his phone. The battery was flat. He collapsed back on to the bed. But he had to get up.

The nurse and doctor weren’t around. He hauled himself up, and struggled into his clothes. He held on to the bed as he got to his feet. His legs didn’t buckle. He took the newspaper and walked unsteadily out of the ward and into the open air. It felt like early afternoon. There’d be a bill to pay, but he could settle that later.

An *okada* was parked outside the gates. Patrice gripped the driver’s shoulders and pulled himself on to the saddle. He had enough strength to say, ‘San Siro.’

Coach Samson came down the steps to meet him and called to Monique. Together they helped him up and sat him at a table and brought him a cold drink.

‘The doctor said you could leave?’ Monique asked.

‘I can’t wait there with all this going on.’ Patrice waved the newspaper.

‘It’s a terrible blow,’ the coach said. ‘The village is in mourning. They had their doubts about the chief – you know about that. Then, they say, he stood up to New Deal, only for this to happen. Now they feel like they’re under attack. And they’ve lost their leader.’

‘What happened?’ Patrice asked.

‘Someone broke into his compound three nights ago, climbed over a wall at the back, and attacked him with a machete. He walked in through the door of the chief’s house. The chief’s uncle was outside, he’s a kind of night-watchman, but he was asleep. He woke and heard the disturbance and walked inside, but the intruder knocked him over as he made his escape. He's a frail old man. He said it was too dark to see anything. I spoke to Alice. She said the chief's body was slashed to pieces.'

Patrice's head was hurting again. 'Like the nursery,' he muttered.

'What's that?'

'Nothing. I'm trying to make sense of this.' He was still sweating. Even fanning himself with the newspaper was an effort.

'Sally got the news out quick,' he said. 'Did she speak to Alice too?'

'It could be. Andre is not talking to anyone. Alice told me he's in a state of shock. He feels guilty because he was critical of the chief before.'

'Wasn't everyone?' Patrice's head began to feel heavy again. 'I suppose Sally was right to link the chief's death to the dispute with New Deal ...'

'One thing is leading to another,' Coach Samson said. 'First the nursery, then the farmers, now this ...'

'Oh, God! I forgot, the reason I went to the hospital.' Patrice was struggling to keep his thoughts straight. 'It wasn't the farmers who attacked the nursery. And whoever it was who killed the farmers, it was the same person who killed your old friend Alex Ebot.'

'What? Le Congo, you're still feverish.'

'I'm telling you, there's a killer on the loose, or killers. And now I see why they left the farmers' bodies by the nursery and decapitated them, even though they were already dead.'

'Already dead?'

'They killed the farmers and hid their bodies. Then they tried to make it look like it was the farmers who attacked the nursery, by leaving Ajebe's cap and phone there. And they left the farmers outside the nursery so it would look like they were killed in revenge.'

'But … the chief?'

'I don't know. I don't know how this fits in. But it must be connected. Do you have Andre's number? We must tell the villagers.'

Coach Samson tried calling.

Patrice carried on thinking. 'I was there when the chief was arguing with the manager. It was a heated exchange but surely …'

'I'm not getting through.'

'Then we must go.'

The coach didn't say anything, didn't move.

'Coach?'

Still the coach didn't move or speak.

'Well, I'm going.'

'Le Congo, you're not in a fit state to go. And there's nothing you can do for them now. Leave them to grieve.'

'We must go. Tempers will be running high. They might do something they'll regret later. Are you coming?'

Coach Samson was looking at the table. 'The thing is, I've got a business to run, and …'

'And what?'

The coach jerked his head and blinked and looked away. 'I'm sorry Le Congo. There's a big match tomorrow, and we need to prepare …'

'I don't believe this. Things could be about to explode. But what's important to you at this time of crisis is the Bakunda

Lions. Nothing else matters. It's fine, Coach, I'll get an *okada*. *No wahala*.'

Patrice stood up and turned to leave, feeling a rush of blood and like his head was about to explode.

'It's not like that,' Coach Samson said, calling after him.

Patrice climbed on to another *okada* and set off.

*

Samson went to serve a customer. It was someone who dropped in now and again. The man must have been sitting there a while, in a corner. He was wearing his usual white tee shirt under his black blazer.

'Hello, sir, I didn't see you there.'

'Good afternoon, Coach, I didn't want to intrude. Our Congolese friend is a determined young man, isn't he?'

Samson jerked his head and blinked.

'He thinks he's on a mission to save the world,' the man said. 'But he should be careful about meddling in other people's affairs.'

Chapter 46

The *okada* took the road all the way to the village, a faster ride than going by the river. They stopped twice so Patrice could get off and be sick.

The second time, the *okada* man said, 'You are not well. I don't want to catch anything from you.'

'You can't catch malaria from another person.'

'Who told you it was malaria?'

'A doctor and a nurse; I was in hospital'

'You suppose to still dey that hospital.'

Patrice hauled himself back on the motorcycle. His head swayed. His vision was blurred. But as they passed the main entrance to the New Deal plantation, he saw clearly that two police pick-ups were parked in front of the wrought iron gates. The men on the back of them were armed with rifles.

When they reached Bafuke, the *okada* dropped Patrice at the first house and sped off as soon as he had his fare. Patrice set off down the main street.

It looked like any other day in the village; women picking up dried laundry off the grass and carrying buckets and baskets on their heads, children with sticks walking after goats. But one thing was different; there were no men.

Patrice wiped his forehead. He felt sick again. He knocked

on Andre and Alice's door. No one answered. He pushed it open and called out. There was no one inside. The bed in the corner made him realise how desperately he wanted to rest.

Further on, at the turning to the chief's compound, he heard voices. It was a crowd, and they sounded angry. He leaned against a tree and tried to vomit, but there was only white bile in his stomach now. He wiped his face with his tee shirt, which was sodden with sweat. He walked on, trying to compose himself.

Twenty or thirty villagers were gathered in a circle outside the compound, taking it in turns to have the floor.

'*I be ready for do anything for defend our village*,' one said.

Another added, 'These people will attack us again. We must sleep with our machetes.'

The statements were greeted with cheers. Patrice saw Alice raise her fist. He looked for Andre but couldn't spot him.

'It has fallen on us to stand up for the memory of the chief and for the future of our village,' a familiar voice declared. It was Francis Akwanga. The chief's previous complicity with New Deal was forgotten now. 'We need to know we can count on one another. *All man ready for fight?*'

'Yes!' the crowd cried, as one.

'*We ready for loss blood for that fight?*'

'Yes!'

'Are we prepared to die for our village?'

'Yes! Yes! Yes!'

A man pointed at Patrice. 'The Congolese is here.'

The crowd turned to face him. It didn't feel like a warm welcome.

'What do you want, Congo?' Francis asked.

Patrice felt suddenly disoriented. 'I've come ... I've got

some information.' He was losing the thread. 'It wasn't Daniel Ajebe and Louis Sone who attacked the nursery. They were dead before that happened.'

'We knew it,' a farmer said. 'They killed them!'

The crowd cried, 'Brutes! Cowards!'

'But …' Patrice tried to make himself heard, feebly raising his arm. '… it's not clear who killed them. Something strange is going on.'

'We know who killed them,' the same farmer retorted.

A woman shouted, 'Don't treat us like fools!'

Patrice turned to see Louisa, Ajebe's widow, standing next to Alice. He tried to catch Alice's eye but she looked away.

'We know who killed the farmers,' Francis repeated, scowling at Patrice. 'And we know who killed the chief. The same people who've taken our land. Leave us to deal with this.'

'Go home, Congo,' another voice cried. 'We don't need you.'

Patrice wanted to protest, but he couldn't find the words. Everyone was shouting at him, their words flying at him like bullets. All he could think about was lying down. Then his legs gave way and everything went black.

It was dark. He was lying outside, under a roof. He tried to lift his head to see where he was but it was too heavy. There were noises but he couldn't make them out. He drifted off again. Then the noises returned; insects and frogs nearby and voices coming from inside the building. The voices were arguing … a man and a woman … Andre and Alice.

Alice was doing most of the talking. She wasn't happy. Patrice remembered the meeting and the hostile crowd - and Andre's absence. Andre said something in reply and a door slammed. A short while later Alice came out on to the porch.

She had a bowl of water and a cloth, which she used to wipe Patrice's face.

'You need to rest,' she said.

'Thank you, Alice.'

'You passed out at the right time. They were getting angry with you! But you need to get away from here, in the morning. This is no place for outsiders now.'

'What are they going to do?'

Alice glanced at the house. 'I don't know.'

'They've got it wrong. Why would New Deal kill the farmers or the chief? It makes no sense.'

'It's too late for talking now, Le Congo.' She patted his forehead with the cloth. 'The people in this village have been pushed too far. You saw the guards, how they treat us. And the police, they're the same.'

Patrice sighed, hopelessly. 'Who will be chief next?'

'That's for the elders to decide. The chief died young, before naming a successor. For now, it will be his uncle, Tabeng Ewang. But he is old and frail. He cannot help us. We are at the mercy of God.'

He slept again. Alice woke him at daybreak and walked with him up the main street to the edge of the village. Patrice was still unsteady. The small wooden houses, with their tin roofs and tidy porches, looked how he felt: fragile. He feared for these people caught up in a conflict with a powerful enemy.

They found the road to Bakunda town was blocked. Armed men in beige uniforms were not letting anyone leave.

'Can't you see this man is sick?' Alice said.

The men said nothing.

Patrice was so feverish that he didn't have the strength to ask why the men had formed a roadblock. He wanted to curl up on the dirt track and sleep. Alice led him back to her house. She told him to wait on the porch, but it was in the full glare of the early morning sun, so he crawled round to the side of the house and sat in the shade.

When she returned, she told him all roads in and out of Bafuke, even the smallest tracks, were blocked; New Deal security guards had sealed off the village. No one was allowed in or out, and the mobile phone mast that served the village had been switched off.

He drifted in and out of consciousness. In his waking moments he heard the villagers gathered by the tree outside Andre and Alice's house - muffled discussions, now and again breaking into arguments. Straining, he leaned his head round the corner and saw Francis was there again in the midst of the group, accompanied by an old man who Patrice guessed was the dead chief's uncle, the acting chief.

He could see why Alice was concerned. Hunched over, the old man's bony fingers clutched a stick for balance. His eyes were glazed. He didn't speak. Despite his impressive traditional robes, cream-coloured with brown and yellow flowers, he didn't look like the leader the village needed at this time of crisis.

'We are prisoners in our own village,' Francis said. 'We are under siege.' The farmer noticed Patrice but ignored him. The villagers' anger was directed elsewhere now.

A four-by-four and a pick-up truck were approaching, their aerials swinging from side to side as they negotiated the gullies and potholes. They pulled up. Six men armed with automatic rifles jumped off the pick-up. The guard Patrice had seen before, with three stars on his shirt lapel, got out of the front of the four-by-four. He stood between the vehicles and the villagers, armed men on either side. Before saying a word, he spat on the ground.

'Last night, as you know, two men from this village trespassed into the New Deal plantation.' He scanned the group of villagers, looking for signs of any reaction. But he was looking at blank faces. 'They attacked two of my men. They beat them with sticks and left them for dead.'

Patrice was sweating again. He tried to make sense of what he was hearing, but he was unable to concentrate; his mind was swimming.

'Now I personally don't care about your dispute with New Deal Plantations. We are here to do a job. But I do care about my colleagues.'

The chief's uncle groaned as if in pain.

The guard continued. 'The attackers were seen running in the direction of this village. We believe they are here now. So, listen carefully. They have until two o'clock this afternoon to give themselves up. Until they do, no one enters or leaves. If they do not, that will be the end of your village.'

He spat on the ground again. Then he and the other guards drove away in their vehicles.

The chief's uncle whimpered, 'Our village. It's doomed.'

'Courage, old man,' Francis said. 'We will see this through.'

The group dispersed. Andre appeared at his door. Alice walked up and hugged him. Francis went across and patted him on the back.

Patrice rolled over and retched. There was nothing he could do. The die was cast. He thought about calling Sally but he hadn't charged his phone. Even if he had, he wouldn't get a signal. Like the villagers, he was forced to sit and wait and see what would happen at two o'clock.

Chapter 47

'Something's not right down there.' Sally waved her phone at her editor. They were in the *Courier* newsroom in Buea. 'I've been trying all morning - I can't get through.'

'You're surprised? With the networks the way they are in this country?'

If nothing else, she thought, Patrice would have rung to keep her updated. 'I think I should go.'

'You've just been. Where's the background piece I asked you for on land-grabs?'

'But it's a moving story.'

'Yes, and you need to explain to our readers what it's all about. Context. The bigger picture.'

Sally went to her desk and opened her laptop. 'The internet's not working.'

'Then go to the cybercafé.'

She stuffed her notebook into her bag and stomped out of the office. 'What kind of place is this?' she muttered to herself. 'How can a serious newspaper not have internet?' She was still tutting when she turned into one of three cybercafés within a hundred metres of the office.

'No light,' the manageress said. Half-a-dozen people inside were getting up from their seats.

'My God, I dong tire,' Sally said. *'This town dey make me craze.'* She walked to the next cybercafé, the World Link Centre, which had its own generator. Finally, she was able to sit in front of a computer terminal with internet and immerse herself in research papers and policy critiques.

She read everything she could find: *The Great Land Grab* by the Oakland Institute in California, which said a rush for crucial food-producing lands by foreign private entities posed a threat to rural economies and livelihoods in poor countries across the globe; *Transnational Land Deals for Agriculture in the Global South – Analytical Report based on the Land Matrix Database,* which revealed that five percent of the agricultural land in Africa (an area, Sally worked out, that was larger than the whole of Cameroon) had been sold off to investors, mostly from Europe, North America, East Asia or the Gulf states; *Land is Life,* a report by an international peasants' movement called *La Via Campesina* into farmers' struggles against land-grabs, which began with what Sally thought was a poignant quote: 'We are not birds that live in the air, we are not fish that live in the water. We are peasants who need to live on land.' Sally read every word of these reports and many more besides.

It's the same pattern, she thought as she sorted through her notes: farmers displaced; forests destroyed; collusion of local community leaders; lack of consultation; meagre compensation. And this was exactly what was going on with New Deal Plantations.

It was well past lunchtime. She rubbed her screen-tired eyes. She remembered the conversation she'd had with Patrice on the way to Bafuke, and her mind turned once again to Douala Manga's story and the German land appropriation plan. The original land-grab. It was the same thing. Nothing had changed in a hundred years. Douala Manga had tried to resist it and was hanged. Only the First World War stopped the appropriation plan going ahead. Now the only resistance came from powerless farmers - because their leaders, Africa's leaders, were prepared to sell the land they came from, the land where their ancestors were buried.

Sally kissed her teeth. She turned her attention to New Deal Plantations, starting with its website, where she was welcomed by photographs of smiling women picking pineapples. She learned that the company was seven years old and operated in Ethiopia and Sierra Leone, as well as Cameroon. 'New Deal stands for Economic Development and Environmental Sustainability through Partnership,' Sally read.

Under a section entitled Putting Communities First, there was a quote from New Deal Vice-President, Thomas Schmidt: 'We work with the not-for-profit NGO, Good for Africa, to see that everyone benefits.'

A photograph below caught her eye. It showed Thomas Schmidt switching on a brand-new yellow generator – in Bafuke Village. Chief Adama Takubi was standing next to him. A caption read: 'Power to the People.'

After more searching, Sally discovered two more things. Good for Africa had been established by New Deal Plantations and was entirely funded by the company, and New Deal itself was a subsidiary of a venture capital company called Thames Rhein Holdings, based in Hamburg and London. 'What do they know about farming?' she asked out loud. 'And what do they care?'

She wrote her article in thirty minutes and emailed it to her editor, under a suggested headline: *Up for Grabs*.

As she was printing a back-up copy, in case there was still no internet at the office, she got a call from Adam Tarkang, her contact in the Bakunda National Park offices.

'I thought you'd want to know,' he said, 'New Deal have blocked all roads into and out of Bafuke. They won't say why, just that a security operation is in progress.'

Sally thanked him for the information and rushed to tell her editor, suggesting again she should go back to the village. This time he agreed, and told her to take Raymond, the photographer.

*

The two o'clock deadline drew closer, but no one surrendered themselves to the guards in the beige uniforms. Patrice was still slumped against the side of Andre and Alice's house, drained and exhausted by fever. The men who were gathered round the tree in front of the house drank palm wine. No one spoke. The atmosphere was melancholy, the bravado from the day before conspicuously absent. It was as if they were resigned to their fate.

At the designated hour, the guards appeared at the top of the main street. They advanced through the village like an invading army, going from house to house kicking in doors, pulling out anyone inside and pushing them along the road. 'Move!' they ordered. 'Now!'

They reached Andre and Alice's house. Ignoring the men outside, they barged through the door. Alice screamed at them to go away. A guard brought her out with his hand over her mouth and shoved her forward. A minute later, Andre was led out, his face bruised.

A guard shouted at the men outside. 'All of you, move!'

'You have no right to treat us this way,' Francis said. 'If a crime has been committed, then call the police. You cannot by-pass the law.'

A rifle was pointed at him. Francis stood his ground, staring down the barrel.

Another guard noticed Patrice. He walked over and kicked his leg. 'Get up!' Patrice struggled to his feet and stumbled over to the men by the tree.

A shot was fired, shattering the palm wine gourd on the ground.

The farmers joined the other villagers being herded like goats at gunpoint. Alice held out an arm for Patrice and they followed. 'They're going to kill us,' she said.

A vision came to Patrice of a shallow mass grave, limbs protruding out of the earth.

The last villager brought out was the dead chief's elderly uncle, Tabeng Ewang. He was pleading with the armed men not to shoot him.

The villagers were taken to the river - two hundred people, the entire population of Bafuke. They were corralled against a steep bank. The guards stood in a row above them, their rifles raised and aimed down at the crowd, like a firing squad. A baby cried. Its voice echoed against the forest on the far side of the river, bouncing across the water.

'You have ignored the deadline,' the leader of the guards said. 'That is your choice. What happens now is up to you. I am giving you one last chance to surrender the guilty men.'

Patrice thought he saw Andre about to step forward. Francis held him back. And it was Francis who shouted, 'Go to hell!'

The chief's uncle was sobbing. A woman began singing a prayer. Patrice was feeling so weak he wasn't sure he'd be able to stay on his feet long enough to be mown down by the bullets. He'd survived twenty years of conflict at home in Congo only to come to die in peaceful Cameroon. He felt his mind drift away from his body and waited for the end by the side of that slow, quiet river.

The leader of the guards gave the signal with a wave of his hand. A sharp noise followed. But it wasn't gunshots. It was an engine starting up, and another, and another. Patrice stood, stunned. The villagers listened, their faces impassive, as the bulldozers set to work. The whining and clattering could mean only one thing. Their houses were being flattened.

Chapter 48

The Bakunda Lions arrived back in town after dark and after a win. Samson drove them round the dusty football pitch in front of the San Siro. Sonny beeped the horn. The players whooped and waved their shirts. The team had every reason to be happy; with other results going their way, a victory in their next and final match of the season would give them the title. Samson was proud of the boys; they'd worked hard and concentrated and got their deserts. But he wasn't joining in with the songs.

He drove past his bar and looked up, trying to make out the faces among the throng of customers. He hadn't heard from Le Congo since he'd let him go off to Bafuke on his own. If it had been any other time, he'd have gone himself, but it wasn't possible yesterday. Now he didn't feel like going with the boys to Tico's house and drinking beer with Tico's father, as he usually did after a match. Instead, after the lap of honour, he pulled up outside the San Siro.

'Papa?' Sonny was looking at him as they climbed out of the car. 'We won. *Why you no dey celebrate nah?*'

'It's too early, Sonny. We still have to win next week's game.'

Sonny feigned a frown, and he and Tico burst out laughing. Samson patted his son's head and the boys ran off.

The bar was busy. A party of teachers had taken over four tables, and there was another group of town hall workers. Adam Tarkang, the national park tourist centre assistant, was there with his manager, Ngwa. There wasn't a spare seat anywhere. Makossa music was playing loudly. The customers were talking and laughing.

'The whole town will turn out for the last match,' Tarkang told Samson. 'The Lions will bring glory to Bakunda!'

'We'll do our best.'

Others congratulated Samson as he made his way to the shipping container at the back, collecting empty bottles.

'*I glad say you dong come*,' Monique said, loading a tray with drinks. 'And about time. *We too get customers today*. See how crowded it is. I can't do everything you know. I'll be glad when the football season's over and you can help me here.' She looked up. 'What's wrong? I thought you won?'

Samson jerked his head. 'Have you seen the Congolese?'

'No. Not today.'

'Is there any news from Bafuke?'

'How would I know about that? I'm too busy here working.'

'I should have gone.'

'Well, you didn't. Take this to the teachers.' Monique thrust the tray into his hands and began loading another.

Samson did as he was told. It was as he was opening the bottles, gazing across the dark football pitch, that he noticed the people heading for the motor park, walking in groups of two or three, with bundles on their heads and backs.

Monique shouted; another table needed serving.

But Samson went over to the steps and looked out. There were a hundred or more traipsing along the road, looking like refugees fleeing a war zone. He walked across the football pitch. As he got closer, he could make out what they were carrying: young children, bulging baskets of clothes and food, rolled up bedding, even tables and chairs. Then he saw people he recognised. He rushed up to Andre and Alice.

'What's happened?'

Andre seemed not to hear him.

'We've been forced to leave,' Alice said. Her eyes were wet. '*They dong destroy all our houses.*'

'What? Why? How?'

'They brought bulldozers.' Her voice was breaking. 'They gave us thirty minutes to collect our things. Then they marched us out of the village as far as New Deal, past their gate. That was it. They said we can never return.'

'But they can't do that. I mean …'

'They say it's because people from our village attacked two guards. They took us to the river. Truly, we thought our last day had come.'

Samson blinked. 'This is terrible.'

'We are still alive. But what are we going to do? We have nowhere to go.' She glanced anxiously at her husband.

From the midst of the crowd, Le Congo emerged, looking ghostly thin, but better than the last time Samson had seen him.

'I'm sorry, Le Congo, I should have come with you.'

'Don't blame yourself, Coach. There was nothing you could have done. Those guards are out of control.'

Villagers were now sitting on the approach road to the motor park. A taxi-driver was complaining to them. '*Wunadey block road for here*,' he said, waving a wad of notes he'd collected from passengers waiting in his car. 'You must make way for us to pass.'

'Where can we go?' Francis Akwanga's voice sounded above the rest. 'We've been evicted from our village.'

'Go there,' the taxi-driver said, pointing to the far side of the motor park.

'No, no, no!' A man marched over from the waiting area, the motor park manager. 'This is not a campsite.'

A group of villagers surged forward. The manager tried to block them, calling to the porters for help.

Samson stiffened his frame and walked across. He raised his arms and spoke to the villagers in a calm voice. 'You can go there,' he said. 'The football pitch.'

The motor park manager and the porters stared at him. 'But, Coach,' the manager said, 'what about the Lions?'

'Look at these people. They need help. This is the only piece of open land in town. Where else can they go? Even here they can't stay for long if a hotel is coming.'

Francis looked humbled. 'Coach, this is generous of you. We will never forget what you are doing for us tonight. And one day we will repay you, because we will go back to our village, despite what those men with guns say. I don't know how, but we will.'

Samson picked up a bag and led the way. 'Come now, before anyone tries to stop you.'

The villagers hauled themselves to their feet and followed. They spread themselves out on the dusty field, rolling out their mats, settling down for a night under the stars.

Returning to the San Siro, Samson told the meat roaster to cook all he could.

'We can't feed everyone,' Monique said, hands on hips.

Samson pushed past. 'They've lost their homes.' He took two crates of beer and carried them across the road for the villagers. He was waiting for Monique to shout at him, but she held her tongue.

Francis and another farmer came to collect the beer. 'Thank you, brother,' he said, and he and Samson bumped fists.

The atmosphere in the bar had gone quiet. The drinkers hardly spoke as they watched the football pitch in the middle of town being transformed into an informal settlement. Many of them patted Samson on the back.

'You're a good man, Coach,' a teacher said, her colleagues nodding in agreement. 'You've done the right thing.'

Ngwa, though, was not happy. 'Is it true it was your suggestion, Coach, that they should use the football pitch?' the tourist centre manager asked as Samson brought him and Tarkang another bottle each.

'They've got nowhere else to go.'

'But the image of the town? What will visitors think when they see such squalor? And what about the new hotel? The developers may have second thoughts about their investment. How will they get these people off?'

Samson felt like spitting in the man's drink. 'They can borrow bulldozers from New Deal Plantations.'

Ngwa frowned and took his bottle. 'I'm thinking of you also, Coach. The way you spoke before it was as if this piece of ground was the most important thing in the world, and now you're giving it up.'

Samson shrugged.

'Papa?'

He looked round. Sonny was there with Tiko.

'Where will we play next week?'

Samson looked across at the villagers and rubbed his hair. 'I don't know.' He jerked his head and blinked.

Chapter 49

'What! You're kidding me!' Josie Mwinga's voice was bellowing out of Patrice's recharged phone as he told her about the eviction of the villagers. 'That is outrageous. My God! But you were there to witness it. That company will have some explaining to do. But …' She paused. 'Patrice, why *are* you still there?'

'I'm on holiday. You said I needed a break.'

'That is kind of you, Patrice. I appreciate what you're doing.' For once his boss sounded contrite. 'You know this is a sensitive issue. The African Union's position is to encourage these land deals. They call it inward investment. That's why I couldn't agree to you staying before. And I still can't officially authorise you to investigate what's going on there. But … let me put it this way, I'm not going to stop you.'

'Thank you, ma'am. I appreciate your unofficial support.'

'Can anything be done for those poor people?'

'That's why I called. You know your friend who works in the Ministry of Justice - do you think they could help arrange for an urgent court hearing tomorrow morning?'

She said she'd see what she could do.

He ate breakfast and took an *okada* into town. The evicted families had made shelters out pieces of wood and cardboard and plastic sheeting. The structures had formed around two 'streets', one between the two goals, the other along the faded halfway line. The goalposts stood like arched entrances to this new village.

Patrice went in search of the man who seemed to be making most of the decisions now and found him sitting on the ground at the edge of one of the penalty areas.

'Good morning, Francis,' he said, not sure what kind of reception he'd get.

'Good morning, Congo. You're feeling better?'

'Yes, thank you. How are you?'

'You can see.' Francis nodded at his things scattered around untidily. He'd made no effort yet to build a shelter.

'You slept in the open?'

'When the rains come I'll make something. If I'm still here.'

'You've got no family?'

'No.' Francis scooped a handful of dust and let it slide out between his fingers. 'Not here. My wife lives with her mother. She has our children.' He looked away, making it plain he didn't want to talk about it.

'Have you thought about what to do?' Patrice asked. 'I mean, about getting back to your village?'

'You have a suggestion?'

'I think you should challenge the eviction in the courts.'

'You think they'll listen to us?'

'I'll speak to all the people here, record their testimonies, and we can apply for an injunction.'

Francis spat on the ground.

'Have you got a better idea?' Patrice asked.

Andre came by with a cup of tea for Francis and squatted next to him. He pointed to the centre circle, where Alice was tending to a pot over a fire outside their new home – a cotton sheet draped over a frame of sticks.

Francis thanked him for the drink. 'Our human rights investigator here says we should go to court.'

'I was thinking the same,' Andre said. 'What they've done to us can't be legal.'

'You'll be wasting your time.' Francis scooped another handful of dust and let it slip through his fingers, like he'd done before.

Patrice looked from one farmer to the other. 'I appreciate there's a problem. The attack on the guards ...'

'You see!' Francis said. 'Our chief has been murdered. We've lost two of our farmers as well. But that will count for nothing. The court will side with the big company.'

Andre got to his feet. 'We're going to hand ourselves in to the police.'

'What? You're crazy.'

'That was the excuse they used to evict us. So ...' He went to his shelter and crawled inside, re-emerging with a young man followed by three children, who watched as their father and their brother said goodbye to their mother and walked over to join Patrice and Francis.

'We talked it over last night,' Andre said. 'We have to do this. What's happened is our fault. My fault.'

A short while later, Patrice accompanied Andre and his twenty-year-old son, Jerome, to Bakunda Police Station, where they confessed to the assaults on two guards at the New Deal plantation.

Patrice spent the rest of the day taking statements from all the evicted villagers aged over eighteen. They had all wondered in the past what would happen to Bafuke following the loss of the farmland around it, but they all shared the trauma of having seen its destruction, and most hoped to return to live and to farm there again.

He'd visited every family and was putting away his pen and notebook when three girls carrying buckets on their heads called out to him.

'Hey, you didn't talk to us,' the oldest said, laughing.

'You don't look eighteen to me.'

'Huh! I'm twenty!'

'Are you looking for a wife?' one of the younger ones asked, prompting more laughter.

'No!' Patrice said. 'But if that's your age, let me ask you some questions.'

'We're going to the river. You can come with us.'

The younger girls sniggered, and they headed for a track that led away from the back of the motor park.

'You're finding your way around?' Patrice asked.

'This is where I went to secondary school,' the older one said. 'Besides, it's not a big town. It's not like Douala or even Bakingi.'

Close up, Patrice could tell she was no child. She had a young face with bright cheeks, but there was a worldly-wise look in her eyes. She said her name was Noela and the younger girls were her sisters. She gave her account of what she'd witnessed the day before in a matter-of-fact way.

'You must feel terrible about what happened to your home?'

'Well, yes and no,' she said, thoughtfully. 'Those guards tried to humiliate and terrify us, and that makes me feel angry. And it's the only home I've ever had, so yes, I am sad as well. And I'm sad for my parents, who worked hard all their lives and built that home themselves. But ... I know this sounds bad ... I wanted to leave that place. There's nothing there for young people, no future at all.'

'Why didn't you leave before?'

'And do what? Where would I go? I don't know anybody anywhere, and I'm not going to the city on my own.'

'Is that where you want to go, the city? Douala?'

'I don't know. I don't want to go and sell groundnuts by the side of the road. But I have no qualifications.'

'You didn't go to college?'

'Pah! How would I pay for that?'

The walk to the river was longer than Patrice had expected. 'Is this where you'll have to come to get water every day?'

'No, there's a tap by the motor park but it's dry right now. Or we can go to the bridge, where the children swim and the women do the washing. We came this way because it's quiet.'

As the river came into earshot, they passed a small shack, set back from the track, on its own, almost hidden against the trees. Beside it were the ashes of a small fire. And hanging from a tree branch was a cracked gourd.

'Huh!' Noela said. 'Ngoti. You know that?'

'Is it for the birds?'

'It's a game, an old game from long ago. Boys throw bamboo spears and try to break the gourd, to show who has the best shot. I never saw it myself. I don't even know if it's a real game. In the old stories, the losers of the game die.'

The mention of bamboo spears caused Patrice to stop and think. He recalled the scene in the farmer's field in the clearing in the national park, and looked again at the shack. 'Do you know who lives here?'

'No. Whoever it is, he is either old or idle.'

Chapter 50

Jeki pressed his face against the wooden slats and peered through a crack, sweating and confused. 'Is Njambe, Jeki la Njambe's father, playing a trick on me? Is this a test?' *Sáŋgó* had told him the more tasks he completed, the more Njambe's spirit would be trying constantly to weaken him. And now here, outside his house, was the Congolese man *Sáŋgó* had told him about, the agitator who was poking his nose into *Sáŋgó's* business. *Sáŋgó* had said the day might come when Jeki would have to deal with him. 'Is this the day? Or is this Njambe causing mischief?'

The girl looked nice. But why was she with the Congolese? And why was he with her, a village girl? And why was she telling him about ngoti? Now the Congolese was looking at Jeki's shack. Jeki kept still, and watched. He could strike the Congolese now, while he had the chance. *Sáŋgó* would be pleased! But no. He must wait for *Sáŋgó's* orders.

The Congolese and the girl carried on down the track, and Jeki slid to his knees in despair. He had no choice but to obey *Sáŋgó*. He didn't want to do these things but *Sáŋgó* had a hold over him. He put his hands over his ears, trying to blot out troubling memories, like what had happened in the forest with the ranger when all this had started.

He thought of his mother. He could always turn to his mother for comfort. He remembered the time he ran to her after some boys had said he was a freak and had thrown stones at him. He felt his mother's arms around him and heard her voice.

Then he remembered something else, something he'd long since forgotten - a conversation they'd had that day.

'Bisá bábané di tá ndē bénumédí bá túmbá,' she'd said, stroking his face with her long fingers. 'We are both outcasts, Jeki. But we have each other.'

'Why are you an outcast, Mama?'

She'd looked away and taken a long time to answer. When she did finally speak, her voice was quiet, and it was as if she was in pain. Even now, as her words came back to him, Jeki had to strain his ears to hear her.

'I was attacked by a man, when I was at college. He was a student, like me. I thought he was my friend. I let him come near me but he took advantage of me. When I got home that night my father asked me what had happened; he could tell I was upset. I didn't want to say. My mother said I must tell them. As a family we should have no secrets. So I told them. And my father said I must leave and never return.'

'Why, Mama?'

'He said I would bring shame on our family. That day, my life changed. Before, I lived in a nice house. We had books to read. My mother would tell me the stories of Jeki la Njambe, like I tell to you. I wanted to be a teacher, like my mother was. But after that, after I left, I couldn't carry on my training. I became a petty trader instead.'

Jeki had never known such sadness as then, when he saw his mother cry.

'It was after I had to run away that you were born, Jeki. Even after that, the man who attacked me would not leave me alone. I never saw him, but I could feel him following us, me and you, or looking at us. He was a bad man.'

Jeki's ears had been burning with anger. He'd wanted to know who the man was so he could avenge his mother. But she said she'd said enough. It was best not to pick scabs, she said; they bleed.

It was strange, he thought, that he'd forgotten about that conversation. A few months later, his mother had died. Jeki had been alone ever since. He'd had to fend for himself, taken odd jobs wherever he could find them, until he got into fights, and then he'd move on. Till he ended up here. He'd built himself this house, like Jeki la Njambe had built his.

Jeki felt his cheeks were wet with tears. He looked around. His house was a shack. But it had held firm against the hardest rain and strongest winds that nature could throw at it. He should be proud. And that's what *Sáŋgó* had said. Whenever he had doubts, he must know they are the work of Njambe, who is for ever trying to undermine him. He must resist them by taking strength from his achievements and his future greatness, which *Sáŋgó* said was inevitable.

He slapped his head to rid himself of bad thoughts. He went outside, climbed the tree, untied the string, and let the gourd drop to the ground. As he was sliding back along the branch to the main trunk, he heard a voice.

'Look, it's fallen.' It was the girl.

Jeki's heart started beating fast. The girl and the Congolese came into view, walking up the track. He manoeuvred himself round the tree. He was out of view, but gripping on to the trunk with his knees.

'Does that mean he's lost the game?' the Congolese asked. 'And will have to die?'

This man thought he was so clever with his jokes.

The girl chuckled. 'Where are my sisters?' she said, looking around. 'Lucille? Cynthia?' There was no answer. She told the Congolese not to wait.

But instead of continuing up the track, he went to knock on Jeki's door. He stood there a long time. Eventually he said goodbye to the girl, and went on his way.

Jeki was straining now to keep hold of the tree. The bark was digging into his thighs and ankles. But the girl was still waiting for her sisters. And then she walked towards the tree, and stooped to pick up the gourd. What was she doing? Why was she holding it like that, inspecting it with such curiosity?

The pain in his legs became unbearable. He lowered himself to the ground. The girl was so interested in the gourd, she didn't hear him. He was close to her. From behind he saw she had a womanly shape he hadn't noticed before. He felt himself drawn to her, like she was pulling him towards her. He stepped quietly … one … two. On the third step the girl turned round, and screamed.

'Wetin you think say you dey do like that?' she yelled, dropping the gourd. 'What are you doing?'

'Shssh', he said. 'I … nothing. I wasn't doing anything. I saw you here … this is my … what do you want?'

The girl took a step back. 'I don't want anything.'

'Why are you here? Who told you to come? Why were you looking at that … that thing?'

She glanced at the gourd and took another step back.

Jeki took a step forward.

'No reason,' she said, sharply. 'I saw it hanging from the

tree before, when we were walking past. It reminded me of old stories we were told ... about Jeki la Njambe.'

He looked from one side to the other. 'My name is Jeki. I am a wrestler.'

She looked at his arms.

He wanted to smile, to reassure her, but he was panic-stricken. 'You told the man about ngoti.'

She looked at Jeki's house. 'The man said he thought we were being watched.'

Jeki felt an itch in his fingers and looked at his open palms. It was as if his hands had a mind of their own. They were pulling him closer to the girl.

'Get away from me,' she said.

Jeki assumed a wrestling pose. He swung at the hips and took another step forward. She stood no chance. She wasn't positioning herself correctly. There were numerous routes of attack. He could pick any one. She looked alarmed. He was ready.

'Noela!'

As he was about to pounce, the two younger girls jumped out of a bush.

'We saw you playing,' they said, and laughed. 'You're playing *pala pala*.'

The older girl turned and ran towards them.

Jeki looked at his hands and arms, confused as to how he came to be standing in this position. He looked up and saw the girl shooing her younger sisters up the track. He saw the broken gourd on the ground and crushed it with his foot.

Chapter 51

Patrice entered the courthouse with his witness/victim statements. Two hours later, he left the building with an injunction. The wheels of justice could turn quickly when one had friends in high places. He went directly to the football pitch, where he found the farmer Francis Akwanga sitting amongst his belongings, and gave him the piece of paper. 'The application has been granted.'

Francis stared at the document, not saying a word.

'It's an interim order, pending a hearing at which the respondents can also be present.'

'We can go back?' Francis asked.

'Yes. For the time being. The judge heard what happened to you. He was appalled.'

For the first time in days, Patrice guessed, Francis smiled, though his eyes were welling up. 'Thank you, Congo. You have given us hope.'

Other villagers gathered round. Francis turned to them. 'This court order says we have the right to return to our village, for now.'

A voice cried, 'Thank God.' It was Alice.

Francis nodded to her. 'We cannot pretend it will be easy,' he said. 'Our homes have been destroyed. But we have our pride. We will help each other. We will work together to rebuild Bafuke.'

There were quiet handshakes and pats on shoulders but no celebration. Everyone there knew it was one thing to be granted an injunction but another for it to be enforced.

'A few of us will go today. To put this piece of paper to the test.'

As the crowd dispersed, Patrice asked Alice if she'd been able to see Andre and their son Jerome.

'I took them food today. It is noisy in the jail and there are rats. But he will be pleased to hear this news ... to know he's done the right thing now.'

*

Sally and Raymond, the *Courier* photographer, caught up with the villagers as they were approaching New Deal Plantations: twenty of them, mostly men, farmers with machetes slung over their shoulders. As if marching into battle. She spotted Francis Akwanga at the front, then she saw Patrice, walking with Alice. She got off the *okada* while Raymond went on ahead to the entrance.

'You left it late.' Patrice said. He greeted her but there was tension in his face – in all the faces.

'We had problems getting here,' Sally said, feeling like she had to explain. 'A French newspaper reporter in Douala said he'd give is a lift but then his editor said he wasn't going to pay expenses. So we had to get a minibus taxi, then ...'

'Never mind, it doesn't matter. You're here now.' He pointed at two pick-ups, manned by a dozen guards in beige uniforms, which had formed a roadblock past the plantation gates. 'These people have to get past that in order to get to their village.'

The marchers stopped short of the roadblock. Francis produced the injunction. 'I have here a court order that entitles us to return to our village,' he proclaimed, addressing the guards. 'Let us through.'

There was silence, except for the birds and the insects and the clicking of Raymond's camera. Then there was a burst of noise from a radio. The guard holding it called to Francis, 'Wait. They're coming.'

Sally looked over into the rows of palms, stocky young trees with trunks a metre high but already spawning arched fronds and bunches of fruit. Behind the large wrought iron gates, a pink earth track, smoother-looking than any of the local roads, cut off at an angle through the trees. A four-by-four approached along it, kicking up swirls of dust. It pulled up, the gates opened, and two men got out of the vehicle.

'Remember them?' Patrice asked.

Sally nodded. The head security guard, who'd showed up after the two farmers' bodies were found, and New Deal's general manager, MacGregor. The two men walked over. Sally pulled out her notebook.

'Good afternoon, gentlemen … ladies.' The Scotsman touched the rim of his straw hat. 'I understand you have a request to enter New Deal property?'

'It's not your land and not a request,' Francis said. 'It's an order. We're serving you with an injunction.' He handed the general manager the document.

'Thank you,' MacGregor said. 'The company will need to verify this. If you'll excuse me, I will take it to our director of security, who is also our director of legal affairs ….'

'You're not taking that anywhere.' Patrice snatched the notice. 'Your company will be notified of a full court hearing, at which point you can raise objections. Let them through, as ordered.'

'I'm afraid I also have orders, from my bosses,' the general manager said.

'Failure to do so will be breaking the law,' Patrice said. 'And, as you can see, the press are here ...'

'No one is trying to break the law, I assure you.' MacGregor went to his vehicle, spoke into a radio, and returned. 'Our director of legal affairs says she would be happy to invite a delegation of representatives to come to her offices. The press are most welcome too. We have nothing to hide.'

Patrice turned to Francis and Alice. 'It's a delay,' he said. 'They're testing your patience. So long as it's not a trap.'

Sally looked at Francis, the unofficial leader of the village now, but new to the role. Francis was staring, eyes narrowed, at MacGregor. Then he looked at the villagers. They were looking back at him. Sweat trickled down the side of Francis' face. He glanced at the guards and their roadblock. His jaw muscles quivered. 'For now, what else can we do?' he said.

They were right to be suspicious, Sally thought. Douala Manga had learned the hard way not to trust the foreign land-grabbers, and nothing had changed since his time. A headline sprang to mind: *New Deal; Same Old Story.*

Chapter 52

'Est-ce que Yaounde vous plait?' she asked. 'Do you like it here in Yaounde?'

'Oui, pourquoi pas? Soon maybe this city will be my home.'

Pierre Mponda was pulling on his trousers. Estelle had come to visit him in Cameroon's capital. She was lying naked on the hotel bed, admiring a stringy silver necklace he'd given her, draping it over her long, pink fingernails. As he tucked in his black tee shirt, he looked out of the window at the presidential palace, a vast complex, though it appeared small from this angle, perched on a distant hilltop. He wondered how far away he was from that place. He was moving in the right direction, but he had to be patient.

'Now I must go. I have a meeting.'

'Does your wife know I am here with you?' she asked, out of the blue.

'Why would I tell my wife about you? I don't suppose you talk about me to your family.'

'Of course I do!'

'You speak to your mother and father about me?'

She laughed. 'Not my mother and father. But my sisters and my friends.'

'What do you tell them?'

She started playing with the necklace again. 'That I know this man who's in government, that's he's clever and he gives me nice things, that he's rich but possibly dangerous.'

'Dangerous?' He slipped on his blazer and checked himself in the mirror. 'Why do you say that about me?'

'You think I don't notice things?'

'Notice what?'

'That you've got a gun.'

He glanced at her in the glass, and patted his sleeve. 'You've been looking through my things?'

'I get bored when you go out. Why do you have a gun?'

'It's a precaution. There are armed robbers around, you know. The streets are not safe at night. I used to be a policeman. That's how I know these things. That's why I have the gun. But it's no concern of yours.'

She gave him a sideways glance. He said he'd see her later and left. As he waited for the elevator, he felt unsettled. Estelle was attractive, but she knew a lot about him. An indiscretion on her part, a loose remark uttered at the wrong time in front of the wrong people, could spell his undoing. If things looked like they were going wrong, those above him would simply cut the rope to save themselves. And he'd fall. He was relieved he hadn't told her who he was meeting that day.

He took a taxi to the Poste Centrale and walked the rest of the way, past the Cathedral Notre Dame and up Avenue President Ahidjo. It was early afternoon and hot, but not as hot as Douala. It never was here.

The Foremost was one of the many cafés on Avenue John Kennedy with narrow terraces overlooking the crowded street where people came to eat a quick lunch. It had emptied out a little by the time Mponda climbed up the three steps and walked inside. The deputy minister was already there, sitting at a table in a darkened corner, facing the wall, looking at his watch.

'*Bonne après-midi, monsieur*,' Mponda said, approaching from behind.

'*Bonne après-midi*, Pierre.'

Mponda took a seat on the other side of the table, which meant he saw the man's head and shoulders in silhouette against the white light outside. Still distracted by the conversation with Estelle, he didn't object when the deputy minister asked if, for once, he'd take a beer with him.

'*Santé*, Pierre! You have news for me?'

'Yes, indeed. Things are progressing as we expected.' Mponda sipped his drink, regaining his composure. He outlined developments in Bafuke village and where he saw things going from here.

The deputy minister nodded. 'Good, very good. Your game is working out as you planned it.'

'Everyone's playing their part. But we must be ready to act. Events are unfolding as we speak.' As Mponda said this, his black phone rang. He cut the call. Then a text arrived. He glanced down. *Call urgent.*

'Excuse me, sir. I must deal with this.' He walked into the street to make the call, and held the phone at arm's length as Thomas Schmidt squawked at him.

'Where the fuck are you, Pierre? The shit is hitting the fan really hard.'

Mponda told New Deal's vice-president to calm down. He'd be with him soon, and he'd sort things out. Afterwards, he made two more calls. One to the divisional officer in

Bakunda. The next, on the cheap phone, to Jeki. Then he returned to the table.

'I must go there.'

'Un problème?'

'As I said, things are hotting up.'

The deputy minister smiled. *'Bon voyage.'*

It was just as well that Schmidt had called when he had, before Mponda had finished his drink. After that, he'd have been obliged to order more bottles. And he needed to have his wits about him.

When he got back to his room Estelle was still in bed, watching a Nigerian soap on TV. 'I have to leave immediately on business,' he said. 'I will be gone a day or two.' He put a few things in a briefcase, including his gun.

'You need that for your business?' Estelle asked.

'I told you it's no concern of yours.' He clicked the bag shut. Then he leaned over the bed and grabbed her by both shoulders. 'Don't talk about this to anyone.'

'I'm not going to.'

'I'm serious, Estelle. Not to your friends, not to your sisters.'

She tried to wriggle free. 'You're hurting me.'

He let go and stood back up. 'Okay,' he said. 'As long as that's clear.'

'I'm sorry.' She sat up, pulling the sheets up around her. 'I think I'll go back to Douala. I'm not sure I like Yaounde.'

'As you wish.' Mponda smoothed down his jacket and checked himself again in the mirror. He wasn't going to waste more time worrying about her. He had other things on his mind.

Chapter 53

'No weapons.' The guard nodded at the machete slung over Francis Akwanga's shoulder.

Francis snatched hold of it by the handle. 'It's a tool not a weapon.'

'Doesn't matter what you say it is or it isn't, you can't bring it on to New Deal property.'

With a flick of the wrist, Francis threw the machete so the blade stuck in the ground with a twang.

It was a defiant gesture, but a gesture was all it was. Patrice sympathised with the farmer, but he knew, and Francis must have known too, that the villagers weren't going to be able to enforce their injunction with a machete. As if to emphasise the point, one of the guards cocked his rifle.

Francis jutted out his chin. But he got in the four-by-four, along with Alice, followed by Patrice and Sally and her photographer, Raymond. MacGregor, the general manager, sat in front with the head guard. They drove off down the smooth track through the palms.

'These trees you see are five years old,' MacGregor said, swivelling in his seat, as if addressing a tour party. 'And up ahead is the mill.'

A gleaming structure came into view, with steel towers and

storage tanks, so different to the ramshackle and dilapidated mill Patrice had seen in the Pamol plantation.

'This is as good as anything they've got in Malaysia,' the general manager continued. 'We're producing the finest quality oil and powering virtually the entire process through biomass waste that we create. Most stages of the milling process are automated now, and operated from the control room we installed last year – this means ten skilled operators can oversee the entire milling process, compared to thirty or so in a conventional mill. Incredible efficiency.'

If the man was trying to impress with his PR sales talk, nobody in the back of the four-by-four was buying it. Patrice saw the muscles in Francis' jaw twitch.

'So, Mr MacGregor,' Sally asked, 'you've displaced thousands of farmers and created ten new jobs?'

'After a process of consultation with local communities, and with the full agreement of the Government of Cameroon, New Deal was leased twenty thousand hectares, of which ten thousand are already under cultivation. There are ten jobs overseeing work in the mill, but there are hundreds of workers involved in the harvest and transport side of things. By the time we've reached full production, in another ten years or so, there will be more.'

'And what do you pay them?'

'Our workers here enjoy a clean and properly maintained state-of-the-art modern mill,' he replied.

Sally tapped her notebook. 'I've been told they turn up each morning at the gate to see if there's any work. And often there isn't.'

'Most staff are employed on contracts that include guaranteed minimum hours per month and accommodation.'

'They get free housing?'

'Yes, there is a bunkhouse for the nursery workers, and we also share the accommodation blocks at the Pamol mill.'

They skirted round the mill and on to a side road which led to an office block. Before they reached it, they passed three rows of whitewashed bungalows, with mowed lawns in front and thatched roofs, and air-conditioning units below the windows. Next to them were a tennis court and a swimming pool. Patrice guessed these were the living quarters for the mill managers, another world from the grim workers' barracks at Pamol.

The office block was a black glass cube, two storeys high. They filed in through the black glass door on to a white marble floor, and the temperature plummeted twenty degrees. Francis glanced around. He looked out of place in his flip-flops, shorts and torn shirt. From the snarl on his face, it looked like he wanted to smash to pieces every pane of glass and every tile of marble.

'Please, follow me,' MacGregor said. They went through a set of double doors into a room with a long wooden table surrounded by steel-framed chairs. 'If you'll wait here, I'll bring the others through.'

A few minutes later he returned, accompanied by a woman with shoulder-length straightened hair, wearing a black skirt suit and high-heeled black shoes. She was carrying some folders. Following her was another smartly dressed woman, but younger, who had a large note-pad.

'Thank you for waiting,' the general manager said, as if they'd had a choice. 'This is Constance Fombum, Director of Legal Affairs.'

The older woman nodded and said, 'Good afternoon.'

The younger woman was not introduced. Patrice guessed she was the other's personal assistant.

Constance Fombum took a seat at the head of the table, her assistant on one side and MacGregor on the other, and invited the visitors to sit as well. The head guard stood behind her. 'I was in conference with London and Hamburg,' she said. 'We're all busy people, so I won't keep you any longer than I have to. Now, I understand you have a document? May I see it, please?'

Francis walked round the table to show it to her, his shoes slapping on the marble. The contrast between the executive and the farmer was stark; her upright posture, his stooped, rounded shoulders; her fingernails, long and manicured, and his, short with dirt beneath them. She took the document, their hands briefly touching the same piece of paper, and looked at him to indicate he could return to his seat. Francis stayed standing where he was.

She skimmed over it and nodded. 'It's as I thought,' she announced, turning to her general manager then to the farmer. 'There's been a lapse in communication, had it not been for which, we would all have been saved a lot of inconvenience.'

'Inconvenience?' said Francis, bristling, stiffening as if squaring up for a fight.

'These things happen in our country, as you know. We are not a developed nation, so a lot of i's are left undotted, and a lot of t's uncrossed.'

'Tell your men to let us through. We want to return to our village.'

'I can't do that,' Ms Fombum said, returning the injunction to Francis and producing another piece of paper. 'You see, your court order is in clear contravention of this eviction notice we were granted two days ago, signed by the divisional officer. This is what I am talking about. The court obviously should have had a copy of this, in which case the judge would certainly not have issued the injunction. Unwelcome though it was for you, our guards here had every right to remove you from your village.'

Francis pulled back his arm, his hand in a fist. He was visibly trembling with rage. Constance Fombum stared at him, blinking. The security guard placed himself between them. Francis lowered his arm, his shoulders dropped, and he trudged back round the table in his flip-flops. His eyes were glazed. He looked like a beaten boxer walking to his corner.

The sight of the farmer being humiliated by this smug company executive made Patrice's blood boil. 'Let's see that eviction notice.'

She held it up but didn't pass it.

'That's a fax. Where's the original?'

The director of legal affairs lifted her chin. 'It's lodged with our country head office in Douala.' Her assistant, who was taking notes, was frowning.

'Why was this not produced two days ago by your thugs when they tore apart these farmers' homes?'

'I'm going to have to ask you to calm down, Mr ...?'

'Patrice Le Congo, from the African Union Human Rights Commission.'

'Human rights?' She patted her hair. 'Well, goodness, let's see ... does that include the rights of security guards trying to do their job?'

'That's a separate issue. The villagers have an injunction.

You can show your eviction notice to the judge at the full hearing. In the meantime, you must let them pass.'

'No, Mr Le Congo. That would be a waste of time. Now, I suggest you all return peacefully to Bakunda. I will see that you are escorted safely off New Deal property.'

The director of legal affairs collected her things and walked out of the room, her black high heels clicking on the polished white marble. Her assistant followed. The head guard took up a position in front of the door.

The sense of defeat in the room was overwhelming. The villagers had been bullied and intimidated, threatened, and evicted from their homes. The arrogance of the director of legal affairs was salt in the wound. Alice went to sit next to Francis, who held his head in his hands. Sally was writing notes. Raymond the photographer was looking over the pictures he'd been taking. Patrice picked up the injunction, an apparently worthless document.

'The courts can make all the rulings they want,' Sally said. 'But the divisional officer has all the power. If he's not on your side, you can't win.'

MacGregor, who'd been silent throughout, coughed. 'Right. I can see we're all getting a little heated, despite our air-conditioning. Let's take you to rejoin your friends.'

There was no tour-guide commentary from the general manager on the drive back to the main gate. The villagers were waiting on the road, expectantly. When Francis and Alice got out of the vehicle, downcast and shaking their heads, the mood changed from hope to anger.

'I be know say we dey waste we time for here,' a farmer said. He made to run at the armed guards but was restrained by two others.

A woman cried out, '*We dong loss our village.*'

The head guard stood before the crowd, raised his gun, and fired two shots in the air. 'Turn around and go back,' he ordered.

Patrice went to join the villagers. It was hard to look them in the eye. He didn't know what to say. He'd been the one recommending the conciliatory approach. It was his idea to go to the courts to get the injunction. Now the best advice he could offer was for them to walk back to town with their tails between their legs, to their makeshift camp on the dusty football pitch.

'No one's going anywhere!'

Everyone turned.

Francis had grabbed MacGregor from behind and was holding his machete to the man's throat. The guards swung round their guns.

Francis glared at them. 'If I see a finger move, I'll cut his head off.'

PART IV

Mbo'a jiba e si mabo bebango nyolo

A thieving dog will always carry wounds
(Douala proverb)

Chapter 54

Jeki stood over his weights once again, preparing himself for the next task. *Sáŋgó* had told him it would be the last. And it was an easy one. The Congolese was weak. Still, Jeki had to be careful. Like Jeki la Njambe's father, this man played tricks with his words. 'Whatever happens,' *Sáŋgó* had said, 'don't let him talk to you.' That suited Jeki. He would take the man by surprise and strike.

He bent over, gripped the bar, lifted it in one clean movement, and held it above his head. He saw himself in the mirror. After this, he would be free of obligations. His career as a champion wrestler could begin, he hoped. He dropped the bar and thumped his chest.

Next, he unfolded the paper packet. The powder had a musty smell and a whiff of *mbanga,* which made his mouth water.

Outside his shack, he crouched by the pot on the fire, added the powder, and stirred. As before, he filled a cup with the *niya,* let it cool a little, then drank it all in one, remembering what the old lady in the market had said: 'That is how you will get the taste of fire.' She was right. His mouth then his throat and his stomach burned as if he'd swallowed hell itself.

He stood before the mirror and saw his arms turn into wings. He flapped them and flew out of the window. As Jeki la Njambe, long ago, had killed Kambo the eagle and shown himself to be master of the sky, so he, the Jeki of today, was flying now, above the town – though taking care not to fly too low over the football pitch or the motor park, in case he was spotted. There would be those who envied his powers and would shoot him down given half a chance. He swooped and glided into the forest, swerving between the trees, dipping under the branches.

The clearing looks familiar. There's the ranger. And there's Jeki! Coming up behind the ranger. Why is the ranger struggling? Keep still! He's not listening, he's waving his arms, kicking his legs and squirming. Jeki tells the ranger that Ajebe the farmer will be there soon. The farmer wants to talk. But where is he? Why is he late? Now the ranger is still. He's dropped to the floor. Now Ajebe is coming. He's Jeki's friend! He watches Jeki wrestle. He knows how strong Jeki is; that's why he asked Jeki to come to help him. But he's not pleased. He's angry with Jeki. What has Jeki done? he asks. Is Jeki mad? Instead of thanking Jeki, he's making him carry the ranger into the forest. Ajebe's a rat!

Jeki circled out of the clearing, and then he was over the river. There would be fish here to eat, but that would come later. First there was other prey to catch.

He rose behind the hotel then swooped again to land in a tree. It was perfect, hidden from view, yet from here he could see the entrance and all the chalets. So it didn't matter that he didn't know the man's room number. He had only to wait.

Chapter 55

Francis pulled MacGregor's head back by his hair. A white light flashed off the blade pressed against the man's neck. The guards held their fire.

The general manager, who earlier had been talking so breezily about the wonders of New Deal's palm oil plantation, was now a trembling wreck. 'Please …' was all he could say.

Raymond was taking pictures. Sally pulled out her notebook. The French newspaper reporter was going to regret not coming. A white man being threatened with a machete was international news.

'Alice,' Francis said, *'come tie this man.'*

'You want make we get more wahala? Things are bad enough for us.'

'Wetin we get to loss?'

'Francis, think what you're doing. *You go join Andre for prison if you continue dey cause trouble.'*

Not all the villagers were so cautious. Three men slipped through the gate. One carried a coil of rubber cord with which he swiftly trussed up the general manager, binding his arms to his body with his hands behind his back.

Francis kept his machete in position. He shouted at the head guard. 'Call the woman. Tell her to come.'

The guard looked at MacGregor.

The Scotsman cried, 'Do it, man!'

The guard walked to the vehicle and talked into the radio, then announced the director of legal affairs was on her way.

Sally noted every detail, making sure she'd have an accurate record of the sequence of events. She glanced at Patrice. He was standing, hands on hips, looking as stunned as everyone else.

Another four-by-four arrived and parked behind the first. Francis stepped back with his hostage.

Constance Fombum got out of the second vehicle and walked to the gate, slipping in her heels as they scuffed the dusty earth. Sweat showed around her temples. Out here, it was she who looked out of place.

'Right,' she said. 'What's this? I thought we had settled everything in the office.'

'We've got your general manager.'

'I can see that. So, before we go any further, I suggest you let him go. Because I can assure you, we cannot enter into any form of discussion under these circumstances.'

This woman had a nerve. Sally looked at MacGregor. He looked like he was about to faint.

Francis turned the blade up, forcing the general manager to tilt his neck further so he was looking at the sky. 'Who says we want to discuss anything?'

'Then what do you want?'

'You.'

He gave a nod and two of the other farmers seized the director of legal affairs and bound her up with the rubber cord.

'Stop this at once,' she said. 'I demand ...'

'Shut up!' Francis cut her off sharp. *'Lock your mop.'*

She stopped talking.

The guards aimed their weapons but still held their fire; the general manager still had a machete to his throat.

'Let's go!' Francis edged sideways with his hostage towards the vehicles, followed by the two men holding the director of legal affairs. 'Come and join us,' he called to the villagers in the road.

A dozen of them cheered and charged through the gate, past the powerless guards. Francis called out again. 'Members of the press, please come with us. We have nothing to hide!'

Sally hesitated, uncertain what her editor would say about going off with hostage-takers, but Raymond was already striding towards the vehicles and mouthing to her, 'Come on!' She followed him. They couldn't miss this.

'And you,' Francis said, pointing at Patrice, 'Congo, human rights man. You can testify that we're not mistreating our prisoners.'

Sally got into the four-by-four with Raymond and Patrice, the same one they'd got out of a few minutes before.

'What are they going to do?' she whispered.

'God knows,' was Patrice's reply.

MacGregor and Constance Fombum were in the middle row of seats. Francis and two other farmers were crouched in the seat behind, holding their machetes against their hostages' necks. Another farmer was at the wheel. He turned the vehicle around and drove it down the track, into the plantation. The rest of the farmers trotted alongside, like bodyguards. The general manager was whimpering and talking about his family. The smartly dressed director of legal affairs was stiff and silent.

As they reached the mill, Francis told the driver to park. Then the farmers led the hostages through the plate-glass entrance doors into a deserted reception area.

'Good,' Francis said. 'Now, Mr General Manager, take us to your fancy control room.'

They filed though a pair of wooden swing doors with glass portholes, then along a short corridor to the factory floor. All around were steaming tanks, conveyor belts, overhead cranes, and a labyrinth of chutes and tubes. A rumble of engine noise and a smell of palm oil filled the sweaty atmosphere. On the far side of the complex, fork-lift trucks swivelled with tubs of palm fruits but apart from their drivers there were few other people. As the general manager had said before, it was mostly a mechanised operation.

Safe now from the guards, the farmers untied the hostages. MacGregor put his hand to his neck and rolled his head round. He led everyone up a metal staircase and along an open walkway suspended from the high roof. Constance Fombum caught a heel in the grilled floor and cursed when it snapped off. She kicked off her shoes and continued barefoot. How the mighty could fall, Sally thought.

Ahead was the control room, the size and shape of a shipping container, with a window overlooking the processing plant. More steps led up to the door.

The farmers and their hostages and their invited guests went in and were greeted with smiles by three men in white coats. The smiles vanished when the farmers raised their machetes and the control room operators realised this wasn't one of Mr MacGregor's tour parties. Francis told them to get out while they had the chance. They didn't hesitate to do as he said.

It was cool in the control room, and quiet apart from a background hum. Computer monitors sat on a long desk beneath the window. Metal casing lined the wall behind, with dials visible through small round windows. There were three chairs.

'This is an occupation,' Francis declared. 'We, the displaced farmers of Bafuke, will not move until the roadblock outside is dismantled and we have guarantees from New Deal Plantations that we can return to our village.'

He pointed at the hostages.

'Only then will we let these two go. In the meantime, we're going to shut down the mill. Mr General Manager, come and show us how.'

Sally watched in amazement as a group of farmers with machetes brought production at one of the largest palm oil ventures in Cameroon to a standstill. As the last machine whirred to a halt and the humming sound faded out, Francis ordered Raymond to take a picture of the farmers gathered round the controls, machetes and fists raised in triumph. Then he told the photographer and Sally and Patrice to go.

'Tell the world what's going on here,' he said.

The door was opened and the three of them left. It was like David and Goliath, Sally thought as they retreated down the metal staircase; the poor villagers taking on the powerful Anglo-German corporation. And it was her scoop.

Chapter 56

It's 2-2, the Lions have come from two goals down ... the ball's played out to the wing, the cross comes in, and Sonny's there to head the ball into the far corner ... he runs to his papa on the touchline and Samson picks him up and hugs him and they jump up and down in celebration together ...

A bump and a bang jolted Samson out of his daydream. He pulled over, got out, examined the puncture, and set about changing the tyre. He'd be late home. But he'd arranged for the final match of the season to be played in Mbimbia, the next town, and he'd found himself dwelling on the possibility that the following day the Bakunda Lions could be league champions. The boys had been working so hard. And with two of them coming from Bafuke, the game had taken on an even greater importance; winning the trophy would give the villagers something to cheer about.

Driving the rest of the way, carefully, through the dust and over the potholes, he felt a responsibility weighing heavily on his shoulders. He jerked his head and blinked.

When he reached the San Siro, Monique was wiping the tables. '*So you dong decide for return for house now,*' she said. 'I don't know why I work so hard at this place. Why is it me who does all the work? Only God can know why I do this.'

'Go sleep,' Samson said. 'I'll finish up in a minute.'

She carried on wiping tables and Samson fetched himself a bottle of Isenbeck and went to sit with the last two customers, Le Congo and the reporter Sally Bintu. They told him the news: the farmers had occupied the New Deal mill and taken two hostages.

'It's a brave action by the farmers,' Sally Bintu said. 'Really. It's sensational.'

Samson thought only a newspaper reporter could see it like that.

The Congolese investigator was less enthusiastic. 'They're desperate. But how will New Deal respond? Every day that mill's not working the company will be losing a lot of money. I'm afraid this won't end well.'

Samson agreed. 'It sounds reckless to me,' he said. 'They'll have to give up in the end. And they'll be in a lot of trouble.'

'These people have nothing,' the reporter said. 'So they have nothing to lose.'

Samson looked over at the encampment on the football pitch. 'They have the love of their families and friends. They must pick themselves up and start again. They can get work on the plantation or do buying and selling. Or they must go somewhere else and seek greener pastures. Kidnapping hostages will get them nowhere.'

Le Congo looked at him. 'I thought you were on their side.'

Samson blinked a couple of times. 'Of course I am,' he said. 'You know that, and I feel for them, in my heart. I have tried to help them. But they should know there's no point picking a fight they can't win.'

The reporter and the Congolese left for their hotel. Samson took the empty bottles through.

'You heard what's going on at New Deal?' he asked Monique. 'These farmers are making a mistake.'

His wife was counting the day's takings. 'No good will come of it,' she said.

'I let them stay on the pitch here, and now they do this. It's crazy …'

'You say they're your friends.'

'They are. Andre is my friend, and he's in jail. Francis is my friend too but he is not thinking about what is best for his people. He's playing a silly game.'

'Huh! You're one to talk. Do you think about what is best for us and our business? No! You only think about your foolish football team.'

Samson dropped the empties into a crate. '*See me foolish. Wetin you know about football sef?* Eh? Tell me Monique, what do you know?' He was shouting. 'You go on at me about this. You think football is just a game, that it's not important. But you're wrong. It's about big things. It's about working together. It's about spirit and camaraderie.' His wife was staring at him. She'd picked a bad moment and hit a raw nerve. But she should understand. 'You don't like football. But look at our boy. He is happy, because he likes to play football. It keeps his body strong. It keeps his brain clean. Through football he learns respect, for his teammates, for himself, for his community, for us.'

Monique kissed her teeth. 'You can be good with words sometimes, Samson, but you are mixing them too much. What I know is football doesn't put food in our bellies.'

'Not everything must be about money, Monique. If the Lions win tomorrow, it will benefit the whole town, and these poor people camping here.'

Monique snapped shut the lid of their money tin. 'You think your league is the World Cup. You take it serious. But nobody else does, not Sonny, not Tiko … for them it *is* just a game. This is not about the community; and don't pretend it's about those villagers either. It's about you. You and your dreams. You know, Samson, it's time you grew up.'

Samson shrugged and went to bed.

Chapter 57

The hotel manager was watching a Nigerian soap with his wife in the restaurant. Patrice went behind the reception desk to get the keys. He and Sally headed into the garden. No one else was around. The only other guest was Raymond, and he'd left the bar before them to get an early night.

They were approaching the guest chalets when Sally clutched Patrice's arm. 'What's that?' she said.

'What?'

'In the tree there. Something moved. An animal?'

Patrice looked at the dark branches, barely visible against the night sky. There was no movement, no flash of eyes. He listened. All he could hear was chirping insects and muffled voices and music coming from the television in the restaurant.

'A cat? Or an owl?'

She stared at the tree. 'It was bigger …'

'Don't worry. Come …'

He walked her to her door and moved on to his own room. As he turned the key, he heard a scraping sound. Coming from the same tree. He looked at it again. Nothing stirred. He opened the door sharply, and once inside he locked it and checked the bars on the windows were secure.

He was exhausted. He washed with the cup and bucket, then turned out the light, crawled under the mosquito net, and lay on his bed, reflecting on the day's events. Once again he tried to piece together all that had happened.

If it was the same person who'd killed the park ranger and the two farmers, it was also likely it was that same person who'd vandalised the palm nursery. And it was possible, given the ferocious way in which a machete had been wielded, that it was also the same person again who'd killed the chief.

The question was, who? Someone trying to stoke up tensions between the farmers and the plantation. But why? These crimes had led to Andre and his son attacking the two guards, and then the eviction of the villagers, and now the hostage-taking and occupation at the mill. Who stood to gain from all this? It was like a hidden hand was at work.

At that moment, on the verge of sleep, Patrice sat up, bolt upright, wide awake. Something was on the roof, bigger than a cat or an owl.

He heard it above the wall behind his bed. A rustling sound. Something – someone? – scurrying up the zinc roof, slipping and scraping. He followed it with his ears as it moved over the middle of the room, to the other side. Then it stopped. There was a different sound, a snap. He remembered the chalet roofs had dormer windows. His heart was thumping. He reached out of the mosquito net for the light, but there was no power. Before he had time to think what to do next, a sound of squeaking hinges and breaking glass was followed by a crack and a cry, as a man came crashing through the ceiling and landed on the floor.

'What the ...' Patrice faltered. 'Who are you?'

The man didn't answer. He rolled on to his hands and

knees. He was dazed. It was dark, but Patrice recognised the figure by its shape. He tore down the mosquito net, twisting it into a thick rope, and jumped astride the intruder, hooking it under his chin.

'I know who you are!' he said. He tightened his hold around the man's neck, astonished as he did by its huge girth.

Still the man said nothing. With Patrice on his back, he rose steadily to his feet. He was not tall, but he was made of solid muscle.

Patrice was powerless. His only weapons were words. 'I've seen you, in the motor park.' As he said it, he realised his assailant fitted the mortician's theory: *a man of unimaginable strength*.

The man ducked his head and threw Patrice forward over his shoulders. Patrice crashed to the floor. He turned as he got to his feet to see the hulk's outline stomping towards him, leaning forward from the waist, his arms out-stretched. Patrice took a step back, then another. But floor space was running out, and he was cornered.

The man sprang forward and grabbed Patrice by the shoulder and twisted him round, so he was facing the wall. The man was behind him, his arms curled around Patrice's chest. And he was squeezing.

'You killed the ranger,' Patrice said, straining his muscles to resist the pressure. He swung his elbows back but they flailed about hopelessly. 'And the farmers and the chief.' He tried to pull at the forearms locked around him, but they were like steel clamps.

The man was unimaginably strong, but it was impossible to believe the troubled porter Patrice had seen in the motor park was a calculating criminal mastermind.

'Someone's telling you to do these things, aren't they?' He sensed a hesitation. 'You're better than this! You've got a talent ...'

The pressure increased again. Patrice was gasping. 'This great strength ... you could be in the Olympics!' It was relentless. He was being crushed in a vice. 'But they're making you do bad things ... to do their dirty work ... because they're not strong and brave like you.' There was a moment's relaxation. 'You're being used. But it's not too late to stop ...'

The grip loosened. The man let go of Patrice and turned. In the dim light, Patrice could see he was shaking. Still he didn't speak. He was sobbing.

'Talk to me,' Patrice said, trying to catch his breath. 'Tell me what's going on. Help me bring to justice those who are really to blame for all this trouble.'

The man walked to the door.

'You can trust me. I will tell the police how you chose to give yourself up.' Patrice stepped forward and pulled on the man's arm – it was like grabbing hold of a telegraph pole. Calmly but firmly, he said, 'Do the right thing.'

The man swiped and caught Patrice on the chin with his elbow. Patrice fell. The man slipped out. By the time Patrice had picked himself up and got to the door to look out, the intruder was gone.

Patrice stumbled to the reception area, which was deserted. He banged on the desk. 'Hello!'

The manager came out, looking sleepy.

'A man broke into my room. He nearly killed me.'

The manager woke up sharp. He went through a door and returned with a machete, and went with Patrice to inspect the damage.

Sally came walking along the path from her chalet.

'You were right, Sally,' Patrice said. 'There was someone in that tree.'

The hotel manager called the police. 'The inspector says they will come first thing,' he said. 'It's late now.'

Patrice tutted. There was a killer on the loose, but catching him could wait till the morning. At least he - Patrice - was alive. 'I've never come across such strength in a man,' he said, rubbing his chin. 'It was dark, but I've seen him before. He's a porter.'

'From how you described it, he fights like a wrestler,' the manager said. 'The way he held his arm out and put his hand on your shoulder, that's what they do.'

'Yes. It was like he had a technique.'

'Wrestling is popular in this part of Cameroon,' Sally said. 'Personally, I don't like it. I was sent to report on a contest in Buea and one of the wrestlers squeezed his opponent so hard, the referee had to stop the fight.'

'That's what this man did to me.'

'The wrestler's name was Jeki,' Sally added with a chuckle.

'Is that a funny name?' Patrice asked.

'Well, I suppose not, but it's unusual. Jeki la Njambe is a character in an old Douala folk story. It's not so well known now but historians cite it as an example of an oral tradition, you know, stories handed down through the generations. Douala Manga actually mentions him in his memoirs.'

'Is Jeki la Njambe a wrestler?'

'He wrestles, he fights crocodiles, he flies with eagles ... he's an all-round hero.'

'Does Jeki la Njambe play ngoti?'

Chapter 58

The effects of the *niya* had worn off. Jeki made his way along the path by the river. He'd spent much of the night wandering in the forest. At some point he'd slept in a hollow by a tree. He'd had strange dreams, but he couldn't remember them. He felt disconsolate and adrift.

His head hurt, from when he fell through the ceiling but also from thinking. The Congolese had recognised him. And he'd said things that were confusing and upsetting. He was trying to get Jeki to release him – Jeki knew that – but there were things he said that were true. Jeki should be a champion wrestler. He'd believed that himself, until recently. Since he'd met *Sáŋgó*, things had changed. *Sáŋgó* had promised to promote him, but Jeki had had only one fight. And since then he'd been too busy with the other tasks.

Jeki turned up the track that led to his home. Dawn was breaking. As he approached his shack, he saw the tree from which the gourd had hung, and felt strangely empty. But he was immediately distracted because coming out of the door to his shack was *Sáŋgó*.

'*I diba á bwâm,* Jeki. Good morning.'

'*A Sáŋgó âm!* My Master! I thought you were in Yaounde?'

'I had to cut short my stay to attend to a situation at the

plantation. I arrived late last night. But this morning I received a call from the divisional officer to say the police have been called out to deal with a break-in at a hotel and an assault on one of the guests.'

Jeki felt *Sáŋgó's* piercing eyes on him.

'Is that a bruise I see?'

Jeki felt the lump with his fingers. He felt himself shrivelling in front of this man who had such a hold on him.

'Jeki, look at me.' The eyes were like blinding laser beams.

'Explain to me how that skinny Congolese could get the better of a champion wrestler.'

'But … but *Sáŋgó* … I'm not a champion. You said you would make me a champion. But it hasn't happened. He said I'm being used. And it's true. You have made me kill …'

Sáŋgó slapped Jeki with the back of his hand. 'I didn't make you kill, Jeki. You became a killer all on your own. That Congolese clown was playing games with you. I told you not to let him speak. Your task was to deal with him, and you failed. Now you must be punished. Get inside.'

Such was *Sáŋgó's* power that Jeki felt compelled to obey, like a child must obey its parent. They stepped into the shack. It looked like it had been ransacked. Jeki remembered the night before, drinking the potion, looking in the mirror, then things spinning round, then him spinning round, trying to take off …

'I overestimated you, Jeki. *O e bwála ká nyaŋgá.* You are weak, like your mother.'

'Like who?'

Sáŋgó's mouth twisted into a mean smile.

'*Nyaŋgó âm?* My mama?' All of a sudden, things fell into place. 'You knew my mother.'

'Your mother was a whore.'

The words made Jeki flinch like a kick in the chest, but he stood his ground. 'You are the man who attacked my mother, who never left her alone, who followed her, and me. This is how you knew where to find me. You are my father.'

'Huh! You might wish that, Jeki, but look at us; you could never be a son of mine.'

Jeki clenched his fists. 'You have used me, like the Congolese said. You said I was like Jeki la Njambe but you didn't believe it.'

'Don't be a fool.'

Jeki was thinking of his mother, who cared for him, the only person who had ever loved him. And then another thought struck him, and he felt calm. For once in his life, he knew what to do.

'A Sáŋgó âm, you are right. You are always right. Jeki la Njambe's spirit is within me, as you said. And as you have set me tasks, like Jeki la Njambe's father set him tasks, so my mission is the same as Jeki la Njambe's: to punish you for mistreating my mother.'

He assumed the opening position, holding his arms out, poised, ready to attack. For once he could look *Sáŋgó* in the eye.

He took a step forward.

Sáŋgó took a step back. 'That was a fairy tale, Jeki. This is real life.' He put his hand inside his blazer and pulled a gun from his trouser belt - and pointed it at Jeki.

Chapter 59

'*Sonny, make we leave this place!*' Samson saw the shape in the bed turn. 'It's the big day! Let's get moving!'

He went to wash. He checked the kitbag. He made tea. Then he picked up the clipboard he used for matches, to write his notes and draw diagrams for the players, and walked out on to the terrace.

So as not to be distracted, he sat in a corner with his back to the scene across the road - where twirls of smoke rose from between the rows of sticks and cardboard and plastic sheeting - and turned his mind to tactics.

He started pulling together strategies that had been forming in the back of his mind while he'd had to deal with other things. The Lions had played today's opponents, Mabengi Kings, earlier in the season and drawn the match. The Kings' main attacking threat was a nimble-footed right-winger, so the first priority was to make sure no passes got through to him. But when he did get the ball, the pressure would be on Moses, the Lions' left back, one of the boys from Bafuke.

Samson glanced round at the encampment. He knew Moses was staying at Tico's house, but his family would be in one of the shelters on the old football pitch. He couldn't dwell on that. He turned to his clipboard. Moses was a good player, but he liked to attack and sometimes got stranded upfield. Samson would have a quiet word with him and explain how important his positional play was going to be today. That was how they'd stop the Kings scoring. The way the Lions would score themselves was simple. The Kings' central defenders were tall, but they lacked pace.

'Sonny,' he called again.

A bleary-eyed teenager poked his head round the door.

'We need to talk about the game.'

His son withdrew into the shipping container.

Samson continued thinking on his own. The trick would be for the Lions' forwards to drop back, play deep, lure the two centre-halves up to the halfway line, then play passes in behind them.

Deep in thought, stirring his tea, Samson hardly registered the police pick-up driving past, then returning minutes later with Patrice Le Congo and Sally Bintu in the front. He half waved but his mind was on the time.

'Sonny, are you ready?'

With twelve passengers in his twenty-year-old Nissan Sunny, Samson had allowed four hours for the drive to Mbimbia, double the time it normally took. The kick-off was at 3pm, but they'd get there early. The boys would have time for a good warm-up, then sit in the shade with a cold drink.

'It's sad we can't play here,' Sonny said as the team set off. He was sitting in his usual place, between his papa and the gear-stick. 'The crowd would cheer for us …'

'It's fate,' Samson said. 'It's God's way of telling you that you still have work to do, that you cannot rely only on the support of our fans.'

'It doesn't matter where we play,' Tico added, encouragingly. He was sitting the other side of the gear-stick, sharing the passenger seat. 'We can beat anyone!'

The boys high-fived and cheered. Those sitting in the boot thumped the side of the car. Samson wished Monique was there to see how these boys wanted to win the league as much as he did.

In the corner of his rear-view mirror, he noticed Moses, the left back, wasn't joining in with the others. He might have unsettled the boy when he'd pulled him aside for a word about the marking job he was going to have to do on the Kings' right-winger. But a few nerves were not such a bad thing. They kept the players on edge. Complacency was their worst enemy, not the opposition.

'You hear that well well, Moses?' he asked, half turning his head. *'You fit defeat anyone if you want!'*

The boy's teammates leaned across and slapped him playfully on his cheeks, and when his face appeared from behind his raised arms and knees, it was smiling.

Samson smiled too. 'We all know what's at stake today,' he said. 'But if we remember all the things we do in training, then we'll win for sure. That's why you trained hard, all those early mornings before school. Now there's this one match, so remember, you never give up! Even if you are losing two-zero with a minute to go, you can still pull level ... why do I say that?'

Sonny answered, 'Because it only takes a second to score a goal!'

Father and son slapped hands.

'Exactly!' Samson loved it when they connected like this, talking about football. 'The game's not over till the referee blows the final whistle.' He looked in the mirror to see if his point had registered with the boys.

A couple of them responded, 'Yes, Coach!'

They bounced and squeaked along the road. They were making good time. A truck overtook them. As it passed, the driver beeped the horn a few times. There were twenty men standing on the open back, clapping and cheering, and Samson saw familiar faces; people who drank in the San Siro and came regularly to watch the Lions play. He beeped back. The young players whooped and hollered. Then Samson saw that among the supporters on the truck were some of the evicted villagers. After all that had happened to them, they were coming to cheer the team. It was humbling. He thought about his conversation with Le Congo and Sally Bintu the previous evening. He shouldn't have said the farmers were beaten. They too shouldn't give up. They had a right to hope. He jerked his head and blinked twice.

Chapter 60

The police pick-up rounded a bend, and Patrice saw the roof of the shack and the tree where the gourd had been hanging.

'That's the place.'

As the words left his lips, a gunshot echoed across the valley.

The driver braked hard. The inspector ordered his men on the back to jump off and take cover. He told Patrice and Sally to get out and hide behind one of the wheels.

They looked from under the vehicle as the police took up positions behind trees, guns raised. The inspector ran from tree to tree, edging closer to the shack. Then he called out, 'This is the police. You are surrounded. Come out with your hands up.'

No one came out.

The inspector called again. Still there was no response. He ran to the shack and stood by the side of the door. With one movement, he swung round and kicked it in, gun in both hands, pointing inside. Then he lowered his gun and signalled for his men to follow.

'Hold your fire,' he said. He waved to Patrice. 'Mr Congo, you can come.'

Patrice walked over with Sally. The first thing he noticed inside was an open window on the far wall. Then a splash of blood on the wall and a puddle of blood on the floor; the source of the blood was lying next to the puddle.

'That's him,' Sally said. 'That's Jeki, the wrestler I saw in Buea'

'It's the man who attacked me last night.' The massive arms were unmistakeable. And now, in the light, Patrice could see his face. 'No wonder he looked so scared at the motor park when the police showed him the photographs of the missing farmers. He'd killed them.'

The room was a mess. A broken chair lay in the middle. Pieces of newspaper and powder substances were scattered on the table. A bar with improvised weights on each end was on the floor in the corner. Patrice stooped to lift it. With both hands he struggled to get one end off the ground. *A man of unimaginable strength*. The mortician's words came to mind again as he glanced at the body on the floor. He shuddered to think how close he'd come to death.

A picture was hanging, torn, on the wall. Patrice flattened it out with his hand. It showed a boy in a loin cloth throwing a spear at a hanging gourd in the forest.

'That's Jeki la Njambe, from the folk stories,' Sally said. 'It looks like he idolised him. But Jeki la Njambe was not a bad character. So … it doesn't make sense …'

'I know,' Patrice said, looking again at the open window. 'What we need to know now is, who killed the killer?'

'That's a good line, Patrice. I'll use it in my report.'

*

Sally set off to find an *okada* to take her to the New Deal plantation, while Patrice went with the police to make a statement. As she walked into town, she tried to call Francis Akwanga, but she couldn't get through. She suspected the signal had been blocked.

When she reached the plantation half an hour later, the security guards had formed a new roadblock before the gate and were not letting anyone through. Police were there as well, but it was the men in beige uniforms who were in charge. A few traders had come, offering snacks to the policemen and a couple of local reporters who'd arrived from Bakingi. Sally wondered why the international press weren't there. Then her phone rang.

'Sally Bintu? Karl Bremmer, Berlin. We've been trying to reach you ...'

It was the first of several calls from newspapers and radio stations from Europe and one from the United States. They asked about how the general manager had coped with the ordeal and how Sally would describe his demeanour.

The fourth or fifth call was from a news agency reporter based in Nairobi, whose name was Frederick. When he started asking about MacGregor, Sally interrupted. 'You know there is another hostage, who's actually senior to him?'

'Sure. But MacGregor was the one they took first, right? And he's the one they got to shut down the mill? So I guess the focus is on him. Now, to check New Deal's statement, it was after the villagers were discovered farming in the national park that they attacked the New Deal nursery and then nearly killed two guards. Is that right?'

'No, not at all. They didn't attack the nursery ...'

'That's what New Deal are alleging.'

'It's not true. They did attack the guards, but that was after the village chief was killed.'

'But it wasn't New Deal who did that, was it?'

'No, but the villagers thought it was. It's confused and complicated ...'

'Yes, well, thank you, you've been helpful.'

'Don't you want to speak to the villagers who've been evicted? I can give you numbers to call.'

'Thank you, but you know the lines are not great, and it's not so easy to understand what people are saying.'

'I can go there later and translate for you.'

'It's okay, really. I've got a deadline, and the story now is the hostage drama.'

Sally didn't say anything.

The reporter in Nairobi softened his tone. 'Hey, Sally, you know how it is. But listen, I can call you later for an update?'

'I thought you had a deadline?'

'I've always got deadlines. You could let me know if anything comes out of the press conference.'

'Press conference?'

'New Deal's. They told me they're holding one today, in ...'

She heard him turning over pages in a notebook.

'... it's a village, called Enjem ... Enger ... I'll spell it for you: N-g-e-m-b-u-m?'

'Oh, that press conference ... yes. Ngembum. I'm going. What time did they tell you?'

'Four o'clock your time. That's in four hours, right?'

'That's right, I'm on my way. But listen, I may not have time to call you, as I've got deadlines myself. Bye now.'

Interesting, she thought. New Deal hadn't told *her* about a press conference. And Ngembum. Also interesting.

*

As far as the police inspector was concerned, the case of the Bafuke village murders was solved. The discovery of a machete in Jeki's shack - with traces of blood on the handle - and the packets of powder left him in no doubt.

'My men have talked to other workers at the motor park,' he told Patrice as they sat in his office at the police station. 'This Jeki was a paranoid psychotic, prone to moods and temper tantrums. Something snapped in him, and he embarked on a frenzied spree of violence, fuelled by drugs.'

'I don't think it's as simple as that. He wasn't acting alone. He was being used to provoke trouble between the farmers and the plantation.'

The thinnest of smiles pulled on the inspector's thin lips. 'Sometimes the simple answer is the right answer.'

'So why did he try to kill me?'

'You cannot know what is in the mind of a madman. Anyway, we are passing all the information to the New Deal people, as they are in charge of security down there for the time being.'

'What? How can you hand over a murder inquiry to a gang of thugs?'

'We are not handing over the inquiry. But with the situation as it is, they need to be kept in the picture. This is what has been decided.'

'Decided by the divisional officer?'

'I am not at liberty to discuss this matter with you further.'

The office was dark, but Patrice could see sweat shining on the inspector's face. 'A lot of orders come from the divisional officer, like blocking an investigation into the death of the park ranger and approving the eviction of the villagers from Bafuke ... now this.'

The inspector's eyes narrowed. 'I understand you have been advising the farmers, and that is generous of you …'

'Did you tell him about the attack on me last night?

'… and I am sorry that you were the victim of an attack. But please don't tell me how to do my job. We have your statement, and we will take the appropriate action.'

'What about finding Jeki's killer?'

'We have already begun inquiries into that. Given his state of mind, we suspect he offended somebody.'

'And they shot him?'

'That's enough questions. I have things to do, so it's time for you to go.' The inspector shepherded Patrice through the police station and out on to the street, into the white light of day. 'I have actually been asking myself, what is there to keep you in Cameroon? The farmers are pursuing a dangerous new course of action – was it your advice, to take hostages and occupy the mill?'

'That's ridiculous. And I'm not finished asking questions. There's something going on here that I don't understand, and I intend to find out what it is.'

'Be careful not to push your luck, Mr Congo.'

The inspector retreated into the station. It was obvious he had his orders, from someone who had their orders; nothing else, like discovering the truth, mattered.

Chapter 61

'Patrice!' He looked round. Sally was calling from a passing *okada*. 'You must come. New Deal are holding a press conference in Ngembum.' She patted the luggage rack behind her as the *okada* pulled up beside him.

'Where's Ngembum?'

'You don't remember it? Douala Manga went there. We have to take a taxi to Mbimbia and then another. And the second road is bad. We must go now.'

Patrice was reluctant to stray too far from the drama at the mill, but a press conference could be an opportunity to get some answers to some questions. 'I'm not a member of the press, you know ...'

'I can say you're my assistant; I was actually hoping you could help me with my research while we're there.'

Despite everything else that was going on, Sally was still thinking about her book on the old Douala king. 'We'll see about that,' he said.

It was nearly three o'clock by the time they reached Mbimbia, where Sally had arranged to meet Raymond. He'd found a car to take them on to Ngembum. The driver had no other passengers, so they had to pay for the empty seats and waited while a boy siphoned petrol into the tank. As they drove out through the town, they passed a football pitch where a match was about to start.

Patrice said, 'It's the Lions' last match of the season.' He craned his neck to look. A crowd was standing round the pitch, a dusty patch of earth like the one in Bakunda. The teams were warming up, the Lions in their yellow kit. He looked for Coach Samson among the mêlée of figures on the touchline and spotted him talking to two of his players, tapping his clipboard.

'No way we no go stop for here, Patrice,' Sally said, as if she was reading his mind.

They climbed the hill out of town and took a turning heading south towards Ngembum. The road was better than Sally had predicted, unpaved but smooth. They saw no other traffic except for a single logging truck, carrying five tree trunks, that came hurtling towards them through the dust. The blast of air as it passed almost knocked the taxi off the road. Further on they saw where the truck had come from: a track that led into a clearing where bulldozers and chainsaws were busy at work.

'This must be part of the New Deal concession,' Sally said. 'They've had to improve the road or they'd never have got the timber out.'

After that, the road shrivelled into a rough track, scarred by deep gullies.

'You see? During the rains, this is impassable. In the old days, Ngembum did all its trade with Douala, and for that they used the rivers. They never built a proper road, and the village has been in decline for a long time.'

Patrice braced himself for the bumps. The taxi crawled along the contours, jolting its passengers from side to side.

It took half an hour to cover the final five kilometres to Ngembum. They arrived to find much of the village abandoned, the shells of long-derelict wooden houses half hidden by creepers and hanging vines. The dwellings that were still inhabited were patched up with off-cuts of wood.

Given the state of the village, and its remoteness, the group of four-by-fours they came across parked in the shade of a large tree looked out of place. One of them, carrying the state broadcaster's initials, CRTV, had a telescopic antenna protruding from the roof.

The venue for the press conference was a circular, open-sided meeting hall with a conical thatched roof that stood in the centre of what was left of Ngembum. The dark wood posts and beams that supported the structure were worn smooth and would have borne witness to important gatherings for hundreds of years.

'Douala Manga could have been greeted here,' Sally said as they approached. 'You can't have read his memoirs carefully if you didn't recognise the name of this place ...'

Patrice wasn't listening. He was taking in the scene inside. A group of men in suits were standing and talking to each other behind two desks placed at the far side of the hall. An elderly man with a string of teeth hanging round his neck was sitting at one of the desks, uninvolved in the discussion going on behind him. Half-a-dozen metal chairs were set out in front. The state TV people were setting up their cameras, one on each side, and wiring up two microphones placed on tripods on the desks.

'You know,' Sally said, whispering to Patrice, 'apart from the CRTV team, Raymond and I are the only press. And I don't think we're welcome.'

Patrice had already noted the stony glares being fired in their direction.

A fly walked across the cloth placed on top of the desks, under the disinterested gaze of the old man with the necklace of teeth. The TV crew indicated they were ready, and two of the men in suits took their places next to the old man. Two men sat on chairs set back from the desks. Patrice could see their faces now.

'Gendarmerie,' Sally said, nodding at one of them wearing a green uniform and red beret. 'Paramilitary police,'

Next to him was a civilian, a middle-aged man wearing a dark blazer and white tee shirt.

'I've seen that other man before,' Patrice said.

'So have I. He was in Buea for the anniversary parade.'

'His name is Pierre Mponda. I met him in Coach Samson's bar. He works for the Ministry of Foreign Business and Investment, in liaison. That's what he told me. Helping foreign investors, making things run smoothly for them. New Deal must be one of his clients.'

One of the besuited men sitting at the desk leaned forward into one of the microphones and coughed. He had a square jaw and deep-set eyes. He put on a pair of glasses, unfolded a sheet of paper, and began to read out his statement. He spoke as if he was addressing a large crowd.

'Good afternoon to you all. Welcome to this press conference that we have organised with our partners, New Deal Plantations. I am Bakunda Divisional Officer Serge Mukam.'

'Well, well,' Patrice thought. 'Speak of the Devil.'

'And here with me are: Chief Arthur ...' He turned to the old man with the necklace of teeth. The chief looked straight ahead. '... Chief Arthur, of Ngembum village, our host today; and Mr Thomas Schmidt, from Germany, Vice-President of New Deal. We are here to update you on the latest developments regarding the illegal occupation of the New Deal mill and the abduction of two managers.'

Another vehicle pulled up outside.

'Ah,' the divisional officer said, 'our last guest is here.'

The frail uncle of the murdered chief of Bafuke shuffled in through the entrance, leaning on his stick, and made his way to the desks, where he took his place next to Chief Arthur. The two men barely exchanged glances.

The divisional officer introduced the late arrival as 'the new and honourable traditional leader of Bafuke, Chief Tabeng Ewang', then carried on with his statement.

'As you know, this criminal incident is causing unimaginable damage to the economy of our division and potentially disastrous damage to the image of our division, and indeed to our nation as a desirable destination for investment. It has therefore been an urgent priority to resolve this matter ... with speed as well as with regard for the law. And I am happy to announce that we have good news.'

The divisional officer paused again with the look of a magician about to produce a rabbit out of a hat. But there was little sense of anticipation in the room. The old village chief was still staring into space, as was uncle Tabeng Ewang. The German man was using a cloth to stem a constant flow of sweat leaking out from under his silvery hair. The man at the back, from the ministry, was fiddling with his chunky bracelet.

'On behalf of Chief Arthur,' the divisional officer continued, 'I am delighted to say that the villagers removed from Bafuke are to be offered resettlement, here in Ngembum. The two villages have historically enjoyed warm and friendly relations, and this new arrangement will be the chance for a new beginning for both. As you know, Ngembum has in recent years fallen on hard times, primarily because of a lack of transport infrastructure. So, as part of this package, it is with great pleasure that I can announce also that New Deal Plantations have offered to upgrade the road from here to Mbimbia.'

Sally raised her hand. 'I have a ques …'

'If you could please wait for the conclusion of the statement, thank you. This offer has been accepted by our friend here, the new and honourable chief of Bafuke, and is being relayed to other representatives of his village, whereupon we now expect the occupation of the mill to end immediately. Thank you, and good afternoon.'

With this, the divisional officer clapped his hands and nodded to the CRTV crew, who switched off their cameras and started packing up.

Sally asked her question. 'What will the resettled people do here in Ngembum, when there is no work here and they cannot farm because, as in Bafuke, all the surrounding land has been leased to New Deal?'

'Well, for one thing, there will be jobs on the plantation, as you know,' the official said, looking to the German man for support and getting an earnest nod of the head. 'But for another, there will be new opportunities with the improvement of the road to Mbimbia, which will enable people to travel and use their initiative …'

Sally waved her pen. 'I would like to ask Mr Schmidt, is it not the case that New Deal would have been upgrading this road anyway, in order to take out the timber when you start felling the forest here?'

The man wiped his face again. 'Yes, well … of course …'

'If I can help here,' the divisional officer said. 'Whatever the plans may or may not have been, the important thing is that the road is going to be upgraded. Now, if there are no more …'

Patrice was losing patience. 'When did you authorise the eviction of the villagers of Bafuke?'

The divisional officer hesitated then glanced behind him at the man from the ministry, frowning as if asking, 'Why is this man here?' And betraying, perhaps, who he took his orders from.

'Why was the eviction notice not presented at the time, as is legally required?'

The official coughed as he tried to compose himself. 'I believe we're straying off the subject …'

'Were you aware the villagers were forced out at gunpoint under threat of death?'

'If you will let me finish, please … What we are looking at now is not what has happened in the past but how we're going to move forward, and as we've been outlining, an amicable solution has been found. So, thank you, everyone, and good afternoon.'

The divisional officer got to his feet, but Sally had another question for the New Deal vice-president. 'It's well known you've bribed local chiefs with promises of college grants for their children, so what have you offered Chief Arthur here and the late chief's uncle from Bafuke?'

Schmidt spluttered and looked at the divisional officer, who gestured for him to get up.

Patrice called out, 'Who killed Jeki the wrestler?'

Seconds of silence passed before the divisional officer said, 'The press conference is over.'

Patrice and Sally made their way out of the hall. Chief Arthur and Uncle Tabeng Ewang left and went their separate ways, neither having uttered a word, and the men in suits and the gendarme in the red beret drove away in their four-by-fours.

Sally tried calling Francis to ask what he thought about the offer of resettlement, but she still couldn't get through.

Patrice said, 'We must get back.'

'But we haven't finished here. I have to find out what the people of Ngembum think about the plan. And then you've got to help me find the spot where Douala Manga nearly got killed by the elephant.'

Patrice shook his head. 'You go sightseeing if you want. I'll get a lift with those TV people ...'

'Hey, Patrice, we go leave small time,' she said. 'We won't be long.'

'Take your time, Sally. I'm going now. You heard what the divisional officer said; they expect the occupation to end immediately – it's a threat.'

Chapter 62

So, this was it. Everything depended on the next ninety minutes. The small band of Bakunda Lions fans were grouped behind one of the goals singing, 'Come on, Lions!' over and over. A few hundred locals had also come to watch the re-arranged championship decider in Mbimbia and lined the edge of the pitch.

The team formed a huddle, before taking up their starting positions. Samson was confident they were well briefed and fit. But he could see too, from the way they were fidgeting, that they were nervous. Had he talked too much about the dangers posed by their opponents? His boys needed to be composed.

The whistle went. After a few minutes there was an early warning for the Lions, when the Mabengi Kings took a clever corner kick, playing it short then passing into the path of an unmarked full back running towards the edge of the penalty area. He struck a sweet shot and hit the right-hand post. Samson clapped his hands. 'Wake up, Lions!'

Mostly he kept quiet during matches, believing the coach's job was in the preparation and there was little he could do to influence the game after kick-off. You had to let the boys get on with it. That was his philosophy. If things weren't going well, he'd make tactical adjustments. His opposite number had a different approach. The Mabengi Kings' coach, a stocky bald man who couldn't have played football himself for at least thirty years, paced about excitedly, barking instructions. Everything he said, he said twice: 'Get in! Get in!' 'Get up! Get up!' 'Pass! Pass!'

As the first half went on, Samson saw his players were struggling to deal with the Kings' danger man, the right-winger, a skinny boy who was skipping past tackles and firing in crosses, creating chance after chance for his teammates. Moses, the Lions' left back, was sticking to his position, but he couldn't cope with the winger's pace and skill. Ten minutes before half-time, the winger got the ball again out by the right touchline. He raced away and Moses was left chasing dust. The Lions' defence was nowhere. The Kings' winger was about to pass to two forwards running unmarked towards the Lions' goal when Sonny raced across.

With the speed he was going, Samson could tell it was going to be difficult for him to control a tackle. 'Careful, son,' he said to himself, and held his breath.

Sonny lunged for the ball, mistimed his challenge, and brought the winger crashing to the floor.

'Red card! Red card!' the Kings' coach shouted, waving his hand furiously.

The referee agreed.

It was a disaster. Samson put his hands on his head and scuffed the ground. It was reckless of Sonny. Now he'd left the rest of the team with a mountain to climb.

Sonny trudged off the field, his head hanging low. *'Forgive me, Papa,'* he said, glancing up. *'Na mistake oh.'*

Samson couldn't bring himself to look his son in the eye.

'Do quick run comot for this field,' was all he could say. 'Hurry off the pitch.'

During the half-time break, the players sat on the ground, drinking water.

'For the second half, your backs will be against the wall,' Samson told them. He pointed at the centre forward. 'Randy, you must help defend. All of you, you must operate as a team. We must keep players back, even when we attack. Running back from their penalty area is a long way when you're a player short.' Out of the corner of his eye, he noticed his son hang his head.

The game restarted with the fans who'd travelled from Bakunda resuming their chant: 'Come on, Lions!'

But most of the play was at the other end, as the Kings launched attack after attack and the Lions struggled to clear the ball out of their half. The few times they did, it came straight back. Samson feared it was only a matter of time before the Kings scored. He rubbed his forehead, trying to ease the tension.

The Lions defended like their lives depended on it, charging into tackles, blocking shots, heading out every corner. And Moses somehow managed to stop the skinny winger running rings around him. But a draw was not enough; the Lions needed a win, so one way or another they had to score. As the game went on, the boys were so exhausted they could barely stand, let alone get anywhere near the Kings' goal.

With a minute to go and the referee looking at his watch, Samson decided it was all or nothing. With a sideways nod, he directed Randy, his centre forward, to abandon his defensive duties and head upfield. Randy hobbled towards the centre circle as the Lions' goalkeeper made yet another clearance.

The centre forward out-jumped two defenders and headed the ball to Tico, who was standing ten metres behind him. This is it, Samson thought; Randy can turn, and Tico can put him through. Randy turned, but lost his footing, and fell to the ground. Samson's head fell into his hand. The chance had gone. The game was up.

But Tico had noticed something Samson hadn't. Moses was bolting up the left wing. As he approached the halfway line, Tico chipped a pass forward, and suddenly Moses was running on to the ball with only the goalkeeper to beat. Samson's mouth dropped open.

'Stay calm, Moses,' he said, not loud – he didn't want to put the boy off, just to will him on – 'take your time … wait for the keeper to commit himself …'

Moses didn't wait. Five metres outside the penalty area, with the goalkeeper coming out towards him, he wrapped his foot round the ball. Like a cannonball fired out of the smoke, the football exploded out of the dust and flew past the flailing arms of the goalkeeper into the drooping net. The San Siro regulars and the displaced villagers behind the goal - along with the rest of the crowd - jumped and cheered in disbelief. Moses stood with his arms aloft then fell backwards on to the ground and was swamped by his teammates. The referee blew the final whistle.

Samson looked to the sky and thanked God. It was as if time was standing still. After all the training, and all that had been going on in Bakunda, and the battering the team had faced on the pitch, the Lions had done it! It might only be a youth football tournament, but it was something; something worthwhile, something joyful! His eyes felt watery. It must be the dust, he thought.

Chapter 63

Sally followed in the footsteps – she believed – of Douala Manga, along a path by the river, the noise from the falls above Ngembum growing louder. Raymond followed her. She'd let it slip that the old king had recounted a visit here in his memoirs. Raymond said her research was sparking his curiosity. She made him swear not to tell a soul.

They rounded a bend and saw the white water cascading in a thick channel over the bare brown rock and crashing and tumbling ten metres into a large pool. There, as if resting after its great exertion, it circled, preparing for the next stage of its journey towards the ocean. Closer to the base of the falls, a fine spray filled the air and the temperature dropped. They stopped to take in the scene.

'It's amazing to think he was in this same place, all that time ago,' Sally said, shouting to make herself heard. 'And he fell in! You can see why he was so impressed by its power.'

'The power of nature. The power of Cameroon!' Raymond was taking photos virtually non-stop.

'That's where the encounter was, with the elephant!' Sally pointed to where the path wound up by the side of the falls. 'He wrote that he slipped as he tried to climb a steep path. It has to be this path here. The elephant nearly trampled him and he fell over the bank and into the swirling waters. It must have happened right here!' She stood, looking down the path, imagining an elephant charging towards her.

Then she looked at the falls. She was trying to think what Douala Manga meant by something else he'd written about his visit to Ngembum: *There are secrets in the forest, with its mighty rivers and waterfalls.* She couldn't figure it out.

'I suppose we'd better head back,' she said. 'I told Patrice we wouldn't be long. But first, let's talk to Chief Arthur. Away from that press conference, he may have more details about the arrangement he's made with New Deal Plantations.'

They found the chief sitting on a bench outside his house, fanning himself with a leaf. They greeted him and he invited them to join him.

'I am Chief Arthur Efoka. I told the divisional officer my name when we met, but he forgot within minutes.' The old man tittered and picked up a stick of sugar cane.

Sally asked him about the offer to let the displaced people from Bafuke come to his village.

'I'm not ashamed,' he said. 'If the people from New Deal want to give me money, why shouldn't I take it? Look at the state of our village. The few of us who remain here now are old people or young children left with their grandparents while their mothers and fathers go away to look for work.'

The chief spoke assuredly and came across differently from the man who'd sat morosely through the press conference. He chomped on his sugar cane with what was left of his teeth. 'If the people of Bafuke want to come here, I'm happy for them. But like you asked, why would they want to come?'

'Chief, you dong live for this village since your mama born you?' Sally asked.

'Yes. My mama born me here seventy-two years ago. My papa and grandpapa them all live for this village their whole life. But they were not chiefs. I was appointed after the family who used to rule this village moved away. You know, in the days before roads, this was an important place, the furthest you could come by river from Douala, because of the falls.'

'Did you ever hear about the German prince?'

'Huh! The German prince!' The old man laughed. 'Where did you hear about that? That woman invented a lot of stories. She'd been working as a prostitute in Douala. She arrived here with a child. But he was no prince!'

'But didn't Douala Manga come to visit them?'

'Douala Manga came here, it's true, more than once. And that's how all sorts of rumours were able to stick. But he didn't come to see that woman, or her child.'

Sally felt a twinge of disappointment. The old man was putting paid to any notions she'd had of being descended from kings. But Patrice was right; she'd allowed herself to be taken in by this story – she didn't even know why. Some silly infatuation with royalty left over from her childhood, perhaps. And the professor in Buea was right too; historical research should be evidence-based. It was actually a weight off her shoulders. She could see things straight now.

'He came more than once?'

The old man smiled broadly, making his otherwise smooth skin crease into soft wrinkles. 'They say the first time, it was to defend the village against an attack by elephants. But he came many times. He was friends with the chief here. The last time it was under cover of darkness.'

'Oh?'

'My grandfather said that.' The chief chewed more cane.

'What else did your grandfather say?' From the way the old man smiled again, Sally guessed her voice was betraying her excitement.

'He said Douala Manga came one night, shortly before he was arrested. He came with people from Southern Nigeria and many canoes.'

'Southern Nigeria? What did he do? Why did he come?'

'The canoes went to the other side of the river; they didn't stop this side, except for a short time when Douala Manga got off and spoke to the chief.'

'And what did he say?' She felt like a child opening a present. She couldn't pull off the layers of wrapping fast enough.

'No one knows what he said. The chief was also arrested by the Germans and sent away to prison in the far north. He died on the journey.'

'What's on the other side of the river?'

'Forest.'

Sally gulped. 'Is there someone who can take us across?'

The chief told them to wait and went inside, returning a few minutes later to say he was making arrangements.

No matter what she'd said to Patrice, a marauding herd of elephants couldn't drag Sally away from this place now.

Fifteen minutes later they set off over the water in a dug-out canoe, powered by the chief's twelve-year-old grandson sitting at the stern with a paddle. Raymond was on the bow seat, taking more pictures of the falls as they came into view.

At the far side of the river, the boy navigated close to the bank, towards the falls, then skirted round the edge of the wide pool below. Sally could feel currents drawing the boat towards the falls but the boy wedged his paddle into the river bed and pushed off it to keep them clear. He moored at the spot where his grandfather's grandfather said Douala Manga had moored his fleet of canoes a hundred years before. The boy told them the only time people came to this side now was to swim in the pool.

Sally jumped out. 'Let's find Douala Manga's secret!'

Raymond chuckled and followed her.

They clambered up an expanse of exposed rock to the side of the falls. From the top, they could walk close to the plunging torrent. Sally peered over the edge. Raymond took at least a hundred pictures. They slid down the rocks and explored the edge of the forest, but there was no sign of a path heading into the trees; no sign of anything.

'If there's a secret here,' Raymond said, 'it's well hidden.'

Sally's shoulders dropped. Her treasure hunt was over.

They waded out with the canoe to get it clear of the rocks in the shallows. Then, as Raymond was taking his position in the bow, he called out, 'What's that?' He was pointing at a shadowy gap in the rock face, by the base of the falls,

The boy shrugged his shoulders. It didn't look like anything to Sally. 'It's okay,' she said. 'We can leave now.'

Raymond said. 'Come on, Sally, let's check it out.'

The boy steered them round the edge of the pool. Seeing the shadow from a different angle, Sally agreed it looked darker and deeper.

The water at the foot of the shadow was choppy. The boy hesitated.

Then it came to her, a line from the memoirs. *'The white man sees darkness.* That's what he wrote!'

'Okay,' Raymond said to the boy, putting aside his camera for once and taking another paddle. 'Let me help.'

They turned the canoe round and headed for the shadow.

The water got deeper. The closer they got, the more strongly the swirls and eddies pulled and turned the boat, and the more clearly they could see there was undoubtedly a crack in the rock.

Raymond paused briefly to catch his breath, but long enough for the front of the boat to spin round and head straight for the falls. Sally gripped the sides and screamed.

The boy shouted to Raymond to do as he had done, and put his paddle the other side. They paddled fiercely, and manoeuvred the canoe so it was sideways on to the falls. But still it was being dragged towards them. Raymond gritted his teeth and strained, frantically pulling across the powerful current. They edged away, the resistance weakened, and with two more paddles they found themselves wedged between a boulder and the rock face.

For now, they were safe – and right in front of what they could see now was the entrance to a cave.

The boy stayed with his boat while Sally and Raymond stepped off and through the narrow opening.

Inside, it was pitch black. Raymond held up the torch on his phone. Further in, and away from the sound of the falls outside, the cave opened out, so that the beam of light got lost in the darkness ahead. He aimed it at the ceiling, and then against a wall. He swung it round, the light catching on damp edges of rock, then on a ledge at around head height.

The two of them edged forward, up a sloping slab of rock, and as they did, they could see the ledge opening out, forming an upper chamber. Raymond shone the torch inside. Sally gasped. What they saw, stacked in neat rows, were a dozen long wooden boxes.

Chapter 64

Pierre Mponda tapped the steering wheel as he powered his four-by-four through the dust thrown up by the divisional officer's vehicle in front. He was trying to work out why the Congolese had asked the question about Jeki. Had he been expecting an answer? For the divisional officer to let something slip? More likely, it was to gauge the reaction – and there had been that moment of silence. But so what? What could he know? Even if he suspected, what could he do? He was still the blind man lost in the forest …

He drove on, swishing past occasional hamlets and schoolchildren walking by the side of the road, carrying home bundles of firewood on their heads. His passenger, meanwhile, was twitching nervously.

'What next?' Thomas Schmidt asked, patting his silver hair. He was fretting about the occupation at the mill.

'That's up to the farmers. I'm sure they'll see sense.'

The German gnawed at a thumbnail.

Mponda's phone pinged. He glanced at it and saw the text was from Estelle. He picked up the phone and was about to open the message when Schmidt cried out, 'Pierre!'

He looked up. A fully laden logging truck was immediately in front of them. He pulled hard on the wheel, skidding and swerving into the middle of the road – missing the logging truck by a whisker.

'Jesus, Pierre, keep your eyes on the road.'

'What's he doing there?' Mponda asked as he pulled over to look back. 'That's one of your trucks.' The truck was stationary. Beneath it, on the embankment, the driver was urinating. 'Why aren't his hazard lights on?'

'Just drive carefully, Pierre, or you'll get us both killed.'

They travelled the rest of the way in silence, following the divisional officer through Mbimbia, where some young footballers were jumping around in the road, almost getting run over, and on to Bakunda town, past the evicted villagers camped on the football pitch, and then finally to New Deal.

The roadblock formed by the security guards had been moved to the top of the road that led to the plantation entrance and was reinforced by a truckload of gendarmes carrying automatic weapons. Among other things, this kept the growing number of reporters away from the gates. There were four or five of them now; one of them was white.

'Shit.' Schmidt scowled, as Mponda pulled up behind the divisional officer's four-by-four.

The Cameroonian reporters headed for the divisional officer's window, holding out microphones. Mponda could imagine the official telling them what a pity it was that none of them had attended the press conference.

The white reporter spotted Schmidt and walked over to Mponda's four-by-four and knocked on the window. Schmidt looked straight ahead. The reporter, a tall, sweaty man with a tufty beard, leaned over the bonnet and stared at Schmidt through the windscreen.

'Herr Schmidt! A few words, please!'

Schmidt cursed again and lowered his window.

'Hans Naumann, *World Report*.' The reporter pushed a recorder in front of Schmidt. 'What will you do if the farmers don't accept the offer to move to the other village?'

Schmidt turned to Mponda who fiddled with his phone, pretending not to be listening. 'The matter is in hand,' the company vice-president said. 'That is all I can say.'

'Will you use force, if necessary, to free the hostages?'

'I can make no further comment at this stage.'

'Herr Schmidt, would you agree that, in evicting these villagers, New Deal Plantations is behaving in the same way as the German colonialists did here in Cameroon a hundred years ago?'

Some of the local reporters had gathered round.

Schmidt's face flushed crimson. 'That is nonsensical! We are investing millions in this country. This enterprise is a partnership. And we have done everything to help these people. We offered them work, and they responded by destroying our nursery. And then they nearly killed two of our guards. But even after this, we are offering our support to the generous proposal to find them a new home in a neighbouring village. You ...'

Up ahead the divisional officer was driving through the roadblock, and Mponda accelerated forward.

The German closed his window. '*Schweinhund!*' he said as he wiped his brow and checked his hair was in place. 'I hate these people.'

Mponda smiled to himself.

They drove to the plantation entrance and straight through to the administration block, where a crisis team had been assembled, working out of the boardroom. A group of managers and two of the guards were looking over a plan of the mill with two senior gendarmes.

The news was bad for Schmidt, as Mponda suspected it would be. The farmers had rejected the offer.

The vice-president clenched his fists, trembling with rage. 'What did they say?'

The head guard answered. 'We spoke to the farmer called Francis Akwanga, who's the ringleader. He said they are not moving anywhere, other than to their village.'

'So what's the plan?'

'That's up to you, sir.'

Schmidt squeezed his cheeks between his thumb and fingers. 'Well, we can starve them out, can't we? How much food do they have in there?'

'They have access to the canteen area which has several freezers. They could have enough to sustain them for days or even weeks. And there are the hostages ...'

'Weeks! This can't go on for weeks. What's happening to the harvest?'

A man in a white coat pointed at the plan. 'We are still picking. If we don't, the fruit will fall. We can keep it in the storeroom for now, on the far side of the mill, but not for long before it rots.'

Schmidt took a deep breath and patted his hair. 'We cannot give in to these blackmailers. What are the chances of bringing the hostages out alive if we use force?'

'It's a risk, but it can be done,' the head guard said. 'A team could storm the control room and take them by surprise.'

'How soon can it be organised?'

'Tomorrow?' The head guard turned to the gendarmes, who nodded in agreement.

Chapter 65

Raymond formed a stirrup with his hands and Sally climbed on to the ledge and crawled across. The boxes were a metre long, twenty centimetres deep and wide, with rope handles at either end. She tried to ease free one from the top row but it was stuck. She pulled at the handle.

Raymond said, 'Hey, Sally, be …'

The box slipped off and crashed on to the rock ledge - and broke open.

'… careful.'

'Oh my God!' Sally reached across, and picked up a rifle. She held it for him to see. 'Guns!'

'Enough for a small army.'

'I knew it!'

'Careful,' Raymond said, pushing the barrel to the side. 'You never know …'

'Sorry.'

'May I see?'

Sally handed the rifle to the photographer.

'Wetin I tell you before?' Sally said, staring at the weapon. 'Douala Manga's secrets! He *was* preparing for an armed rebellion.'

'It looks like it,' Raymond said. 'And with the help of the

British. This is a Lee Enfield Mark III, standard issue for the British army during the early twentieth century.'

'Well, we don't know if the British knew about this,' Sally said. 'You can't jump to conclusions. The chief didn't say anything about white people being on the canoes.'

Raymond shrugged. 'Is there ammunition?'

He pointed his torchlight from one side to the other. At one end of the boxes of rifles were two square boxes. Sally dragged one of them over, and Raymond used a pocket knife to open the lid. It was full of small paper parcels tied with string. He opened one. 'The .303,' he said, holding a pointed bullet between his thumb and forefinger.

'Douala Manga said he didn't want the British to rule in Cameroon, and he was a man of his word.' Sally was thinking aloud. 'But that doesn't mean he wouldn't take their guns to stage his own rebellion. So maybe these did come from Nigerians, who stole them from the British. I mean, who knows? My God!'

'But why hide them here?' Raymond asked.

'Well, they would be safe. I suppose he wasn't ready, so he kept them here while organising the rebellion. And then he was arrested, and the chief here, Ngosso Din too … and nobody else had the authority, or the courage – who knows what – to continue. Who else even knew about these guns? *The sceptre lies hidden* – till now!'

Raymond took the rifle closer to the cave entrance and examined it in the grey light. 'Beautiful and deadly,' he said, propping it against his shoulder, unlocking and locking the bolt and clicking the trigger. 'It's supposed to be accurate up to five hundred metres. I wonder …'

'Raymond, wetin you think you dey do so?'

He dropped the bullet in the magazine. Then he stepped outside the cave.

Sally climbed down from the ledge and followed, at a distance. She heard Raymond call to the canoe boy to cover his ears then she watched as he aimed high into the trees on the far side of the wide river pool and fired. There was a flash at the end of the barrel and a loud crack that echoed through the cave.

'Wow!' the photographer said as he came bounding back.

'Come on, Raymond. Leave that, and start shooting with your camera.'

She got back on to the ledge, and Raymond took a series of pictures as she posed next to the boxes, with two of the rifles from the first box, and a couple of packets of ammunition, on her lap.

In the darkness and relative silence of the cave, and with the old rifles in her hands, it was like they'd gone back in time. The farmers' occupation at the mill, the eviction of the villagers, and their camp on the football pitch were of a different world. Sally was there with Douala Manga and Ngosso Din and the gun smugglers from Nigeria a hundred years before; she imagined how it was for them as they braved the torrents of the waterfall, canoes weighed down by the heavy boxes, stashing their weapons, hoping, believing, that they were about to launch a rebellion against the German colonialists. She felt a rush of triumph and elation; here was the proof that Douala Manga was the true resistance leader she'd always wanted him to be.

'Are you going to report this to the police?' Raymond asked.

Sally gave a short shake of her head. 'They might arrest us.'

'What about the chief?'

She put her finger to her lips. 'Let's keep it quiet for now, Raymond. We'll have to talk to our editor about how to handle this.'

They put the rifles back in the box and replaced the lid and made their way out to the canoe. By pushing hard off the rock wall, the canoe boy was able to get them clear of the drag from the falls, and soon they were paddling peacefully across the river towards the village of Ngembum. Sally slipped the boy some banknotes and made him promise not to talk about the gunshot. They stopped at the chief's house to say goodbye, and then they were in their taxi, on their way to Bakunda and the present-day resistance struggle that was unfolding at the palm oil plantation.

*

It was dusk by the time Patrice reached New Deal. He got the *okada* to drop him before the turning that led to the main entrance, out of sight of the guards at the roadblock. He slipped through the barbed wire fence and scampered between the young palms on all fours. He made for the stretch of road between the mill and the office block, which was bordered by other, taller trees, and arrived at it opposite the whitewashed bungalows that served as management accommodation.

The mill was at one end of the road, a dark shadow. At the other end, lights were on in the boardroom. He could make out figures standing round the table. Guards with guns were stationed outside both buildings.

While he was watching, the door to the office building opened. Two men stepped out and began walking in his direction. Patrice darted behind a tree. As the men neared, their voices became clearer; one spoke with a French accent, the other German. Patrice recognised them both.

'Do these gendarmes know what they are doing?' New Deal's vice-president asked as they approached the gate to the first bungalow in the row.

'They have a special unit to deal with situations such as this, trained in France.'

'I'm telling you, Pierre, this will have to be well planned. Whatever happens, we must be ready with our story.'

'Story?'

'Don't give me that innocent stuff, Pierre. It must be made clear that force was only considered as an option after the farmers threatened to harm the hostages.'

'Of course, of course ...'

Patrice watched them enter the bungalow and close the door behind them. But as he stepped out from behind the tree, the door opened.

'Who's there?' It was Pierre Mponda's voice.

Patrice froze.

A light shone in his face.

'Mr Le Congo. This is a surprise. What are you doing here?'

He thought about running, but then he thought, why should he? 'I could ask you the same question. Does liaising with foreign companies extend to co-ordinating paramilitary hit squads?'

'What's going on, Pierre?' The silver-haired German appeared at the door.

'There's an intruder.'

'Jesus! Guards! Come!'

Instinctively now, Patrice took a step back.

'Wait there, Mr Le Congo.'

'You know this man?' the German asked.

'You don't recognise him? His hair? He was at the press conference. And we've met before. He told me he found Cameroonians to be hospitable, but it seems he's overstaying his welcome.' Mponda turned to Patrice. 'You haven't answered my question. What are you doing here?'

'I want to talk to the farmers.'

A four-by-four arrived. Three guards in beige uniforms got out. And the police inspector from Bakunda.

Schmidt said, 'This man is trespassing. Search him; and detain him while we find out what he's up to.'

'I think I can persuade them to end the occupation, peacefully. But you must guarantee their safety.'

For a while, no one spoke. Then the German asked, 'What do you think, Pierre?'

Mponda tutted. 'Do you trust such a man, who comes sneaking through the bushes like this? You've made your offer. The farmers have rejected it. No doubt, Mr Le Congo, the rights of hostage-takers are enshrined in that charter of yours. But it's too late for talking now.'

'I know him,' the police inspector said as a guard frisked Patrice and bound his wrists together with zip tie handcuffs. 'He's been nosing around and stirring up trouble. And he doesn't like you people either,' he added, talking to the guards. 'This morning in my office he described you as a gang of thugs.'

Mponda grinned. 'You should have taken my advice, Mr Le Congo, and gone to Douala. There you could have been enjoying fresh fish and sleeping in a comfortable bed. I fear tonight will not be so pleasant for you.'

The inspector smiled one of his thin smiles.

The man from the ministry returned with the German to the vice-president's bungalow, set amidst its lawn and spotlights. Leaving the security men to set about their prey.

The inspector struck the first blow. He swung his baton and whacked Patrice in the side. Kicks and punches followed, to the stomach, head, legs, groin …

Patrice didn't know how long it lasted. All he was aware of at the end was being thrown into the back of the four-by-four.

When he came to, he was on an earth floor. There was a stench of over-ripe oil palm fruits. The air was close and sticky, and it was pitch black. He heard a bolt slide across a door, and a padlock click. A vehicle drove away. After that, the only sound was the scuffling of rats.

He'd had the senses beaten out of him, and he didn't know where he was, but he was conscious enough to know that if he didn't escape, the farmers in the mill were going to be massacred. The press conference in Ngembum had been a charade. The plan was clear: no one was getting out alive.

Chapter 66

Samson noticed the logging truck at the top of the hill, but he didn't pay it any attention. He'd stayed behind after the match to sort out some formalities with the league officials and was walking along Mbimbia's main street, past the football pitch, to the bar at the bottom of the hill, where the Lions were celebrating. As he got closer, he could see the boys, still in their yellow kit, jumping about and singing with the fans on the terrace in front of the bar. Sonny was there amongst them, forgiven completely for the careless tackle that had got him sent off. Samson chuckled. He hadn't had a chance yet to give his son a hug.

It was beginning to sink in. The Lions were the champions. And Moses, from Bafuke, had scored the winning goal. How fitting! How beautiful football could be!

The engine whined, and Samson looked up again at the truck, which was now crawling down the hill. It was carrying a vast load: five tree trunks, strapped together, bulging out either side of the trailer and above the yellow cab in front. The hydraulic brakes were hissing on and off. The gears were grinding as the driver changed down. Then the hissing stopped. There was a terrible crunch and a screech of metal being torn apart as the truck gathered speed.

The driver sounded his horn, repeatedly. Samson started running. If the footballers and the supporters had heard the truck hooting, they must have thought it was joining in the celebration, because they cheered and clapped. They weren't looking at it. They couldn't see it was heading their way.

Samson was waving his arms and yelling his son's name, but the boys only responded by waving to him. He was trying to point to the danger behind them, but they kept on waving. Then there was another crunch as the driver tried again to engage the gears but failed. This time everyone at the bar swung round. And they saw the giant torpedo careering towards them.

There was a bend in the road at the bottom of the hill as it passed the bar, but for now the truck was on a collision course with the crowd outside. There was panic. Some stayed rooted to the spot; others began to scatter, bumping into each other as they ran in different directions.

Samson was looking for Sonny. He couldn't see him. 'Sonny! Sonny!' he shouted, running, straining, stretching. Then he skidded to a stop. He was too late. There was nothing he could do. The truck was going to plough into the terrace. He put his hands up, to shield his eyes, as he cried out his son's name again. Through his stretched-out fingers he saw figures scamper across the road, then others dive for cover inside the bar.

At the last moment, the driver tried to steer his truck round the bend. Had he kept its course, those in the bar might have been able to jump clear. But now there was no escape. It was going too fast to carry its heavy load and flipped over on to its side. The tree trunks were thrown off, as if catapulted, and rolled and bounced chaotically across the seating area before clattering into the building and demolishing the flimsy wooden structure instantly.

Samson scraped his hands over his head, looking on in horror. He heard moans and cries and loud cracks as pieces of wood snapped and sections of wall fell to the ground. He was saying his son's name again, but now more to himself than anyone else. He looked across the road. Three boys were sitting against a wall, hands on their heads, staring at the disaster scene in front of them. They were safe. They were Bakunda Lions players, and Samson was thankful. But Sonny wasn't with them.

He walked forward as the cloud of dust thinned out. The first thing he saw was the sawn end of one of the tree trunks, with the words New Deal stencilled in white. He tried to move it. It didn't budge. Then he saw another trunk, lying diagonally across the remains of the bar building. All around it were bodies. The red and white plastic chairs and tables lay scattered.

He knew what it was he should do; move from body to body to find out who was alive and if they could be helped. But all he could think about as he searched frantically through the debris was his son. He kept hoping, imagining Sonny popping his head round a corner, calling out, 'Hey, Papa!' He must be here, he told himself; he must be alright. But with every second that passed without finding his boy, his heart sank deeper.

The first two bodies he came across were dead. He didn't know who they were. As he was moving to the third, a woman ran in from somewhere. She said she was a nurse; she'd called the health clinic that was nearby; the doctors were coming in an ambulance. She was talking to him, asking him if he was hurt. But he wasn't hearing her properly. He was looking at a pair of football boots - boots that he recognised because he had bought them for his son. He saw the legs, sticking out from under the tree trunk. They looked so small, like a little boy's. They weren't moving.

'Sonn ...' His voice broke before he could finish saying his son's name. He walked round to the other side of the trunk. And now, through streaming tears, he saw his boy, his body crushed beneath ten tons of timber. His left shoulder was jutting out, and into the side of his face. His eyes were closed. Samson cupped his hands round Sonny's cheeks. They were still warm. For a split second he thought the impossible and checked for a pulse. It wasn't there. His head dropped. He pressed his cheek against his son's forehead and sobbed.

What he'd have done then to get his son back. He'd have given an arm, a leg, his life, anything. And to think he'd scolded him for something so stupidly small as a bad tackle ... it was unbearable. The boy had been trying his hardest, and he'd been doing it for his papa, because he knew how much the match had meant to him. *Get off the pitch.* That was the last thing he'd said to his son.

He felt a hand on his shoulder and saw the nurse on her knees, checking, like he had, for a pulse. Then she stood up and moved away. He heard her speaking to a doctor.

'Ten dead. Four seriously injured, two over there, two behind there. Twelve others with minor injuries.'

'Thank you, nurse.'

They moved off to do their work, and Samson was left with his son to confront his grief and agony. But then the nurse's words sank in; he had to check on the rest of the team.

He forced himself to stand. He heard angry voices. A mob

had gathered round the truck driver. His cab was half on its side. The door had swung open. The driver was leaning out, mopping a gash on his forehead, looking confused. The crowd were shouting at him.

'Murderer!' they cried, pointing fingers. A man wearing a baseball cap grabbed hold of the driver by his jacket and yanked him out of the cab.

A old woman yelled, 'Do away with him!'

Samson felt his fists clench. Only the knowledge that he was needed to care for his players stopped him joining the mob.

*

As their taxi came over the brow of the hill, Sally and Raymond saw the devastation below; the tree trunks strewn all around like fallen skittles; broken walls and rubble; a truck on its side.

Sally struggled to take in the scene. It was as if a bomb had gone off. Raymond got his camera ready. As they got closer, they saw the boys in their yellow football kit.

'It's the Bakunda Lions,' Sally said. 'Where's the coach?'

The taxi parked by a small ambulance, and they got out. Before they had a chance to look for Coach Samson, they were distracted by a commotion. A crowd of people were by the fallen truck. A man was on the ground, being beaten with sticks and rocks.

'Murderer,' a woman shouted, stony hatred in her eyes.

'I didn't …'

'You're the driver. You did this.'

The mob tore off the man's clothes.

'Please,' the driver said. 'Have mercy ...'

Another blow struck the side of his face, and he slumped on to his stomach.

'We must stop this,' Sally said.

Raymond held her back. 'Don't get involved, or they'll kill you too.'

A pastor stepped into the circle formed by the crowd. '*For God e name, I take beg oh. Wuna stop for kill this man like this. Wuna leave make court try the man.* Let the law ...'

The woman who'd been shouting cut him short. 'There'll be no justice then. New Deal will pay the police and this murderer will walk free. You know that's how it is. *Court no fit guarantee any justice for this matter.*'

People started slapping the pastor and pulling at his clothes. He pushed and shoved in order to break free and beat a retreat. Away from the crowd he started praying.

A man produced a tyre. He and two others squashed it down over the driver's shoulders. Then petrol was doused over him.

'We can't do nothing,' Sally said.

'This is what happens when people don't trust the police,' Raymond said. 'In Douala they kill thieves like this.'

They, and the crowd, looked on as the match was struck. The air filled with black smoke, the smell of burning rubber, and the screams of the truck driver.

Sally reeled away and went from one horror to another, as she saw bodies being lifted out from the bar area and taken to the side of the road, where they were laid out in a row. It was then that she saw Coach Samson, walking with a football-kitted young body draped over his outstretched arms.

'Coach ...'

The big man looked up. From the bloodshot state of his eyes, and the way his shoulders hung low, Sally feared the worst.

'Your son?'

'He's over there, he didn't make it. Like this one. Three of my team didn't make it. It's not only Sonny ...' He laid the body he was carrying next to the others. 'This is Moses. He's from Bafuke. He scored the winning goal ...'

'I'm so sorry,' Sally said, feebly.

Coach Samson was looking over to the black smoke. 'They didn't have a chance ... and all because ...' The muscles on his face were twitching. 'Are they trained, these drivers? I mean, are they instructed properly? Do they know they are driving a dangerous weapon?' He jerked his head. 'This driver ... I'm sorry, I don't mind they killed him. But I don't blame him. I blame New Deal. They're the ones. They've brought nothing but trouble to this place.'

The coach crossed the road to where the survivors of his football team were assembled in silence. He held out his arms as he approached. The boys went to him, and they all embraced. Not long before, Sally thought, they'd have been celebrating their victory; never could joy have turned to sadness so quickly and so completely.

But she had work to do. She took out her notebook. Raymond was taking photographs. They'd stumbled upon another story.

'It's not the first time this has happened,' she said. 'There was a crash like this a few years ago. That was a logging truck. It crashed into a bar in Mutengene. You remember?'

'They don't learn,' Raymond said. 'And they don't care.'

The photographer said he'd go to Buea that evening and

drop his pictures off at the office. Sally asked him to tell their editor she'd send through the words later, along with an update on the situation at the New Deal mill. She said their report on Douala Manga's guns would have to wait.

Sally found Coach Samson again and asked if there was anything she could do. He asked her to take some of the boys with her to Bakunda; he'd stay till his son's body had been freed from beneath the tree trunk. So she shared a taxi with three young players and three of the displaced villagers who'd come to watch the match.

No one said a word during the two-hour journey, but a current of seething anger zinged around the car like a bolt of electricity. It made Sally suspect that if there'd been any doubts before about the farmers' occupation of the mill, the whole village would be behind them now. She tried calling Patrice but she couldn't get through.

Chapter 67

Pierre Mponda woke early with a sense of anticipation. He showered and walked across from his guest bungalow to the office block. He glanced the other way, at the mill, and noticed the storeroom to the side.

'Self-righteous fool!' he said to himself.

A single room was lit on the ground floor of the glass cube, in a corner, and against the blinds Mponda saw the silhouette of a man sitting with his elbows on a table and his head in his hands. He guessed the day had not started well for Thomas Schmidt, Vice-President of New Deal Plantations. They'd been up late together drinking brandy, but it was clear Schmidt was suffering from more than a hangover.

It had been an unpleasant evening in Schmidt's bungalow. With the television tuned to a German pornography channel, conversation had taken place against a background of electronic music and groans. Then news came of the accident in Mbimbia and the lynching of the truck driver.

Reports from the scene had suggested the truck's brakes failed, but Schmidt had insisted the driver was to blame. 'It's up to him to make sure his trailer is securely loaded,' he'd said. 'It's the man we passed, who parked his truck without hazard lights to take a piss. You cannot get reliable drivers here, Pierre. And the roads! If you want a decent road in this country, you have to build it yourself. I tell you, Pierre, this place is not easy.'

Mponda had thought of the victims of the crash, but not for long. That was life. There were winners and there were losers. His main concern had been for the likely impact of the accident. He'd calculated it should work in his favour. All in all, as he entered the office building, he had the feeling the endgame was about to play out.

The German's manner had evolved from indignant to disconsolate. He pushed a fax across the table. It was the front page of the news magazine *World Report*. The headline, above a graphic photograph of the scene of the crash, was a quote from Schmidt himself: *"This is a Partnership".* Next to a report about the accident was another article, headlined: *Land Grabbing: the New Colonialism.*

'What the fuck is going on?' Schmidt asked. 'Two of our people are taken hostage at knife-point, and these liberal shits write about colonialism.'

Mponda held a straight face. 'Relax, Thomas. This will all be sorted out soon. I understand the gendarmes are ready.'

Schmidt picked up the fax, scrunched it into a ball and threw it into a bin.

Chapter 68

A slither of sunlight let Patrice know it was daytime. It also suggested there might be a way out. The light was coming from a window high up below the roof. It was possible to reach it by scaling a stack of storage shelves. The problem was his hands were tied.

His stomach rumbled. He couldn't remember the last time he'd eaten. Definitely not since he'd been in this shed. Bunches of palm fruits were piled up in a corner. He'd been staring at them, supposing that they were, in theory, food. He didn't feel inclined to find out, but he wondered how long it would be before he'd have to.

Then he looked again at the storage shelves and thought of another use for the oil palms.

He picked a few of the fruits, placed them on the floor, and stamped on them, over and over, creating a greasy red pulp. Then, kneeling, his hands still bound together, he smeared the lubricant around his wrists and the zip tie cuffs. Slowly he eased the cuffs off.

His body ached from the beating the night before, but now he was able to haul himself up the shelving network to reach the window and crawl through. Outside, it backed on to a bank, so he could lower himself to the ground without having to jump. He made his way round to the front and looked out from between the shed and a warehouse, across an open area to the mill.

Two trucks were being unloaded into barrows, which Patrice followed with his eyes as they were then wheeled into the warehouse. And then, by an open gate in the perimeter wall, he saw Sally. So, she'd come, after all. But now was not a good time for her to be here. It was too risky.

He turned and went round behind the warehouse, till he reached a point where he could see the gate, and Sally at the gate could see him. He put his finger to his lips. When the coast was clear, he went across and signalled for her to follow him out through the gate. They crouched against the perimeter wall.

'Sally, what are you doing here?'

'Patrice, what's happened to your face? And what's that smell?'

'I had a rough night, you could say - and nowhere to wash. But what are you doing here?'

'What do you think I'm doing here? I'm trying to find out what's going on. They're not letting anyone in through the front, so I got an *okada* to drop me by the river, and I came through the plantation ... But what *is* going on?'

'You must leave. Immediately. They're going to send in a Gendarme special unit. The farmers won't stand a chance. I'm going to warn them. I'll do what I can to persuade them to end the occupation.'

'Well, I'll come with you.'

'Sally, it's dangerous. The gendarmes could come any time. If they come when we're there ...'

'So, let's get moving. This is my story, remember.' She

patted him on the hand and smiled. 'Let's hope we make it out alive!'

Patrice looked at her askance. 'Okay,' he said. 'It's up to you.' It seemed like, for Sally, life was a game. But it wasn't his job to tell her what to do. It occurred to him that, actually, they had something in common: stubbornness.

When the coast was clear, they slipped inside the gate and ran along a road between the perimeter wall and the main processing area, where the control room was. There was no door to the building on this side, but there was a long, covered conveyor belt that rose in two stages and entered at an upper level. Access was by a loading bay, from where – when the mill was operational – the fruit could be tipped straight from the trucks on to the belt. They stopped and looked around. They were about to run to the loading bay when they heard a rumble and saw a truck coming round a corner at the far end of the complex.

They ducked behind two large waste bins. From there they watched as the truck approached. It had a tarpaulin roof.

'That's a troop carrier,' Patrice said. 'The gendarmerie.'

Sally bit her lip.

Patrice shuddered at the thought of a truckload of paramilitary police being let loose on a few farmers armed with machetes. 'Murder squad.'

The truck came to a halt at the conveyor belt. Half-a-dozen men in black combat uniforms and balaclavas jumped out. They inspected the loading area, peering up the conveyor, then looked around. Two of them looked directly at the waste bins. Patrice and Sally swung their faces away from the gap they'd been looking through. They looked at each other, listening, waiting, trying not to move. The men walked over and looked inside the bins. Then they got back in the truck and drove off.

'Okay,' Patrice said. 'Now we go.' He and Sally crossed to the loading area. But as they stepped on to the belt, there was a shout. Then footsteps. Two New Deal security guards in beige uniforms were running in their direction.

'*Merde!*' Patrice pulled on Sally's arm, and they scampered up the conveyor belt, skipping over the steel plates and awkward cross-struts. At the top, the belt turned at right angles and they followed it into the building, trying to get their bearings and catching their breath. Patrice spotted the metal grated walkway on the far side. 'The control room's over there.'

They raced down a ladder fixed to the wall, then across the factory floor. Their footsteps echoed round the otherwise silent interior, bouncing off the tanks and other metallic surfaces like gunshots. There was another shout, but by now they were on the steps to the control room, taking them two at a time. They hammered on the door. It opened and closed again behind them.

Bizarrely, in contrast to the gathering tension outside, the atmosphere inside the control room was calm and quiet. Patrice felt like he and Sally had burst noisily into a library.

There was a stale smell of sweat and a dozen unwashed bodies. The room was overcrowded, but those inside looked comfortable enough, sitting on the floor, leaning against walls or machine cupboards. The two hostages were sitting together and looked more bored than distressed.

Francis got up from one of the swivel chairs. 'We saw you coming,' he said, nodding at the window that looked out over the factory. He needed a shave and, like Patrice, a shower. But he seemed relaxed considering the circumstances.

Patrice took another look round. He knew that Francis, too, was stubborn. If pushed too quickly, too hard, the farmer would dig his heals in. 'You rejected the offer of resettlement?'

Francis spat on the floor. 'What is there for us in Ngembum? We'd be worse off there than we were in Bafuke.'

'Yes. The offer was not realistic.'

'We heard old Uncle Tabeng agreed to it, but New Deal and the divisional officer are playing with us.'

'I know. And you're right. But listen, you've got to get out of here now, while you have a chance. Gendarme special forces have been sent to end the occupation …' Patrice glanced at the hostages and lowered his voice '… at any cost.'

'It's a bluff,' the farmer said. 'They won't risk the life of a white man.'

'Francis, we've seen them. They're here. New Deal are going to say you threatened to kill the hostages.'

Other farmers came closer to listen.

Francis looked at the two New Deal managers. He no longer showed open hostility towards them. 'They're our insurance policy,' he said. 'But if it's true New Deal would rather let them die than let us have our land, what can we do? Let them come and kill us all.'

The other farmers exchanged glances. One of them spoke. 'If we had a chance, I would fight with you. Francis, I would give my life for our community's future, like you. But not like this, like lambs waiting for slaughter.' There were murmurs of agreement.

Patrice said, 'Don't give up, Francis. Make a tactical retreat. Regroup. Live to fight another day.'

Francis let out a long breath, as if he was seriously thinking it over. Surely, Patrice thought, he had to see sense.

Below them, the flurry of activity from the guards that followed Patrice and Sally's arrival had petered out. All was ominously still. But inside the control room, Patrice sensed the earlier calm had been replaced by an air of anxiety.

'What's that?' A farmer who'd been sitting in another of the swivel chairs was standing now, pointing through the window at the factory floor. Everyone turned to look. A fork-lift truck with a tub full of bunches of palm fruit was speeding down an aisle, heading their way.

Francis asked the general manager, 'What's going on? You said the plant was shut down.'

'It is, I swear.'

The fork-lift came to the end of the aisle, turned, and was now face-on as the farmers watched from the control room high above. The operator was wearing blue overalls and a blue baseball cap pulled over his head. He drove forward then stopped at the bottom of the metal staircase, lowered his load to the ground, and got off.

'What is this trick?' Francis asked. 'What's in there?'

The operator turned and looked down the aisle he'd driven up, then across in the other direction. There was near silence in the control room, just the sound of fast breathing and sweat trickling over stubble.

'It looks like this is it,' Francis said. He crossed the control room, pulled MacGregor to his feet, and pushed the general manager's face against the window, with his machete at the man's throat.

'No, Francis,' one of the others said. 'Don't make things worse than they already are.'

He put his hand on Francis' shoulder, but the farmers' leader elbowed him away.

'This is a trap,' Francis said, the muscles in his jaw twitching. 'Who's that man?' he asked MacGregor.

At that point, the fork-lift operator looked up.

'I … I don't know,' the general manager said. 'He's not one of our men.'

But now they could see his face, everyone else knew who it was. The man signalled with a wave that he required assistance. Then he began lifting the fruit bunches out of the tub. Three farmers went to help.

Patrice was wondering if, after all, the fruit was edible, when the man wiped his brow, leaned into the tub and pulled out a long wooden box, holding it by rope handles at either end.

'What the …' Patrice didn't finish the sentence. Whatever it was that was going on, he could tell when he looked into the vacant gaze of the man below – even from that distance – that something inside him had changed, catastrophically. In body, that man was Samson Eta; bar owner, football coach, friend, even. But in mind, he was no longer there.

Chapter 69

Sally's head was spinning. 'Douala Manga's guns …' She spoke as if to herself, as if to confirm this was what she was actually seeing. 'Raymond must have told him about them.'

No wonder she hadn't been able to get hold of the photographer. She'd been trying all day. In the end, she'd called her editor, telling him things were getting tense and Raymond had to come back. Her editor said Raymond had been working late, processing his pictures from the crash in Mbimbia, but he'd tell him to return when he came into the office. Her editor had actually thanked Sally for her report. 'You've done well,' he'd said. It was the first time he'd ever praised her work. And he'd faxed over a copy of that morning's *Courier* front page; the headline read: *Footballers Felled.* Below it was Sally's bylined story, with Raymond's photographs.

Sally told Patrice how they found the hidden arsenal and about the tragedy after the football match, showing him the fax she'd been sent. 'We were passing just after the accident. The coach lost his son.'

She checked her phone - still no signal at the mill.

'Come on, quick!' Coach Samson was hurrying the farmers who were carrying two boxes of rifles up the stairs. He was following with one of the square boxes of bullets. Half a minute later, the guns and ammunition were in the control room. The coach stood in the doorway and announced, 'A gift from King Rudolf Douala Manga Bell!'

'Oh my God,' Sally said as it dawned on her that it was her search for Douala Manga's secrets that had led to this. Why had she involved Raymond, anyway? She'd always felt there was something cavalier about the photographer. But for him to tell Coach Samson, in the state that poor man was in the previous evening … he had no right to do that.

Francis picked out one of the rifles, his eyes on stalks. 'Where did you get these?'

'God showed me where to go.' For once, Coach Samson wasn't twitching.

Firmly, Sally said, 'These weren't meant for you.'

'They were meant for all Cameroonians,' the coach said. 'Douala Manga was planning to fight the Germans.'

'They're not yours!' She was shouting now, at Coach Samson and at Raymond, wherever he was.

'Thank you, brother,' Francis said, ignoring Sally. He was handling the rifle in a way that suggested he knew how to use it. *'I think you just come in time to save us.'* A couple of farmers cheered in support. 'This is the first I am hearing of this Douala king, but I am grateful to him. And now we can finish his work!'

Coach Samson looked round the faces in the room. 'God is on your side.'

Sally turned to Patrice. He shook his head in despair.

'Wait!' The farmer who'd appealed to Francis before held up a hand. 'These guns are a hundred years old. They're no match for what the gendarmes have.'

'Take my word for it,' Coach Samson said, 'they work.'

Francis popped in a bullet and made as if to shoot through the window, but then lowered the gun. *'Okay, make we make things easy for everybody here.* Anyone who wants to leave can do so now; the rest of us will stay and fight.'

There was silence. Finally, Patrice spoke up. 'Francis, this is madness. You want to do the honourable thing, but this is suicide. Get out, while you still can.'

'Thank you, Congo, but your advice, your tactics, they've got us nowhere ...'

'But Patrice is right,' Sally said. 'You've made your point. The occupation and the way New Deal have been treating you has made front page news in Germany ...'

'Front page news!' Francis picked up the gun again and pointed it at Sally, who raised her hands. 'What does that get us?' the farmer shouted. 'Nothing. We're not stupid, and we're not doing this to be famous in the newspapers. We want our village.'

Patrice said, 'You won't get your village if you're dead.'

Francis lowered the gun, and his volume. 'Enough discussion. It's time to decide. Who's in and who's out?'

Coach Samson and two farmers crossed the room to stand by Francis. The rest made for the door.

Francis turned to the hostages. 'You two, go with them.'

MacGregor, the general manager, let out a squeak. Constance Fombum, the director of legal affairs, looked dazed. MacGregor helped her to her feet, and they joined the others, who were filing out of the room.

Sally and Patrice were the last to leave. As they stepped through the door, she looked at the men staying behind; she still couldn't believe what was happening.

'Come on, let's go.' Patrice put his arm round her shoulders to usher her out. 'While *we* still can.'

*

No one spoke in the control room as Francis Akwanga handed out the rifles and packets of bullets. They loaded up three rifles each. Samson sat on the floor, leaning against the closed door. He calculated: five hundred rounds between four; a hundred and twenty-five each. Not enough to win a war, but still plenty to cause serious damage; more, even, than an out-of-control logging truck could cause.

That was all he'd been thinking about since … since whenever it was the photographer had told him about Douala Manga's guns, since when he hadn't slept. It was like a dream now: driving his car to Ngembum, waking the chief's grandson, the confused look on the boy's face when Samson said he wanted to go to the cave by the waterfall; then slipping about in the dark with the heavy boxes, almost causing the canoe to capsize; the drive back in the early hours, with no other traffic nor any people on the road, just the road itself, the red dust on the grass on either side, caught in the headlights, the black sky and visions of Sonny's face appearing on the windscreen; then finally, driving to the plantation, making three journeys on foot with the heavy boxes, hiding them outside the mill, spotting the fork-lift, hitting the operator on the head, pulling him off, hiding the boxes under the fruit …

The photographer was a good man. He'd promised to send pictures to a magazine in Germany, so the people there would know how New Deal Plantations was operating in Cameroon.

He'd been sickened by what he saw, literally. Samson had witnessed him vomiting at the scene of the devastation in Mbimbia. But the photographer hadn't lost his son. He hadn't waited till late into the night to see them finally shift the tree trunk; he hadn't had to carry his dead son to the makeshift mortuary at the clinic.

It was after Samson had left Sonny there that it hit him. It was God who'd sent the photographer to meet him. Walking to his car, he knew what he had to do. His world had turned upside down. Football ... the Indomitable Lions ... He used to love his country – he'd wanted to travel across the world to see the national team. Now he laughed at that. How could he be proud of a country that sold its land, the people's land, to foreigners?

He looked at Francis and the others at the window. While he, Samson, had lost his son, these farmers had lost the things that mattered to them; their village, their place, their history. He could have - should have - done more to help them. But they had a chance now to restore their pride. It was going to end here, but not without a fight.

Samson joined the others, and the four of them linked themselves together, arms round shoulders, and watched from the window as those who'd left descended the metal steps; and watched as the first farmers reached the factory floor and a dozen heavily armed men ran out from a corridor at the side and surrounded them.

The gendarmes were wearing black balaclavas instead of their usual red berets. They ordered the farmers to lie, face-down on the ground, in a row, with their hands behind their necks. Those still on the stairs were told to finish their descent and join the others on the floor.

'You stay there, no one moving,' one of the armed men ordered, clearly the commander. 'Woman, white, here.' The two hostages were led by one of the gendarmes into the corridor at the side, out of sight.

'Let's get ready,' Francis said. He and the two other farmers crouched below the window, rifles in hands.

Samson took a rifle and positioned himself by the open door. He spotted Le Congo and Sally Bintu still on the walkway above the factory floor, pressing themselves against the wall. Evidently the gendarmes hadn't seen them.

All was quiet. Samson felt his middle finger on the trigger, moist from sweat. But he felt calm. He didn't need to jerk his head or blink. He was ready. He looked along the top of the barrel, lined up the front sight.

The gendarme commander walked slowly in front of the farmers lying on the ground. Even from the control room, Samson could see the farmers trembling. The commander stopped at the end of the row. 'You are scum. You bring shame on your country. This is what happens to traitors.'

He signalled to one of his men, who stepped forward with a large pistol and, at point-blank range, fired a bullet into the head of the farmer lying at the feet of the commander. It was the farmer who'd told Francis they'd have no chance staying in the control room. His head bounced up then smacked on to the floor. There was a cry from one of the others. The gunman aimed at a second farmer. There was another shot – but not from him. From Samson. The gendarme with the large pistol dropped to the ground, struck in the heart by a hundred-year-old bullet.

The other gendarmes looked up, startled. Then Francis and the two farmers with him smashed the window and opened fire. Samson himself fired four more times. Despite the explosion of noise, he felt no distraction. Three more gendarmes fell, while the rest, including the commander, retreated into the corridor at the side.

The surviving farmers didn't move.

'Stay on your guard,' Samson said to the others in the control room.

Two more gendarmes jumped out in front of the farmers below and fired automatic weapons at the control room, then jumped back. There was more breaking glass. Samson heard a cry behind him but he didn't take his eye off the entrance to the corridor. When two other gendarmes darted out and raced across the floor, he followed them with his sight and fired twice, bringing both of them down.

There was a pause. Samson looked behind. One of the farmers next to Francis had been hit in the shoulder. Francis helped him to the floor. He tore off part of his shirt and pressed it against the wound.

'They killed that man in cold blood,' Francis said. 'It was an execution.'

Samson looked at the dead farmer and the others still lying next to him, hands still clasped together over their necks. It was as if they were waiting for their turn. 'They're going to kill them all.'

Francis shook his head. '*I sorry them.* But they should have stayed with us. We will die too, but with dignity and valour; not like lambs but like lions.'

Samson felt for his pocket and pulled out a photo of Sonny and kissed it. 'I hope you'll forgive me,' he said. '*We go soon be together again, so no mind.*'

Chapter 70

There was silence, but the sound of gunfire still echoed in Patrice's ears. He knew it was only a matter of time, seconds even, before the gendarmes returned to deal with Coach Samson and finish off the farmers. And he and Sally were sure to get caught in the middle. It was partly his fault that these farmers were here at all, and Sally, too. It was on him to try and get them all out. And it was now or never.

He skipped lightly down the steps, beckoning Sally to follow. At the bottom, he strained his ears; he could hear voices from the corridor, but they were muffled, as if they were coming from the reception area the other side of the swing doors at the far end.

'Let's go,' he said to Sally. Then he called to the farmers on the floor, 'Get up and run, while we have the chance.'

The farmers raised their elbows to look up, but they didn't get up. They seemed to be paralysed by fear.

'Now!' Patrice glanced urgently to the side. He could see heads through the porthole windows in the doors at the end of the corridor. 'Come on, let's go!' He kicked a couple of the farmers in the legs and pointed towards the far side of the mill. It was from there that Coach Samson had approached on his forklift, so there had to be an exit. 'This way.'

The farmers got to their feet, but they all gathered round their colleague who'd been shot. 'We must take him.'

'No!' Patrice shouted. 'There's nothing you can do for him. Run, before you all get shot.'

The door in the corridor swung open.

'They're coming!'

The farmers looked, then turned and ran. Patrice and Sally went with them. A burst of gunfire followed. Bullets pinged off the machinery. The farmers kept running. Shots were being fired from above as well. A bullet zinged past Patrice's head, so close he thought it brushed through his hair. He dived behind a large tank. He turned to see Sally escaping with the farmers. Catching his breath, he peered back. The gendarmes weren't following. They were still in the corridor, pinned there by Coach Samson and the others in the control room.

Another gendarme came through the swing doors carrying a different kind of weapon on his shoulder: a grenade launcher. He trotted to the end of the corridor, swung round and took aim. He was greeted by several rounds from the old British rifles. A couple clipped the wall the gendarme was using for cover, but he was still standing. With a pop, he fired the missile. In an instant, the control room exploded into rolling red flames. The rest of the building was engulfed in heat and smoke and choking fumes.

Feeling his way past the machinery, Patrice waded through the darkness, the way Sally and the farmers had gone. As the visibility improved, he broke into a run. He breathed a change in the air, and then he was out in the open. Coughing, he made for the gateway in the perimeter wall where he'd met Sally earlier. She was waiting for him outside.

'The farmers?' he asked.

'They've gone, they got away ...' She pointed into the plantation.

The two of them looked at the mill. Thick smoke was billowing out of the sides and the roof.

In the falling dusk they walked round to the main road and came across Coach Samson's car. The key was in the ignition. He must have known he wouldn't be coming back.

They drove to Bakunda town and parked outside the San Siro. It was mid-evening; the bar was closed. But Monique was there, sitting alone on the front step. They told her what had happened.

It took some moments for the news to sink in. She had lost her son and now her husband. Clearly, she was in shock. 'My God,' she said, eventually, disbelievingly. 'Like a fool, I am waiting for him here since yesterday. And he is doing this! He didn't even call me to tell me about Sonny. I heard it from Tico's father. I tell you, that man Samson thought only of himself. And his stupid football. Look where it has got us. What about me? How am I going to manage this place by myself?' There was anger in her voice but tears in her eyes.

Sally put her arm round the woman's shoulders.

Two customers walked up but saw the bar was closed and moved on.

Shouts sounded from across the road, from the evicted villagers' encampment. Then more shouts and wails. Patrice braced himself and headed over. Three women were gathered outside one of the ramshackle structures. They were looking at a sheet of paper and crying out.

'Dem dong kill them oh!'

'Our husbands ... *dem dong die!'*

'Can I see?' Patrice asked.

It was a statement signed jointly by Bakunda Divisional Officer, Serge Mukam, and New Deal Plantations Vice-President, Thomas Schmidt:

Peace Restored

This evening, a unit of the National Gendarmerie successfully brought to an end the illegal and violent occupation of the New Deal Plantations Bakunda Mill. The two hostages were rescued, unharmed, and are now being cared for by New Deal medical staff, and their families have been informed.

In the course of the rescue mission, however, the Gendarmerie were ambushed and six of their men were lost, shot down without warning by the militants staging the occupation. In the ensuing battle, the ringleaders were killed, some by gunfire, the rest in an explosion they set off in the control room in an attempt to destroy the entire mill. Structural damage will take some weeks to repair, during which time the mill will remain closed.

New Deal Plantations wishes to express its sincere thanks to the Gendarmerie, who bravely put their lives on the line for the sake of peace, and the company expresses its heartfelt condolences to the families of those who died. It also wishes to express its thanks to the Government of Cameroon and the people of Bakunda District for their unyielding support in the face of this attack, and the company commits itself to continuing the warm and prosperous relationship it has worked so hard to establish in this country.

Patrice walked back to Sally at the San Siro. 'You need to read this.'

Her eyes darted across the lines. 'They can tell all the lies they want,' she said. 'I'm going to tell the world the truth.'

Chapter 71

Two weeks later, Pierre Mponda was sitting at the back of the Foremost café in Avenue John Kennedy in Yaounde. He was early for his meeting. A newspaper lay folded on the table, the headline visible: *New Deal Expelled – Minister Arrested.*

He smiled. Everything had happened more quickly than he'd anticipated – brought to a head, ironically, by that naïve young reporter's so-called exclusive story about the gendarmes' botched operation. His plan had even surpassed his own expectations. Protests in Germany by environmentalists and anti-capitalists had snowballed, causing New Deal's share-price to tumble. Cameroon's government became nervous about its association with the company. When a bank statement was leaked to the press showing New Deal had paid two million euros into the account of the minister of foreign business and investment before being awarded its concession, the government had to act. The concession was withdrawn, immediately, and the plantation handed over to Pamol, to be managed on behalf of the Cameroonian nation. In a gesture of goodwill, according to today's report, so as not to frighten future potential partners, New Deal Plantations was being compensated an unspecified amount for its investment in land clearance and local infrastructure.

The deputy minister walked in and took his usual seat, with his back to the rest of the café. He was carrying a large briefcase. 'You've done well, my friend,' he said, a big grin on his face.

'*We've* done well. Thank you, and congratulations, sir … or should I say, Minister?'

The man held up his hand. 'That's still to be confirmed.'

Mponda chuckled. 'This could never have happened without your support, sir.'

The deputy minister noticed the newspaper on the table and tapped the briefcase. 'Cash is best. It leaves no trace. I'm afraid our erstwhile superior had become careless in that regard. But he also made another big mistake.' The man stared across at Mponda.

'Yes?'

'He was greedy. He didn't share his good fortune with those around him.' He handed over the case.

'Thank you, sir.' Mponda stroked the smooth leather.

The man chuckled. 'Hard-earned, if I may say.' He leaned forward. 'It's as we agreed: ten million for New Deal, one each for us. Look inside if you want!'

Mponda clicked it open and saw the wads of euros. He resisted the urge to touch them.

'What will you do with it?' the deputy minister asked.

'Enjoy it! I'm actually thinking of proposing a joint venture with a Chinese investor I've been advising. He wants to build a hotel in Bakunda, and I've found him the perfect location.'

The deputy minister ordered a beer and asked Mponda if he'd like one. Mponda declined, but his boss insisted. 'Come on, my friend. Join me in celebration. You deserve it! We deserve it!'

When their bottles of Mutzig arrived, the deputy minister proposed a toast. 'To development!' They clinked bottles and laughed.

'It happened as you predicted, Pierre. But tell me, honestly, were you surprised by how little fight New Deal put up to stay? They have lost a lot of money.'

'Not at all. I explained to Schmidt that his share-holders might not be happy with the offer, but they wouldn't be happy either if they knew the details of the company vice-president's expense claims for his nights out in Douala. And neither would his wife!'

'What happened to the Congolese?'

'Don't worry about him. He has his suspicions. But he can't prove anything.'

'But he got close?'

'Actually, it's true, things nearly took a different course. If we hadn't caught him that night, he might have got the farmers to change their mind and leave peacefully. By the time he reached them, it seems it was too late. Fate had intervened!'

'So, some luck was involved.'

'Even the greatest chess players must take risks.'

They drank two more bottles each. By the time Mponda reached his room, he was tipsy. With a smile on his face, he stumbled in. Seconds later there was a tap on the door. He wasn't expecting visitors. He kicked his briefcase under the bed then carefully edged the door open.

'Hello, stranger.' It was Estelle. Her lips were parted, her cleavage inviting in a figure-hugging dress.

'What are you doing here?'

'I missed you. Aren't you glad to see me?' As she spoke, she pressed her forefinger into his chest and scratched her pink nail downwards.

'Mais oui, pourquoi pas?' His head was swimming. He thought when she'd said she was leaving for Douala she didn't intend to return. But since she was here … he let her finger continue its journey and pulled her into the room. She dropped her purse on a table and undid his belt. Slobbering and fumbling with her breasts, he tried to kiss her. But she pushed him away.

'You've been drinking,' she said. 'I thought you didn't like alcohol.'

He laughed. 'I've been celebrating a deal.'

'What kind of a deal?'

'An important one. Now I can buy you another necklace.' He leaned again to kiss her, but she moved to the side.

'How can you do business if you're drinking? That is not professional.'

'Huh! You don't believe me? Sit, here. Come and sit.' He patted the bed then stretched under it and brought out the briefcase. 'You don't think I'm capable of doing business?' He opened the briefcase and let the contents fall on the bed.

'Oh my God!' Estelle picked up a wad of 100-euro notes. 'How did you get this?'

He took off his blazer. 'I'll tell you after.'

'Oh no,' she said, wagging a finger. 'Tell me first.'

'It's a long story.'

'I'm not in a rush.'

He went to the minibar and poured a whisky. She gave him a disapproving look. He didn't care. He sat in an armchair and looked up at the ceiling. How did he do it? He really was extraordinary …

'It was so easy,' he said, taking a sip, feeling the whisky burn. 'There was a village chief; he was a drunk and a fool. I arranged for his children to go to college, and in return he gave up his ancestral lands.'

'This all came from a village chief?'

'That's just the start. Making money like this is about seeing opportunities. Two farmers from his village went to him one day and told him about something unfortunate that had happened. They were worried a ranger was going to find out they were farming in the national park, and they asked a young wrestler they knew to scare him off. But the wrestler used too much force and killed him.'

Estelle frowned.

'To most people, that's something bad, tragic. To me, when the chief told me about this, I saw an opportunity. You see? He saw a problem; I saw an opportunity. How? Because I happened to know where to find this wrestler. I simply persuaded him to do some favours for me, and an irreversible chain of events was set in train ...'

He took another sip of the whisky and swilled it around in his mouth, reflecting on his genius.

'... that's to say, nature took its course. You see, people are easily led. They are prepared to believe anything if it's what they want to believe. In this case, simple villagers and an international company were as gullible as each other. They were pieces on a chessboard.'

Mponda went to sit next to Estelle. She tried to pull away, but he held her with one hand and with the other he tucked some banknotes into her bra. She picked out the banknotes and threw them down.

'I don't want this kind of money,' she said.

He'd had enough of her rudeness. 'How dare you come here trying to seduce me, then reject my generosity!' He slapped her.

'That was the wrestler who killed those people in Bakunda,' she said as she held her cheek. 'It was in the newspaper. I heard you talking to him on the phone. You made him do those things?'

'You're a fool, Estelle. Like everyone else.'

'And then the wrestler was killed. He was shot.' Estelle shifted away from him. 'And the village was destroyed ...'

He turned and lunged forward on top of her, pushing her on to her back, holding her by both shoulders, as he had a few days before. But this time he moved his hands to her neck, and pressed hard with his thumbs. This stupid woman. Why was he even talking to her? He pressed harder. She struggled. He kept up the pressure, until her arms dropped, and she was still. Breathing heavily, he loosened his grip. Then out of the stillness, her hands sprang up and she stabbed her long, pink nails into his eyes. He let out a squeal. Estelle pushed him off her and jumped off the bed.

'I'm going,' she shouted. Through a blur, he saw her run to the door and take her purse. Then she stopped and reached into the cupboard. 'You killed the wrestler, didn't you?' She turned and pointed his gun at him.

'Put it down, Estelle.' Pierre Mponda wiped his eyes. He could just make out she was pulling the trigger.

Chapter 72

A white sun was struggling to burn through the cloud that filled the late afternoon sky. The San Siro had reopened, and from the terrace Patrice was keeping half an eye on the motor park, waiting for a signal from the taxi-driver to say he had a full car and was ready to go.

Across the road, the evicted villagers were preparing for another evening; girls were bringing buckets of water from the river, women were tending to fires outside their shacks. A few men were sitting and talking. The farmers who had escaped from the mill had all dispersed, going to stay with relatives till it felt safe to return. No one had taken up the offer of resettlement in Ngembum.

'So, you're actually going?' Sally asked. She'd come to write a follow-up story.

'Finally, yes,' Patrice said. 'This time it's for real.'

'Are you sure your boss still wants you?'

'Yes, she's pleased with me, unofficially. She says she hopes this episode will force the African Union to rethink its position on land-grabbing.'

The football pitch itself was no longer under threat. According to Ngwa, the tourist centre manager, the Chinese businessman was now going to build his hotel inside the national park, on the land cleared by the farmers from Bafuke. It would attract visitors from all over the world, and there'd be jobs for local people, he said. Bakunda had to look forward, not back.

Sally's report had been the undoing of New Deal's Cameroonian operation, and there was jubilation when it was announced the company was being kicked out of the country. But there was to be no inquiry into the actions of the gendarmerie.

'That's Cameroon,' Sally said. 'The special forces are too powerful. We live with corruption at every level.'

The latest edition of the *Courier* carried news of the murder of Pierre Mponda, the man from the Ministry of Foreign Business and Investment who'd been advising New Deal. A maid found him in a hotel room in Yaounde, along with ten thousand euros.

Sally said there was probably more than that. 'The police will have helped themselves to plenty, for sure.'

The report said police believed a woman had been staying in the man's room until a few days before his death. The murder weapon, a gun, was found at the scene. It was a police-issue firearm belonging to the victim, who was a former policeman.

'It must have been a crime of passion,' Sally said. 'If she left all that money behind.'

'So, he did have a gun …' Patrice commented, a lot of puzzling things suddenly making sense.

Sally didn't hear. 'What was he doing with all that cash? Since when have civil servants been paid so well? And in foreign currency?'

'… the gun he used to kill Jeki.'

'What?' She heard that. 'How do you know that?'

'Go and talk to the mortician at the hospital here. Tell him you're there unofficially, and promise you won't quote him on anything.'

Sally screwed up her face. 'Hey, Patrice. Are you sure you're not a reporter?'

'It all fits. He was always there, in the shadows, stirring things up. He told me I was wasting my time. He said I should go to Douala, even suggested a hotel. He wanted me out of the way. When I didn't go, he played me along, until I got too close. But I see now, he was playing everyone along.'

'But how did he get that money?'

'It's in the newspapers. New Deal received compensation. That was probably Pierre Mponda's cut. Or part of it.'

'You agree there was more?'

'He took a lot of risks for ten thousand euros.'

Sally took out her notebook and scribbled a few lines. 'So who else was in on it, Patrice? The divisional officer?'

'I don't think so. They didn't strike me as co-conspirators when we saw them at the press conference. All along, I've been trying to think, who stands to gain from this? And now I'm thinking, who would have the power to arrange for such a payment to go to Mponda.'

'And?'

'Again, I think the answer is in the newspapers.' He pointed at a photograph in the *Courier*.

'Huh! The new minister. The former deputy minister. That actually makes sense. He and Mponda were sitting together at the reunification event in Buea.'

'You'll have to be careful how you go about proving it.'

'Thank you, Patrice. Even I can work that out.'

There was little activity at the motor park. Patrice ordered an Isenbeck. 'Don't forget to send me a copy of your book,' he said.

'Yes ... though I don't know. Maybe there won't be a book. Now the discovery of Douala Manga's guns has been reported ... and then, what they were used for ...'

'I thought you wanted to set the record straight; tell the full story of a national resistance hero?'

'You know what I think now?'

'Tell me.'

'I think Douala Manga hid those guns while he tried to rally support for his resistance struggle. But what he found was, other Cameroonians weren't prepared to die for him.'

Poor Sally, he thought. After all her research, and taking so many risks, she sounded crestfallen. 'But you've got all that material from his memoirs ...'

'We'll see,' she said, flicking at her hair. 'I'm actually thinking that I might be better suited to journalism than academic research after all.'

'What about your DNA test?' Patrice asked, with a smile.

She frowned. 'It's expensive, you know, and the results are not always conclusive. Anyway, maybe some things ... you're better off not knowing.'

It was Alice, from Bafuke, who brought Patrice's beer to the table. Monique had invited her to stay for as long as Andre and Jerome were being kept in detention at the police station, and Alice was now working at the bar. Following the recent turn of events, they were hoping the charges against Andre and Jerome might be dropped.

As Patrice put the bottle to his lips, a four-by-four drove

past and circled round to park by the football pitch. Two men in suits and a policeman got out and walked into the encampment.

'Are the villagers going to be evicted for a second time?' Sally asked.

'They should leave these poor people be,' Patrice said, tutting. 'They've had enough trouble.'

'I'll see what's going on.'

As Sally left the bar, Ngwa, the tourist centre manager, entered.

'Mr Le Congo, how are you?' He was looking glum. 'You are leaving, I hear.'

Patrice nodded. 'News still travels fast in this town.'

'You have finished your investigations?'

'I've written my reports. Though some details are going to need updating.'

The man slumped on to a chair and called to Alice to bring him a bottle of *Trente-trois*.

'Have you heard about the hotel?'

'Yes, I saw in the newspaper. I thought you'd be happy.'

'No. It's not happening. We heard today, the local partner has pulled out, and now the Chinese are having second thoughts.'

Another piece in Patrice's jigsaw slotted into place. But before he had time to ask Ngwa if he knew any more about it, their conversation was interrupted by shouting from across the road.

'What's that all about?' the tourist centre manager asked.

A crowd was growing outside one of the shacks, around the two men in suits and the policeman. Men were cheering and punching their fists in the air, women were ululating.

Sally emerged from the middle of it and came running up to the San Siro. 'Alice!' she said. 'Patrice! It's incredible. Bafuke is saved!'

'What's this?' Alice was serving Ngwa his beer. 'What do you mean?'

'It's true,' Sally said, breathless, excited. 'An anonymous benefactor has set up a trust fund with nearly a million euros to rebuild the village and to lease back from Pamol all the land taken from the farmers.'

'Are you sure about this?' Alice asked, taking a seat to steady herself.

'Yes, yes! Those men are solicitors. They are managing the fund. They showed the letter of instruction and the bank statement.'

'Who is the benefactor?' Ngwa asked, not sounding like he was sharing the delight of the moment.

'They can't say. It's a condition of the arrangement that their identity cannot be revealed. They said it's someone who was very upset by what happened and was in a position to help.'

Tears trickled across the smile on Alice's face. 'Oh, my goodness! Thank the Lord!'

Monique came over. 'Perhaps it means my Samson didn't die for nothing.'

'Yes,' Alice said. 'He was a good man.'

The two women hugged.

'Go and join the others,' Monique said. 'At last, there's something to celebrate here.'

Alice walked across the road and into the encampment.

Patrice saw his taxi-driver waving and signalling that he'd drive round to pick him up. Sally waited with him by the roadside. 'Monique is right,' she said. 'The coach didn't die for nothing. Neither did Francis or the others.'

Patrice raised his fist. 'Modern-day resistance heroes?'

'Yes,' she said. 'Headline: *V for Villagers and Victory!*'

The taxi arrived. The driver took Patrice's bag and fitted it into the boot.

'You're flying tonight?' Sally asked.

'No, in the morning. I'm spending the night in Douala, in the hotel Mponda recommended! The Alexandre. A night of luxury ...'

'The Alexandre?'

'Yes.'

'Oh my God ...'

'You know it?'

'... was it him? Was it her? But how ...?'

Patrice squeezed into the front of the car.

'Wait ...'

'Bye, Sally. Good luck!' Whatever it was she was on to, he didn't want to know. It was time, finally, for him to go.

THE END

Postscript

For the most part, *Pala Pala Killer* is set in 2014, when the 'unresolved Anglophone issue', so called in the novel by the newspaper photographer Raymond, referred to a mostly peaceful campaign for greater autonomy in the English-speaking regions of Cameroon. Two years later, after demonstrations against perceived marginalisation led to a violent response from security forces, this campaign turned into an armed struggle for independence. Since then, thousands have died and hundreds of thousands have been displaced. It's fair to say that, like many observers, Raymond and the young reporter Sally Bintu probably underestimated the strength of feeling among the Anglophone community and the speed at which the 'issue' could turn into a crisis.

PL June 2023

Acknowledgements

For historical research I relied heavily on the following works: *Le procès du roi Rudolf Duala Manga Bell, martyr de la liberté* by Joël Kondo; *Douala Manga Bell/Héros de la résistance douala* by Iyé Kala Lobe; and *Middlemen of the Cameroon Rivers* by Professor Ralph Austen and Jonathan Derrick.

I must also thank Professor Austen for his time and for sharing with me his research into the stories of the mythical folk hero Jeki la Njambe, as laid out in *The Elusive Epic: Performance, Text and History in the Oral Narrative of Jeki la Njambe*.

I am indebted to Brendan Schwart, formerly of Greenpeace, for his expertise on land-grabbing. And to my friend Katrin Albrecht for her German. And to my former BBC colleagues, Veronique Edwards, Randy Joe Sa'ah, Francis Ngwa Niba and Omer Songwe for their knowledge of everything to do with Cameroon and their patience in sharing it with me.

Lastly, thanks to my friends and family once again for their support – my wife Sharon, for keeping faith in me, my daughters Ella and Holly for their sharp-eyed reading, and my brother Mark and friend Sarah Temple-Smith for their editorial advice.

Thank you, Dear Reader

I hope you enjoyed *Pala Pala Killer*. If you did, it would be a great help to me as an independent writer if you could take a few minutes to revisit the site where you purchased it and leave a review. Just a few words and/or a star rating could be enough to nudge the title up the rankings.

BUKAVU BLUES

A macabre murder. A country torn apart by conflict. A man determined to stop the bloodshed.

Seeing his people suffer for too long has left human rights defender Patrice Le Congo feeling weary and cynical. But when schoolteacher Aurélia Mukunda turns to him for help after a mutilated body is found in a village, he can't say no.

His inquiries lead him on a perilous journey to the heart of a seemingly never-ending war that's brought death and destruction to eastern Congo.

After more murders threaten to derail a crucial peace conference, the killers abduct Aurélia, and Patrice is faced with two challenges: save the teacher and save his country.

Bukavu Blues **is the opening novel chronicling the investigations of Patrice Le Congo – a series of crime thrillers with a global political dimension.**

'A blistering and eye-opening read. Highly recommended.'
Amazon Five-Star review

'Captivating political intrigue at its finest.'
Amazon Five-Star review

COLD CHOP

The Investigations of Patrice Le Congo #3

Ghana, present-day ... amid a scramble to exploit Africa's renewable energy potential, the body of an engineer is found, electrocuted. The police say it's an accident. The man's daughter says he was being threatened by people who want his land.

Ghana, fifty years earlier ... at a time of coup plots and Cold War politics, a young woman is killed by a hit-and-run driver. The police don't get involved in this case either.

The two victims are related; could their deaths be too?

***COLD CHOP* IS COMING SOON!**

About the Author

Peter Lewenstein was born in London. He was a journalist before turning to fiction, first in print, then for the BBC World Service, where he produced and edited the popular radio programmes *Network Africa* and *Focus on Africa* and travelled widely across the African continent, reporting on elections, war and everyday life. He is a member of the Alliance of Independent Authors.

Printed in Great Britain
by Amazon

31544837R00223